⑦

monkey business

MONKEY BUSINESS INTERNATIONAL
(ISSN 2159-7138 (print)
ISSN 2326-8786 (ebook)
ISBN 978-0-9972480-2-9)
IS PUBLISHED UNDER LICENSE AND BY ARRANGEMENT WITH WE'VE INC., TOKYO, JAPAN.

PUBLISHED ANNUALLY BY A PUBLIC SPACE LITERARY PROJECTS, INC. 323 DEAN STREET, BROOKLYN, NY 11217. PRINTED IN CANADA BY THE PROLIFIC GROUP. ISSUE 07, 2017.

POSTMASTER
PLEASE SEND CHANGES OF ADDRESS TO A PUBLIC SPACE, 323 DEAN STREET, BROOKLYN, NY 11217.

EDITORS
Ted Goossen
Motoyuki Shibata
MANAGING EDITOR
Meg Taylor
CONTRIBUTING EDITORS
Brigid Hughes
Roland Kelts
MARKETING MANAGER
Tiffany Ferentini
ART EDITOR/DESIGN
Lissi Erwin
PRODUCTION MANAGER
Rachel Holscher/Bookmobile
LOGO
Seiichi Suzuki
COVER ILLUSTRATION
TAKORA Kimiyoshi Futori

PUBLISHED WITH THE SUPPORT OF THE NIPPON FOUNDATION'S READ JAPAN PROGRAMS

Supported by
日本財団
THE NIPPON FOUNDATION

GENERAL INFORMATION

BOOKSTORES
Monkey Business is distributed exclusively through Ingram Periodicals and Nippan IPS.

CONTACT
For general queries, please email monkeybiz@apublicspace.org or call 718.858.8067.
A Public Space is located at 323 Dean Street, Brooklyn, New York 11217.

the monkey speaks

Kinokunizaka is a long slope in Tokyo.

—Back in 1967, when I was in junior high, I found these seven words in our English textbook. They were the opening sentence of a simplified version of Lafcadio Hearn's "Mujina," which was in turn a retelling of one of the many Japanese folktales that Hearn's Japanese wife, Setsu, had recounted to him.

Just a simple sentence. It was, however, so different from what I'd encountered till then in English textbooks—*"This is a pen!" "How are you?" "Fine, thank you, and you?"*—that I felt something pulling at my heart. I couldn't have articulated it at the time, but I think I sensed a *story* in that short sentence.

And that's the game I've been playing for fifty years: finding stories in sentences written in English.

In 1989, I started a new game: to convert that pull in my heart into my own language. I began translating into Japanese English sentences by American and British writers: Paul Auster, Rebecca Brown, Joseph Conrad, Stuart Dybek, Steve Erickson . . . over the course of a quarter century I've covered every letter in the alphabet except U, X and Z!

In 2011, I started another new game with my North American friends: to help them convert into English the pull *they* feel in their heart when they read Japanese sentences. And what a fun game it was. As far as I was concerned, our *Monkey Business* couldn't be more aptly named.

What a fun game it still is, for all of us writers, translators and editors—with more than a little help from our friends in America, Canada and the UK. We've launched our new issue in North America every year, and we have repeatedly been invited to literary festivals in the Philippines, Indonesia, and Singapore: the Monkey King is making his journey to the West!

—Motoyuki Shibata

Many years ago a boy lived down by the sea, where the great green waves came riding in to break on the shore in clouds of salty spray. This boy, Urashima, loved the water as a brother . . .

I was a little boy of five or six living in the scraggly woods of upstate New York when I read this line in an illustrated book of Japanese fairy tales retold for children by Teresa Peirce Williston and published in 1904, the year Lafcadio Hearn—whose "adult" versions I read years later—passed away. I loved that little book. Like all my favorite reading at the time, it took me from my rural isolation to an exciting, more colorful world of dream and fantasy. I had not yet seen the ocean with my own eyes, but I could imagine it breaking on Japanese shores thanks to a chain of storytelling that linked Setsu's sources, to her, to her husband, to Teresa, to me.

All of us involved in *Monkey Business*—writers, translators and editors—take great pleasure in being part of that chain that carries stories back and forth across the ocean, to and from Japan. It is a team endeavor, led by our valiant Monkey King. We hope that you will enjoy our stories as much as we enjoyed bringing them to you.

—Ted Goossen

Maybe it started when I was eight with the discovery of a leather-bound book of Edgar Allan Poe stories in the library of a big old house—I'll never forget the illustration of "The Tell-Tale Heart" and the strange pull of that story, at once horrifying and fascinating. Then Alice and Huck, and much later Tanizaki and Gogol. I tried my hand at translation—a few Shiga Naoya stories and attempts to make Kyogen funny in English. By that time I was living in Tokyo, working at Weatherhill, editing books on Japanese architecture, pottery, tattoos. Making books, which is what I've been doing ever since.

In recent years I've circled back to fiction, especially Japanese stories in translation. This issue of *Monkey Business* marks the tenth collection with Ted, starting with a few anthologies in the mid-1990s. It's a rare treat to work with Moto and Ted, and with the Monkey King leading us, we look forward to getting into all sorts of trouble in the years to come!

—Meg Taylor

This issue is available in both paper and ebook format and can be purchased at http://monkeybusinessmag.tumblr.com/store.

monkey business

volume 07 | 2017

translated by David Boyd

ORACLES AND MIRACLES

HIDEO FURUKAWA

DESOLATION GIRL WANTS TO BE A WEATHER ORACLE WHEN SHE GROWS UP

So this new girl transferred into our class and I guess she was on a research vessel with her dad when they fell into the ocean or something and after they dropped into the stormy sea they drifted ashore on a desert island where life was like super brutal so we called her Desolation Girl.

Desolation Girl had this amazing aura and we were all spellbound from day one so we didn't pick on her because we sort of knew that she would mow us all down if we gave her the chance so instead of hazing her or whatever we welcomed her with open arms and did our best to understand her.

It was a really big deal during lunch the second week when Desolation Girl flipped out over the typically Japanese way that the menu mixes Japanese and Western food and when our teacher heard that he nodded in total agreement and I guess that information got back to the lunchroom resulting in Desolation Girl swapping email addresses with three of the school cooks which only deepened our profound respect for her.

But when Desolation Girl made a move for the class fishbowl twenty-one or twenty-two of the thirty of us watched wide-eyed even though she wasn't like torturing the pop-eyed goldfish or anything but she was actually mixing some mystery fluid into the water for a couple of days and after that the fish started breeding like crazy which literally blew us away.

There were whispers in class that the liquid in question was really soy sauce or maybe some Asiatic miracle condiment called fish sauce but Desolation Girl just snickered and wouldn't tell us what it was even though she gave us this look that told us we were on the right track and fish sauce was actually pretty close which made us think that the substance had to be piscine in nature.

After a month or so rumors started going around that Desolation Girl was really good at making a particular dish and even the boys got wind of the fact that it was lasagna but it was the girls who figured out that her secret was using fish sauce instead of meat sauce so the girls were the toast of the classroom for like three days straight.

"It takes clams," Desolation Girl told us, "loads and loads of clams."

The principal repeated those words the next Monday morning during assembly.

We got the feeling that the educators had pretty much given us license to ask Desolation Girl anything we wanted so we had her fill out a detailed questionnaire through which we learned that her favorite food was preserved eggs and that she could speak Dutch and that she wanted to be the one in charge when cleaning the classroom.

Because Desolation Girl was really good at music we asked her if music was her best subject but she sort of tilted her head and said well I can do a pretty mean punk rock version of the national anthem at school functions but that's not technically a subject now is it and with that we were once again blown away.

At some point we started talking about what we wanted to be when we grew up and it looked like we were all thinking about our own answers or whatever but we really wanted to know what everyone else was going to say and most of all we wanted to know what Desolation Girl wanted to be.

"You know on TV," Desolation Girl started. Now even the teacher was holding his breath. "They have weather forecasts, right?"

Right right, we said.

"Right? Weather shows, weather guides. You probably think each one of them—every program on every channel—is forecasting, right? Well, they're not. It's a lie. About one in eight isn't forecasting at all. They're *prophesying*. You know what I mean? Everyone? Sensei? Forecasts miss the mark, all the time. Because they're just speculating. But prophecies never miss. I mean, they're prophecies. You know how some weather shows are just spot on? Those are prophecies. Those weather guides that never stray? Prophecies. Those people pretend to be forecasters. But they're more than just people. They're beyond people, beyond human. For them, 'probability' means nothing, because they can make things happen! That's what I want to do when I grow up. And give people hell, like, 'Here's a sneak peek at the weather to come. . . . See how bad things will get? Gales and tidal waves and heavy snow and blizzards—better be careful! There's a blizzard on the way, so it's high time to repent! Mankind is living in sin! S-I-N!' And I'll have these weather maps that are way better than the normal ones, like, 'WEATHER ORACLE MAPS.' Yeah, I think I can get humanity to the next stage. Well, everyone, what do you think?"

We were with her, a hundred percent. Our teacher felt the same. So—under his enthusiastic supervision—we sent a glowing recommendation to the Japan Broadcasting Corporation.

THIS IS A POLITICAL FICTION

They discovered a door while cleaning out a guestroom closet on the second floor of the Official Residence of the Prime Minister. Asked about the unidentified door, the Secretary to the Minister of Construction and the Government Building Department were baffled: "There's no door there in the plans." Residence Security was promptly summoned to investigate. They had assumed that the so-called "discovery" was probably just some kind of hoax but were shocked to find that:

—the door could be opened;

—bomb detectors found nothing unusual within a 10-foot radius (before or after opening the door); and

—there was a room on the other side of the door, and that room was full.

No equipment was needed to confirm that the room was full. It was full of paper. The doorway was blocked by a wall of paper, which they subsequently dug into.

They excavated the paper.

What was on the paper? Secret treaties. Nothing but. Enough damning intel to bring down two—maybe three or four—nations. Japan would obviously be one of them. This room shouldn't have existed. It wasn't in the plans. The Residence was built on a slope. While the building opens on the first floor on the west side, it opens on the third floor on the east side. Almost directly beneath the east entrance, one floor beneath it, was the door. There should have been nothing but dirt on the other side of that door—but this was dirt of a different kind: a white hole of international intrigue.

Dirty documents were wheeled out by the barrow. For analysis, storage and other purposes.

Needless to say, the Prime Minister was present—as were the Chief Cabinet Secretary and the Vice Secretary. Yet not all cabinet members were apprised of the *facts.* They remain in the dark to this day. The Minister of Defense, the Minister of Foreign Affairs and the Minister of Education, Culture, Sports, Science and Technology were the first to be admitted to the "inner circle." Meanwhile, in the basement the Residence Crisis

Management Team was more alive than it had been in decades. Its sole concern: "THE DOOR ISSUE."

Then things took a sudden turn:

—they had tunneled almost 10 feet into the wall of paper;

—at which point, a different kind of document began to emerge; and

—these buried documents did not appear to contain any state secrets.

Now everyone was at a complete loss. These deeper documents appeared to belong to the category of writing broadly known as fiction. More specifically, narrative fiction. But looks can be deceiving. Dark secrets were likely to be lurking beneath the fictional surface. At this point, the Metropolitan Police Department and the National Police Agency (acting under the guidance of the National Public Safety Commission) were no longer of any use. How could they be expected to read between the lines to uncover the secrets within? So the Agency of Cultural Affairs stepped up to the plate, and the Minister of Education, Culture, Sports, Science and Technology—i.e., the head of the Ministry to which the Agency was a special body—emerged as the right-hand man to the Prime Minister and the Chief Cabinet Secretary. Or, if you consider the Chief Cabinet Secretary to be the Prime Minister's right-hand man, then the Minister had become the man to the immediate right of the Prime Minister's right-hand man.

By this point, sacrilegious messages in the fiction had become a major concern, which only further solidified the Agency of Cultural Affairs' standing as *the foremost authority on decoding the excavated text.*

Then the Diet convened for a number of extraordinary sessions, in which it was concluded that:

—public education shall no longer promote the act of reading;

—the sale and distribution of books (or any other manner of reading matter) outside the designated zones shall be strictly prohibited; and

—a model Japanese citizen is one who is well aware that reading in "public" (on trains, etc.) is utterly disgraceful.

This was, in effect, a ban on reading. But the group most affected by this prohibition (i.e., "the youth") was sick and tired of being forced to read, so the catchphrase READING IS WRONG swept the nation, meeting virtually no resistance at all.

But the Prime Minister kept reading. He read the excavated text. It would have been remiss of him to do otherwise. Yes, he read out of duty. But he found nothing but fiction in the fiction. It was overwhelmingly fictional. Nevertheless, here were words, written on paper that *shouldn't exist*, hauled out of a room that *shouldn't exist*. There simply had to be more to this text than met the eye.

So the Agency of Cultural Affairs prepared a manual for the Prime Minister. This text would allow him to read the excavated text "logically" (i.e., with complete disregard for its so-called artistic, poetic or literary qualities), to suss out:

—its hidden codes;

—its religious transgressions; and

—its subversive potential.

Now the Prime Minister found nothing but nonfiction in the fiction.

Flash to the House of Councillors' Budgetary Meeting, when the Prime Minister answers all—on live TV, same as always. The Prime Minister stands there on the dais, in front of three microphones. One for the hall, one for the Japan Broadcasting Corporation and one for commercial networks. There's a pitcher and a glass of cold water on the podium. Behind the Prime Minister are the Minister of Defense, the Minister of Foreign Affairs, the Minister of Education, Culture, Sports, Science and Technology, and all the other brains of the present cabinet. The Prime Minister looks down at the papers he's been handed—notes to guide his answers—when it hits him:

—read this as fiction and a code emerges;

—read this as fiction and it violates all that is holy;

—read this as fiction and it sows the seeds of anarchy.

"What power!" He exclaims.

The words slip out of the Prime Minister's mouth—into the set of microphones. "We need to harness this power . . . To protect our nation, our people, our planet . . . Planet? Did I say that? Fiction, don't die on us!"

EMERGENCY EXIT MUSIC

The story you're about to hear contains just one miracle. One real miracle.

One object occupying two spaces (or, worse still, more than two spaces) is an impossibility in this world. Granted, it's no problem for you to be in Place A at 8 a.m. and in Place B at 11 a.m. But when you're in Places A and B at 11:30 a.m. on the same day, then you've got a real problem. It's an even bigger problem if witnesses can place you at both scenes—if you interact with people in both places, if you're caught on film in both places. Well, being in two places at once is a big problem *for you*. Yet for some reason, we tend to let that sort of thing slide when the duplicitous object is nonhuman. Take, for example, a calico cat at Shinjuku Culture Center and Hanazono Shrine at 11:22 p.m. on July 10, 2016. At the Culture Center, the animal was seen yawning; at the shrine, she was seen clawing at a sacred tree. There is ample evidence (even DNA, if that's what it takes) to prove that the two cats were one and the same. Still, no one really cares. And why is that?

Because it's a cat. Not a human.

No one even notices when an inorganic object is in two places at once.

A door appears—a single door—in Osaka and in the Kushiro Wetlands. Not two doors of the same model. The exact same door. But this shocks no one. In Kushiro, the presence of the door was confirmed by a number of eyewitnesses: a supervisor at the Regional Development Bureau, park personnel, a group of tourists, a nature photographer. The officials were convinced that the door had to be some sort of a hoax—a prank. They filed their reports, and that was that. Meanwhile, the visitors thought the door was a piece of artwork—or maybe a monument. And that was that.

In Osaka, however, the door was a huge problem.

Because it stood at the crossroads of a busy intersection in Umeda, Kita Ward, it was disrupting traffic, so the City of Osaka tried to have it removed. They used every piece of heavy machinery they had at their disposal, but the door wouldn't budge. What the hell was going on? Wasn't it just some door in the middle of an intersection? And, while we're on the subject, why was the door there in the first place? How did it get there? Who put it there? The authorities needed to get to the bottom of this. They went back to the surveillance footage, closed off the intersection, rerouted traffic. TV crews flocked to the scene. Then came the crowds. The TV crews pointed their cameras and microphones at the crowds, but learned nothing of value. There were rumors that the Self-Defense Forces would be sent in at any moment.

Four hours after the door's appearance, twenty-three men and women in Osaka, Hyogo and Nara—people of all ages and walks of life—began to feel something strange happening in their armpits. They itched. Soon their shirts no longer fit. Something was there, a growth that hadn't been there before. Well, more like a pair of growths. Like wings. It seems reasonable to assume (or imagine) that had they kept growing, they would have become a fine set of translucent wings.

All at once, these twenty-three people felt a sudden urge to *get out*. They had to get through that door, right away.

They descended upon Umeda. All at once. But it was clear that the twenty-three had not coordinated with one another beforehand—each moved independently.

They came to the intersection, from the east, the north, the south and the west.

They broke through the police blockade—half were apprehended in the process. The others kept moving toward the door. One made it, then two. Three. More. As soon as the door opened, or moved at an angle suggesting "opening," a song filled the intersection. Almost as if there was an invisible "room" on the other side of the door, a room where music was playing. The TV crews caught the whole incident on tape.

Two, three, more people disappeared behind the door. The moment they stepped inside the invisible room, they vanished. Into thin air. Needless to say, the door in Osaka was the door in Kushiro. So when the door moved as if opening in Osaka, it did the same thing in Kushiro. In other words, it opened. An Ezo deer grazing nearby saw it happen. It was a buck with a magnificent set of antlers, measuring a good 70 centimeters across. The same music was playing in Kushiro. The same piece. And it was coming from the same invisible room.

The buck raised his antlers, opened his eyes wide, then—with total determination—made his way to the door. Yes, he walked through the door. Right through it, Then he vanished. And, as soon as he did, so did the door. It disappeared. Needless to say, the door in Kushiro was the door in Osaka, so when it disappeared in Kushiro, it disappeared in Osaka, too.

Okay—this story contains just one miracle. What is it? Keep in mind, there can only be one.

THE MAGICIAN

translated by Ted Goossen

TAKI
MONMA

Someone seemed to be visiting the main house.

Although we called it the main house, it was not a separate building: rather, it and our home were under the same roof, connected by an L-shaped corridor. When I ducked through the small door in the courtyard wall next to the bicycle shop, the entrance to my home was straight ahead, while the entrance to the main house was on my right. In short, I had to pass the entrance to the main house to reach my own. Originally it had been a single residence, and one could pass freely between the two sides, but now the hallway was blocked by a pile of wooden tea crates where it turned at a right angle. For some reason, though, we had a proper toilet and kitchen in our home as well. It was an odd sort of dwelling. The stack of boxes was there just to block the sight lines, so it didn't reach the ceiling; as a result, I had a good idea what was taking place on the other side. My mother and I lived so quietly, though, I doubt they could tell what we were up to.

A sliver of a garden with a single paulownia tree was squeezed between our kitchen and the veranda of the main house, so when I opened the kitchen window that day, I could see our neighbor's wife squatting beneath the tree. She seemed to be crying. I felt I shouldn't be watching, but I hesitated to close the window, thinking the sound might give away my presence. When I turned to leave, though, she stood up, wiped her face with her apron, and went back inside. Not long afterward, I heard the engine of the small truck that farmers used to peddle their vegetables, so I stepped outside to buy some just as the visitor was leaving. It must have been the wife's father, for the child was waving and calling, "Bye-bye, Grandpa."

I was still in high school, but I shopped for vegetables like a regular housewife. I made sure dinner was waiting for my mother when she got home from her job at a small sweet shop owned by one of our relatives. After dinner, she took a package of sweets from work to the people in the main house. They were our relatives too, but so distant I could never remember the precise connection, however often I was told. When she left, I sat down to study. She had already cleaned up the dinner dishes. I offered to do that too, but she refused. "You cook dinner for me, so I'll do the cleaning up," was the way she put it. When I persisted, she told me to "hit the books." I wasn't the type of student who slacked off until exams came around—I was constantly preparing and reviewing. Yet all those hours didn't seem to make me a more efficient student, since I blundered my way through my classes. My mother was blind to that, though: as long as I was sitting at my desk, she was content. I looked at the schoolbooks and notebooks spread out before me. This time I felt sure I'd have no trouble concentrating. Then, out of the corner of my eye, I saw a black something scurrying away. "Not again," I thought with a slight shudder. My attention had been captured by whatever it was: I turned off the lamp and shifted the desk so I could look down into the crack between it and the wall. Nothing there. It's still a bit too early in the year, I murmured, moving the desk back in place. When summer came around, the bugs would be larger and more brazen, scampering up the shadowy part of the wall where my lampshade blocked the light. I would hurl sharp pencils at their backs, but they were always too quick. I would move my desk and the pile of books next to it but still be unable to spot anything. They were glossy black roaches—"oil bugs" was the term we used for them. If it wasn't an oil bug, then what had just cut across my field of vision? I felt at once relieved and somehow a bit disappointed. And that white magnolia in the back garden—would it be blooming yet? We called it our back garden, yet it was actually part of the garden of the hospital behind our house, beyond a bamboo fence. When the father in the main house was ailing, the doctor had squeezed through a break in this fence to see his patient. He had recommended an operation from the beginning, but the old man had refused. "The guy thinks I'm a potato or turnip," he complained. "He just keeps saying 'Cut, cut.'" By the time he finally agreed it was too late. The problems in the main house had begun with his death. My mind drifted on, freed from the schoolwork in front of me. I imagined the white magnolia in full bloom, the cherries that would follow . . . Two cats were making love near where the break in the fence had been.

The old man's son, whom I called Niisan,[1] was repairing a flat tire in front of his shop, where the main house faced the street. A number of brand new bicycles were lined up

1. Girls and women often call somewhat older boys and men Niisan, literally "older brother."

inside. He was good with his hands, and fixing flats was one of his specialties. He was less good at concentrating on his work, though—he liked to sit and have a smoke in the chair reserved for customers or, if the weather was good, leaning in the entranceway. On my way home from school, I had no choice but to pass in front of the shop to reach the side door. "Welcome home," he would greet me, and I would reply "I'm back." He had long eyelashes and striking eyes that turned down somewhat at the corners. I glanced at them as I passed and was surprised again by how clear they were. He worked in his father's shop after demobilization, but during the war he had been employed in a munitions factory until he was called up for active service. At the factory, he had turned out one defective product after another, some of which he carried home and hid to keep them out of sight. When his father caught wind of this he gave him a good thrashing. Recognizing that the fault was his, Niisan did not turn against his father, nor did he resist his punishment. Working in his father's shop, therefore, presented no particular problem: he simply did as his father instructed, and the customers liked him. A younger, more intelligent-looking brother lived in the main house as well. That brother said that he wanted to go find work in Tokyo. The father planned to eventually pass the shop on to his elder son, and help the younger son either open a shop of his own or find work nearby. The elder son married a fine young woman who proved able to get along with everyone, including the younger brother. In fact, she seemed to get along better with him than with her own husband. Observing this, the father began to worry that the two of them might be hitting it off a bit too swimmingly, so he assented to his younger son's dream of going to Tokyo. He had been concerned that the big city was too dangerous, but that worry evaporated when his son told him he was applying to become a policeman. Which was, in fact, what he became.

Niisan was just leaving his shop one day when I got back from school. "Welcome home," he said. Before I could say, "I'm back," though, his wife stepped out of the house and asked where he was going. "Be right back," he called, jumping on a bicycle and pedaling away. His wife clucked her tongue in extreme annoyance. Pretending that I hadn't seen, I slipped in the side door. I was later than usual. The reason was my problems with math, which that day had me completely baffled. It felt like I was falling farther and farther behind. So I had gone to the staff room to ask my teacher to explain it to me one more time. He was just getting ready to leave. But when he realized I had a question, he pulled up a chair, sat down and opened the textbook.

"So what's the problem?" he asked.

"Everything," I replied.

"Everything?"

He began to jiggle his leg in a jittery sort of way. I've irritated him, I thought. He was the elder brother of a girl in my class—it hit me then that I should have asked her. The two of them looked very much alike. In fact, the similarity was striking—it was incredible how much members of the opposite sex could resemble each other! I had whipped up my courage to go to the staff room; yet I spent the whole time distracted by one thing and another, so that in the end I didn't learn a thing. I trudged along lugging my satchel, which felt heavier than ever. *I shouldn't have continued on to high school,* I thought. *I should be working beside my mother, making sweet bean paste.* Then, when I finally got home, Niisan flew off on his bicycle before I had a chance to say, "I'm back." He looked as if his wife had caught him with his hand in the cookie jar. Come to think of it, someone had once commented that Niisan and I looked alike. His wife had asked me to bring him home from the local bar where he hung out. When I got there, a woman emerged from the *noren* curtain hanging in the front door. "He's not here," she said. "You must be his little sister. I can see the resemblance." "Like hell you can," I thought. Maybe that's where he was off to this time—to see her.

There were frequent amateur theatrical contests in those days, and in one of them Niisan won first prize. For a magic act. I wasn't there, so I don't know exactly what he did. Still, it must have been pretty spectacular if he won. It was hard to reconcile that image with the way he looked bent over a flat tire. Apparently he made friends with other amateur entertainers in town, and the bar became their gathering place. It was shortly before his father's stomach pains began, and the shop was still managing all right. When his father's condition worsened he quit going out and stayed close to home, as one might expect. Yet his bedridden father continued to worry about the future of his family—his wife, his daughter-in-law, his grandchild. "His heart isn't really in the business," he fretted about his son and heir.

The father died. Niisan went on his best behavior. The shop continued on as before, the young wife pitching in to help (she learned how to fix flats and so forth), and her mother-in-law serving tea and chatting with the waiting customers. Nevertheless, the proceeds seemed to be tailing off, so Niisan's mother went into business on her own, buying fried tofu from a friend of hers and selling it on a downtown street in a nearby town. Why fried tofu, I wondered? I mean, you could get that anywhere.

When the father was alive and well, there had been lively after-dinner gatherings in the main house—we could hear them from next door, the sound traveling from their living room, down the inner corridor and over the tea boxes piled between their space and ours. I was invited to join them at New Year's, along with friends of the two sons. We played card games—*karuta, torampu* and *hanafuda*—and the father handed out prizes to the winners, since he didn't allow betting. When my mother saw him the next day she was sure to thank him for inviting me, and for the gifts I had received. "Not at all," he would reply with a laugh. "Just trying to keep my boys away from the nightspots." Things became quieter, though, when the younger son went to Tokyo. His big brother had never been one for family parties, tending to excuse himself with a "be right back."

Math wasn't the only class that gave me a hard time. So did my home economics class in Japanese-style sewing. I had to choose between it and cooking, and was about to go the cooking route, since it didn't require any homework, when friends warned me that it involved calculating calories. It was that word "calculate" that drove me into sewing. When I had passed the entrance exam and entered the school back in the sixth grade, it had been all girls, so the presence of home economics courses was quite natural. The school system changed the following year, which meant I continued on to high school after only three years. Some kids quit at that point, and I thought maybe I should do the same, so my mother went to consult with the father in the main house. "I've been in business for many years," he told her, "and there've been times when I didn't know how the devil I was going to pay the wholesaler, but I always got by somehow. I'm sure you'll manage somehow too—it's just three years. Don't let her quit school." So I decided to stay on, following his advice. A lot of things were changing around that time. My high school started accepting children from other towns, some of whom were boys. So we stopped being a "girls' school." The old ways still lingered, though, which was why I got stuck with sewing. Yet even there, "calculating" reared its ugly head. You needed to calculate your measurements and your estimates. I told my mother I would be better off making bean paste in the sweet shop with her.

"Don't take making bean paste so lightly," she chided me. "It requires a lot of training."

As a matter of fact, the daughter of our relatives who owned the sweet shop was one my classmates. It had already been arranged that she would marry one of their employees—he would take her family name, and the two of them would inherit the business. She was very good in all her classes; even her sewing projects were perfect. And she was nice. "If she can do it, so can I," I would think, watching her. But that enthusiasm never lasted long. I was more like Niisan, and I guess some of my classmates were like me too. We would get together after class or during the lunch break to discuss our plans.

I listened in while my classmates talked about their futures.

“I’m moving to Tokyo after graduation,” someone might offer. “I want to have as much fun as I can while I’m young and then settle down and get married.”

“You’re not going to college?”

“Entrance exams are hard—it’s quicker to pick up some secretarial skills and find an office job.”

“There are all kinds of colleges. Find one that’ll let you in.”

“I could care less about college.”

It had been because of the advice from the main house that I had stayed in school, and I doubted there was money for me to go on to college. I knew full well what the other girls were talking about, and had made my decision—I was going straight to work after high school.

I brought my overdue sewing project home with me and spread it out on the table. I quickly tired of it, though, and sat there vacantly worrying about my future. After a while, I wandered out into the garden, where I saw the wife next door sitting in the window mending some clothes. I wandered over and watched her hands as she worked.

“Is everything all right?” she asked. I told her how much trouble my sewing project was giving me. I couldn’t broach the subject with my mother, but with her it popped right out. “Bring it here,” she said. Then she did the whole thing for me, ostensibly teaching me as she went along. She stretched the garment over the clothes rack when she finished to make sure it didn’t become baggy. “You fold it once before you wear it,” she explained. Just then someone entered the shop. “Yes!” she called, quickly straightening up what was lying around before going out to the front. She hurried right back, though, removed the garment from the rack and pressed it to my chest. “I’ll show you how to fold it later,” she said, whereupon two men strode into the room. I slipped out the back way into the garden. From there, I could see what was going on inside through the lattice window. The men asked her where the stock was being kept, and she told them in the storehouse. One of the men went out, presumably to the storehouse adjoining the shop. The other walked around the room, placing tags on all the furniture before moving on to an inner room. I guessed he was tagging the items from her trousseau, everything she had brought with her as a bride. She stood there, straight and stiff, through the whole process.

The shop was closed after that. The wife had been raised on a farm, so she was able to supplement their income somewhat by working in the fields on the outskirts of town.

But she's so good at sewing, I thought. Niisan was no longer in front of the shop to say, "welcome back" when I arrived home from school. I thought he might be in the house, but when I passed through the side door and by their entranceway, it was locked, and the windows and veranda were shuttered as well.

"Isn't anyone left in the main house?" I asked my mother.

"The wife's away working," she answered.

"Where? What about her little boy?" I rattled on. It turned out the wife was taking the child with her whenever she landed odd jobs. But her needlework is amazing, I thought again. Niisan's mother had apparently gone to Tokyo to confer with her younger son. I couldn't imagine, though, that he would toss away his policeman's job and come back to take over the family's failing business.

That night, when I peeked through our kitchen window, I could see a light in the main house. There was a dim glow behind the pile of tea crates stacked in the corner of the hall.

The firebombing of Tokyo had driven my mother and me from our home. My father was at the front, fighting the war. She had grabbed me, and we had boarded a train at Ueno Station that was so crammed it seemed some people might be pushed out the windows. We had shown up at the home of these distant, distant relatives. There had been no prior visits, no real communication between our family and theirs; yet their father welcomed us, expressing relief that we were safe. "You can have the rooms my mother used in her final years," he said. Indeed, before the day was out he had stacked the tea crates at the turn in the corridor, separating our space from theirs.

My father's ashes arrived shortly before the war ended. When my mother shook the urn we could hear little bits rattling around inside. There was no news of my mother's brother, also at the front. She wrote to him constantly, worried that, since none of us remained in Tokyo, he wouldn't know where to find us. She was convinced, though, that somehow he would make his way to where we were.

We went to the station each evening after the surrender, hoping to greet him when he got off the train. We have to be there, my mother said. He may know the station's name, but he has no idea where we live. We weren't the only ones waiting—many families from the area had sons and brothers returning from the front. The benches were always full. Some waited for a week, and some for just two or three days, but when the last train pulled out we all went home. One night, exactly a month after the war was over, my mother's brother—my uncle, in other words—stepped down from the train. He was no longer the fresh-faced youth we had seen off to war, however. He stayed with us for a week and then returned to Tokyo. My mother fretted over him as if he were her own child. Only when a letter came from him telling us where he was staying did she relax.

The generosity of the late father of the main house explained why my mother felt so beholden to his family. Once again, she took a small box of sweets from work and went next door to see how things were. I was supposedly studying at my desk, but I felt on edge, so I stood on my tiptoes where the tea crates were stacked in the hall and tried to see what was going on the other side. I could make out Niisan's voice, the first time I had heard it in a long while. The voices of his wife and my mother too. I could tell which of them was speaking, but not what they were talking about.

A few days later, on my mother's day off from work, she announced she was going out. At first, she wouldn't tell me where she was heading—I "didn't need to know" was how she put it—but on the way out she let it drop that her destination was the bar where Niisan had been spending so much of his time. I sensed there might be trouble. Then, several days later, I heard my mother and Niisan's mother, who had just come back from visiting her younger son, talking in the garden.

"Thank you for pitching in while I was gone," the son's mother said, handing my mother a gift from Tokyo.

"I wish I could have been of more use," my mother replied. "But I'm not very good at that sort of thing. I don't think I helped at all." I could tell she was almost in tears. "I heard the proprietress boasted she was going to squeeze his inheritance out of him."

"We don't have any inheritance to be squeezed out of."

I listened eagerly to their conversation. "What can you expect from a fool like that," his mother said at the end.

"But the woman was a real beauty," my mother added, unable to hide her admiration. "She was tying up her sleeves when she came in and sat down—her kimono was *meisen* silk, and her obi was wide and fastened in a seashell bow. Any man would fall for her."

Why did my mother have to go there, I wondered.

Niisan resurfaced at last. The shutters on the windows and veranda of the main house were open again, and I could see him moving about inside. The shop doors were still closed, though, so we didn't exchange greetings when I returned from school. He didn't even seem to notice when I slipped through the side door and passed by his entranceway. I lethargically changed out of my school uniform. A heavy melancholy flowed over the stack of tea crates into our house, filling it. I opened our kitchen window. The young wife was squatting beneath the paulownia. I blinked and she was gone. In fact, she had left some time before for her parents' house, her child in tow. So that was why her father had showed up back then. Someone told me he had said, "Why should I waste my own hard-earned money on someone who refuses to work hard!" In fact, however, he may actually have been hoping his son-in-law would buckle down and do what was necessary to preserve his family. But when he thrust divorce papers in his face and told him to take them to city hall, his son-in-law simply said "yes" and did as he was told. Most likely the father-in-law had expected some resistance, perhaps a plea for "one more chance," but if that were the case, his plan had laid an egg.

When I checked that evening, a light was burning beyond the tea crates. Niisan and his mother were in there alone. I really wanted to know what they might be talking about, even imagined I could hear their voices, but when I listened more closely I heard nothing. Maybe my ears were playing tricks on me.

"What are you doing!" my mother scolded me. She was wiping her wet hair, fresh from the bath. But she knew I was worried about what was going on in the main house, so she added, "He's leaving tomorrow."

"Who? Niisan?"

"Yes."

According to her, Niisan had collected his things from the shop and the house and then tried to leave, but his mother had stopped him. "Don't run away like a thief in the night. Wait till tomorrow and then go," she had said. "And don't come back. You needn't send word, even if you die."

"If I die the police will let you know," was his apparent rejoinder.

Niisan left the next morning, not early but when everyone was up and around. Carrying a big suitcase.

For the first time in ages I saw Niisan's brother, the policeman. My mother and I had moved back to Tokyo shortly after my graduation from high school. My mother's brother was living in company housing; the younger brother bunked in the police dorm. They went out for an occasional drink, solitary bachelors that they were. My mother and I found a small room off an entranceway to rent. I got to see the policeman because of a letter sent to him by Niisan, inviting his younger brother to attend a performance of his magic show. "It's just a short set between acts, but please come anyway," he wrote. My uncle asked my mother and me to accompany them. She had promised to meet her friend that day, but she encouraged me to go. She and her friend were trying to open a Western-style dressmaking shop. They were dead serious about it.

My uncle and the policeman were very considerate, coming all the way to the station closest to my home to meet me. Then we set off, our only guide the almost indecipherable address and map Niisan had enclosed with his letter. We had to change trains several times to get there. I left the navigation to them and sat looking out at the Tokyo cityscape passing by the window or at the fascinating outfits some of the women on the train were wearing. The station where we got off was far from the city center. I trotted after my uncle and the policeman, who were turning the map this way and that, trying to figure out the route.

Finally, we arrived at our destination. The "theater" turned out to be a rundown strip joint. The policeman seemed at a loss what to do. He went up to the man working the door and conferred with him for a few moments, trying to pinpoint when Niisan would be performing. The arrangement was that we would attend that "interval" and no more. If I hadn't been there, they would probably have gone straight in. Then again, he was a policeman.

"Shall we have a drink over there in the meantime?" asked my uncle.

"No, that wouldn't work. We'd end up missing the act."

After that exchange, the three of us stood there uncomfortably.

At last the doorman gave us the thumb's-up, and we walked through the door, them first and me following. The curtain was still up, and the shouts and catcalls from the audience hadn't subsided. My chaperones could hardly grab me and cover my eyes, so they just looked away from the stage until the curtain finally went down. When it went up again a few seconds later, there was Niisan standing on the stage, dressed in a swallowtail coat. He started out with some sleight-of-hand, and wrapped up his routine by sending a dove flying into the air. Then the curtain descended again. It was the first time I had seen him do magic tricks. The first time I had seen him on stage, period.

We were all very quiet when we left the theater. Each of us entertained our own thoughts—the policeman had his, my uncle had his, I had mine—but no one put them into words.

My uncle spotted a stall by the side of the road. "Want to eat some *oden*?" he asked me. I looked at the policeman. He nodded, so we ducked inside the flimsy awning. My uncle and the policeman drank a glass of warm *shōchu,* while the man running the stall served me some of the steaming food. Even so, it was an outdoor stall, and our backs were cold. We knew my mother would worry if it got too late, so the two men called it quits after a single glass.

"We gotta get this girl home," my uncle said, cuffing me lightly on the side of the head. I wished the night could last forever. The three of us cut a sharp figure as we walked shoulder to shoulder down the busy street towards the station, me in the middle, collars over our ears and hands plunged deep in the pockets of our overcoats.

translated by Michael Emmerich

ALICELAND

MAKOTO
TAKAYANAGI

The dream was composed like a tower of layers without end, rising upward and losing themselves in the infinite, or layers coiling downward, losing themselves in the bowels of the earth. When it swooped me in its undulations, the spiraling began, and this spiral was a labyrinth. There was no vault and no bottom, no walls and no return. But there were themes repeating themselves with exactitude.

—Anaïs Nin, *Winter of Artifice*

To the Alice in my heart.

1. EXISTENTIAL PRINCIPLES

Aliceland is, as you might judge from the semblance of its name to those of places such as Iceland or Ireland, an island country. You must not, however, call up an image of an isle surrounded on all sides by ocean. Were you, instead, to envision a solitary spot of land suspended in the great blackness of space, or floating in the lightless depths of the earth, you would be at least partially correct.

Either way, there is no disputing the fact that Aliceland is airborne, or afloat—that, more exactly, it is adrift in a universe of the imagination. Aliceland's adriftness stands as the first principle of its being.

And just as an energetically spinning top will sometimes seem to be at rest, Aliceland's adriftness is, in the end, a pretense. The superficiality of its detachment is its second existential principle.

2. SIZE AND LOCATION

Since ancient times, myriad hypotheses have been advanced regarding Aliceland's size; some declare it tiny as a poppyseed; others claim it is larger than the universe itself. There is no knowing which of these many interpretations is right. After all, no unit of measurement exists by which we might assess the country's dimensions.

One proposal—an epoch-making view, much discussed of late by our compatriots, that contains all those that preceded it—holds that the country is forever in the throes of a cycle of expansion and contraction, that it expands from poppyseed size to larger-than-the-universe size and then shrinks back down again. It is said, furthermore, that insofar as everything in this country grows and shrinks at the same rate, we do not feel it happening.

Many theories have been offered up, as well, concerning the country's location. Broadly speaking, these fall into two categories: those that argue Aliceland is to be found drifting someplace on earth, and those who say it is not restricted in its drifting to the limited area of the planet.

3. FOUNDING / BOOKS

Aliceland's establishment as a country is said to have been nearly concurrent with the emergence of the human race. This is suggested by, among other things, the existence of an ancient hieroglyphic text describing its origins. Researchers are currently struggling to decipher this manuscript, but it is a daunting task, as each animal it depicts is invested with its own sacred meaning—the crested ibis is the symbol for wisdom, for instance. The cow is patience, the falcon is bravery, the baboon is wit.

To be sure, a certain faction is utterly convinced that the manuscript is fake. But if this were true, then all the books in this land of ours must be forgeries as well. Or rather, we live in a land in which books are not books if they are not forgeries (incomplete, unfinished, disordered forgeries).

4. OCEAN, RIVER, LAKE

Whenever you turn into a narrow alley in Aliceland, you see the blue of the ocean. This is true no matter what direction you turn in, or into which alley; so long as the alley is narrow, you see the ocean. No one can say for sure whether it is an actual ocean. There is the scent of the tide, it is true, but to some this faint odor recalls not water but blood. Perhaps the truth is that it is the scent of an ocean of blue blood.

The riverwaters flow with considerable force from the ocean to a lake at the heart of Aliceland, into which they pour. Beneath the lake, a channel leads back to the ocean. Thus, however far upstream you and the waters may venture, you never escape that bloody scent, and the waters never cease their circulation.

5. "THE DROWNED"

The rivers are home to the drowned. "The drowned are not men who sink into the water and suffocate. They are an altogether different class of being—persons possessed of a startling ability, when left for a time in the water, to adapt to that environment. Their ways are bizarre, and—though they, too, take pleasure in frolicking in the water—diametrically opposed to those of fish. Fish, it is widely known, always swim against the current; those dreadful victims of aquatism simply drift lazily along just beneath the surface. In their encounters with land-dwellers, they exhibit the most scrupulous manners: polite nods, exaggerated bows, respectful summersaults, and so on. These demonstrations are utterly lacking, however, in societal value."[1]

6. MIRROR / SKY

In every mirror in this land, a clear blue sky is reflected. And yet there is no sky overhead. The sky exists solely in the mirrors. I should perhaps say, so I am not misunderstood, that we are not talking here about pictures of the sky affixed to the mirrors. The sky reflected there, only in those mirrors, is the bona-fide, nonexistent sky. The very sky the Belgian painter in the frock coat and bowler hat painted, but also a living sky in constant motion.

Occasionally, someone flits across the mirrored sky. Naturally, you will not see anyone overhead when you look up. Glancing back down at the mirror, however, you now see reflected there a crowd of people comfortably riding the wind. All of them are the frock-coated, bowler-hatted painter.

7. QUEEN ALICE

No one has ever seen the face of our ruler, Queen Alice. Photographs of her—it has been confirmed that she is female—do exist, but each shows a lady of a different age and appearance. It is impossible that they are all one and the same woman.

Naturally, there are times when Alice reveals herself to subjects. She appears before the populace on "Alice Day," in the nude. Her face, of course, covered by many veils.

Alice's figure, at these times, is so unsurpassed that . . . but we must not talk of such things. Her beauty is beyond words, and we are forbidden by law to describe it. We are permitted only admiring sighs, which spread outward in concentric circles until they cover all the land.

8. ALICE THE SACRED VIRGIN

We call Queen Alice by another name, as well: Alice the Sacred Virgin. Some say she is 10, some 16, some 127; her true age is unknown. She sleeps, it is said, with anywhere from a few thousand to as many as ten thousand men in a single night, thus living up to her name.

That which she desires above all from her mates, though, is eternity. Everyone knows this. If you are prepared to accept her price for eternity, Alice the Sacred Virgin will lie with you whenever you like. It is not our responsibility if she leaves you ruined.

One theory holds that this land was formed from the bodies of such ruined men. At night you can hear, coming from no place in particular, an eerie sound that could be the wind or their sighs.

9. LIGHT / WOOD

There is, in Aliceland, an esoteric sect whose members are capable of becoming light when they think of light, and wood when they focus on wood. As a rule, they sleep as wood from dusk till morn, then diffuse all across the land, as light, from morn till dusk.

If just before dawn you were to visit the forest where the trees (these people) sleep, all together, you would find that there are branches about a meter above the earth protruding from the trunk of every tree, and in the crook of each branch is a vagina-shaped opening from which a white, milky liquid that smells of chestnut blossoms seems, only just now, to have trickled out. The liquid gives off a light that never dims.

No sooner does the sun rise, however, than the forest dissipates into the air, leaving a cluster of brightly (sometimes glaringly) shining lights that scatter almost immediately, leaving nothing behind.

10. PLANTS AND ANIMALS

The vast majority of the flowers in Aliceland are iris or amaryllis. Their petals are formed of ice, and they bloom in the depths of night, only to melt as the temperature rises each morning before anyone is up and about. The plants' official names are Alice Ice Iris and Alice Ice Amaryllis.

There are, in Aliceland, many lice and mice. Their sizes are reversed, however—the lice are as big as mice, the mice as tiny as lice—and so they are known officially as Alice Lice Mice and Alice Mice Lice respectively. These creatures are visible to us, but we cannot touch them. They are not accustomed to being touched, so if we try they simply smile oddly at us and fade away.

11. FACE-CHANGING DAY

The first day of the New Year is Face-Changing Day. People set out together for the central plaza. When the midnight ringing of the bells heralds the coming of the New

Year, each of us gives thanks to the face he has used over the past year, then removes it. The faces are classified by gender and age, and numbered. The lottery to assign faces begins. Nothing could be more exciting.

We draw lots in an orderly fashion, one by one, showing our joy or sorrow at the results. We are thrilled if we receive a beautiful face, and terribly disappointed if we get an ugly one. When the lottery is over, we don our fresh faces and trade comments on each other's looks. We commiserate with some, noting that there is no helping it, we have to live with our new faces until next year, and they walk home with drooping shoulders; others go off full of excitement, chattering and laughing. Thus, in Aliceland, is fairness maintained in the distribution of looks.

12. NEWSPAPERS

Everything relating to the future, however how great or small—above all, things that will take place tomorrow—gets written up in the newspaper, so our actions are prescribed by what we read there. To put it more precisely, we have no choice but to follow the newspapers.

Suppose an article reports that, "A young man, despairing, committed suicide by jumping from a tower. No one present attempted to stop him, though his intentions were evident; they just looked on in silence." Since this is what the newspaper says, those who find themselves on the spot the next day will find it impossible to help, even should they wish to. The coercive force of time strips them of the freedom to behave as they might like.

The bookstores start selling newspapers at exactly the same time each morning. People line up to purchase their copies, read them as if they are competing to see who can finish first, then head off each in his or her own direction looking relieved to have learned what the following day holds. No one knows who writes the articles. Many, of course, stubbornly refuse to join in, and do not read the newspaper at all.

13. SONGS

First, I ask that you listen to this song, which our countrymen have secretly gone on singing through the ages, right down to the present day.

Alice and Teres, siblings though they be
Alice and Teres were wed

But the weight of their sin
Drove Teres from home
Astride a white horse, lute in hand
Roaming the provinces, traveling at night
Has he come to the ends of the earth?
Died in a field, in the desert?
Murdered in the secret forest?
Yet Alice waits. She waits
For Teres's return
Alice and Teres, siblings though they be
Alice and Teres were wed

14. TERES

As this song indicates, all manner of hypotheses and suppositions are bandied about regarding Teres, Queen Alice's brother and husband. Most claim that he has gone off to wander in the real world.

The most widely accepted, though, is that his apparent disappearance is merely a ruse, and in fact he is being held under duress in the castle. This does not in itself refute any of the other conjectures—that he was killed in the secret forest (by Queen Alice herself, no less!), or fell sick and died 2,300 years ago, or took his own life in a fit of madness.

Some have gone so far as to suggest that Teres never existed in the first place, or—in a sense this seems the most reliable theory—that he is simply a ghostly vision of Alice herself.

In any event, the image of Teres casts a dark shadow on this country.

15. QUEEN ALICE'S (FAKED) MONOLOGUE

"The next moment I saw everything in natural colors, only the colors were misplaced. I knew then that I was out of my mind. I looked for my brother and when I found him he was staring at himself in the mirror. I looked over his shoulder, into the mirror, and I could no longer recognize him. He was a complete stranger. I called him by name, I shook him, but he continued to stare at his image in the mirror. At last I understood that he didn't recognize himself either. My God, I thought, we've both gone insane. The worst of it was, I didn't love him any more."[2]

16. THE CASTLE

The castle in which, according to one hypothesis, Teres is confined stands atop a small hill, such that it is visible from all across Aliceland—or, from the other perspective, such that one can gaze across all Aliceland from the castle.

Nonetheless, the castle is all but impossible to reach. It seems close enough, and yet the distance separating you from it never narrows, however far you travel. At some point, you realize that the castle you had seen in front of you just a moment before has suddenly disappeared, only to appear again, jutting up from its hill, directly behind you.

Occasionally, chance will lead someone all the way there. But once you enter the castle, you find that it is a labyrinth inside, one from which you will never again emerge. Queen Alice is, they say, the only one able to come and go as she likes. So there are no guards. None are needed.

17. "BIRDS"

The castle is home to an enormous number of birds, all of just a single species. "The bird is purely metaphysical—a quaternary type of the genus dodo, having a tiny, dorsal aperture through which it delivers homilies on the nature of all things. As a species it is extinct; as an eidolon it retains its corporeality—but only if maintained in a state of equipoise. The wings, you will observe, are almost atrophied—because in the pseudocatalepsy of the dream it does not need to fly, it needs only to imagine that it is flying. The bird is definitely not obscene and has never been known to foul its nest. It lays a speckled egg about the size of a walnut whenever it is about to undergo metamorphosis. It feeds on the Absolute when hungry, but it is not a carrion bird. It is exclusively migratory and, despite the vestigial wings, flies incessantly over great imaginary tracts."[3]

18. HOBBYHORSES

The hobbyhorse is our principal mode of transport. Depending on the rider's imaginative energies, the hobbyhorse can soar through the sky or dive to the sea floor; some claim to have traveled as far as the underworld or the millenarian Kingdom of God.

The vibrant coloring of the hobbyhorse heads might at first glance recall a carousel horse; the great difference between them is that the hobbyhorses of this country move through time as well as space. In this sense, they function much like time machines, though you might not think it from their form.

A hobbyhorse is simple to ride. You straddle its body, grasp the handles that extrude sideways from its head, then close your eyes and envision the place and time you plan to visit. If the vision you call up is insufficiently real, then of course your hobbyhorse will remain in the here and now.

19. HUMAN-POWERED AIRPLANES

Those who are unsure of their imagination but are confident in their physical strength are provided with human-powered airplanes. Because this is the more realistic mode of transport, people who fly these planes must obey air traffic signals and laws, speed limits, etcetera. You might picture the human-powered airplanes as something akin to winged bicycles that fly when you pedal them.

In actual fact, flying these things demands almost inconceivable reserves of energy, since the sky you are navigating doesn't exist. For some years now, pilots have been required to obtain Human-powered Airplane General Flying licenses, and training schools were established. At these schools, special machinery and drugs are mobilized to strengthen to an extraordinary degree the thigh, stomach and back muscles, though regrettably this training is matched by (or perhaps prompts) a proportional decline in imaginative power.

In contemporary Aliceland, then, it is becoming possible to split the country into two categories as far as transport is concerned: the hobbyhorsers (a sizable majority, at least by the numbers) and those who prefer human-powered airplanes (sizable in terms of the strength required).

20. BOY HUNTING

Once a month, on a night when the full moon shines across a cloudless sky, they hold a boy hunt. About a hundred boys are stripped and released into a field. Dogs with human faces are unchained and set after them. The human-faced dogs run with all their might in pursuit of the boys. Dog-faced humans amble along behind them.

The boys run extremely fast, but there is no escaping the human-faced dogs, so tenacious are they in their pursuit. When the human-faced dogs have encircled the boys, the dog-faced humans finally catch up and, slowly taking out their knives, slice off the boys' ears and noses and hollow out their eyes. Then, carefully, slowly, they peel off the boys' skin.

Oddly, each time there is a boy hunt ten or so of the loveliest boys go missing, along with precisely the same number of human-faced dogs. Neither the boys nor the human-faced dogs have ever been seen again.

21. GIRLS / DOLLS

The girls are at least a little luckier than our boys. Once a year, on Alice Day, the finest, loveliest girls are kidnapped while they sleep by some unknown hand and ferried away to the castle. There, they are kept as living dolls. The process of living-dollification demands a highly refined technique and the administration of a precisely measured blend of drugs (one rumor holds that Teres himself is the doll maker).

The sleeping, dollified girls, stored in large vacuum-sealed bottles, are secretly offered up for sale. They fetch extremely high prices but move so quickly that it is near impossible to get your hands on one (needless to say, this is because at night the dolls go back to being girls).

Though the supply cannot meet the demand, it is simply not feasible to scale up production while simultaneously maintaining quality. Still, the notable decline in recent years in the population of appropriately lovely girls is beginning to pose serious difficulties for doll lovers.

22. NUMERALS

In Aliceland, special importance is attached to the numeral 1. Indeed, 1 is essentially the only numeral that exists. This is because people regard 1 as the origin of everything, and see all the numerals from 2 on up as mere repetitions of it.

In truth, though, one numeral is accorded more respect—or perhaps one should say that people are secretly in awe of it—and that is 0. This numeral, in actual fact, rules our country. The 0 of absence, of emptiness, of eternity, which has neither beginning nor end—this numeral beyond numerals seems, somehow, intimately connected to Aliceland's principles of existence. Compared to 0, people believe, 1 is just a momentary blip, a pretense.

23. COLORS

In this country, no one heeds the order of colors. For instance, "The grass was violet instead of green; horses were blue; men and women were gray, ashen gray, like evil spirits; the sun was black, the moon was green."[4] The colors of things are susceptible to change, moreover, from one day to the next, and depending on the time. Grass that was purple a week earlier may now be flaming red, and twenty minutes later turn a perfect, spotless white. While these changes may seem, at first, to be the result of an insurrection on the part of the colors themselves, they are in fact governed by rigorous laws.

There is a moment in Aliceland, as the air grows clear and sharp and the temperature rises, when everything seems to fade. Borders grow vague, causing certain things to liquefy while others evaporate altogether, assuming a gaseous form. Afterward, a peculiar spiritual energy lingers in the air. At such moments, Aliceland itself is stripped of the very basis for its existence and is transformed into a country that is nowhere.

24. EXISTENTIAL PRINCIPLES

Aliceland, as a country, is infinitely and eternally open, temporally and spatially, to everyone (there is, of course, a question as to whether the concept "country" as we know it is in any way appropriate in this instance). It is a world in which the infinite inhabits a single point; an instant holds for an eternity; and the part is the whole—*or so it seems.* This, in a nutshell, is Aliceland.

And so in Aliceland a grain of sand is a boulder, and it is a mountain (the reverse is also true). A drop of water is an ocean. All people are a single undying person, and each tree is every tree. The essences of things are revealed to the greatest possible degree, and as a consequence essences lose their meaning.

Aliceland exists in reality (setting aside issues of space and time). There can be no doubt about that. Though neither believing nor doubting falls any longer within the realm of our responsibilities.

ENDNOTES

1. Alfred Jarry, "Les mœurs des noyés."
2. Henry Miller, "Astrological Fricassee."
3. Henry Miller, "Burlesque."
4. Henry Miller, "Astrological Fricassee."

The quotations that appear in this story were slightly modified by Makoto Takayanagi.

translated by Jeffrey Angles

EVIL FLOURISHES BUT ITŌ ENCOUNTERS JIZŌ IN BROAD DAYLIGHT

HIROMI ITŌ

These deadlines that come once a month are a lot like menstruation.

My friends who are the same age tell me that they've gone through menopause or are on the verge. But for me, it hasn't stopped yet. I've spent these last forty-some years with my menstrual blood. Once a month. Once a month. Once a month. I'm completely used to it. I've grown close to it—in fact, I know how to live with it far better than I know how to live with my own husband. I ought to treat the installments of *The Thorn-Puller* that I submit once a month to the literary magazine *Gunzō* like I treat my menstrual cycle. I ought to just keep writing, linking one installment to the next like my periods that just keep on coming.

My mother's suffering, my father's suffering, my husband's suffering.

Loneliness, anxiety, frustration.

Various forms of suffering pour down upon me, but these days my suffering is no longer suffering. When I use the suffering that pours down upon me as material for my writing, I become preoccupied with observing suffering and talking about it, and when I talk about it, I find myself forgetting that suffering causes pain. And so what's really happening? Isn't Jizō answering my prayers and removing my thorns?

The miasma arising from my sick husband's anger was growing worse, and I struggled with the very thought of it. My return to California grew closer by the minute. I had no choice to but to face him. I had to face the question of where we'd go from here, if our family might even separate and go different ways.

Because I was in Japan, I had plenty of friends to talk to. Every one of my friends had something wrong in their lives. Some were having trouble with men, some had conflicts with their families, some faced financial troubles.

I had all sorts of female friends who would sit down and listen to me. All I had to do was open up. The problem was that no one really knew what my husband was like. True, some of them had met him. A few had even exchanged pleasantries with him and said, let's get together again sometime. To them, my husband might look a little disheveled, but when he opened his mouth, he seemed to be a pleasant, intellectual, well-brought-up, quiet *gaijin*. Huh? *Gaijin?* Why the slang term to refer to a foreigner, you ask? Well, what's the matter with a *gaijin*'s wife calling her husband a *gaijin*? He is a *gaijin*—an "outsider"—after all. I couldn't think of him in the abstract as just a "foreigner." He was a stranger; it was my mistake to let someone like him in and start living with him under the same roof.

I didn't know what to do with myself, so I gave in to my daughter's feelings. I'm talking about my other daughter—Aiko's half-sister. She had left the nest and was now living elsewhere, but in some ways she was still right behind me, listening to my feelings, and even sharing her frustrations about men with me. At the time I separated from her father, she was about the same age as Aiko is now. She had been through all sorts of suffering, not all of which had been entirely necessary. The bitterness and sweetness she'd tasted along the way had matured her, so she was the first one I turned to this time. She listened obligingly at first, but before long, she wrote me the following message.

>> I feel sorry for Aiko, but to tell the truth, I think it's okay to be a little selfish and call it quits. Then you'd be living in a way that's true to yourself. It makes me excited just to think about it.

She was barely twenty years old, but there she was talking to me like she knew everything. My rage suddenly boiled over. I felt like an on-demand water heater that had been in storage for the last twenty years. I might not have boiled over anytime recently, but suddenly my daughter had pushed my buttons. I clicked Reply and began angrily jabbing at the keyboard.

> Keep quiet when it comes to things you don't know anything about.

> When have you ever seen me living in a way that *wasn't* true to myself?

> Come to think of it, have I ever shown you how I act when I'm really being true to myself?

So I was left living in turmoil, not knowing where to direct my indignation and resentment.

I'd gotten to thinking.

Maybe I'd go back to California. Without making a big deal out of it, I could take the money out of our savings account and send my most important books to the place where my older daughter—yeah, the cheeky one—was living. I could leave everything else behind. Abandon it all. Just grab my passport and hard drive, meet Aiko in front of her school, and whisk her away on an airplane.

Or maybe I'd find a cheap apartment somewhere nearby and move in. Aiko could go back and forth, or maybe move in with me and go visit her father on the weekends. She'd be just like all the other kids with divorced parents. After all, Aiko's friends went back and forth between their parents, spending one day with their mothers then the next with their fathers.

The other day Aiko said, Mom, please, I should get a cellphone. So-and-so has one, she brought it to school, it had a long strap on it. So-and-so—you know, that other girl—she's also got one.

I told her, kids don't need such things, cellphones are nothing but trouble, a cellphone wouldn't do you any good, but Aiko held out and argued back.

Our teacher let so-and-so and so-and-so have them, our teacher said it'll help them stay in touch with their parents because their parents are divorced. So, *Okaasan* (she said that in Japanese), the first morning I take my cellphone to school, I want to hang my Tamagotchi from it (she said that in English).

I'd gotten to thinking.

One of those simple little cabins for surfers would be enough for me, I'm Japanese, I've lived in tiny, single-room, 75-foot-square apartments before, I could sleep in just a few square feet and use a few more square feet for everything else. If I did that then maybe Aiko was right, maybe it would be hard on us if she didn't have her own cellphone. Still, when I tried looking up prices on the net, I found that those simple little cabins for surfers are ridiculously expensive, especially considering they have so few conveniences. And if I were to leave Aiko, her Japanese wouldn't get any better—it would just grow worse, and soon we wouldn't even be able to talk as mother and daughter any more. When that thought hit me, a cloud passed over my heart, and I felt despondent. As the classical poet said, *This is the darkness of loving a child.*

I've started to notice something odd. I hear people talk about Jizō all the time. Here, there, everywhere. No one knows that I've been thinking so much about the Thorn-puller, yet everyone seems to be talking about Sugamo and the power of the Jizō located there.

One of the nurses by my mother's bedside said to her, Itō-san, Sugamo, just think of Sugamo. Her words "Sugamo, just think of Sugamo" seemed to be some form of encouragement.

Sugamo. The word took me by surprise.

Seeing my reaction, the nurse said, your mother talks about Sugamo so often. Actually, I'm fond of the place too. I've got a daughter in Tokyo, so every time I go there, I make sure to visit Sugamo. That's why I promised your mother that if she gets better, we'll go there together. You know, *Sugamo* is a secret little word that we share, just the two of us.

As the nurse said this, my mother, who can only communicate with facial expressions, smiled and nodded.

I told the nurse, I haven't been to Sugamo for quite a long time.

How many years had it been since I'd been there last? Even so, I'd been thinking recently that I'd like to pay a visit.

The nurse said, you know the honey shop near here? They've got a branch on the street that leads up to the Jizō temple. It sells honey and all kinds of stuff. Well, they started selling "sudden dumplings" too. It was like the Tokyoites were imitating us or something—as they ate them, they kept saying how great they tasted in their funny Tokyo dialect, how nice the texture was, meanwhile they kept buying them and gobbling them down as if "sudden dumplings" were some kind of Sugamo specialty.

Let me interject here. A "sudden dumpling" or *ikinari dango* is a Kumamoto specialty. You take a slice of raw sweet potato, some red bean paste, wrap them in dough, then give your creation a brief, sudden steaming—that's why it's called a "sudden dumpling." I could imagine how surprised she was to find them for sale in Sugamo, more than halfway across the country.

Clearly, she was surprised. In fact, she said, I couldn't have been more surprised than if I was in Hell and ran into Lord Jizō myself! So I did what anyone would do, I bought some and ate them—those same little treats I've been eating ever since I was a little kid. And ever since then, *ikinari dango* always makes me think of Sugamo.

I was talking to a certain poet's widow when suddenly she said, well, why don't we meet in Sugamo then? That'd be perfect. From there, we can go visit my husband's grave.

That surprised me. What are the chances she'd suggest Sugamo as a meeting place?

I had only met her husband, the poet, once while he was alive. (I will refrain from using honorific language when writing about him. There is a part of me that really wants to show my respect, but I have the feeling that if I use the codified language Japanese use in such situations, I won't sound sincere.) Even at that first meeting, I was completely in awe of him. He was a famous poet, after all, and I pricked up my ears to take in everything he said. Every sound he made sounded familiar; in fact, his manner of speaking reminded me of my grandfather Tatsugorō, my uncle Tatsuo, my uncle Kazumi, and all my other male relatives (none of whom were still living). But then I realized, no, it wasn't his voice that sounded like them. It was his pronunciation. Changing the first sound in my name—*hi*—to the Tokyo pronunciation—*shi,* he whispered, my wife's reading your work, *Shi*romi-chan. His distinctive Tokyo accent made me feel as if I had ascended to heaven.

He died not long after that. I was off in California keeping myself busy when it happened. When I managed to get my next book out, I sent a copy to his wife, even though we hadn't met. In response, she sent me a postcard expressing her thanks in generous but not at all flowery terms. Again, the next time I published a book, I sent it to her, and once again, I received another postcard. Once again I sent a book, and once again I received a card. That continued for over ten years. It was like a long, thin thread of connection had formed between the two of us, even though we'd never met. But I hadn't received a postcard lately. Judging from the age of the poet at the time of his death, I guessed she probably wasn't any spring chicken either. She might be growing old and having problems as well. I began to worry. A little while later, the postcard I had been expecting finally arrived. I wrote her a card back: *I was worried when no postcard arrived. I'm pleased to hear there is no change on your end. I write books to make a living, but when your postcard didn't arrive, I began to feel like maybe the real reason that I write all these books is because I'm really hoping to hear from you.*

A box of chocolates arrived from her. I called her on the phone to thank her, and in doing so, I heard her voice for the first time. Like her postcards, her speech was quick, generous and concise. Her accent wasn't as strong as her deceased husband's, but I could still detect traces of a Tokyo accent. While I was talking to her, the thought came to me—*Sugamo. Sugamo again!* Her husband's grave was located there. Once I had tried to find his grave on my own. If you're walking from Sugamo Station, you reach the temple where he is buried before you arrive at the shop-lined street that leads to the Jizō temple. I managed to find the graveyard, but the graves were packed so tightly together that I couldn't find his.

I told her that I'd gone there, but that I hadn't been able to find it. I told her, I must have some sort of karmic connection to Sugamo. I've been thinking about the Jizō temple constantly, and I'd really like to make a trip there to see it again.

Oh really? Well, why don't we meet in Sugamo then? That'd be perfect. I'll invite so-and-so—here, she mentioned the name of a poet who was a mutual friend of ours.

It had been thanks to that particular friend that more than a decade before, I had met the dead poet in the first place. The poet's wife sounded so happy that I could imagine her jumping for joy. Why don't we go visit his grave together?

I don't remember exactly when, but at some point years before, my husband came to Japan to spend some time with me. We were out with our daughter Aiko, who was still little at the time, when we passed a small statue of Jizō standing alongside a city street. I stopped, bought a stick of incense from the little window beside him (a stick and a candle cost a measly ¥20), and gave them to him as an offering. Aiko and I would sometimes do that when we were out on our own. When my husband saw us, however, he began berating me: *it seems my wife is giving my daughter some sort of religious education without consulting me!* It took quite a while to clear up the misunderstanding.

In fact, we only really managed to clear it up the next time he came to Japan. A friend of mine took him to a bunch of places. They were at a Shinto shrine together when she threw a coin in the offering box and pressed her hands together in a gesture of prayer. He asked, who are you praying to? Not looking the least concerned, she answered, to anyone who listens to me. Later, back in America, my husband repeated that story over and over again: *There's nothing stranger than what passes as faith among the Japanese. You might call it religion, but it's not religion as we know it.*

Personally, I have no strong feelings about religion one way or the other. But it's a whole different story when it comes to Jizō. I'm not sure whether to call it "habit" or what exactly. It's like how I want to use Japanese when I really want to express myself, like how I want to eat when I get hungry . . . Jizō is like that for me. I keep coming back to him because it's the natural thing for me to do. There is a part of me that wishes that I could be like my grandmother, the shaman, and pray and pray and pray so ardently that I fall into a trance. But since I can't, well, the next best thing is to buy a good-luck charm and keep it close.

I told my mother, Before long I'm going to Tokyo, so I'm going to go to Sugamo while I'm there. I'll pray to Jizō and ask him to remove your thorns of suffering.

My mother said, if you're going there, buy a good luck charm for me. She said, they sell them just inside the temple gate. The *migawari* "scapegoat" charms are the best—they take away troubles on your behalf. They've also got *omikage* "portrait" charms that have images of Jizō on them that you swallow to heal yourself from the inside out, but the "scapegoat" charms work the best.

It won't work if you just carry it around, my mother told me. You have to roast the charm little by little and eat it. It's like the bark of the "relationship-ending hackberry tree." You take a piece of bark, grind it up, and put it in miso soup or something. That's what makes it work. Mother was referring, of course, to the tree located on Iwanosaka, long known for its ability to help a person end their relationship with anything or anyone causing them trouble.

Mother said to me, if you want to break up with a man, you should walk along the road that goes in front of the Sugamo Jizō temple. Keep going toward Kōshinzuka until you reach the tram tracks. The grave of Oiwa is right where it stops. That also works. (Oiwa is a famous ghost from Kabuki. Her husband betrayed and then poisoned her, so she returned as a ghost and took revenge on him and his lover.)

I say to mother, but isn't Oiwa's grave in Zōshigaya?

No, she insisted, no, the demon-mother goddess Kishimo is in Zōshigaya. Oiwa's grave is in Kōshinzuka.

Get off at Kōshinzuka and walk in the opposite direction from the Jizō temple. It's right by the tram tracks. That time you had that problem with that guy, I worried myself sick. I went there to pray for help, and sure enough, that did it—the two of you split up.

She was right. When I was twenty-two, I had a love affair that broke my heart. The experience was so painful that I cried in front of my mother more times than I care to remember. Still, I would never have dreamed of asking Oiwa's ghost to help us break up. After that, I had a string of painful love affairs. Come to think of it, I've never had a painless one. I wondered how many times mother had gone there to pray, hoping that she could help me end the relationship. There was no way of knowing which of her prayers had worked. It wasn't as if there was anything I could specifically identify that happened as a direct result of her prayers.

I've done lots of bad things in my time. I couldn't help it. If a woman wants to be her own person, she doesn't have any choice. She has to steel herself and do some down and dirty things—that's the reason I've experienced so much pain. There have been times I felt like all the enlightened beings in the universe had turned against me. I've had trouble with my partners, with my children and with my current husband. No sooner did I work free of those than a new set of problems with my parents came along.

When I was a little girl, about once a month someone would take me by the hand to the temple. It didn't matter if I felt like the enlightened ones were looking down upon me. When we arrived, I'd put my tiny hands together in prayer, and my mother or my grandmother would rub, rub, rub, rub the smoke from the burning incense all over my hands, legs and head as I told myself, everything will be fine as long as I trust in Jizō. And now, I thought, he's still there waiting for me.

The poet's wife and I decided not to meet on the twenty-fourth—the most popular of the three monthly pilgrimage dates. We met on the nineteenth, a blustery spring day.

Sugamo looked different to me than I had remembered. My most recent trip had been ten years before when I brought an American poet and his wife to see the place. That visit fell on one of the monthly pilgrimage days. The whole place was packed, and I grew exhausted trying to lead them through the crowds. They tried to comfort me, commenting, this is still better than Disneyland. This place fulfills the need to believe in something, it keeps local culture alive.

I bought some flowers in a shop near the station. I was worried I'd be late for my rendezvous with the poet's wife, so I didn't take the time to choose them properly. I just grabbed three bouquets of smaller chrysanthemums—white, yellow and reddish purple—from the bucket by the entrance, went inside and asked the florist to bundle them together. He responded, if you want those colors, why don't you take these instead? He went over to a bucket with fresh chrysanthemums of various colors.

Now then, you wanted white, yellow and red, right?

Well, how about if you just give me all white?

Okay, white then. You want me to wrap them up together, right?

He spoke with a rich Tokyo accent. It had such a familiar ring.

The wind was blowing through the temple grounds where the poet's wife was waiting. Moments later, the poet Mr. So-and-so showed up, followed by yet another poet. Together, the four of us went to visit the grave. The cherry trees were in bloom. The other visitors in the graveyard were carrying buckets of water to clean the gravestones. Near the entrance, someone was selling bundles of *ashibi* branches and flowers of various colors. On his sign, the vendor had written *asebo* instead of the ordinary word *ashibi.* When I stopped to reflect, I realized it was the equinox, when we go to pay our respects to the dearly departed. I'd totally forgotten. She called to her husband under the gravestone, *Mii-chan, Shiromi-chan has come to see you.* The way she pronounced my name was halfway in between *shi* and *hi,* giving off just the faintest whiff of Tokyo dialect.

Thank you. That was a really nice meal.

I bowed and said, well, I think I'll be off.

Where are you going next?

I thought I'd go to the Jizō temple and get one of those *migawari* "scapegoat" charms for my mother, I answered.

Mind if I go with you too? Mr. So-and-so chimed in. It feels like it was meant to be.

I bowed and said, well then, we'll be off.

As we parted, everyone said that we ought to get together sometime.

The poet and I walked side by side. It had been ages since we'd seen one another.

It probably sounds disrespectful to be calling him "Mr. So-and-so" just to preserve his anonymity. After all, he's much older than me, and we're really, really close, but it had been ages since I'd seen him. We saw each other more often in the past and used to talk on the phone frequently. He loved to talk trash—mocking people's foibles and sharing gossip. Then he'd break off to recite a newly written, always sincere little poem, peppered with classical allusions. His voice would become as strong and clear as a boy's, and I'd listen, my heart swelling with appreciation and affection. In those days I never had new poems. All I had were piles of old ones, so I never had anything to recite in response.

Today, the manuscripts of his poems were in his backpack, and he carried the kind of walking stick you might use for mountain climbing. He leaned forward as he walked, and the cluster of tiny bells at the end of his walking stick jingled with each step as if casting some kind of spell.

I asked him, is this your first time visiting Sugamo?

He answered, no, it isn't.

I told him, I came here once with an American poet. You know who I mean—that guy and his wife. It was the twenty-fourth and the place was so packed you could hardly move. We bumped against strangers with every step, and lord help us if we got lost! He wanted a statue of Inari-san, the fox god, and so even though it was super crowded, we stopped to buy one at that shop that sells religious goods in front of the temple.

The poet nodded and said, he must have found it very exotic.

There were fewer people on the approach to the temple than you'd encounter on one of the special pilgrimage days. There weren't too many stalls either, and no crowds of ladies jostling against each other to get where they were going. Grocery stores, plant stores, flower shops.

I commented, it's early in the spring, but all they're selling are chrysanthemums.

To that, the poet responded, it's the vernal equinox. Chrysanthemums make the best offerings.

But why? It's not the right season. It's spring.

It's so that you can offer up a flower with a long stem. They say that back in ancient times, when Mahākāśyapa was rushing to see the Buddha, he encountered a Brahmin on the road who showed him a single flower—a keepsake from the funeral of the Buddha, who had attained nirvana a week before. That is how Mahākāśyapa learned of the Buddha's death. A flower with thorns leaves a thorn sticking in the soul, but if a flower can't dispel evil, then the one offering it might be the next to be consumed by death. That's why the chrysanthemum is best—it has no thorns, yet can dispel evil.

(A pharmacy, a shop selling salty Daifuku mochi, a clothing shop, a pickle shop, a shop selling *senbei* rice crackers, a shop selling undergarments, a shop selling knitted goods, a shop selling *tsukudani* simmered side dishes, a shop selling sweets made from sweet potatoes, a fabric shop and the honey shop where my mother's caretaker went. A shop selling kumquats, a shop selling Chinese medicine, a shop selling ginger, a shop selling goji berries, another shop selling clothing, a shop selling beaded handicrafts, a shop selling eels, a restaurant selling soba noodles, a parlor selling sweets, another shop selling *senbei*. A shop selling wooden clogs, a shop selling shoes, a shop selling work clothes, a shop selling shawls, a shop selling *furoshiki* wrapping cloths, a shop that cleans kimono, a shop selling clothing, a shop selling fabric, a shop that provides acupuncture and moxibustion services, a shop selling peppers and spices, and all over the place, people selling bundles of incense.)

The poet was transformed as we walked.

An incense vendor stood there with his face covered.

The poet's whiskers disappeared.

His spine slowly straightened.

His walking stick grew into a staff as tall as he was.

Surprised, the incense vendors all bowed in respect.

The creases in his face smoothed, and the streaks of white in his hair disappeared. His face grew younger and younger—as he walked forward, eyes shimmering with curiosity, he looked like a boy of fourteen or fifteen. He grew plumper, no longer gaunt. His chest swelled, grew thicker, for a moment, I thought I saw his breasts jiggle slightly. In other words, he had become both man and woman, yet at the same time, neither. In previous lives, the poet had certainly been both a woman and a man. The poet was a bodhisattva who felt so sorry for humankind that he had decided to transform himself into Jizō to inhabit the six realms of existence and help alleviate our suffering. Jizō was walking beside me.

I bought a bundle of incense. We walked through the temple gate, and I threw my lit bundle into the gigantic cauldron of burning incense.

How strange.

I hadn't been here for years to pray, and yet I still remembered how to do it.

First you wash your hands to purify them.

Then you throw your incense into the cauldron to burn.

As a visitor, you always get trapped in the crowds, but you can't let that bother you, unless you push your way through all the people, you'll stay trapped and won't be able to get close to the big incense burner, once you're there, you use your hands to fan the smoke toward you, then rub it on any part of your body that might be afflicted—be it your head, face, shoulders, breasts, fingers or throat. Next, you proceed to the temple's main building, toss a coin or two into the offering box, and pray.

Ordinarily, you'd get into the long line to wash the statue of Kannon in front of the temple after that, but we skipped it that day. My poet-friend-turned-Jizō stood there with his backpack and staff and watched me silently as I prayed.

We left along the same street that we had come. I talked about the problems that I'd been having with my husband. The people walking past us produced a quiet but steady noise, but I ignored them.

And so, I don't know if I can go back, I don't even know if I even want to go back.

Jizō asked, why on earth did you do such a thing?

I've got to level with you about a couple of things.

Jizō nodded, that's fine, you can tell me anything.

And so I started telling him all sorts of things—about my husband's erections (or his lack thereof), about my husband's willingness to go down on me (or his lack thereof).

It's clear that there's some sort of problem between us, but we're not able to talk it out. I'm not able to tell him my true feelings.

Jizō nodded. Sure, that makes sense.

But if we can't talk those things over, my husband asks, then what kind of couple are we? I only hope we can spend time together without getting in each other's hair, but he doesn't seem to feel the same way, it's like there's something he believes in, some Judeo-Christian delusion—or ideal perhaps. The romance between a husband and wife ought to be eternal and unchanging—at least that's what he seems to think. That doesn't leave any room for growing older or dying, but in reality, that's what's happening—we're getting older and dying little by little. He gets dragged down by that feeling and keeps on complaining, *I can't get it up anymore, I can't get it up, I just can't get it up.* It's not like it's anyone's fault he can't get hard. When our eyes meet every morning and every night, we don't even smile at one another. It's like we're on pins and needles.

We crossed to the opposite side. The crowds of people going to worship the Thorn-Pulling Jizō were already behind us, and we were walking down the kind of shopping street you'd find in front of a station, filled with ordinary people coming and going. There were none of the big piles of chrysanthemums we had seen in the roadside stalls just a few minutes earlier. Instead, there were rows of potted plants—flowering quince, small flowering peach trees, Calanthe orchids.

Jizō commented, it only makes sense, we're all the same, he's no spring chicken, the fact he's been able to do it this long is impressive—it's like a dream come true—there's no need for him to feel bad about anything, but of course, telling him that won't make him feel any better, plus, I can't imagine anyone saying that to him in the first place.

Then Jizō turned to me and said, I've got some advice for you.

Here's what you need to do. Praise his work, praise it to the skies. Tell him his work is far more impressive than his penis. You've got no idea how much more a man prefers having his work praised. Praising someone's work is much more important than praising his cock.

Jizō said, tell him this—*I've been too embarrassed to say it until now, but you've got no idea how much your work has influenced my poetry.* It's probably true too.

As soon as we descended the stairs to the platform in Sugamo Station, Jizō resumed the form of the poet, carrying his backpack filled with handwritten poetry and his walking stick. Bent over as before, he disappeared into the crowd boarding the train for Komagome. I stood there for a long time, hands pressed together as if in prayer, as I watched the green train retreat into the distance.

Author's note: Throughout this chapter, I have borrowed the voices of several people and made them my own. For instance, I drew inspiration from a poem in the late twelfth-century anthology *Ryōjin hishō (Songs to Make the Dust Dance)*: "As I pass through the ephemeral world / I am spurned by countless enlightened beings / to the same extent that I labor in the mountains and on the sea / I know not what shall become of me in subsequent lives." In addition, I have borrowed language from the food writer Moeko Akatsuka, Yōko Yoshioka (the wife of the poet Minoru Yoshioka) and the poet Mutsuo Takahashi.

translated by Paul Warham

OUR BATHROOMS AND THE GREAT SEA

KEITA JIN

Essentially, what it boils down to is this. We believe that our world is made up of countless bathrooms that hang suspended on innumerable strings from the canopy of the heavens. And from the bottom of each bathroom the long, thin metal pipes of the water system extend downward, their number beyond calculation, bending and twisting until they vanish from sight into the depths below. After these pipes have made their winding way down through the Sewage Plant, past the Water Treatment Center and all the other myriad facilities too many and various to mention, they eventually come together again when they empty into the great sea that is situated at the center of the world.

My own bathroom is 1.8 meters by 1.8 meters. The ceiling is a little over 2 meters high. I believe these are the standard dimensions. I'm very fond of my bathroom and its clean and simple design—with a milky-white plastic tub that takes up half the space and a simple tap that juts out unceremoniously from the pipes behind the wall.

Once or twice a day I take off my clothes and turn on the tap, filling the tub with hot water. As I watch the swirl of gurgling water, I allow my thoughts to turn to the vast sea that presumably lies at the far end of all the pipes. If only I could detect even the faintest tang of salt on the steam that rises from the tub, my fascination with the distant sea would doubtless be even stronger. Sometimes in my reverie I ponder the legendary stories of those who dared to leave their bathrooms behind. They ventured out into the world, never to return. Sometimes I wonder who could have told such tales of adventure and derring-do if none of these people ever came back. But this is a question that no one can answer.

Afternoons are when we chat, using the showerheads as receiver-transmitters. We press our ears against the showerheads and eagerly catch up with the latest news.

By listening through the drains to the sound of the tides as they rise and fall, we hope to discern the shifting seasons and the passage of time. But the voices that I hear through the showerhead are very faint, and sometimes I am unable to say for certain whether what I am hearing is truly the sound of other voices like mine or just phantom echoes, auditory hallucinations conjured up by my own hopes and fears. All of us are fascinated by what goes on in the world beyond our bathrooms. In particular, we are always eager to learn more about the great sea.

One day not long ago, I happened to notice that several shards of ice had fallen from the shower onto the floor. Winter is here again. A gush of steam from the shower melted the ice to nothingness almost instantly, but that brief glimpse was enough to make me realize that another year has passed. How many years, how many decades, has it been now? Within days, the familiar rumors started to come down the water pipes again—the same rumors that always circulate at this time of year. *The sea is freezing.*

If this is really true, it would surely presage the onset not of an ordinary winter but of something more like an Ice Age. Were that to happen, the constant movement of the hot and cold water from the bathrooms to the sea and from the sea back to the bathrooms again would come to a halt, and the universe would succumb to heat death.

And if the sea did freeze, presumably our bathrooms would freeze over too. But no. These stories are a kind of bad joke. They come around year after year at this time. At least, that's what I prefer to believe. So I hunker down in my tub, as we all hunker down inside our tubs, curled up against the cold air that whooshes through the pipes, and I continue to tap out these fragile signals to my brothers and sisters beyond the pipes, though none of us has any way of knowing whether they ever get through.

SOME ANIMALS AND THEIR HOUSING SITUATIONS

HELEN GURI

Nov. 30, in the year the St. Helena Giant Earwig was declared extinct

I had expected the bunny to be enormous, but it turned out to be only the regular size. I had confused the kind it was—Holland Lop—for another kind—Flemish—when I was googling, I guess because Holland and Belgium are so close together, if you are thinking about distance from a certain perspective, as a rabbit never would.

Flemish rabbits, also known as Flemish Giants, are the size of sheepdogs, fat children, but taller, longer when stretched out, and I imagined the bunny would lie next to me in bed like a softer, sweatless, riskier version of my ex with a heart rate up to 325 beats per minute.

The bunny's name is Frog, and he is the size of a boxing glove with ears.

Dec. 7

Frog's been hopping around the pale green apartment demolishing lettuces in a beautiful systematic way, and I've been watching him as an example of how to live. He's perfect at it. A glad little equation.

But today he stopped. First hopping, then eating. Now he no longer poos his gem-like droppings. Drool mats the fur along his jaw and throat, and makes a dark trail down to his shoulder.

I should clarify that Frog is not my bunny. What's mine are two sweaters, four T-shirts, a sports bra, eight pairs of slightly stretched-out underwear, a pair of jeans, a pair of too-tight beige cotton-polyester blend pants that I have not yet realized make me look naked from the waist down when I am seen from a distance, a raincoat, a staticky zip-up fleece, black socks with holes in the toes, my favorite red woolly socks, and spongy white athletic socks with dirty bottoms.

Four rechargeable batteries and a charger and a dirty

laptop and a charger and a vibrator and a charger and an ancient orange flip phone and a charger and a small electric blanket you don't charge just plug in for instant romance.

A vial of concealer and small squirt bottles of soap and shampoo and two tinted lip balms and some books and receipts and new and previously chewed gum and a rust-colored reusable menstrual cup and a papier-mâché necklace I dropped in the toilet once and an empty fraying black suitcase on wheels.

I had some money, too, but I spent it—almost all of it—on fixing up my ex's house, for reasons I guess could best be described as cultural. It happened effortlessly. My ex is supposed to pay me back, and I mostly believe he will, but he hasn't yet. We have disagreed about some things. The amount. Right now it's tense, like in the nineteenth century.

Not having my money gives me these melodramatic feelings. Or maybe they are just dramatic feelings. It depends whether the feelings are only inside me or whether they are externally justified. If they are valid in the present or just historically. Anyway I'm broke and homeless. That's the feeling.

Frog belongs to Soft Force, a young stranger with good posture who rented me his apartment at a discount this month in exchange for keeping Frog alive, and now Frog is dying. I should clarify that Soft is not wealthy, objectively, as far as I can tell, and I am not completely poor—others are far more broke and homeless, and I think about them increasingly, identifying a little *(what if, what if)* but mostly just wanting to hold them and not be them, as my ex held and did not want to be me, and I can't tell yet if this hypocrisy is the first step toward love or just the same old violent tantrum, a means or illusion of control—and no one knows for sure about Frog yet, but still everything is relative and I have these feelings.

Dec. 8

What belongs to Frog is a special threadbare towel that people use to wrap him up in like a sausage in the event of an emergency.

The sausage goes in a cat carrier that normally belongs to the neighbor's cats. I apply my lip balm but forget the concealer, and we wait by the side of the road in the rain in these states of half-convincing disguise.

The cab driver tenses as I slide Frog in across the back seat.

"It's a bunny," I offer.

"Oh."

Frog's tension, which because of his various casings as well as his status as a tiny animal can only be known by inference, is different from the cab driver's, having to do with his body as opposed to possessions. Some cab drivers own their cabs. Others lease them. It feels important to consider whether this particular cab driver owns this particular cab, whether any of us in this situation is really free.

It occurs to me that I have no personal reason to be tense, but am present as a kind of bowl.

When we arrive at the clinic, the cab driver presses his palm into the meat of the seat cushion where Frog was, checking something. I find the way his hand moves to be kind of sensuous. Vulnerable. Like me.

The cab driver took a shortcut to get us here, a route I didn't recognize, and it occurs to me while the vet is talking—she recommends exploratory surgery—that this city, where I used to live, very near where I grew up, is no longer mine. After the breakup I wanted to come back, to double-check. But to be honest I feel kind of lost here.

Still, there is something electric about paying for things just by saying a man's name.

Nothing alive belongs to anyone. Everyone is constantly learning this and forgetting this, and learning and forgetting this and learning.

Dec. 9

When I load my late-night bread into its cannon, the kitchen light dims, and when the toast hops out, brightness.

I'm learning about electricity and I'm learning about Force.

Force has a liquor cart stocked with gin and an array of special glasses. It is dustless.

The real skulls of two animals, one a cow I think, with big friendly sockets, are on the wall.

China plates and tiny framed pictures of men and dogs and an even coat of hospital-room green paint are on the wall.

A steel mesh bookcase containing a number of books that look good to me, that maybe one day I'll read, as well as a bunch of books I am actively avoiding, plus two guides on how to be a gentleman, is on the wall.

I invite my sister over to get drunk on cheap red wine and learn to be a gentleman.

I pull some records—*The Kick Inside* and *Pet Sounds*—from a low shelf. It's okay to leave them on the floor because the bunny's not here right now.

Sex according to the guides is exactly what you'd expect.

Modern gentlemen should always wear the most expensive socks they can afford.

The irony is that I always wear the most expensive socks I can afford. They are from the drug store or Loblaw's or my birthday or, once, on an impulse, the Running

Room. At any given moment, the vast majority of the world's population is impeccably gentlemanly in terms of socks.

Now we are rummaging in the closets. We find some drugs, no, herbs, no, natural cleaning products or something nasty-smelling to sprinkle on plants. The smell is a mystery. The mystery is Soft's.

Dear Soft I am wearing my socks all over your floors and into your mushy bed sometimes at night because it's cold and I am lonely.

Wearing socks and tearing through your kitchen cabinets in search of food. Don't you have any food. Soft I have just been dumped. By a man I lived with until he went crazy and stopped loving me. You'd have to be crazy not to love me. What the fuck is the deal with all this empty space plus a parcel of dried fish.

Soft, no seriously. Where is your secret bulk section, your hint-of-lime chips.

Please Soft I'm begging you. Some heavily salted caramel kettle corn for my sister she's done nothing wrong at all.

For fuck's sake, Soft.

If I stand on this chair.

If I kneel on your damp countertop in these cute athletic socks with dirty bottoms, like a real gentleman.

If seeing me on my knees like this would turn you on.

If the posture of my begging could at least illustrate something. How it is you got promoted from person.

Yeah when I snoop inside your closets it's a kind of prayer. Your diary a holy book. Just because I can't locate your stack of vintage pornographic magazines does not mean you don't have one.

The Kick Inside makes me think of the quickening.

Dec. 11, in the year of the only remaining Rabb's Fringe-Limbed Tree Frog. He is male. The last known female died in 2009. He's held on a while, though, maybe he'll make it through another year.

When I pick Frog up from surgery his chin is shaved, which makes him look like an imaginary order of monk.

Rabbits' teeth grow continuously to sustain the continuous eating rabbits must do to live. Any interruption is grave.

Frog's teeth grew so long on one side they pierced the gum, which healed, and then was pierced again, and healed, and was pierced and healed at such rapid intervals the processes merged, so the more appropriate term might be *peeled* or *hearsed*, and made an abscess.

Between the stitches are ugly gaps. At these I am to aim syringefuls of iodine three times a day. Sucked up from the bottle it is like cherry juice or dilute blood, a measured red quantity of jewel. Over time I expect it will turn Frog pink, since he is mostly white, and the process imprecise, like basting.

Other syringes, full of medicine, are to be aimed in general at Frog's mouth.

I chase Frog around all evening with the syringes. Near midnight he backflips out of my hands and thwacks his little horse skull on the edge of the glass coffee table. *Oh sweetheart.*

On the verge of Dec. 12

The internet suggests rabbits can be tricked into eating medicine if the medicine is stirred into a fruit puree such as baby food. I go to Shoppers Drug Mart and buy three kinds. It is midnight, but they are open, because Shoppers Drug Mart is a place like the human brain, either awake or dreaming, processing something.

The clerk's face is oddly pigmented, with darker and paler sections, like a map. He is handsome. No, he is neither sexy nor unsexy. He is himself. While I am reaching into my raincoat pocket for my credit card I have a thought. The clerk, naked, wrapped in a towel, arms pinned to his sides, kind of mummified, struggling ineffectually. Meanwhile I'm pressing a syringe of baby food between his lips. *Heyyy sweetie* I say in the thought. *Gorgeous hold still.* His breath becoming all appley. Not a sex act per se but one of those elliptical activities people sometimes still pay each other for. In this scenario who would pay whom.

And meanwhile he is thinking things too. He must think I've given birth. I have given birth to a baby and it's back at home, waiting for me to return to it with this miniature mushed-up orchard and my perverted mind.

Frog loves baby food. I am pretty sure if he could choose, he would eat nothing but baby food. But it gives him diarrhea.

Dec. 13

The landlord is an old man I have not met yet, but who inquired about my character and the nature of my shoes (loud or quiet) before I came. Setting him aside, as is easy to do with the elderly, the living room is first Soft's, and then mine, but right now it is Frog's meadow.

In the meadow I squat surrounded by a smattering of bunny poop while Frog licks my bare legs or jeans devotedly. I tithe him a percentage of my cut-up apple and let him eat the edge of a rare book. I am far enough down the line to inherit Soft's possessions that I offer everything freely. I am not too fussed about the condition of the wooden couch legs or the edges of the record album covers. I wear my white socks, which Frog seems to view as company. He gets really excited and starts to hop around between my feet, like in a herd. The new sole purpose of my white socks is bunny lingerie. I suddenly feel so great in them. I worry I will step on Frog but also want to prance.

In theory I have the power to do things Frog does not like, but in practice I do not. There is no way to be liked while squirting iodine straight into the eyelet of a wound, which is what is currently required.

I don't especially mind whether I make myself unlikeable to Soft, who has a giant painting of himself and his girlfriend in their swimsuits on the wall of his office that I practice the following conversation with:

—Hi Soft.

—Hi.

—I know you have just spent a thousand dollars on your bunny but you need to spend more.

—Why?

—Because it offends my sense of myself as a loveable person to continue to try to wrestle your bunny into various inescapable holds when he does not want to be held. Also it is exhausting, and no holds are inescapable, it turns out.

—If I were there I could totally show you some inescapable holds.

—I would rather you show me your credit card number.

Soft is mostly naked in the picture, which gives me an advantage.

Dec. 15

When I drop Frog off at the vet's the second time, he has to sit on the waiting-room floor in his cage while I fill out some forms and explain about the baby food. During that time he makes friends with a cat who is loose in the office. By "friends" I mean that Frog makes nibbley faces at the cat through the bars, and the cat marks Frog's cage all over with the scent gland at the corner of its mouth, possessively. They are about the same size; Frog is an old buck of ample girth, and the cat is petite, although a predator. Perhaps this is the relationship model that will solve everything.

Dec. 16, in the year the last known Forest Skink, named "Gump," died in a zoo

While the bunny is being boarded at the vet's, I read excerpts from the latest leaked report about American modes of torture. Americans kept people in "stress positions" for long periods of time, so it felt like their limbs were breaking. Americans induced the sensations of drowning. Americans prepared thoughtful, culturally appropriate meals, and then put these in the blender so they could be infused into their captives' rectums. This last activity was said to be for the captives' own good, like medicine. Because otherwise, Americans said they feared, the captives might starve themselves to death, in protest of the conditions.

Dec. 17

Alice Notley says, "Don't alliterate or you'll go to hell." I am doing something far worse: walking around the apartment singing Tori Amos's "Playboy Mommy" with the bunny in mind.

You seemed ashamed
Ashamed that I was
A good friend of American soldiers

The use of the word "friend." What Tori means is most likely not love but the performance of particular acts of care in exchange for something in a situation of precarity.

Also "soldier," synonymous here with "man."

All these tiny hooks in language holding a very big thought together like a net across the world.

Dec. 18

The bunny has been picked up from the vet's by a female friend of Soft's, Noelle, who works as a veterinary assistant and so knows how to flush out wounds. I have noticed that men are often surrounded by a constellation of helpful women with different skill sets. Do they collect them consciously, I wonder.

Frog's vet is a young woman, and all of her assistants are young women. All of the women involved in flushing out Frog's wound perform a carefully choreographed series of trade-offs and competent hand motions that spell a gently glowing suggestion in the night sky.

Soft's apartment was very tidy when I moved in, with all the objects put away in places far from where they are needed (the toaster in a cabinet, the toothbrushes behind a mirror, the dish rack below the sink, the bunny's cage in a corner of the office). I have moved all of the objects to exactly where they are needed. The bunny, although not presently present, lives in the center of the living-room floor.

Dec. 20, in the year the Quiver Tree was unable to grow or disperse quickly enough

Living in another person's house is like wearing their atmospheric outfit over time. I feel these little gusts. My body slips into position. So this is what it's like. Or is it.

My clothes are all wrong for me. But Soft's are even more wrong—huge. They have basically no purpose except in an emergency.

Then Gillian bikes over in her cycling shoes with clips on the bottom. She doesn't have anything good to walk in. Don't worry, I say, and dig out a pair of Soft's leather boots. I know exactly where he keeps them. They are just like my boots, but three times bigger. Gillian looks like she's in a fairytale as we stroll up the road to get lunch.

When my soup comes I mention that I might start calling myself a lesbian, to see if the word changes anything. I'll probably still just fuck whoever, as usual, I hedge. But I would like to give the women a promotion.

Gillian agrees. She still loves men. For some reason I worry that if I'm not careful I might ruin this for her. I'm a very persuasive speaker.

Gillian's feet are so big right now I can't stop looking. Do they feel big, I wonder. On the inside.

Dec. 21

There is no bunny here right now, but there is a jar of pureed carrots with a picture of a baby's head on it. Yesterday I was almost lazy enough to eat the carrots instead of buying food. Today they are sitting on the counter as incriminating evidence when the landlord appears at the kitchen window, suddenly as an animal, and raps his small, wild, manly fist on it.

I'm at the table in the living room, sitting in my sweaty nightshirt, braless as a real live nymph or cow, very visible. "Hello," I say over my shoulder, wishing my head could swivel all the way around, like an owl's.

Pets are not allowed in the apartment, and luckily, none are here.

Dec. 23

Now here is a bunny, carried out to my mother's car by Noelle, who is covered in a gentle down of stray hairs of many different colors, and whose sweatpants have been perforated, as if by an adoring wolf pack, to a kind of coarse lace.

I'm spending Christmas with my mom in the suburbs, and Frog comes as my date. The drive is long in rabbit-time. When we arrive my mom serves carrots, apple pieces wrapped in kale (almost like sushi), and a grape. Three grapes. Frog eats everything while we watch, hungry to see him satisfied, and it does not take long before he gets spectacularly sick, his diarrhea leaking all over my mom's pale carpets, all over the ancient towels we lay down over them.

Frog licks his paws and moves them in circles, grooming, until the whole of him is an evenly mottled shitty grey-brown. My sister spends the evening sitting beside him with a damp washcloth, attempting to undo a particular matted clump on his forehead we refer to as his "poonicorn horn." My mom buffs him dry with a Kleenex. He is so loved, and he has never looked worse. I make him hay salad to calm his stomach. Hay salad is hay snipped into tiny pieces with celery leaves and shredded kale mixed in as an incentive. It drifts on the carpet until we are in a kind of prairie on which Frog is the last living bison.

Frog with his luxurious, soft, streaked coat, that is heaven to run my fingers through even now, is the literal aftermath of one of those toilet paper commercials featuring a fluffy white creature people are meant to desire, unspeakably, to rub against their assholes.

Dec. 27

Frog's ears never go above half-mast, but they spend a lot of time there, sticking straight out like a propeller when he grooms.

Frog's ass is as flat as a frying pan from, I guess, so much sitting on it.

Of earth, water, air, fire, Frog's element is earth, but not all of it. Carpet is a type of earth. Tile and linoleum and polished wood are earth. Of these only carpet is inhabitable.

What happens when Frog finds himself on tile: panicked pawing-kicking as if he might drown.

I do not know what Frog would do in water.

Dec. 28

My ex had clinical anxiety. This fact does not explain everything. But some parts of our relationship were a tile to him.

Today I take the three towels that are in Soft's closet and lay them down in the tiled hallway, which connects to the carpeted office and bedroom. The way dreams connect to new landscapes that are really just the same familiar landscapes. Frog begins to race along the towels and into each new, maybe long-forgotten space.

Eventually Frog gets to the bathroom. He pauses, craning his neck out over the cool, ocean-blue ceramic floor with my stray hairs scattered over it like drawn-on waves. He twitches there a moment. Then he jumps.

If a man is someone you do things for, then a drowning man is not less of a man but more of one. Nothing is manlier than sheer panic.

Dec. 29, in the year there were five remaining Northern White Rhinos

My sister comes over again. She's fascinated by the giant swimsuit painting. Who wouldn't be. She discovers a date on it, and it suggests that the woman in it could not possibly be Soft's current girlfriend but has to be his ex.

Then she finds a signature. The painting of Soft in his swimsuit turns out to be not of Soft at all, nor of any of his girlfriends, barring a huge coincidence, but a poorly executed early work of an artist who has since become talented and famous.

I had thought Soft was keeping the ugly painting out of love, or possibly vanity, but maybe it's more like an investment.

As to the question of why Soft bears such resemblance to the young man in the painting:

a) Soft was drawn to the painting because he saw himself in it;

b) I see Soft in the painting because Soft is everywhere around me;

c) All young men are Soft.

Dec. 30

Soft's kitchen is not the full size a kitchen longs to be. I spend a lot of my time in it swearing. Everything is put away in neat interlocking stacks that do not like to be disturbed. Frog is either used to the sound of sudden crashes, or he is deaf, or he hears on a different frequency altogether. Or for him the kitchen is an unreal place whose events are mythological and therefore not frightening.

Kitchens are traditionally feminine spaces that women have longed to either escape or upgrade the cabinetry in. But Frog wants nothing so desperately as to get in. I extend his towel-road as far as the cabinet below the sink, so we can keep each other company while I stand aimlessly, not cooking.

Frog hops to the end of his road and sits facing the fridge. He spring-loads his hind legs and waits, I assume, for the white door to open.

Frog is too fragile, too masculine, too tiny, too edible to ever do his share of meal preparation, but I don't begrudge him this fact. Nor his suicidal determination. The absurdity of our situation is a product of culture.

Dec. 31

It is five in the morning, and someone has put their running shoes in the dryer. *Thunk-thunk-thunk-thunk.* No, someone is jiggling my doorknob. He is persistent. Could it be the landlord. Meanwhile I'm rummaging in one of my dream-rooms.

I haul myself upright. There is no one. I walk out to the living room. Frog is lying twisted on the floor of his cage, kicking his legs out behind him, trying to stand up. Feet thumping percussively against the food dish. His efforts have carved deep circles in the bedding.

It's too early to do anything, and too late, but I know it is my role to remain in denial about *too late* until the very end. This is the premise of my work. I sit listening because it's hard to watch. *Thunk-thunk-thunk.* At seven I call Soft, then the vet. Then I shower, circling my palms up under my armpits in a gesture that seems in this moment to symbolize life.

White socks go around in the dryer until they are dead, and so does Frog. By the time I am clean he is dry. And fluffy, in an elegant tangle like a scarf, though still very stained. I feel around for a heartbeat anyway.

Jan. 1, in the year after Plectostoma sciaphilum was a snail that lived entirely on one Malaysian hill. A cement company wiped them all out.

I have this feeling like I hosted a party and it went really wrong. Everyone went home early or died.

Tori Amos knows my feeling. "Don't judge me so hard, little girl, so you got a Playboy mommy," she sings to her miscarried baby.

As if dying is just another snarky thing that people do to one another, that *women* do to one another, passing judgment for bad hostessing.

In the Christian myth of creation, Force invents mortality as a punishment. The behavior to be punished is Eve's. Either (a) she serves Adam substandard food, or (b) in the story, substandard food symbolizes sex, and Eve serves it. The moment where death first becomes a possibility is also the beginning of shame.

Tori is ashamed. And in Tori's description the dead baby is ashamed too, of Tori. Everyone in the song is ashamed except possibly the American soldiers, whose feelings are not described.

Soft's diary, which I am not proud to have read, but which I cannot deny knowledge of, is mostly an account of services provided to him. Sandwiches and how good they were. Lobster rolls. Blow jobs. Concerts. People who gave him rides or painted his apartment for him. His feelings are not described. It's an incredible document. I wish that I could publish it. I think that it would captivate its audience, who would intuitively understand that for a certain kind of young man with a certain amount of money—a man who is not and never will be an American soldier, but who at the same time completely *is*—these transactions are indistinguishable from life itself. The diary is life itself.

later

Victim Index

1. The rest of the world
2. Rabbits in fiction
3. Frog
4. Dead babies
5. American soldiers
6. Me
7. My ex
8. Soft Force (but I read his diary)
9. The vet
10. The landlord
11. American soldiers
12. Soft Force
13. This list is endless and loops back on itself, like the universe

& later

I am lying on my back humming my vibrator down past my navel and into my thicket. It is the kind with two heads, one longer (for stimulating the G-spot) and one shorter (for stimulating the clitoris), that people refer to as a Rabbit, though mine is a knock-off and so is technically called something else. I have forgotten the name.

I am trying to masturbate in a lesbian way. I'm unfocused. Pick a woman, I tell myself. Anyone. Think of her. But my feelings make a kind of constellation.

In the galaxy there are stars enough that when a rabbit dies you can find its outline in the sky, even if the rabbit is a hunchback or has its legs sticking out at a broken angle.

The galaxy hums when you turn it on, like a machine, and rabbits can breed and die and be born again as often as necessary. Some live their whole lives in captivity.

Rabbits are related to horses in a distant way that rabbits would never think about, or maybe they do.

The galaxy is outside me, and inside too.

Horses can bolt like lightning.

But when the stars run out of batteries I plug them in.

A rabbit is the softest thing to rub against.

My relationship with my ex was an open one. I am thinking of a woman I fucked a little sometimes, with permission. But permission is a room that no longer exists. Where is she now.

The toast pop-pops like a firework until the night sky is lit.

There is no limit to how much you can learn about electricity.

Jan. 2

Do I want the rabbit cremated, asks the vet.

It's not my decision, I say, and text Soft. His number's always right on top these days.

In the children's story *The Velveteen Rabbit*, a toy bunny is sentenced to be burned after coming into contact with a human child's scarlet fever. Because desire as funneled through the narratives of our culture burns all the lesser creatures.

When I was small my dad taught me how to build a fire. He said the most effective method is to pile the wood exactly like a house, and I have remembered this. I am good at fire.

For a bonfire, pile the wood like a mansion.

The word bonfire has the word *bone* in it. It does not mean a good fire, from the French. It means a fire intense enough to burn bones.

later

A theory. Alliterative crochet loops.

A playboy bunny is a kept creature.

A playboy mommy is a kept creature who in turn keeps a creature, and is lousy at it. Maybe because of real estate—she doesn't have a place of her own in which to keep a creature, so must do so in a place belonging to someone else, which is every place, including the ones in her body—or maybe more because she is keeping the creature for aims that are not her own but belong to someone higher.

Doing something for a higher purpose has a positive connotation in our culture, but nobility of purpose and height are not actually correlated. A better correlation: higher/hire, as in a playboy mommy is a caregiver for hire, like a mercenary, a mercenary of care.

When a playboy mommy keeps a creature, the creature often dies. Or it doesn't, but we expect it to.

Because the higher purpose of our society is violence.

When a creature dies, we look at its caregiver and call her a playboy mommy and say *that's why*.

A playboy bunny starts off as just a regular bunny in the wild, but upon being discovered comes to live in a mansion. A mansion sounds large, but is really just anyplace belonging to someone, a gentleman, in which bunnies are brought to live and collect. The lighting is usually nice, cozy. A mansion is widely considered a desirable place to live. And a playboy mansion, a place where desire lives.

I used to live in a mansion belonging to my ex. Now I live in this mansion I am renting. It's modest.

A mansion is not desire's only habitat but a structure built on top, an overlay. Because desire comes from creatures, who are constantly everywhere on the surface of the earth.

In the taxonomy of creatures, there have been some errors. A playboy mommy and a playboy bunny, for example, are exactly the same. It is only the Madonna/whore binary that maintains the illusion they are separate.

If I slide open this binary's partition, everything comes rushing into focus and I get ten seconds of total insight: I died just now, of neglect. I mean of caring very hard within a structure beyond my control. Anyway, I would like to register my death as a protest. Not just against the ones immediately above me, but at the highest level.

translated by Ted Goossen

ON WRITING SHORT STORIES

HARUKI MURAKAMI IN CONVERSATION WITH MOTOYUKI SHIBATA

THE MURAKAMI METHOD

Haruki Murakami—I never write short stories singly. When I decide to write them, I always write a number. Six or seven at a stretch.

Motoyuki Shibata—Why is that?

Haruki—That's the only way I can do it. I guess I'm basically a writer of novels, but once I'm in a short story writing mode, I can turn one out every two or three weeks. That's how it was for *Men Without Women* [2014], and *Strange Tales from Tokyo* [2005] and *after the quake* [2000] were the same. All were written in a single push, without stopping.

Moto—Even your early collections give the feeling of being unified. It's my impression that they became even more so following *after the quake*.

Haruki—That's because I set a theme at the beginning. If I did it in a more haphazard way—writing a story on request for one literary journal, let's say, and then a different story for another—I wouldn't be able to unify them in my mind.

Moto—You set the theme, but that doesn't mean you know how the stories will end before you start, does it? Do you enjoy the process of finding out as you write?

Haruki—You bet. I'm not certain how a story will turn out, for sure, but I only have to wait two weeks to find out, and it's great fun getting there. With a novel it's more like two years! That's one reason short stories are easier. If I don't switch off my engine but keep it in idle, I can jump from one story to the next without a pause in between. It helps to have a trigger as well. With *Strange Tales from Tokyo,* for example, I made a list of twenty-odd key words before I started; then I would choose several to weave the first story around, several others for the second story, and so forth. It was pure improvisation.

Moto—That reminds me, I think I was there the first time you used a word processor. We were at the Shinchōsha office, and you'd brought your new machine with you. I remember the first words you typed on it were something like, "I was walking in the forest when out jumped a bear . . ." and then you just kept going. That impressed me a lot. So that's how a writer works, I thought. Stories just pop up!

Haruki—It was a brand new Fujitsu. You're right, that was my first time. I'm not quite like the poor guy in Stephen King's *Misery,* but it's true: if someone asks, I can pretty much whip off a story right there on the spot.

Moto—Could you do that when you were a child?

Haruki—No. Only after I turned thirty.

Moto—Did it feel like something had been unlocked inside you?

Haruki—Maybe I've got a touch of schizophrenia, like Grace Paley. (laughs) It does strike me as strange, though. I mean, I had no training at all. In the old days, I sometimes took a short story and developed it into a novel, but I haven't done that recently. People have asked me if I plan to do that with several of the stories in *Men Without Women,* but that's no longer something that interests me. I think the role that short stories play in my writing has changed.

Moto—Do you think that has to do with the fact that your short story collections seem to hold together at a deeper level now?

Haruki—I think my stories are more self-contained than they used to be. More self-sufficient. The story that was the basis for *The Wind-up Bird Chronicle,* "The Wind-up Bird and Tuesday's Women," looked like a finished story, but in fact it wasn't. That's why I felt like going back to it. But there may be no stories of that sort in *Men Without Women* and *Strange Tales from Tokyo.*

THE NEW YORKER AND KINDLE'S "SINGLE STORY" SYSTEM

Moto—There's a big difference between the publisher-centered Japanese system, where writers are initially commissioned to write stories for specific journals, and the author-centered American system, where writers prepare their stories first and then go about marketing them. Do you think this results in a marked difference between the stories produced in Japan vs. those published first in the U.S.?

Haruki—This is just my personal view, but I think the two types of short stories are aiming at something slightly different. I sometimes get tired of the sort of stories creative writing programs foster, where writers put themselves at the center of whatever they write. Then again I often find the stories in Japanese literary magazines just as dull. They all seem to follow the same template. Since the U.S. is a less homogenous society, you find more writers who are intent on breaking down the system. Japanese publishing houses are mostly based in Tokyo, so the range of opinions is very limited, and everything begins to look alike. Everyone slips into the same groove, so to speak. You could say even the journals or "containers" eventually take on a single color. There should be some types of stories that don't fit very well into those containers.

Moto—Either way—whether it's the American author-based system or the Japanese journal-based model—there seems to be an unspoken pressure to write short stories in a particular way. So you're put off by stories that don't oppose those models?

Haruki—When I read American stories about the writer's family, or the suffering of minorities, my reaction to be honest is, not again! Of course there are other kinds of stories. But the "not again" variety seem to find the most favor in creative writing programs. Having said that, when I get my weekly *New Yorker,* I sometimes find an interesting story, but when I leaf through Japanese literary journals I'm unlikely to turn up anything.

Moto—The *New Yorker*'s stories are not always my cup of tea, but when an author writes a good story, that's where the agent takes it first, so they're in a privileged position.

Haruki—They have first option on many stories, which ensures the quality of the stories they publish.

Moto—Looking at it from another angle, a Japanese writer *could* make a living writing short stories for journals, whereas an American writer can't. They could until about fifty years ago, though. Writers like Jack London and William Saroyan made good money from the start that way.

Haruki—F. Scott Fitzgerald did as well.

Moto—Now it seems only the *New Yorker* and *Harper*'s pay a substantial fee.

Haruki—*Esquire* doesn't publish short stories any more either. Magazines like the *New Yorker* and *Esquire* rely on middle-income subscribers, the same people who read short stories, so when the middle class takes a hit, subscriptions go down and short story readership dwindles. Young people today don't read magazines. Japanese literary journals don't rely on the subscription system, and not that many people read them anyway. Seen in this light, the situation faced by short story writing in America may be more acute. Still, my American agent is always after me to write more short stories. She loves them because she can sell them quickly.

Moto—All the same, writers in the United States are encouraged to make their name writing novels.

Haruki—For sure. Get known from your novels, then turn out the stories—that's an agent's refrain. Another issue these days is Kindle's new strategy of marketing short stories individually. I've been approached by them, too. They want to take one of my stories and sell it separate from the rest, like selling a hit single off a CD. I've turned them down, though. A writer wants all the stories in a collection to be read, I've explained. But maybe that's the wave of the future.

Moto—Let's leave Salinger's *Nine Stories* as nine stories, right?

ONE STRONG POINT IS ENOUGH

Haruki—In my opinion, a short story really only needs one outstanding feature to be successful. Grace Paley's stories are a case in point. I don't think my early stories are very good. Yet rereading them makes me realize that, yes, there is something about them that stands out. I might not be able to write that way any more, even if tried. For that reason, they may stick in the reader's mind. For example, a lot of people like the story "The Last Lawn of the Afternoon," but I can't stand it. If I were to write this story again I could make it a heck of a lot better. Nevertheless, it has its own strong point.

Moto—You can't stand that story? Really?

Haruki—Short stories are like that. Novels are written over a very long time span so it won't work if you rewrite only a part, but you can rewrite a whole story. Remember the reading I did not long ago in Kōriyama of "On Seeing the 100% Perfect Girl One

Beautiful April Morning"? Well, when I read it aloud to myself before the event I ended up changing a lot. I did the same thing the night before I read, "Blind Willow, Sleeping Woman" in Kobe. It's hard to go back and read my old stuff. I'd like to think it's because I'm becoming a more skilled writer, the way Raymond Carver did over time.

Moto—Do you have any advice for budding short story writers about what to do, and what not to do?

Haruki—The most important thing is to develop your own system. My system seems to have been more or less in place from the beginning. When I wrote "A Slow Boat to China" and "A 'Poor Aunt' Story," I started with the title and let it lead me where it wanted to go. I was curious where that might be.

Moto—And have you worked like that ever since?

Haruki—More or less. Of course there are cases where I haven't started with the title. "On Seeing the 100% Perfect Girl One Beautiful April Morning," for example, was sparked by actually walking past a girl when I was out on a stroll. Basically, I approach short story writing as a kind of game: most of the time, I'm experimenting to see what kind of tale I can spin out of this phrase or that fragment. Other writers may not proceed that way, but I find it the most fun. I think that's the key—you need to reach down inside yourself to come up with a system that is uniquely yours. Put another way, avoid writing like everybody else. Write a story in a way that only you can, even if it's not very good at the beginning. That's the way that Grace Paley and Raymond Carver did it too.

SHUFFLE DRIVE

TOH
ENJOE

translated by David Boyd

Nowadays, everybody agrees. The shuffle drive is the best way to travel between galaxies—but the technology has not always been as reliable as it is today. In fact, in the past, the shuffle drive was responsible for many tragic accidents. The following is the record of one such incident.

WAYS TO SHUFFLE

There are many ways to shuffle. Take, for example, "the perfect riffle." This refers to any shuffle in which a deck of cards is split into two identically sized packets and interleaved in alternating order.

In such a shuffle, it makes a difference which packet you lead with. Experts use the term "in shuffle" to describe the action in which cards 1/2/3/4/5/6/7/8 are re-ordered 5/1/6/2/7/3/8/4. The term "out shuffle" describes the action in which the same cards are re-ordered 1/5/2/6/3/7/4/8.

It was fortunate that the drive's early developers decided to shuffle out rather than in. Fortunate because, even in the best-case scenario, the so-called "in-shuffle drive" would have to pass through fifty-two spaces—the number of playing cards in a standard deck—before returning home. Of course, such an epic journey would have to change the traveler in some fundamental way. Can we say with any certainty that he made it home at all?

THE RECORD

00

ONE MORNING; IN THE MIDDLE OF THE NIGHT; IN THE KINGDOM OF HEARTS; YOU AND ME; WE DISCOVERED IT; WE DRAFTED IT; THE SHUFFLE DRIVE. GOING GOING GOING GONE; FROM HERE TO INFINITY; AND WHERE IS WHERE; AND WHEN IS WHEN; NO ONE KNOWS; INTO CHAOS WE ALL GO.

IT WAS MORNING; THAT NIGHT; IN THE KINGDOM OF CLUBS; YOU AND SHE; YOU MADE IT; YOU IMPLEMENTED IT; THE SHUFFLE DRIVE. BANG BANG CLANK CLANK; GALAXY MEETS GALAXY; AND WHAT IS WHAT; AND WHO IS WHO; NO ONE KNOWS; INTO CHAOS WE ALL GO.

WAY BACK WHEN; WHEN WAS THAT; IN THE DISTANT FUTURE; TIME AND TIME AGAIN; IN THE KINGDOM OF DIAMONDS; IN THE KINGDOM OF SPADES; HE AND YOU; YOU AND I; YOU IMPROVED IT; WE DESTROYED IT; YOU REBUILT IT; WE UNDID IT; THE SHUFFLE DRIVE.

THE SHUFFLE DRIVE. CRUNCH SNAP CRUNCH SNAP; BUMP CRASH BUMP CRASH; ALL BROKEN UP; WHEN UP IT CAME; OUT OF ORDER; WHERE IT ALL BEGAN; OUT OF THIS WORLD; WHEN IT ALL ENDED; NO ONE KNOWS; NO ONE KNOWS; INTO CHAOS WE ALL GO. INTO CHAOS WE ALL GO.

01

ONE MORNING; WAY BACK WHEN; IN THE MIDDLE OF THE NIGHT; WHEN WAS THAT; IN THE KINGDOM OF HEARTS; IN THE DISTANT FUTURE; YOU AND ME; TIME AND TIME AGAIN; WE DISCOVERED IT; IN THE KINGDOM OF DIAMONDS; WE DRAFTED IT; IN THE KINGDOM OF SPADES; THE SHUFFLE DRIVE.

HE AND YOU; GOING GOING GOING GONE; YOU AND I; FROM HERE TO INFINITY; YOU IMPROVED IT; AND WHERE IS WHERE; WE DESTROYED IT; AND WHEN IS WHEN; YOU REBUILT IT; NO ONE KNOWS; WE UNDID IT; INTO CHAOS WE ALL GO. THE SHUFFLE DRIVE.

IT WAS MORNING; THE SHUFFLE DRIVE. THAT NIGHT; CRUNCH SNAP CRUNCH SNAP; IN THE KINGDOM OF CLUBS; BUMP CRASH BUMP CRASH; YOU AND SHE; ALL BROKEN UP; YOU MADE IT; WHEN UP IT CAME; YOU IMPLEMENTED IT; OUT OF ORDER; THE SHUFFLE DRIVE.

WHERE IT ALL BEGAN; BANG BANG CLANK CLANK; OUT OF THIS WORLD; GALAXY MEETS GALAXY; WHEN IT ALL ENDED; AND WHAT IS WHAT; NO ONE KNOWS; AND WHO IS WHO; NO ONE KNOWS; NO ONE KNOWS; INTO CHAOS WE ALL GO. INTO CHAOS WE ALL GO. INTO CHAOS WE ALL GO.

02

ONE MORNING; IT WAS MORNING; WAY BACK WHEN; THE SHUFFLE DRIVE. IN THE MIDDLE OF THE NIGHT; THAT NIGHT; WHEN WAS THAT; CRUNCH SNAP CRUNCH SNAP; IN THE KINGDOM OF HEARTS; IN THE KINGDOM OF CLUBS; IN THE DISTANT FUTURE; BUMP CRASH BUMP CRASH; YOU AND ME;

YOU AND SHE; TIME AND TIME AGAIN; ALL BROKEN UP; WE DISCOVERED IT; YOU MADE IT; IN THE KINGDOM OF DIAMONDS; WHEN UP IT CAME; WE DRAFTED IT; YOU IMPLEMENTED IT; IN THE KINGDOM OF SPADES; OUT OF ORDER; THE SHUFFLE DRIVE. THE SHUFFLE DRIVE.

HE AND YOU; WHERE IT ALL BEGAN; GOING GOING GOING GONE; BANG BANG CLANK CLANK; YOU AND I; OUT OF THIS WORLD; FROM HERE TO INFINITY; GALAXY MEETS GALAXY; YOU IMPROVED IT; WHEN IT ALL ENDED; AND WHERE IS WHERE; AND WHAT IS WHAT; WE DESTROYED IT;

NO ONE KNOWS; AND WHEN IS WHEN; AND WHO IS WHO; YOU REBUILT IT; NO ONE KNOWS; NO ONE KNOWS; NO ONE KNOWS; WE UNDID IT; INTO CHAOS WE ALL GO. INTO CHAOS WE ALL GO. INTO CHAOS WE ALL GO. THE SHUFFLE DRIVE. INTO CHAOS WE ALL GO.

03

ONE MORNING; HE AND YOU; IT WAS MORNING; WHERE IT ALL BEGAN; WAY BACK WHEN; GOING GOING GOING GONE; THE SHUFFLE DRIVE. BANG BANG CLANK CLANK; IN THE MIDDLE OF THE NIGHT; YOU AND I; THAT NIGHT; OUT OF THIS WORLD; WHEN WAS THAT;

FROM HERE TO INFINITY; CRUNCH SNAP CRUNCH SNAP; GALAXY MEETS GALAXY; IN THE KINGDOM OF HEARTS; YOU IMPROVED IT; IN THE KINGDOM OF CLUBS; WHEN IT ALL ENDED; IN THE DISTANT FUTURE; AND WHERE IS WHERE; BUMP CRASH BUMP CRASH; AND WHAT IS WHAT; YOU AND ME; WE DESTROYED IT;

YOU AND SHE; NO ONE KNOWS; TIME AND TIME AGAIN; AND WHEN IS WHEN; ALL BROKEN UP; AND WHO IS WHO; WE DISCOVERED IT; YOU REBUILT IT;

YOU MADE IT; NO ONE KNOWS; IN THE KINGDOM OF DIAMONDS; NO ONE KNOWS; WHEN UP IT CAME;

NO ONE KNOWS; WE DRAFTED IT; WE UNDID IT; YOU IMPLEMENTED IT; INTO CHAOS WE ALL GO. IN THE KINGDOM OF SPADES; INTO CHAOS WE ALL GO. OUT OF ORDER; INTO CHAOS WE ALL GO. THE SHUFFLE DRIVE. THE SHUFFLE DRIVE. THE SHUFFLE DRIVE. INTO CHAOS WE ALL GO.

04

ONE MORNING; YOU AND SHE; HE AND YOU; NO ONE KNOWS; IT WAS MORNING; TIME AND TIME AGAIN; WHERE IT ALL BEGAN; AND WHEN IS WHEN; WAY BACK WHEN; ALL BROKEN UP; GOING GOING GOING GONE; AND WHO IS WHO; THE SHUFFLE DRIVE.

WE DISCOVERED IT; BANG BANG CLANK CLANK; YOU REBUILT IT; IN THE MIDDLE OF THE NIGHT; YOU MADE IT; YOU AND I; NO ONE KNOWS; THAT NIGHT; IN THE KINGDOM OF DIAMONDS; OUT OF THIS WORLD; NO ONE KNOWS; WHEN WAS THAT; WHEN UP IT CAME;

FROM HERE TO INFINITY; NO ONE KNOWS; CRUNCH SNAP CRUNCH SNAP; WE DRAFTED IT; GALAXY MEETS GALAXY; WE UNDID IT; IN THE KINGDOM OF HEARTS; YOU IMPLEMENTED IT; YOU IMPROVED IT; INTO CHAOS WE ALL GO. IN THE KINGDOM OF CLUBS; IN THE KINGDOM OF SPADES; WHEN IT ALL ENDED;

INTO CHAOS WE ALL GO. IN THE DISTANT FUTURE; OUT OF ORDER; AND WHERE IS WHERE; INTO CHAOS WE ALL GO. BUMP CRASH BUMP CRASH; THE SHUFFLE DRIVE. AND WHAT IS WHAT; THE SHUFFLE DRIVE. YOU AND ME; THE SHUFFLE DRIVE. WE DESTROYED IT; INTO CHAOS WE ALL GO.

05

ONE MORNING; FROM HERE TO INFINITY; YOU AND SHE; NO ONE KNOWS; HE AND YOU; CRUNCH SNAP CRUNCH SNAP; NO ONE KNOWS; WE DRAFTED IT; IT WAS MORNING; GALAXY MEETS GALAXY; TIME AND TIME AGAIN; WE UNDID IT; WHERE IT ALL BEGAN;

IN THE KINGDOM OF HEARTS; AND WHEN IS WHEN; YOU IMPLEMENTED IT; WAY BACK WHEN; YOU IMPROVED IT; ALL BROKEN UP; INTO CHAOS WE ALL GO. GOING GOING GOING GONE; IN THE KINGDOM OF CLUBS; AND WHO IS WHO; IN THE KINGDOM OF SPADES; THE SHUFFLE DRIVE. WHEN IT ALL ENDED;

WE DISCOVERED IT; INTO CHAOS WE ALL GO. BANG BANG CLANK CLANK; IN THE DISTANT FUTURE; YOU REBUILT IT; OUT OF ORDER; IN THE MIDDLE OF THE NIGHT; AND WHERE IS WHERE; YOU MADE IT; INTO CHAOS WE ALL GO. YOU AND I; BUMP CRASH BUMP CRASH; NO ONE KNOWS;

THE SHUFFLE DRIVE. THAT NIGHT; AND WHAT IS WHAT; IN THE KINGDOM OF DIAMONDS; THE SHUFFLE DRIVE. OUT OF THIS WORLD; YOU AND ME; NO ONE KNOWS; THE SHUFFLE DRIVE. WHEN WAS THAT; WE DESTROYED IT; WHEN UP IT CAME; INTO CHAOS WE ALL GO.

06

ONE MORNING; WE DISCOVERED IT; FROM HERE TO INFINITY; INTO CHAOS WE ALL GO. YOU AND SHE; BANG BANG CLANK CLANK; NO ONE KNOWS; IN THE DISTANT FUTURE; HE AND YOU; YOU REBUILT IT; CRUNCH SNAP CRUNCH SNAP; OUT OF ORDER; NO ONE KNOWS;

IN THE MIDDLE OF THE NIGHT; WE DRAFTED IT; AND WHERE IS WHERE; IT WAS MORNING; YOU MADE IT; GALAXY MEETS GALAXY; INTO CHAOS WE ALL GO. TIME AND TIME AGAIN; YOU AND I; WE UNDID IT; BUMP CRASH BUMP CRASH; WHERE IT ALL BEGAN; NO ONE KNOWS;

IN THE KINGDOM OF HEARTS; THE SHUFFLE DRIVE. AND WHEN IS WHEN; THAT NIGHT; YOU IMPLEMENTED IT; AND WHAT IS WHAT; WAY BACK WHEN; IN THE KINGDOM OF DIAMONDS; YOU IMPROVED IT; THE SHUFFLE DRIVE. ALL BROKEN UP; OUT OF THIS WORLD; INTO CHAOS WE ALL GO.

YOU AND ME; GOING GOING GOING GONE; NO ONE KNOWS; IN THE KINGDOM OF CLUBS; THE SHUFFLE DRIVE. AND WHO IS WHO; WHEN WAS THAT; IN THE KINGDOM OF SPADES; WE DESTROYED IT; THE SHUFFLE DRIVE. WHEN UP IT CAME; WHEN IT ALL ENDED; INTO CHAOS WE ALL GO.

07

ONE MORNING; IN THE KINGDOM OF HEARTS; WE DISCOVERED IT; THE SHUFFLE DRIVE. FROM HERE TO INFINITY; AND WHEN IS WHEN; INTO CHAOS WE ALL GO. THAT NIGHT; YOU AND SHE; YOU IMPLEMENTED IT; BANG BANG CLANK CLANK; AND WHAT IS WHAT; NO ONE KNOWS;

WAY BACK WHEN; IN THE DISTANT FUTURE; IN THE KINGDOM OF DIAMONDS; HE AND YOU; YOU IMPROVED IT; YOU REBUILT IT; THE SHUFFLE DRIVE. CRUNCH SNAP CRUNCH SNAP; ALL BROKEN UP; OUT OF ORDER; OUT OF THIS WORLD; NO ONE KNOWS; INTO CHAOS WE ALL GO.

IN THE MIDDLE OF THE NIGHT; YOU AND ME; WE DRAFTED IT; GOING GOING GOING GONE; AND WHERE IS WHERE; NO ONE KNOWS; IT WAS MORNING; IN THE KINGDOM OF CLUBS; YOU MADE IT; THE SHUFFLE DRIVE. GALAXY MEETS GALAXY; AND WHO IS WHO; INTO CHAOS WE ALL GO.

WHEN WAS THAT; TIME AND TIME AGAIN; IN THE KINGDOM OF SPADES; YOU AND I; WE DESTROYED IT; WE UNDID IT; THE SHUFFLE DRIVE. BUMP CRASH BUMP CRASH; WHEN UP IT CAME; WHERE IT ALL BEGAN; WHEN IT ALL ENDED; NO ONE KNOWS; INTO CHAOS WE ALL GO.

08

ONE MORNING; IN THE MIDDLE OF THE NIGHT; IN THE KINGDOM OF HEARTS; YOU AND ME; WE DISCOVERED IT; WE DRAFTED IT; THE SHUFFLE DRIVE. GOING GOING GOING GONE; FROM HERE TO INFINITY; AND WHERE IS WHERE; AND WHEN IS WHEN; NO ONE KNOWS; INTO CHAOS WE ALL GO.

IT WAS MORNING; THAT NIGHT; IN THE KINGDOM OF CLUBS; YOU AND SHE; YOU MADE IT; YOU IMPLEMENTED IT; THE SHUFFLE DRIVE. BANG BANG CLANK CLANK; GALAXY MEETS GALAXY; AND WHAT IS WHAT; AND WHO IS WHO; NO ONE KNOWS; INTO CHAOS WE ALL GO.

WAY BACK WHEN; WHEN WAS THAT; IN THE DISTANT FUTURE; TIME AND TIME AGAIN; IN THE KINGDOM OF DIAMONDS; IN THE KINGDOM OF SPADES; HE AND

YOU; YOU AND I; YOU IMPROVED IT; WE DESTROYED IT; YOU REBUILT IT; WE UNDID IT; THE SHUFFLE DRIVE.

THE SHUFFLE DRIVE. CRUNCH SNAP CRUNCH SNAP; BUMP CRASH BUMP CRASH; ALL BROKEN UP; WHEN UP IT CAME; OUT OF ORDER; WHERE IT ALL BEGAN; OUT OF THIS WORLD; WHEN IT ALL ENDED; NO ONE KNOWS; NO ONE KNOWS; INTO CHAOS WE ALL GO. INTO CHAOS WE ALL GO.

[FINISHED IN 0.1 SECONDS]

MR. QUOTE

BY SATOSHI KITAMURA

1. IT WAS ALL GREEK TO THEM

Mr. Quote went out for a walk one afternoon.

He came upon a colleague from the university, and in no time they fell into a philosophical discussion.

At one point Mr. Quote cited a maxim by the Greek philosopher Approximandros to support his argument.

Later, Mr. Quote stopped by a tavern for a gin and tonic before heading home.

Mr. Quote noticed that he was being followed.

—You there, wait a minute!
An old man in a tunic and sandals caught up with Mr. Quote.
—You got my words all wrong!
—Excuse me?
—I've never said such rubbish!
—I beg your pardon?
—You misquoted me!
—Mr. Approximandros? Is it really you?

Approximandros had been dead for more than two millennia, but since he was often misquoted, he had found no peace in the grave. Overhearing Mr. Quote mangling one of his maxims was the last straw: he decided to set the record straight once and for all.

At home in his study Mr. Quote noted down what Approximandros had to say: endless maxims and theorems. When they were done he promised the old man that he would publish it at the earliest opportunity.

Just then Mrs. Quote called them to dinner.

She served roast chicken and boiled potatoes, accompanied by a bottle of good wine. Approximandros was surprised and touched by this unexpected hospitality. He became quite mellow, cheerfully cracking a joke or two, though it was all Greek to his hosts.

It was past midnight when they hailed a cab and saw the great philosopher off. Everything turned out all right in the end. Mr. Quote was grateful to his ever-dependable wife, Ann.

MR. QUOTE

2. HOLIDAY IN SCOTLAND

Mr. and Mrs. Quote went to Scotland on holiday.
They took a rowboat out on a quiet lake. Birds circled overhead, the water rippled gently, and hills rose in the distance beyond the shore.

The view reminded Mr. Quote of a poem he had read a long time ago. Was it Wordsworth? Keats? Or was it older? A passage from *The Faerie Queene*?

Then again, perhaps it was from the ancient Greek or the far shores of Asia . . .

Japan? China?

It must be something I read when I was very young. But it couldn't be a children's book, since even as a boy I didn't see the point of reading a book full of pictures. What a little snob I was!

I thought I was above such foolishness, but in truth I longed for those books. They looked so alluring. I wanted to tumble down the hole with the rabbit in a waistcoat . . .

I had no friends. I was afraid of other children. Books with difficult words were my armor. I always hid behind them. I was a lonely child . . .

What was I thinking about? Oh, yes, it was a poem. Its name is on the tip of my tongue. How frustrating that I cannot remember! Am I getting old? I hope not.

Heading back on the coach, it suddenly dawned on Mr. Quote that when he was five or six, his parents had taken him to the very same lake. After a boat ride, young Quote had written a poem about it. "So it was me!" he exclaimed. Mrs. Quote beamed at her husband.

MR. QUOTE

3. I SING, THEREFORE I AM

Mr. Quote was fascinated by birdsong. He wished he could sing as birds did and understand what they were singing about.

One day he came across a medieval manuscript in the university library titled *Master Bird Songs in Four Weeks* by St. Francis of Assisi.

After mastering the basics, Mr. Quote tested his skill in the garden the next morning. When he chirped *Hello, good morning!* a blackbird turned round and replied, *I like your accent.*
It worked!

Encouraged by his success, Mr. Quote continued with his studies. Soon he was able to have everyday conversations with all the birds in the neighborhood. They were charmed by this mammal who spoke their language with a funny accent.

The more he understood the birdsong, though, the less musical it sounded. Songs became talk, and the birds were a pretty talkative lot. While strolling in the woods Mr. Quote sometimes felt as if he were walking through a crowded beer hall.

Although he had many interesting conversations with birds, some of what they said was outright silly or vapid. Sometimes he felt embarrassed or even alarmed. Mr. Quote kept a wide berth from a few of them.

One day when Mr. Quote came home he saw a gang of rogue ostriches abducting his wife. He ran after them as fast as he could, but he was no match for them. One of them threw an egg at him.

Mr. Quote woke up. He had fallen asleep on the couch.

So it was a dream!
Mr. Quote went out into the garden where the birds were singing their evening songs. To his great relief, he didn't understand a single note.

MR. QUOTE

4. HAM AND CHEESE AND INFINITY

When he was a young boy Mr. Quote's mother often sent him to the local delicatessen to buy ham and cheese. The shop had a tiled floor with an intriguing pattern. Young Quote couldn't help but gaze at it every time he went in. The pattern repeated itself endlessly as if it would spread beyond the limits of the walls. He felt giddy. When he returned home his mother would cut generous slices of the ham and cheese to make a sandwich for him.

In his teens Mr. Quote excelled in mathematics. He had an unusual grasp of numbers and equations, which he handled the way a soccer player handles a ball. Naturally he majored in math at university.

It all started when Mr. Quote attended a lecture on infinity. He was fascinated by the subject: from that day on he could think of nothing else.

One morning he awoke to find that the world had grown strange. Whichever way he turned, everything was covered in the same pattern as the floor of the delicatessen from his childhood.

Tumbling Block, he learned, was the name for the pattern. Thus he tumbled onto infinity. The harder he tried to grasp it, the more he got lost, like an explorer in the midst of a trackless desert. He was starved for clues. He was starved for ham and cheese too. He had to eat. In particular, he had to eat ham and cheese sandwiches—that seemed to be the only way to keep infinity under control. So he ate day in and day out.

Infinity had a huge appetite.

One day Mr. Quote's mathematics professor noticed that he had inflated so much he could barely enter the classroom. He took Mr. Quote to see another professor in the medical school.

The doctor diagnosed him with a typical case of infinititis and advised him to refrain from mathematics and ham and cheese sandwiches.

"You need to exercise and change your program of study to something less demanding."

So Mr. Quote took up table tennis and literature. Soon he got his figure back.

That was almost twenty years ago.

The other day he walked past the delicatessen on the way to visit his elderly mother. He was tempted to go in and look at the floor but thought better of it.

Lately Mrs. Quote had been immersed in knitting something. That evening she announced she had finished it and gave it to her husband. It was a vest with a Tumbling Block pattern!

Feeling apprehensive, he put it on. It was slightly tight around the waist, but he looked good in it. They had just finished dinner when Mr. Quote was struck by an overwhelming desire for ham and cheese sandwiches.

5. THE DRAGON AND THE PRINCESS

Among his many literary achievements Mr. Quote is probably most famous for his translation of *Golbolbough,* popularly known as *Waiting for a Knight,* an epic engraved on hundreds of clay tablets. It is considered as old as *Gilgamesh,* if not older.

The story opens with the abduction of a princess by a dragon (Golbolbough). The dragon expects a knight to appear at any moment, seeking to rescue the princess. So he prepares to fight the knight by doing exercises (running, stretching, weight-lifting) and eating well (bears, wild boars, vipers, and fire). But to the bewilderment of both the dragon and the princess, no knight comes to her rescue.

In the meantime the princess is bored. She happens to be a first-class chess player—indeed, she always carries a chess set with her. To kill time she teaches the dragon how to play the game. As a matter of fact, a substantial part of *Golbolbough* is dedicated to chess: its rules, moves, tactics, even its etiquette.

The dragon quickly becomes absorbed in the game. He progresses rapidly under the guidance of the princess. He learns to think and begins to see things in perspective. He even expresses doubts about his fame-seeking abductor career. On the other hand the princess finds an ideal pupil in the dragon and tutors him enthusiastically. Towards the end of the book, one can detect a new camaraderie between them.

The book ends abruptly, however, with the appearance of a rather nondescript knight who approaches the dragon from behind and slays him in a single blow.

There have been disputes over the authenticity of the ending, according to Mr. Quote in his introduction. Some claim that the last few tablets were made from a different type of clay, while others point to textual discrepancies. The whole book is a political satire, one scholar speculates, but it is hard to prove because we know so little about the political context. Perhaps some professional chess players destroyed the last tablets to keep the more ingenious moves to themselves. Another theory goes that certain "moves" between the princess and the dragon were deemed inappropriate. "In any case, it is a great shame," writes Mr. Quote, "that we can never know how the game between the princess and the dragon really turned out."

SEALS

ANDREW COWAN

Seals were rumored.

"Do we know where we're going?" asked Becca.

"You're navigating," said Alan.

"I am," she confirmed. "I was . . . I've lost us on the map."

He met her gaze in the rear-view mirror, her deadpan expression. After a moment she bowed her head and resumed her scrutiny of the A–Z on her lap. Since they'd left the dual carriageway the roads had become progressively narrower, every fork and junction leading them deeper into the countryside, into uncertainty. The gaps in the hedges revealed brown fields, the beginnings of crops. Dwellings were few, half-hidden by trees. Spring sunshine briefly brightened the road.

"Is this it?" he said. "Where that car's going?"

"Which car?"

"That one, the white one!"

But it was already too late. The white car swung left from the road and he glimpsed a flint cottage, a trampoline cage in a garden. He checked his speed, eased off on the approach to the next corner, accelerated out of the bend.

"No, that wasn't it," said Becca.

"Thanks," he replied.

Beside him sat Becca's mother, mutely observing the scenery, clutching her dog in her lap. Her name was June, though even now, a year since they'd been introduced, he shied from calling her that, just as she shied from calling him Alan. His car was small and felt sluggish with the additional weight of her. Each time he shifted down a gear his fist on the gear-stick knocked into her hip, which caused her to wince. He'd stopped apologizing.

"What's this sign?" said Becca. "Coming up."

He braked sharply and June let out a noise, a gasp or a grunt. She tightened her hold on the dog.

"Any good?" said Becca.

"Couldn't see it."

The dog began panting, and June pressed down on its head. "Just settle," she said.

"You're going too fast again, Alan."

It was Shelley, Becca's daughter, sitting directly behind him. He'd almost forgotten she was there. She hadn't wanted to come, hadn't spoken for almost an hour. He pictured her slumped against the window, sullenly watching the world as it hurtled past them, heading in the wrong direction, back where they'd started from.

"How's anyone supposed to see in time?"

"It's okay," said Becca. "I've found us again. We're very close now."

"You should get a TomTom," said June, as if confirming an opinion she had shared with him earlier.

"Don't need one," he said. "I've got Becca."

He glanced at June quickly—the thin line of her lipstick, the irritated tuck of her chin—and smiled to himself.

A tractor was approaching in the opposite lane and he swerved across to the verge as it bounced by them, hauling a trailer of turnips or beets. Mangelwurzel, perhaps. He had learned that from a crossword this morning as he sat waiting outside Becca's tiny terraced house. Fodder crop (12). Whenever June came to visit he wasn't allowed to sleep over, not even on the sofa-bed; there wasn't enough room for him. Whenever she came to visit he would complete one crossword after another. He had books of them everywhere. The irony wasn't lost on him. As his latest therapist had told him, a crossword provided the obvious place to channel his anger, all the cross words inside him.

"Is this it?" said Becca. "I think this must be it."

"Yup," he said, "this is it."

And now that they were here it was obvious: a signboard displaying a silhouette of a seal, and another car—a mud-spattered 4x4—indicating right to turn in, its blinking red light oddly luminous for this time of day. A mist was forming, and seemed to thicken as they bumped along the track to the car-park, a rutted enclosure of gravel surrounded by trees and sandy scrubland. There were eight or nine other vehicles. As he unclipped his seatbelt he adopted a robotic voice, how he imagined a TomTom might sound: "You . . . have . . . reached . . . your . . . destination."

Becca closed the A–Z.

June continued to gaze straight ahead. "I shan't get out, if you don't mind."

"Oh." Alan looked at her, more relieved than sorry, then found himself saying, "Are you sure? Seems a shame to have come all this way. . . ."

"Mum," said Becca more forcefully, "you can't just sit in the car. What will you do?"

"There's the radio. There's Snowy." She fondled the dog, now balled in her lap. It was a fluffy white crossbreed, two years older than Shelley, with fish-smelling breath and a cataract in each eye. "You won't be gone long, will you?"

"Not too long," said Alan. He hesitated to open his door. "But maybe Snowy needs a turn around the car-park?"

June considered the dog, which lifted its milky gaze to her. "Do you need a widdle?" she asked it.

"Nanna," said Shelley, "he needs a walk. He's *obese*."

"You aren't obese, are you?" said June.

"He needs exercise," insisted Shelley. "Then he wouldn't be so aggressive." She reached an arm between the front seats, displaying the red mark on the back of her hand.

The dog had nipped her the previous evening. Seeing him curled beside June, soft and furry as a cuddly toy, Shelley had swooped to embrace him. The bite was instant, a nip, and Shelley had screamed. Teeth bared, hackles visible, the dog had leapt to the carpet, ridiculously yapping, and Shelley had screamed louder, determined to compete with him. Startled from her near-slumber, June had shouted at the dog to be quiet, shouted repeatedly, then Becca had charged into the front room, her sleeves rolled, suds on her hands. "What the fuck is going on!" she'd yelled, which is when Alan had bent to lace up his shoes; it was time to head home, back to his parents' old bungalow, where the quiet was constant.

"So can we take him, Nanna?" asked Shelley, sweetly wheedling now.

"Alan can always carry him if he gets tired," said Becca.

"Sure," agreed Alan, and distractedly watched as a young couple emerged from either side of the 4x4, identically dressed in chequered caps, waxed jackets, corduroys, hiking boots. They released a pair of handsome black hounds from the rear of their car, clipped leather leads to their collars, and set off into the mist, the track through the trees.

"Oh, go on then," sighed June, and reached for the radio knob. "I'll survive."

Alan took the dog from her, and said, "We'll just be ten minutes or so," but June didn't respond. Shelley and Becca clambered out after him, and June continued to stare straight ahead, the car swelling with the noise of the radio, her gnarled, puffy hands now empty in her lap. But she wasn't his problem; she wasn't his mother. His mother was long gone.

Patiently he escorted the dog across the car-park as it enquired at each rut in the ground—delicately sniffed, lifted its leg, waddled on—and when at last they reached the sandy track through the trees he said, "Shall I take him back now or what?"

"No," urged Shelley. "Keep going."

"He seems happy enough," shrugged Becca.

The trees were straggly and stunted, fading into the mist, and Shelley suddenly broke into a run. "Snowy, Snowy, Snowy!" she called, waving her arms. Becca jogged after her. Alan let go of the lead. Momentarily enlivened, the dog began to pursue them, but the sand was too much. It flopped to its belly, heavily panting, and waited for Alan. He scooped it up, tucked it under his arm. It smelled of June's perfume.

"Why did we bring your mother here?" he called. "She'd never have managed this."

"Had to get her out of the house," said Becca.

Flush-faced and smiling, she and Shelley tramped backwards as he walked along the track towards them. Like a colt and its mare, they were so plainly mother and daughter, long-limbed and slender, with the same sharp features, narrow eyes, dark curly hair. But if Shelley was a smaller, more gangly version of her mother, there was scarcely any resemblance between Becca and June. As if Becca had willed herself as an adolescent not only to hold different opinions, different preferences in everything, but to manifest those differences in her appearance, she had grown a head taller than her mother, and retained the narrow hips of a girl, of her own twelve-year-old daughter, while June was short and increasingly rotund; Shelley would have called her *obese*.

Becca's father was tall, with the same features, same hair, though Alan had not met him, and supposed he never would. A secondary school teacher, he'd become involved with one of his sixth-formers when Becca herself was just twelve. The girl had completed her A-levels, but the relationship hadn't survived her first term at university. Becca's relationship with her father hadn't survived his affair with the girl. He'd lost his job, his wife and daughter, his girlfriend, and become a private tutor, an educational consultant, finally a teacher of English as a Foreign Language, living now in Korea. June had found any number of replacements; there was always some new man for Becca to get used to. June referred to them as her "gentlemen," but claimed finally to have had enough of them. She was too old. Snowy, she said, was the only company she now needed.

"Foggy," remarked Becca as they emerged to the beach.

He nodded. "It's called fret," he said, and hesitated, glancing at Shelley. "It's when moist warm air passes over a cooler surface, like the sea. The moisture in the air condenses."

Shelley sighed and walked down to the shore. Becca smiled at him.

"Sorry," he said.

"No, it's good. You know things. It's educational."

For a few moments they stood and listened to the shush of the waves, shingle hissing at the shoreline, gulls screeching above. Footsteps clacked along a ridge of pebbles, and a party of walkers passed by them, muted patches of colour fading into the mist, becoming like a memory of people, a dream. They were heading left to right along the beach; he guessed that meant south.

"What's that smell?" asked Becca.

Alan pointed behind her. The bin was red and pockmarked with rust, displaying a symbol of a defecating dog. She grimaced. He pretended to offer June's dog to the bin.

"Oh, don't," Becca said, as if she would like nothing better.

"Mum!" called Shelley then. "Come quick!"

Folding her arms, Becca stepped down to the shoreline, the scummy brown sea, and Alan came after her, still cradling the dog.

"Look!" said Shelley.

There was no horizon, no sky, but the seal was starkly visible, barely ten yards away from them. Its mottled head bobbed in the waves. Its eyes were enormous, fathomless, black. As if the fog had receded especially for them, they stared at each other. Sunlight softly gleamed though the mist. A minute went by; another. The seal regarded them steadily; its gaze was transfixing. It might have been beckoning, calling them in. And then it was gone. It submerged, and they waited, scanning the water. "There!" cried Becca, pointing into the murk.

"Where?"

The seal was small and indistinct now, many yards further on and further out, but seemingly still watching them. Oddly elated, Alan wrapped an arm round Shelley's shoulders, drew her into his side. "A seal!" he exclaimed.

"Mum!" she complained.

"He's just being friendly," said Becca.

Alan lowered the dog to the sand and offered Shelley the lead. He was tolerated now, he supposed; she was slowly coming to accept him. Every other weekend she would pack her rucksack and go to stay with her father and his new family, and though something of her former grudgingness would be evident each time she returned, he had stopped fearing that she could sense his self-consciousness, or smell the sex on him. He was the first "gentleman" that Becca had allowed into her own life—or her bed—since Shelley's father had walked out on them, eight years before. Shelley was bound to be suspicious of him; it was bound to take time.

They set off along the beach, but the dog was unused to the exercise and couldn't be hurried. Several times it sat down, refused to continue. Shelley soon became exasperated. "Mum, can you take him?"

"Here," said Alan, and held out his hand. Shelley relinquished its lead, let it drop to the sand.

Becca glared at her. Shelley gave a small shrug, seeming to stifle a smile. Half-squatting, the dog shuffled around in a circle.

"Any poo-bags?" asked Alan.

"Hundreds," said Becca, and produced a fistful of nappy sacks from her anorak pocket: scented, coral-pink. Alan tucked a hand inside one of them and stuffed the rest in his back pocket. They waited for the dog to stop circling.

"This, by the way, is canine magnetoreception," he told Shelley. "Snowy won't do his doos until he's properly aligned with the earth's magnetic field."

Shelley shifted her weight to one hip and folded her arms, her posture exactly mirroring her mother's.

"Fascinating fact about dogs," he added.

"Not interested," she replied.

Alan imitated her shrug, and stooped to pick up the excrement. He inverted the bag, knotted the ties. Then grinning, he held it out on his palm. "Would you like to carry it, Shelley? It's lovely and warm."

Becca had once compared a bag of Snowy's warm feces to the feeling of cupping his balls. She liked to clutch them when he came.

"Mum," complained Shelley, "he's disgusting!"

Becca looked at him coolly. "Yes, he is," she said, and took the bag from him. She looped the ties around a finger, let it dangle by her side, and offered her free arm to Shelley. They walked on ahead of him.

Alan continued to carry the dog, his hand supporting its chest, its legs on either side of his forearm. He could feel its heartbeat on his palm. He didn't mind it. He was comfortable here, enveloped in the fog, the sounds of the seashore. Even as a boy he had never stripped off at the beach, sunbathed on the sand, plunged into the sea. The horizon didn't interest him, the endless roll of the waves. He didn't swim or surf or build sandcastles. The beach wasn't a place for play or contemplation. Instead he would stare down at his feet, scanning for bones, shells, pebbles with holes in, souvenirs of having been here, of this excursion having happened. His elderly parents—who weren't really his parents, who had adopted him—would sit on their deckchairs and wait for him to come back to them.

These days he worked for the local authority as an education officer in the museums service, and spent hours hunched over cabinets, studying artifacts, relics. He liked to be purposeful, even during his breaks. He still liked to discover things, and to know things. One day he had discovered Becca kneeling in one of the galleries, surrounded by children. She was the new artist-in-residence. They had taken their lunch together, sitting in the tiny staff kitchen, eating from plastic boxes. Weeks had passed before he'd dared to ask her out, many weeks more before she'd brought Shelley to visit him at home.

He hadn't yet made a start on the redecorating, and most of his parents' belongings remained where they had always been: their furniture, glass ornaments, framed photographs; the crockery in the cupboards, the coats and scarves on the hat-stand. Becca had compared it to a mausoleum, which was when, smiling, he had shown them the collection of bones in the conservatory. There was a ram's skull with horns, a sheep's skull, the jaw of a horse still containing its teeth, the delicate beak of a gull, an assortment of vertebrae. He had found them on his walks in the countryside. But there was also the skull of a small deer, and another of a badger, animals he had glimpsed from his car, dead by the side of the road. Eventually he had gone back for them.

"Can we leave now?" said Shelley.

"I'm sorry," said Becca, touching his arm. "Would you mind?"

"No," he'd said, "of course not," and picked up his car keys. He guided them out through the bungalow, avoiding the plates of food he had prepared in the kitchen.

Becca was calling to him now. He recognized the shape of her, standing with Shelley near a cluster of boulders. They seemed to have stumbled on something. He lowered the dog and dawdled towards them, stooping, picking up stones, discarding them. "What is it?" he said.

Becca pointed. He looked. The mounds on the beach were not boulders but seals, dozens and dozens of them, lolling about in the sand. The colony continued into the mist, becoming invisible, and he noticed several other small huddles of people, standing quite still, including the couple from the car-park, their dogs constrained on short leads. Despite the fog, there were cameras, smartphones.

"Fuck," he said, and Shelley smirked at him.

A small seal lifted its head, lazily observed them, and he thought of the seal that had appeared to them earlier, how special that moment had seemed, and how meaningless now. There were so many of them, and no two were exactly alike. They had the appearance of dogs, their faces, the way that they yawned, rolled onto their backs, scratched at themselves. He edged closer. "Be careful," said Becca, and he stood very still. June's dog seemed oblivious.

Their pelts were various shades of gray and brown, mottled, speckled or blotched. Those nearest the water were darker, glistening wet; those nearest the people were duller and fluffier, coated in sand. Their claws were sharp and very long, their flippers almost useless on land. He peered through the mist to the sea, and saw a hefty bull seal hauling itself out of the water, belly-flopping onto the beach. A smaller seal waddled down to the waves, skimmed the final few yards, gracefully plunged. And now that he could see them he also became aware of their smell, the stench of rotten fish, and the sounds they were making, the ghostly howls, plaintive wails, the groans and coughing barks. It seemed Snowy had become aware of them too, and was straining on his lead, pulling to get away from them. Annoyed, he yanked it back.

"So, what do you know?" asked Becca.

"Yeah, Alan. Go, Alan," said Shelley.

Their arms were still linked. Their curls had become damp in the mist.

"Well . . . They come ashore to give birth. That happened a couple of months ago, I think. The mothers are called cows. They're mammals, warm-blooded. Everyone knows that. They feed their pups on milk. And the males are called bulls." He looked around. "There aren't any now, but when they're born the pups are white. They have to moult before they can go in the sea, because they're not waterproof—the cows leave them to fend for themselves, and about half of them die in their first year, something like that. Also, if the pups stray too far from their mother some other seal will attack them. They don't adopt strays. They're pretty nasty to each other, even the cute ones."

He paused, tried to think of something else.

"That one's not cute," said Shelley, and gestured towards an enormous bull seal, three or four yards away. It was slumped on its side and displaying its penis, a lurid pink tube. Another, smaller bull was sidling towards it.

"We'd better watch out," said Alan, and took a step backwards. Becca and Shelley stepped with him.

For some moments neither seal looked at the other. The larger of the two rolled onto its belly, concealing its penis, and he was glad about that. The smaller seal yawned, displaying its teeth, its cavernous maw. Suddenly it reared. The seals lunged at each other, and all at once they were wrestling, butting and writhing. Each attempted to bite the other one's neck. They might have been playing. They might have been attempting to mate. But soon the smaller seal found itself caught, clamped in the larger seal's jaws. Its flesh was torn, red-raw. Briefly they paused. The injured seal appeared to submit, then struggled and ducked and pulled itself free. It ought to have fled, but instead it returned. It continued to fight, and again it was caught. Blood ran down its neck and speckled the sand.

The surrounding seals ignored them. Some of the onlookers edged closer and attempted to film them.

"Can we go now, please?" said Shelley. "This is gross."

Becca nodded, and looked to Alan. "Mum will be wondering," she said.

"Let her wonder," he said. "This is interesting."

Becca held up the poo-bag. "I want to get rid of this."

"And she'll be missing Snowy," said Shelley.

"Let her," he said. "She's a grown-up, she'll survive, remember."

"That's really selfish," said Shelley. "And childish."

"So you take him!" snapped Alan, and held out the lead, but Shelley barely glanced at it. She pushed her hands in her pockets.

Becca gazed at him steadily. He wasn't to do this, he knew. He had to be patient. "Coming?" she said at last.

"In a minute," he insisted, and watched as they trudged off, mother and daughter, kicking through the sand in their plimsoles. He waited until the fog had enveloped them, then turned back to the grappling bulls, but the spectacle was no longer so fascinating; it no longer held him. Like their encounter with the solitary seal in the sea, it was merely something he'd witnessed, something he could talk about later. The dog whimpered at his ankles. June was sitting alone in his car. Soon Becca and Shelley would be sitting there with her.

He surveyed the scene a final time—the seals, the fog, the spilling sea—then picked up the dog and set off along the shoreline, where the sand was damp and easier to walk on, and almost immediately he came upon a seal and its pup, both of them dead. They must have been there for some time, and he must have walked past them earlier. He lowered the dog and crouched to examine them.

The only other time they had come out to this coast—last June or July—there had been sunshine and a blustering wind, blue skies but no seals. That was a few miles further north, where there was a protected site for Little Terns. The birds nested in the sand. A pair of wardens in green tabards had sat on fold-out chairs beside a smart little hut, keeping watch on the dog-walkers. They had used binoculars. He remembered how the birds had described the shape of the wind as they'd swooped over the sea, seemingly black with the sun behind them, suddenly white as they wheeled around. And he remembered the remains of the creature he had found at the tideline. It was five or six feet long, and entirely decomposed except for its head, which was rubbery, black. He'd thought it resembled a sheep. Everything else was vertebrae. He'd wondered if he might take it home. He'd called Shelley over to look at it, and her face was disgusted. That weekend she should have been visiting her father, but something had gone awry. "I think it's a conger eel," he'd told her. "They can grow a lot longer. They're prehistoric. Predators. They lurk in the dark and wait for their prey—they'll go for anything, even humans. They can take quite a chunk out of you." He was smiling. Without warning Shelley had stamped on the eel, crushed the skull under her foot, and walked away from him.

Later Becca had suggested it might still be too soon for him to think of moving in. He was beginning to think it might always be too soon.

The seal pup was small and badly decayed. Its skeleton was almost entirely revealed, its flesh scoured clean, but the mother was preserved in her pelt, seemingly intact. Her eyes were closed. She might have been sleeping, her body shielding the pup. He stared for several seconds to be sure. She did not move. Her flippers were rotting, he realised. Months might pass before she was stripped to the bone; perhaps the tide would reclaim her. He looked around in the fog, scanning the beach, then the sea, and thought he saw something out there, a dark shape in the haze.

He shuffled nearer the pup. Still crouching, he placed one foot on its torso. The skeleton crunched under his weight, the bones surprisingly brittle. He gloved a hand inside a poo-bag and gripped the top of the head. He assumed it would detach quite easily, but he had to twist and wrench to loosen it. He kept twisting, and tugging, until finally it made a noise like fabric tearing. The skull came free, but not cleanly. It was attached to several inches of spine. He had not wanted the spine. The tearing noise had disturbed him, and now he wasn't sure if he wanted the skull.

He stood and examined it, then gazed disconsolately down at the seal, lying alongside what remained of its pup. He couldn't repair it, reassemble the body, leave it just as he'd found it. He shouldn't have touched it. He had desecrated something, he knew. That was how Becca would see it. "You didn't?" she'd whisper. She might even cry. June would certainly judge him; Shelley would probably hate him. But animals die, he might say. They turn to rot; their bones are all that remain. He had merely picked up some bones from the beach.

He thought of the eel that Shelley had stamped on. He thought of his collection at home. After a moment he drew a second poo-bag from his pocket and used it to sheathe the remnant of spine. He might be able to hide it. He might be able to slip it in the boot of the car, pretend it was something else: driftwood perhaps. He picked up the end of the lead, but still the dog refused to come with him. He tugged, and it resisted. Its paws were damp and gritty with sand. June wouldn't want it on her lap. He was carrying the skull and spine of a seal pup, and neither Becca nor Shelley would want that in the car. And of course it would smell. The journey home would take them an hour. It was hopeless. He yanked on the dog's lead, yanked on it too hard, and the collar came free.

"Oh, fuck it," he murmured, and stuffed the lead in his pocket. He set off up the beach. The dog could follow him. He quickened his pace to encourage it, as much as the sand would allow him, and headed for the red metal bin by the trees. Becca would have deposited the poo-bag in there. He hesitated, then lifted the black rubber lid. A smell of dog shit breathed out. He dropped the seal skull inside, and let the lid fall.

It need not have happened; he need never mention it, or attempt to explain what he had done. He took a long breath and peered back through the mist, which was beginning to lift now. Snowy had not followed him, and the girls would be wondering what had become of them. He would need to apologize for having taken so long. He might offer to drive them further up the coast to the nearest resort: they could eat fish and chips on the pier in the sunshine. There might be amusements. The day was not yet lost to them.

"Snowy!" he called, and hastened back down to the shoreline, where the squat little dog was sitting just as he'd left it, tilting its head to the sound of his voice. The dead seal and the remains of its pup lay a few feet away. He stopped. The sea darkened and swelled. There was something approaching; perhaps their seal was returning. The dog did not move. He could see it quite clearly, the breeze lifting its fur. A torrent of sunlight poured down through the haze, and he watched as a gargantuan bull seal reared up from the waves, splashed onto the beach. Its red maw was gaping. It might have been yawning.

translated by Sam Bett

A PEDDLER OF TEARS

YŌKO OGAWA

Eighteen was the last year I made a living selling tears. Among my best customers at the time were a violin instructor at a music college, a clarinet player in the circus, and a flamenco guitarist.

My tears were all the rage. Musicians considered them indispensable before a big performance, and sometimes things would go so awry during a rehearsal that I would have to rush out with an emergency delivery.

"Damn, that hits the spot!" they would say. "What would I ever do without you?"

I went wherever I was needed, whether studio or concert hall, city square or music store, a musician's house, his summer home or where his lover lived. I'd even make calls in the middle of the night. Three hundred sixty-five days a year, with no days off. You never knew when an instrument might go wonky. Changes in the weather were always a factor, but the intensity of the stage lights, the temperature of the audience, and especially how the musician was feeling could easily turn the tone sour. That's where I came in.

I had one customer, a renowned cellist, who asked for something beyond the ordinary dose. He thought my sheer presence was good luck. What he really wanted wasn't tears so much as knowing I was there.

"I'm here, sir," I would whisper, standing with him in the wings, and rest my hand on his back. The moment I did this, his tension slipped away. He would give me a reassured smile and step out into the spotlight.

Even on nights he didn't need my tears, he paid me what they would have cost and then some just to have me stand there in the wings. But he played the cello so magnificently that I was always moved to tears.

I wasn't interested in working with professionals alone. My tears were more than a commodity. If I walked by a child struggling with her recorder at the edge of a schoolyard, or found a pedal organ abandoned at the dump, I sprinkled the instrument with tears. As long as I could be of service I didn't hesitate to give my tears away, even when there was no money to be had.

At some point, I'm not sure when, I realized that my tears had power over music. When I rub them on an instrument, its tone instantly improves, no matter what it is. The notes of a worn and battered xylophone or a rusty triangle will come to sound as though they are drifting up from the bottom of a deep cave. Once I fixed a broken music box. A few tears on the lid and its gears began to turn again.

I'm not sure why. Once a scientist from some institute asked if he could analyze my tears to see what they were made of. I refused. What good could it possibly do? My tears were my own business, and no one had the right to tell me how to use them. I tremble just thinking about being laid out in a laboratory, surrounded by strange drugs and devices, while total strangers stare down at me and siphon away my tears.

In the beginning I saved up tears until I had enough to sell and took them to an old man in the neighborhood who ran a music shop. But word got out, and people started asking me to sell to them directly, and on a regular basis. I began to take orders on my own, circumventing the old man without realizing how cutthroat his operation was. When I told him I was suspending our relationship, he went berserk and set off on a mission to ruin my life. He stuffed spoiled giblets in my mailbox, hung a dying crow from my doorknob, chucked sea cucumbers at my windows—abuse like that. Perhaps he was trying to make me weep and steal my tears. My house reeked of death, and when my neighborhood association complained, I knew I couldn't live there anymore.

So I made up my mind to head out on the road. There was no other way to escape that venomous old man. Even if I relocated he was bound to track me down and beset me with more foul presents. As long as I had my tear ducts and my tear sacs, all I needed was my body. That gave me the freedom to roam. There was no problem left to solve. To sell my tears I would have to become a wanderer.

Once I heard of a famous violin whose maker had mixed human blood into its finish. I guess every generation has a special few who possess the ability to mediate the instrument and the soul, just as there are those who effortlessly intuit the feelings of animals or hear the voices of the trees. Blood lasts. Once it penetrates the wood, it can only sink deeper into the grain. But tears are different. Their lifespan inside an instrument is pitifully short. Like sound, they're soon sucked up into pockets of air.

As long as the instruments want me, I'll shed tears until the day I die.

I keep all my mementos from my days selling tears safe inside a candy tin secured with a pale peach ribbon. Postcards sent back from tours, a cassette tape recorded just for me, a sheet of music given as a birthday present. A broken string, concert programs, photographs, a handkerchief. The postcards offer glimpses of far-off cities, places someone like me would never have a chance to visit. In the corner of the sheet music is a poem, a confession of love. My initials are sewn into the handkerchief.

These days, I never untie the ribbon. My memories of all my loyal customers have slipped into the past. I hate to say it, but if I opened the tin today I'd probably find wormholes in the programs, the cassette unspooled, what was once a beautiful melody now no more than a crashing stream of noise.

The cellist who considered me his good luck charm died ages ago. I heard he breathed his last seated in his studio, his beloved cello in his arms. They say that when they found him it looked like he was giving it one last kiss. I can only hope that the residue of even one of my teardrops still lingered in the cello when he kissed it goodbye.

Life changed abruptly for a reason so simple it's embarrassing to admit. So simple I'm not sure how to put it into words. What can I say—I fell in love.

One day, just before I turned nineteen, I met a man. I was on the way home from delivering tears to one of my regulars, the circus clarinetist. As I walked alone back to the railway station along the road from the sports complex where the circus had raised their tent, I heard a strange music. Strange is the only way to describe it; I had never heard anything like it before. I considered myself fairly good at recognizing instruments by their sound, but these instruments eluded me. I had to know what I was hearing. I found myself drifting in the direction of the sound.

Five musicians were camped out beneath a poplar tree. At first I wasn't sure where the music was coming from. I thought it must be coming from a radio, and they were only dancing to it. And who'd think otherwise? They weren't holding any instruments, and they were all half-naked.

Then it clicked: they were a body band. Every sound I heard was coming from some part of their bodies.

The girl standing in the middle was whistling. She played lead. To her right was a guy in a thong playing percussion on his butt cheeks. To her left another one blocked and unblocked his ear holes with his palms. A fourth member plucked his hair, its strands the length of his arms. Together they made quite the ensemble.

When I first saw him he was outside the circle, dancing even more bizarrely than the rest. However odd the others were, I could basically connect their movements to the sounds they were making. But not him. No matter how hard I tried, I couldn't zero in on the locus of his energy. All he did was flail his limbs around like macaroni.

Few had stopped to hear them play. Everyone was probably at the circus. They were quieter than a normal band, bafflingly quiet, and to be honest they could have used a little flair. The handful who had gathered watched from a distance with bemused expressions, listening more out of puzzlement than appreciation.

The band finished their song, something from a film score, perhaps, or a foreign lullaby. The light patter of applause only drew attention to how forlorn they looked. You could see a few coins at the bottom of the hat they had set out. There was no question they were pros. But no one went over to add a coin. Without any comment, no signal whatsoever, the band launched into their next song.

The wind was up, so it took me some time to figure out that the song was . . . a jazz standard? I'd never heard such timid jazz in all my life.

I was hopelessly distracted by the man with the flailing limbs—I tried in vain to make out his sound, the part he was playing. It pained me that even with ears so attuned to the differences among instruments I couldn't hear him.

Sweat flying, he whipped his hair about as if possessed. His ankles, his knees, his waist, his wrists, his neck—all twisted in unthinkable directions. The shadows of the poplar leaves raked and heaved across his naked back and chest. It was as if he was squirming under their caress.

At last my ears latched onto a sound—his sound—running softly underneath the melody. He was snapping and popping his joints together to the rhythm of the beat, playing them like castanets. This man was a maestro of the joints.

Without warning, a man tore through the circle of musicians, gesticulating wildly.

"Stop it! Stop! You can't just set up anywhere you want. Go on now, get out of here."

He seemed to be affiliated with the circus. Somehow he thought the band was interfering with their show. He chewed them out and prodded the joint maestro in the chest.

Caught off guard, the maestro fell flat on his ass. I rushed over to help him up. When I see an instrument being handled roughly, I can't help but come to its defense.

"Enough with the fighting!" I railed against the circus man. "What are you so upset about? These people aren't doing anything wrong. They're only playing music. Quiet music. So quiet you can barely hear it."

The members of the band were aghast at my intrusion, which seemed to have shocked them far more than the circus man's violence.

"We're fine. Thank you. Don't worry about us . . ."

The joint maestro's voice had the same reserved quality as his hidden castanets. This was the first moment that we shared.

After that, I followed the body band wherever they went. Since I couldn't make music with my own body I never stood onstage. I worked behind the scenes, tuning the band with my tears.

I had to give up selling tears to my old customers. It's not like my supply was endless. Even I had limits. I had no other choice. Since I didn't have enough tears to go around, I gave everything to the band (but really, if I'm honest, mostly to the maestro). My tears could make a desperate man resort to rotten gizzards, but from then on the maestro was the only one I would shed them for.

The body band was always on the road looking for places to perform. My lifestyle barely had to change. It was a just a matter of an independent contractor signing up for a full-time gig.

"I had no idea that tears were this warm," the maestro said to me, lying on his back.

"I know. Fresh tears are even warmer than the rest of the body. It's because you squeeze them out from deep inside."

"They're so warm . . ."

I climbed on top of him and blessed each joint, rubbing my tears into his skin. All I had to do was blink and my eyes would fill again with tears of joy. I could touch him to my heart's content.

"All the tears I've ever sold were cold—I've. I could never make fresh tears like this for anyone else. What do you think that means?"

He didn't respond. Transfixed by the sensation of the tears, he couldn't hear a thing I said.

For someone who lived off physical labor he was surprisingly slender. I guess any extra muscle would have trapped the sound of his joints inside his body. When I touched him, it felt as if my fingers were meeting bone, as if there were no skin or veins or fat between his hardness and my hands.

His joints were wonderfully articulate, their movements so intricate I imagined each had its own independent thoughts. If you watched him up close during a performance, you could almost see the tiny bones beneath his skin as their bumps and grooves meshed fluidly.

Each emitted a distinctly different sound. A subterranean rumble rose from the sockets of his thighbones, while the first joint of his pinkie finger was like a little bird sighing. The sounds ran the gamut, and he combined them readily and endlessly.

"Doesn't it hurt?" I asked once, worried.

"Doesn't bother me," he said offhandedly. "It's not like I'm working my joints harder than anyone else. I just catch the sound with my lymph system so you can hear it."

I imagined lymphatic fluid vibrating throughout his body, beckoning me. His was the most amorous music I'd ever encountered.

Indeed, what instrument could be more understated than the joint maestro's castanets? The violinist or pianist scrapes his strings or beats his keyboard in bursts of virtuosity for a grand display of sound, but joint castanets are hidden in the body and amplified by lymph as meager as the tears behind your eyes. My tears were the perfect complement to such a precious instrument.

His joints sucked up my tears like sand: my tears penetrated the tiniest crevices, smoothed the movements of his bones, and cleansed his lymph of all impurities. I forgot at times what I was there for, and found myself yearning to smother his joints with kisses. Curbing this desire proved exhausting. Should they be exposed to a stray breadcrumb, a piece of chapped skin, or worst of all saliva, my tears would be unfit for use. I had to sequester myself.

When the tuning was over, he didn't say a word, but he made my favorite of his joints sing—his left ankle. I would hug his left foot to my head and press it to my ear. It was as if I was hearing a single tear drop into a pool, deep within a cave. This was my reward for all my modest service.

A body band can only perform in certain kinds of places. It was rare for us to play a proper concert hall. At best our gigs were on the roof of a department store or in a community center. Most of the time, though, we were out in the open, like on the day we met.

If we were at a park or plaza, we made our preparations in the shade. The band stripped down, did some stretching exercises, discussed the set list. My job was over after tuning up the maestro, while the other four members—the whistler, the ear gong, the hair harp and the bum drum—rubbed each other with tears from a chilled bottle I had prepared.

After passing them the bottle, I watched from a bench on the periphery. I claimed that I stayed away because I was new to body bands, but the truth is I didn't want to touch anyone except the maestro. But he was a good man, and helped the others all he could. He cleared out the ear gong's ears, held a mirror for the bum drum, and combed stray hairs from the back of the hair harp's neck.

The one thing I could not abide was when he rubbed the whistler's lips with tears. Why did he have to be so nice to her? Couldn't she find her lips herself? Sure she was the face of the band, but wasn't playing lead enough? And remember, those were my tears on his fingers! The same tears that mingled with the maestro's lymph were soaking into the whistler's lips. My heart raced—I could hardly breathe.

I withdrew from the others and crawled into the green world behind some bushes. I crawled in there to cry. Shedding tears calms me like nothing else.

I drew a custom-made vial from my pocket. An acquaintance at a glass shop had fashioned it especially for me. The tube is curved into the letter U, and the two ends—which perfectly match the space between my eyes—can be plugged with rubber stoppers. When I hold the bottle to my cheekbones I can catch tears without losing a drop.

Given my high standards, though, I rarely if ever try to collect tears standing up. The tears that run through my eyelashes or the corners of my eyes get tainted with impurities and thus cannot be used. So I get down on all fours. That way the tears drip straight from my eyes into the bottle.

Beyond the bushes, I could hear the band readying their instruments. I pictured the maestro and the whistler working to harmonize the sounds coming from their bodies. Drop by drop, tears filled the bottom of the U. On my knees like that I must have looked like I was vomiting.

Someone snuck up on me. "Are you alright?" she asked.

"Yeah, I mean no, I'm fine. Don't mind me," I said through my tears. "Hey look, that body band out there's about to play!"

Not to brag, but the caliber of the band's music has gone way up since I joined. Their sound is more substantial, their rhythm more relaxed and forthright, the general feeling they give more robust. Their faces are alive, even at rest. The atmosphere is brighter, and the number of coins in the hat has increased with the crowds.

The whistle girl swings her head and whistles, bright with confidence, convinced that all these changes are her doing. The bum drum's butt cheeks glimmer in the sun. The hair harp produces a vibrato so compelling honeybees draw near, and the ear lobes of the ear gong have turned a rosy pink. But I know better. The band sounds wonderful because of the maestro. Because of the tears I work so lovingly into his castanets.

But I'm not satisfied. Tears vary tremendously depending on what provokes them. Tears of happiness, tears of sadness, tears of distress, tears of regret . . . each having its distinct flavor. When I first started selling tears I mixed them together in the same bottle, regardless of variety, but I soon began to notice their color, density and texture depended on what had made me cry. Naturally, this also altered their effect on instruments.

The cheapest tears are those you cry while cutting onions. As a novice I sometimes resorted to this method when I was swamped. Just because I sold tears for a living didn't mean that an order of 15 cc of tears for a concert, for delivery the same night, was going to be easy to fill. I always kept a few onions in my purse for these emergencies.

Onion tears are the lowest grade a professional can offer. Good tears well up from deep within the body, near the center of the soul, while onion tears slide from the surface of the eye, no more than a response to circumstance. Plus they're adulterated by the onion juice.

What then, you may ask, are the highest-quality tears?

The answer: tears of pain. Pain that drugs can't touch. A shooting pain that brings you to your knees in agony. Pain you'd never revisit if you could avoid it. Nothing is as pure as the tears you shed in pain of this intensity. Tears of sadness or regret are exposed to whatever grime has adhered to the heart, while tears of physical pain come from the flesh itself.

Such tears can only flow when the body is besieged. Their taste is free from calculation, jealousy or self-indulgence. And the greater the sacrifice, the happier the instrument.

To my dismay, I had summoned tears of pain only a few times in my life, and then from a toothache or a migraine. Nevertheless, their performance was astounding. The night that renowned cellist was decorated by the Queen and played the greatest solo concert of his life, his cello had been tuned with tears of pain.

I needed tears of pain for the joint maestro. The whistle girl and the rest of the band would be fine with normal tears. That was enough to satisfy them. Even onion tears would do.

But the maestro was special. The music he played was so restrained. Were it not for my help, who would hear the rills of clear lymph coming from deep within his body? Not the whistler, that's for sure. You couldn't count on her to do more than stand there with her head in the clouds, puckering her lips while the maestro moistened them with my cheapest tears.

I resolved to sacrifice anything to reap the highest quality tears of pain. My tear ducts and my tear sacs were all I needed on this journey. I was prepared to give up everything else.

First, I cut the little toe from my left foot. I could rub the maestro with my tears just fine without it. As he lay waiting to be tuned, I sat beside him with a kitchen knife, took aim, and dropped it like a guillotine. To hide my moans I shot both hands over my mouth. I was happy to see that suppressing my screams made me cry even harder. I dripped tears onto each of his joints, taking care not to sully him with blood.

Next I took the little toe from the right, then the next toe from the left, chopping my way across both feet. The tears of pain were more orgasmic than I could have dreamed. The pain made my hair stand on end; I couldn't breathe. I felt like I was going to puke. But my eyes, now moist, narrowed in a smile. When I was finished he would play his ankle for me, and its tone would take me to the brink of oblivion. It was getting harder every day to stop myself from kissing him.

Once my toes were gone I went after my lips. Without lips there'd be no kisses to hold back. No jealousy when he touched his finger to the puckering whistle girl.

I gave up my calves, my earlobes, my nipples, and my tongue. There were so many things I could sacrifice, and this knowledge gave me great solace. I said goodbye to my ovaries, my vocal cords, my cheeks, my urethra. I had to stifle myself to hold back the tears of joy. The maestro was getting tears of pain and pain only.

Soon there will be nothing left of me but tear ducts and tear sacs. But that's all I really need. What more is there to a wandering peddler of tears?

translated by Christopher Lowy

PETER AND JANIS

TOMOKA SHIBASAKI

I know it was February. I had taken an entrance exam at a university in Kyoto and was returning home on a Hankyu express train.

The doors opened at Katsura Station. Heading from Osaka to Kyoto that morning, some surprisingly chilly air had rushed into the train the moment the doors opened at that same station. It reminded me that Osaka and Kyoto are not the same. There is a marked change after you pass Mt. Tenno, almost as if you are entering a different country. Now I am used to the Kyoto climate, so when the doors open I'm not surprised or anything—*It's cold* is all that registers.

It was nearly dusk, but there was still light outside. Several seats were taken by people who had boarded the train with the chilly wind. The seat next to me, too, was occupied. A young white man had sat down. Once the doors had closed and the train began to move, the rays of the setting sun and the heater blasting away at our feet made the car uncomfortably warm. I would board this train again the following day to take another entrance exam at a different university. I doubted I'd pass that one either. At least that was the impression our high school had left us with. *It's weird,* I thought to myself. *I have no idea what I'll be doing two months from now.*

I had been staring out the window at the houses, apartments, rice fields and pachinko parlors passing by, a collection of sights I remembered from the few times I had traveled to Kyoto. A baseball team was lined up in a field attached to a school filled with students I did not know. When we drew close to Mt. Tenno, the late winter sun divided the dull green mass of trees into clearly defined areas of light and shadow.

Excuse me, the foreigner sitting next to me said in Japanese.

Though he seemed to struggle a bit with his

pronunciation, his *excuse me* suggested he had grown more or less accustomed to saying it. I looked at him.

My name is Peter Jackson. I'm from Canada, and I do the work of God.

I see, I replied.

His blond curls were nearly transparent in the sunlight, and his eyes were green. When they gazed into mine, though, I didn't feel as if I were being looked at. Even before he said anything I imagined he was connected to some church or other. People with similar expressions sometimes came to our house. They were always in groups of two. It seemed as if this person was on his own.

He wore a khaki coat and had an orange nylon backpack on his lap.

Hello, he said.

Hello, I said. I didn't tell him my name was Yamada.

I'm twenty-three years old. How old are you? he asked, his calm smile never wavering.

Eighteen.

"Eighteen!" he exclaimed in English. His whole face registered surprise—his muscles danced, and his eyes widened. *Really,* he said in a slightly high-pitched voice, *I thought you might be twenty.*

Pure flattery, I thought. I'm usually mistaken for someone younger; in fact, I've only been mistaken for someone older twice before.

The railway straps and hanging advertisements swayed in rhythm. Outside the window, I could see someone bringing in laundry from their veranda.

Were you at school?

The plump woman sitting across from him was glancing at us curiously. If the roles were reversed I'd probably look, too.

Umm, for an entrance exam . . . to take a test to enter university.

"For test of university?" I thought to myself in English. That's not correct. Then again, I doubt I did well on the English exam I took just a little while ago.

Oh, that's an important day. I hope all your dreams come true, he said with a large, approving nod. I bet he really means it, I thought. He is a servant of God, after all.

I looked away, feeling I didn't really deserve his sincere blessing. Directly across from me was what appeared to be a grandmother with a grandson of about four in tow; she was talking to the boy while pointing out the window at something just behind our heads. Two people were situated on either side of them, all four of whom were dozing.

The warm air blowing into the car from just below their legs had probably put them to sleep. I was sleepy, too.

I'll try hard again next year.

I'm sure your effort will be rewarded, he said earnestly.

We arrived at the next station and the doors opened. A middle-aged man wearing navy-blue work clothes sitting on the seat in front of us jerked awake just before the doors closed as if someone had startled him. He checked the station name on the platform column just behind him, leaped to his feet, and hurriedly exited the train just as the doors were closing. He got caught in the closing doors and they reopened with a clang, closing the next time nice and snug. Once safely outside, he ambled off in the opposite direction.

What are you going to study?

Peter's eyes were a pale green. It was as if you could look right into them. How could one see with such eyes? It was a mystery to me.

Philosophy or art history.

Peter tilted his head to the side. Their light green color made me feel as if I could almost make out every cell in his eyes.

"Philosophy? And history of art," I said in my best English.

I had no idea how much Peter understood, but he nodded with an *ahh.*

That sounds difficult, Peter said, and this time I nodded, adding, *I suppose.*

How long will you be in Japan? I asked, fingering a button on my pea jacket.

As if looking for the answer, Peter glanced up at the hanging ads swaying above his head before answering. *Six months?* he said as if trying to confirm it with himself.

One overhead ad, whose typography mimicked a fissure or crack in the ground, predicted the occurrence of a major earthquake and giant tsunami within the next four years that would devastate Japan and claim 3 million casualties. The button on my coat came off.

"How about Japan? How do you think about my country?" I asked in English.

Peter broke into a smile.

It's a great place! he said in Japanese.

His blond eyelashes looked bristly.

It's beautiful, and everything is very convenient. Everyone is very nice.

As if suddenly remembering, he opened his backpack and took out a business card. The name of some church and sect were printed on the white rectangle, but the distinctions were lost on me. Peter flipped the card over, where "Peter Jackson" was printed in katakana. I saw he was holding a ballpoint pen in his right hand.

I had someone think of a Japanese name for me, he said as he began to write. The lines trembled with the shaking of the train. I followed them with my eyes as if tracing a path leading out of nowhere.

On the back of the business card he had written four kanji: *pi* 美 beautiful; *ta* 多 many; *jaku* 弱 weak; and *son* 損 damage. At the upper right-hand side of the kanji for "beautiful" was a diacritical mark indicating that it should be pronounced *pi* instead of the usual *bi.* I stared intently at those correctly written, yet awkward, kanji.

Who taught these to you? I asked.

A friend, Peter said.

Sensing my reservations about his Japanese name, he frowned, his eyebrows forming an inverted V-shape. Westerners have such expressive faces.

Did I make a mistake?

Well, they aren't wrong, I answered.

I started going through different kanji in my head, thinking I should teach him some other ones. Then again, perhaps it was deliberate. Just as baseball players put numbers associated with bad luck—like 42 and 49—on their uniforms, maybe because Peter was a young monk-in-training he had chosen kanji with negative connotations.

What're you going to become in the future? A sensei?

Since he asked, I had to say something:

I want to live a virtuous life.

I had come across this phrase in the ethics portion of the standardized university entrance examination a month earlier. The phrase had really flustered me when I came across it at the very start of the test—if I don't score high enough that would be the reason. Since no noticeable reaction came from Peter, I went on:

A novelist, I said in Japanese. "Author," I added in English.

Maybe my pronunciation was bad: Peter gave a vague smile.

"Novelist," I tried again.

Oh, fantastic! Peter enthused.

I transferred to a bus at Osaka Station. I wanted to sit in a single-row seat or by the window but they were all taken. I took an aisle seat. Janis was sitting on the window side. When the bus started moving Janis—all the while looking out the window—asked:

You heading straight home?

Well, I hesitated, looking up at the numerous tall buildings twinkling in the already darkening azure-blue sky. I continued, *I think so.*

Ah.

Janis was still looking out the window. She wore her sheepskin coat and a rainbow scarf. Her sheaf of wild brown hair was all over the place. Janis seemed to be watching the moving cars in the lane next to us.

Last year I saw a film about you, I said, following the cars with my eye. *Remember the live scene where you recalled that the girl living a floor below you had a boyfriend and you didn't? You said, "I noticed the chick downstairs was getting up early in the mornings, so I decided to wake up early too."*

Janis didn't say anything. I had seen the documentary on Janis at a venue lined with folding chairs on the first day of summer vacation.

I really liked that. "You know what you gotta do every time you're not getting what you want? You gotta try hard!"

The Japanese word for effort, 努力 *doryoku,* had appeared onscreen with the English word *try* written directly above just as Janis launched into "Try (Just a Little Bit Harder)." I loved that moment. Janis, with one of her elbows against the window, finally looked at me.

Hey, are you trying?

I don't know.

The only person who knows if you're trying is you!

Yeah . . .

Janis got off the bus at the third stop and headed west along the promenade running beside the Dojima River. I moved to the window seat. I locked eyes with a dog on the sidewalk.

Back at home those four kanji came to me: *pi* 美 beautiful; *ta* 多 many; *jaku* 雀 sparrow; *son* 村 village. I was content: it sounded like the name of a disciple of the famous Rakugo performer Katsura Shijaku 桂枝雀 or possibly a haiku poet. I didn't contact the church on the back of the business card.

Some years later I watched a film in which a high school girl in New Zealand kills her mother. The name of the director was Peter Jackson. Some years later, that same director would make *King Kong* and another very long film about little people who travel long distances to throw away a ring. That Peter doesn't look anything like the Peter I met on the Hankyu Railway, though.

PRIVATE TOUR

BARRY
YOURGRAU

I arrange to lead an invasive tour of a psychologically troubled person's disorderly private space.

"Wait, so who actually lives or works in there?" asks a tour signee all at once, suspiciously. He has the aggressive and overweight presence of a business type.

"Well, in fact," I tell him, "I do."

"Wait a *minute* now," says the guy. He takes a step back showily. "What kind of weirdness is going on here? This place is yours?"

"Nothing 'weird,'" I tell him, coloring. "Why not 'unusual' or 'distinctive'? Even perhaps a little 'desperate'?"

"Cause it's *weird*," he says. "Hey everybody!" he cries to the group. "Guess whose place it is we're going to? *His*."

The others all turn around, staring at me like cows being approached by a naked farmer. There's slow-witted confusion and bewilderment.

"Now see here," I tell him, badly flustered. "Nobody's forcing you to come along, okay? If you have a problem, I'm sure they'll refund your money. Okay?" The prospective loss of income though is a bitter blow to my parlous budget.

"You bet they will," he informs me. "Hey, everybody!" he cries (he obviously was a town crier in a previous life). "Get your money back, this is some sort of scam. Or at least it's very very *weird*."

"Excuse me, what are you doing?" I snarl at him.

"Heck, if it's weird—it's cool!" says a tall gangly guy with long drab hair on which sits a sweat-faded baseball hat. He grins goofily, in would-be trickster approval. "Count me in," he says. "Me too," chips in a middle-aged lady in a sunhat with fuzzy little balls on its brim. Others add their dittos.

"You're all a bunch of ignoramuses," the troublemaker declares.

"Just go and get your money back and clear off," I tell him.

"Just look alive, everybody!" warns an elderly voice from the back of the group. "These troubled types can have a lot of rage going on when anybody else handles their stuff."

"He's right," I advise them grimly. "Like I said earlier. *No touching anything.*"

"There's even the threat of suicide or the like!" the voice adds.

Many faces with half-opened mouths stare at me. I grit my teeth.

"All right, if you've paid up, then let's go!" I announce.

And in this manner our tour commences.

translated by Jeffrey Angles

AM I A DOCTOR?

AOKO
MATSUDA

A timid voice piped up, small and quiet in the darkness. "Am I a man?"

Only a single beam of light pointed toward the voice.

A moment later, voices spoke from all directions.

"No."

"Wrong track."

"Nuh-uh."

There was a short silence, then "Not necessarily. Wouldn't you all agree?" The new voice spoke with a certain degree of confidence.

After a short pause, the others assented.

"Well, I guess."

"That's true."

"Sure."

The speaker who had asked the question so timidly nodded in a somehow quizzical way. "Hmmmm . . ."

"Am I am a woman?"

"Of course." The answer came from the darkness nearby. It was deep and raspy. There wasn't a lot of moisture left, so everyone's voice sounded as parched as a dead tree branch. Needless to say, the air in the room was dry as bone.

The other voices chimed in, using more or less the same tone. "No mistake."

"I see." The voice sounded as if it hadn't dried out completely.

The next time a voice spoke in the darkness, it was cut off immediately. "Am I—?"

"Not necessarily. Wouldn't you all agree?" It was the same voice that had spoken so confidently before.

One could sense confusion hanging in the air.

"Really?" This was voiced by the person who had asked the question a moment ago. Clearly, he (or maybe *she*) felt that this blunt interruption had cancelled out the assurance that he (or maybe *she*) had felt just a moment ago.

"Well, I guess it's not impossible."

"Now that you say it, I do seem to recall something like that in a movie once."

"Oh, I know the one you mean. I saw it too. Got me all excited."

"Yeah, the girl I was going out with at the time got all worked up over it. I went to see it with her, but the movie left me in a foul mood." The raspy laugh echoed softly in the darkness.

"Huh?" The person asking the questions wasn't sure what to think. After the interruption, he (or maybe *she*) tried to get back to the main point, but someone else had moved the conversation in a completely different direction.

"Keep giving those kinds of answers, and you'll wreck the entire game."

I did what I had been doing this whole time. I turned the flashlight in the direction of the voice. There was no electricity in the building. Hardly any buildings still had it. After shining the flashlight on several faces (all shook their heads from side to side to show they weren't the one who had spoken), the thin beam of light fell upon a face that seemed to be floating there delicately.

The speaker continued. "Okay now. When you play a game, you're supposed to follow certain guidelines. You could probably answer, 'Not necessarily' to just about any yes-or-no question, so you have to tell yourself, 'Well, usually that's how it is.' After all, even the simplest things become difficult if you don't make generalizations. We're just playing a game, after all."

"Sure, makes sense. I was just trying. . . ." The person who had so spoken so confidently a moment ago no longer seemed very confident of anything.

I quickly turned the flashlight to illuminate their faces. Almost everyone was looking down in embarrassment. All of them had a piece of paper attached to their foreheads, partially obscuring their faces. The sight reminded me of the white-faced zombies you see in Chinese films. What were they called again? *Jiangshi,* if I remember right.

The speaker who had lost confidence just a moment before started speaking again, this time with renewed courage. The piece of white paper hanging over the speaker's features swayed with each breath in and out.

"I don't like to do that—make generalizations so things are easier to understand, I mean. I hate it when people ignore things that don't fit into the molds they've got in their minds. When someone did it, I'd always hold my tongue. I stayed quiet even though I probably shouldn't have—because I was a teacher. If someone generalized for the sake of simplicity, a sad expression would come over some students' faces. Still, I pretended not to see—as if I didn't notice. I thought our games would fall apart if I didn't give simplistic, stereotypical answers, and the class would screech to a halt. But I regret that now."

I guessed that under the white paper the speaker was biting dry lips. Blood oozed out. . . . At least, that's what I imagined.

Here and there, I heard people speaking up in agreement, but I gave up turning the flashlight to illuminate each one.

"I know that feeling."

"Me too."

"Everyone here probably has the same regrets."

"We get it."

The person who had advocated simple answers so as not to halt the game spoke up again as if trying to patch things up. "I've got the same regrets too, I've got to admit."

Realizing the conversation might go on for a while, I turned the flashlight in that direction. The speaker had forgotten to hold up their piece of paper, perhaps because of all of the commotion. The paper was outside the frame of light.

"A few moments ago, when we were trying to get the 'stripper' to guess their profession, someone asked the same question. Stripping wasn't only a woman's job, of course. There were men who used to do that too. There used to be clubs where you could go to watch men take off their clothes. We all know that, right? And before that, we tried to have the 'stewardess' guess their profession. It's hard to generalize about that profession too. A long time ago, people used to say that was a woman's job, but things changed over time. We started calling them 'flight attendants.' We all know that too, right?"

The speaker's lips were trembling. In the light from the flashlight, his (or maybe *her*) face shone dully like a firefly.

"So yeah, I've also got regrets. I don't know why I didn't do more of the things I could have. You know, before it was too late. . . . I was old enough to know better, but I acted like I didn't care. Why'd I do that? It doesn't really matter anymore, does it, given our current situation? There aren't any young children with futures stretching before them. The only folks left are us hard-headed adults, and it's all over for us. If ever there was a time to play games, to be uncritical and unthinking, this is it, isn't it?! Let's just enjoy ourselves. Come on, let's have some fun."

The speaker gave a self-conscious grin and stopped. The room fell silent again. I switched off the flashlight completely. Darkness descended over the room.

We heard pounding footsteps over our heads. It sounded like shoes running above us. They didn't seem too far away. I imagined a pair of tough, black leather shoes dashing by, kicking up puffs of dust. The leather shoes were connected to a pair of khaki trousers. The khakis were connected to a khaki-colored jacket. I tried to imagine the face that came with the jacket, but I couldn't. The person wearing the khaki pants, khaki jacket, and black shoes had no face. A faceless person.

The person who had lost confidence broke the silence, confidence seemingly restored. "Good idea. Let's just have fun."

A series of voices piped up as if trying to reinforce the positive mood.

"You're right. Let's have fun."

"Come on, let's play."

But suddenly another voice rose to upset the equilibrium the others had been trying so hard to maintain. "Mind if I say something?"

I traced a zigzag through the air with the flashlight before reaching my destination.

After confirming that the beam had settled on them, the speaker continued. "What I want to say is that we can leave the question of sex aside, right? If we think hard, we can still figure out what our profession is and win the round, even if we don't ask about gender. We've said, 'not necessarily' too many times already."

A certain lull fell over the room as everyone wondered why they hadn't thought of that. A moment later, words of agreement filled the darkness.

"Good idea."

"You're right."

"Let's play the game that way. Might as well."

"You know, I should apologize for giving away your answer a moment ago. Sorry, everyone." The speaker sounded truly apologetic.

Other voices chimed in, overlapping one another.

"No problem. We can do it over."

"We've got plenty of time."

"How about if we start again?"

Someone started ripping pieces of paper out of an old notebook, one for each person there. Another person passed their hand across the surface of the table to locate the tiny pencil lying there. In the darkness, each person felt for the edges of their paper and wrote something on it before passing the pencil to the person seated next to them. Once everyone had traded the pieces of paper, we held them up and pasted them to our foreheads.

"Do I sell things?"

The word *firefighter* floated in the darkness. Everyone simultaneously answered with a big "no." I shifted the beam of the flashlight to the person seated right next to me.

"Am I a historical figure?"

"No." The word *ghost* was written on my neighbor's piece of paper.

Someone in the room muttered, "It's not fair to try to make someone guess that." Not knowing what to think, my neighbor let out a nervous "Huh?"

I moved the beam of the flashlight to someone else. They asked, "Do I save people's lives?"

Everyone held their breath for a moment. Taken by surprise, everyone responded, "Yes," at once, like a conditioned reflex.

Hearing that, the person asking the questions grew confident and fired back, "Am I a doctor?"

"That's right!"

Everyone started clapping. It was the most excited the group had been the whole evening. Of course, we couldn't raise our voices too loudly. It would be curtains for us if we were discovered.

"How'd you get it so quickly?"

"Inspiration, I guess you could say. The question just came to me."

"Amazing."

"It's a new record. Fastest round ever."

"Good job!"

The person who had guessed correctly stretched out a hand toward me and said, "Say, you with the flashlight. You're probably bored. Want me to take a turn holding the light?" The flashlight was the only source of light in the room, and I was being asked to give it up.

"Thanks."

I flexed my hand, stiff from holding the flashlight, then rolled up my sleeve.

"Do I sell people dreams?"

"No." *(Bank employee.)*

"Do I take care of growing things?"

"Yes." *(Animal caretaker.)*

"Does my job involve desk work?"

"Yes." *(Lord Yama, Judge of the Dead.)*

"Do I maintain something?"

"Yes." *(Lighthouse keeper.)*

"Am I a hard worker?"

"No." *(Stay-at-home shut-in.)*

"Does my job attract people's attention?"

"Yes." *(Serial killer.)*

The game proceeded smoothly. A doctor, eh? It was funny to me I had managed to correctly guess the profession I'd been given in the game. A doctor. In fact, I used to deliver pizzas. Day in and day out, I put round pizzas in square boxes, delivered them to customers—that's how I made my living. I didn't really think too much about my job at the time, but just remembering it now made me long for the good old days.

For us, time was a crossword puzzle. We could fill it in with these games we played so single-mindedly, but we never quite knew when it would end. How much time had passed? I tried to remember, but couldn't. It seemed ages since anyone had looked at a clock. We had started out playing a different game—one person said a word, then the next person had to say a word that started with the last letter of the previous one, and so on. We played that for quite some time, but at some point, we found a pencil and paper in a drawer and started the game we were playing now in which we assigned each other professions and then tried to guess what they were. In this game, we changed jobs over and over. We were presidents and singers and businessmen.

"Does my job involve heavy work?"

"No." *(Nun.)*

"Is my job artistic?"

"Yes." *(Action figure manufacturer.)*

"Is my job a bad one?"

"Yes." *(Politician.)*

"Do I wear a uniform?"

"Yes." *(Nun.)*

"Do I always work in the same place?"

"No." *(Pilot.)*

"Am I an athlete?"

"No." *(Nun.)*

"Am I . . ."

"Hold on. What kind of job is that?"

One person was sitting there happily, sleeves rolled up. A murmur of confusion rose as the flashlight illuminated the piece of paper hanging from their forehead.

"You're right. Weird."

"What's that?"

"Oh, my goodness."

"You've got to be kidding."

The person whose turn it was to ask a question was thoroughly confused by everyone's reaction. "What's going on?"

On the piece of paper were the words *penguin-petter.*

"Nothing, it's not a joke."

I quickly turned the flashlight in the direction of the voice. This was a serious matter. A calm face floated up in the light. Everyone could tell, even in the darkness, that all attention was focused on the illuminated face.

"I made that profession up. For years that was my dream job, but it didn't exist so I had no choice but to do something else. I think it's a real shame nobody does it. That's why I like to pretend it actually exists." With that, the speaker smiled a little.

"What were you thinking?"

"You made it up?"

No one could contain their laughter. Of course, everyone tried to keep the volume down.

Someone outside the flashlight's beam asked, "So tell me. Exactly what kind of work does a penguin-petter do?" The tone of voice revealed that the person asking the question thought the whole thing was hysterically funny.

The response was serious and measured. "It's just like it sounds. A penguin-petter pets penguins."

"Huh . . ."

That set everyone's imagination going. At least, that's what I thought was happening. A part of me wished it was possible to put a comic strip bubble over everyone's head so I could see what they were picturing.

"Wouldn't that be the same as a caretaker in a zoo?" someone asked.

I had been so busy trying to imagine what a penguin-petter was that I had completely forgotten my responsibility as bearer of the flashlight. I quickly sought out the speaker's face with my light.

"No. All they do is pet penguins. Nothing else. It's an extremely specialized profession—they're just penguin-petters."

Everyone started asking questions, hoping to give the images in their head a more concrete form.

"Can both men and women do it?"

"Why not? Petting penguins has nothing to do with gender."

"I see. What kind of salary would they get?"

"If all they do is pet penguins, I doubt they'd expect very high wages. Caretakers and the rest probably wouldn't be very understanding at first. They'd say, 'Huh? What the heck?' just like you guys. But it's important for zoos to have happy penguins. When penguins sulk and hide, the visitors are disappointed, and the zoo loses out in a big way. Penguin-petters would put all their energy into petting penguins to ensure that wouldn't happen. Before long, others working at the zoo would come recognize how important penguin-petters are!"

"What kind of qualifications would you need to become a penguin-petter?"

"The only thing they'd need is a real love of penguins."

Everyone was thinking the same thing: *What a cool job! I want to give it a try!* The thought of the penguins' wet feathers, their cute little heads and necks, the water sliding off them to pitter-patter onto our boots—all penguin-petters would wear boots, of course—it was all so charming. Almost before I knew it, everyone had turned to the inventor of the penguin-petting profession and offered up a small round of applause.

The inventor seemed embarrassed. "Sorry for saying something so weird. We'll have to start the game over."

"Not at all. This is a game-changer. *You're* a game changer!"

"Yep, right on!"

Everyone praised the penguin-petter's audacity, which seemed to embarrass the penguin-petter even more. He extended a hand to me and muttered, "Now, it's my turn to hold the light."

The game got much wilder in the next round. Everyone wrote down their ideal profession. It was as if we all had been set free, as if the last thread connecting us to reality had broken. We wrote down jobs that no one, other than the person who originally wrote them, could possibly guess—our dream professions. There wasn't a single ordinary job among them. On one hand, I felt bad that I had started this, but on the other, I was glad everyone was having so much fun.

I turned the flashlight on the next person. The words "bug notifier" hovered in the darkness. In Japanese, the words "notification from a bug" means "a feeling in one's bones" or a "hunch," but it was hard to imagine how "bug notifier" might translate into a profession.

"What kind of job is that?" This question came from a completely different part of the room.

Then from still another direction, a voice piped up, "Let me explain . . ." The person with the piece of paper on his forehead just grinned and leaned forward to listen like everyone else.

"You know how no matter how carefully you proofread, typos always manage to creep into books? Well, a bug notifier would read book manuscripts really carefully looking for the 'bugs'—the typos in other words—that inevitably find their way into print. They'd find typos and report them to the editors. Lots of bugs just slip by. In an ideal world, professionals would carefully catch bugs one by one. After all, when you're reading a book and you find a typo, you always feel let down, right?"

"What kind of salary would a bug notifier earn?"

"They'd work solely by commission, earning a certain amount for each typo they find. Of course, bug-notifiers would have to work hard all the time just to make ends meet. If they fell on hard times, I imagine everything would begin to look like a typo to them, even words that are completely correct. Of course it'd be a real problem if the bug notifiers made that mistake, so they'd have to be on their toes all the time."

"That job would drive me nuts."

A number of people nodded and murmured their agreement. It sounded like a tough profession to me too.

"But I like detailed work. That's the kind of job a loner could do for a long time. I could have done that till I got old."

The would-be "bug-notifier" let out a sigh. Someone had once told me he had been in the sales department of a human resources company.

Not too many people seemed to be getting on board with the idea until someone else chimed in. "No, I get it. I also like work that involves lots of details." That evened out the scales considerably. I shined the light in the direction of the voice.

"You know those strings in snap peas and the white strings in mandarin oranges? Lots of people think it's a pain to take them out. Apple peels and sticky chestnut husks too. But I love that kind of work. When my son grew up, he thought it was such a pain to peel his food that he stopped eating things that needed to be peeled. I got stuck peeling everything for him, but to my surprise, peeling made me really happy. I wish I could concentrate on that. Just peeling one chestnut after another for my son."

The happiness in the speaker's voice reminded everyone of moments they had been happy too. As we realized how far away those memories were, though, a heavy weight began to press down on our hearts.

I quickly shifted the beam of light to the next person's face.

Recorder of street corner conversations.

Delighted cries rose from all over the room. Someone chimed in, "That one sounds interesting, just judging from the words alone."

"Yeah, I can imagine that one."

For a moment, people muttered among themselves about what they thought it meant. As the murmur of voices subsided, the inventor of the profession began to speak. I turned the flashlight in their direction.

"I've been thinking about that job for a while. You know how you used to hear interesting conversations in the city? Nobody paid attention, and the conversations simply disappeared. What a shame! There were times when you'd pop into a café, stop by a supermarket on the way home, or sit at your chair at work, and you'd overhear amazing conversations, so wonderful they seemed like small miracles. Sometimes the speakers didn't even seem to realize how amazing their conversations were. So I started taking notes, thinking to leave a record behind, but once I gave it a try, I realized how good I was at transcribing conversations I'd overheard. I could record them perfectly in my notebook—never missing a single word, or even a single breath. I got obsessed with recording conversations I overheard in the streets. If only that could be my job, I thought. It's the only work I ever really wanted to do."

As we listened, everyone started to recall snippets of conversation overheard on street corners. Sometimes they were interesting, sometimes they were incredibly boring, sometimes they were about things we never would have dreamt up on our own, but as we reflected, we realized how many of those little exchanges remained hidden in the recesses of our minds. How could we have forgotten them until now? I should have made notes too. I should have recorded them for the world to hear. I bet I was the only person who'd ever heard them.

Someone spoke up, "All of these jobs sound really interesting." The speaker sounded as if he was having a hard time containing his emotions. His comment was quickly seconded by the others.

"You're right, it's a shame none of these professions ever existed."

"True. Even if they did exist somewhere, they weren't things we could've really done."

"For years I didn't feel like there was any job I really wanted to do."

"Same goes for me."

"That was the way it was right up to the point there weren't jobs anymore."

"Yep."

"If I'd known how everything would turn out, I would've just gone ahead and invented a job."

Maybe I wasn't the only one. Maybe everyone ended up doing a job they didn't want to do. I wondered why there'd been so few jobs we really wanted. Why did we all have to *become* something? That question bothered me. Constantly. It especially nagged at me as I grew into adulthood, but now I was realizing maybe that feeling was universal. My heart flooded with emotion as I moved the flashlight from person to person, illuminating each of the speakers in turn. How many spare batteries were left? I began to worry, then realized it was silly to worry about a little thing like that in our current situation.

Designer of collars
Planner of measures to protect left-handed people
Composer of hummed tunes
Thursday carpenter

I took back the flashlight role after telling the group about my idea for "planner of measures to protect left-handed people." Our world was primarily made for right-handed people, so I thought it made sense to have people who worked to make things a little more accessible to left-handed people. Right-handed people probably don't notice, but most things are designed for folks like themselves. You can see it in just about everything—automated machines that accept train tickets on the right-hand side, vending machines that dispense on the right. Even the designs on teacups are meant to be viewed with the handles to the right. I worried no one would understand, but fortunately there were a number in the room who were left-handed, and my proposal was warmly welcomed.

Right before our eyes, new professions were being born just like that. We no longer stuck paper on other people's foreheads. We kept our sheets of notebook paper, holding them up and describing the professions we had invented. We were all surprised to learn how many unknown, undiscovered jobs were slumbering deep within our imaginations. I moved the flashlight from person to person, illuminating the dream professions we had written upon the white sheets, and the smiling faces of the inventors who had created them. At a certain point, I realized I was wielding the flashlight not so that everyone could see, but so that *I* could see—*I* wanted all of these professions to be burned into my memory. The handle of the flashlight was slick with sweat, but that didn't bother me a bit.

Dream programmer
Manager of a shop with no style in particular
Framer of postage stamps
Secretary to a company president who is a cat

The handle of the flashlight was getting sticky. The middle-aged fellow who had the flashlight until just a minute ago must sweat a lot. I wiped the flashlight against my clothes. I had taken hold of the light but was still mulling over how much I would have liked to have had one of these jobs. I was the one who had written "framer of postage stamps." I imagined myself looking at the striking foreign postage stamps that customers brought in and carefully selecting the right material and color to frame each one. I'd find the perfect frame—one that matched so well that it was impossible to imagine any other. Of course, I would have been happy to frame domestic stamps too, but there hadn't been many designs worth hanging on the wall in recent years.

I had just graduated from college but had never worked—not even once. I majored in a subject that required a lot of classes, which made me too busy for a part-time job. I wish there had been something I could've done, whether I liked it or not. I just wished I could have become *something*.

But as fate would have it, there I was in that room that night, playing the game with all of the others. I shone the flashlight on them, one by one. It seemed like none of this could possibly be happening, but it was. There was an unpleasant sound overhead, and dust and particulate rained down from the ceiling. Something stuck to my face, but I didn't know what it was, so I shook my head from side to side to dislodge it. When I couldn't, I wiped my cheek with the palm of my hand. I wondered for a second what my face looked like. I heard someone gulp in the darkness.

"If someone discovers these pieces of paper way off in the future, I bet they'll get a totally distorted picture of what our era was like."

The voice sounded almost cheerful. It was sort of loud and had a particular tone, as if the speaker was trying to draw us in. Others started chiming in, as if adding beads to a necklace the first speaker had started to string.

"These jobs are all so weird."

"I bet they'll think, 'The guys who wrote these things were crazy—no wonder their civilization collapsed.'"

"It's kinda fun to imagine."

"Maybe we should write down more weird jobs to distort the picture even further!"

"Yeah, let's come up with even more surprising ones!"

We began to laugh, imagining future generations puzzling over the jobs we had invented. The darkness spread out in front of us, but we imagined we could see one another's faces clearly. For a moment, we all seemed happy. We weren't *guessing* we were happy. We *knew* we were. None of us had ever dreamed we could be this happy again. As I shone the flashlight on each one of their forms—each of the voices—one by one, I realized how happy I was to have ended up holding the flashlight.

That's it. I should take one of those pieces of paper and write "flashlight holder" on it. I stretched my hand out into the darkness, searching for pencil and paper.

Right at that moment, there was a loud noise like something exploding—louder than any sound we had ever heard before. And with it, the lights came on in the basement where we were seated. In the dark, I had imagined I could see everyone's face clearly, but strangely, now that the lights were on, I couldn't see a thing. I'm not sure why, but not a single sound could be heard. I thought to myself, "Damn, it's bright!"

translated by Michael K. Bourdaghs

THE CARLYLE MUSEUM

SŌSEKI NATSUME

In a corner of the park a speaker delivers an oration to passersby. Along comes an old man, the hat atop his head tapered like a kettle, a faded overcoat over his hunched shoulders. He halts to watch the speaker. The speaker abruptly abandons his oration and in determined fashion approaches the humble scholar. The two stare at one another. *Aren't you Carlyle?* the speaker asks in a thick, rustic accent. *None other,* the provincial scholar replies. The speaker asks again: *the one they call the Sage of Chelsea? Well,* comes the answer, *I suppose some call me that.* The speaker guffaws loudly. *But a "sage" is a kind of a bird.*[1] *What a rare treat to encounter a human sage!* The humble scholar replies, *You are right—a person is after all a person, so why take the trouble to label me a sage? I'd prefer they think of me as just another man.* With this, he too begins to guffaw.

Whenever I stroll through the park before dinner, I stop and sit on a bench by the river and gaze at the far shore. London's famous fog is especially thick near the river. As I look out, chin resting on the handle of my cherry-wood walking stick, the shadowy fog creeping along the thoroughfare on the opposite bank thickens; from the ground up, the five-story buildings that line the street gradually fade from view behind its trailing haze. What remains in the end is a vague brown shadow in the distance, as if the world of the future were being summoned up before my eyes. At this moment, in the very depths of that brown I spy a flickering of dim lights. On the third floor, fourth floor, fifth floor: gas lamps are being lit. Taking up my cherry-wood stick, I head back to my boardinghouse. As I walk, I invariably recall the story of Carlyle and the orator. This place buried in thick, dark fog is Chelsea, where that provincial scholar once lived.

---

1. This likely refers to a sage sparrow or sage grouse.

Carlyle is no longer with us. Surely the orator is dead as well. But Chelsea remains, today as always. In fact, the very home where Carlyle lived for so many years is preserved in all its dignity. How many proprietors have come and gone since Cheyne Row was built in 1708, I have no idea, but it remains today just as it was then. When Carlyle died, civic-minded volunteers took the initiative to collect the furniture and books he used during his lifetime and put on them display in its various rooms. Thus, today we enjoy the good fortune of being able to visit whenever we please.

The list of noted literary figures with ties to Chelsea stretches back as far as Thomas More. It includes such later figures as Smollett and, reaching down to Carlyle's day, Leigh Hunt. Hunt's home was near Carlyle's, and Carlyle's journal records that Hunt came calling the very evening that Carlyle moved into the house. It is also known that Hunt presented Carlyle's wife with a bust of Shelley. In addition, George Eliot's house and the estate where Rossetti lived sit nearby along the road facing the riverbank. All, however, have changed hands over the years and are presently occupied, so we cannot visit them. Only the old haunts of Carlyle are open to visitors, to anyone willing to pay sixpence.

Cheyne Row is a small lane branching south from the thoroughfare that runs along the river. Carlyle's house is toward the middle on the right-hand side, No. 24.

One morning, during my usual routine of sitting by the river and peering through the fog at Chelsea, I abruptly decided to cross the bridge and knock on the front door of the famed hermitage.

Calling it a hermitage suggests a forlorn place. Or, at least, a place harboring a sense of the refined, the elegant. But there is nothing delicate about the Carlyle hermitage. It is perfectly square, a four-story house built so close to the road so that you can knock on the door while standing in the street.

The building stands straight and square, with nothing protruding or indented. It looks almost as if they had chopped off the chimney of a great factory at its base and dumped it here, simply adding a roof and windows.

This is the house Carlyle finally came upon when he first arrived in London from the north He had searched and searched in the west and south of the city; he looked as far north as Hampstead, yet he couldn't locate a suitable home. Finally he came to Cheyne Row and saw this place—but lacked the courage to decide immediately upon it. He was a fearless denouncer of the myriad fools populating this world, but hunting for a house stumped him. To his wife, whom he must have counted among those fools of the world, he reported the particulars, hoping to ascertain her wishes. Her response: "Keep them *both* open if you can till I come—and if you are constrained to decide that you may not let both or either slip thro' your hands do it with perfect assurance that Goody will approve your choice."[2] In matters of literature Carlyle wrote as if he alone was capable of rendering judgments, but when it came to choosing a house he seems to have felt the need for his wife's approval, and so he waited with folded arms until she could reach the capital. She arrived four or five days later. Thereupon the two of them searched east and west, north and south, until they concluded that Cheyne Row was right for them after all. They moved in on June 10, 1834, and we know that the canary their maid carried in its cage during the move chirped the whole time. It appears that his wife settled on this place only because none of the other options much appealed to her; at any rate, this square chimney of a house with its annual rent of ¥350[3] welcomed the new household. And it was in this house that Carlyle—a bit like Cromwell, a bit like Frederick the Great, and a bit like a factory chimney—lived out his square-and-proper life, composing his celebrated biographies of Cromwell and Frederick the Great, declining the pension that Disraeli arranged for him.

I stand on the stoop outside the front door of this square house and use the ogre-faced knocker. In a moment a plump, fiftyish woman opens the door from within. *Come in,* she says. She takes it for granted that I've come to see the house. The woman pulls out a kind of registry book. *Your name, please,* she says. During my stay in London I end up making a total of four visits to this house, and each time, I recall, I signed the registry.

This day is the first time I record my name. I write as neatly as I can, but as always produce an ugly scrawl. Flipping back through the pages, I find not a single Japanese name. I might be the first Japanese to visit: this silly thought somehow makes me quite happy. *This way, please,* the woman says, as she opens a door to the left and we enter a room facing the street. This was the parlor. Various objects are arranged around the room. Paintings and photographs hang on the walls—mainly portraits of the Carlyles. In the room behind this stand bookcases designed by Carlyle himself. They are crammed with books—difficult books and flippant books. There are ancient-looking books and books that look as if no one could ever read them. In addition, there are two medals, one silver and one bronze, both cast in celebration of Carlyle's eightieth birthday. No one thought to make a gold medal, apparently. These medals and the other commemorative

2. Jane Welsh Carlyle letter to Thomas Carlyle, 26 May 1834.
3. Sōseki converted British pounds to yen for his Japanese readers. According to *Carlyle's House Catalogue* (London: Carlyle's House Memorial Trust, 1900), the source that Sōseki relied on for the information given here, the annual rent was £35.

objects are effortlessly persistent in the way they sit eternally steadfast and unchanged: how strange it feels to see them in stark contrast to the mortality, fleeting as smoke, of the man they honor.

We go up to the second floor. Here too is a large bookcase overflowing with books. Again, many appear to be books that no one could read, books I've never heard of, forbidding books. I count 135 volumes. This room was also apparently once used as a parlor. On display are a letter from Bismarck to Carlyle and an official decoration from Prussia—connected, it seems, to his biography of Frederick the Great. Over there is his wife's bed, an exceedingly awkward and plain-looking thing.

Tour guides everywhere are the same, no matter the country. For some time now, the woman has been delivering a point-by-point explanation of the room's pictures and furnishings. Not trained for fifty years as a professional guide, perhaps, but nevertheless exceptionally polished. On and on she goes, seemingly without having to think: *On such-and-such a date, such-and-such took place.* Her fluid delivery carries its own modulation and rhythm. These are so fascinating that I find myself listening only to them and end up not catching her meaning. At the start I tried to make appropriate responses and queries, but this quickly becomes bothersome and I end up adopting another attitude: you go right ahead and talk all you like, I'll stick to looking around at my pleasure. She seems not to care if you listen or not; she just keeps talking: *On such-and-such a date, such-and-such took place*—conscientious, and without a hint of impatience.

I lean out an east-facing window to take in the neighborhood. Directly below is a garden of about one-tenth of an acre. On both sides and to the back it is enclosed by a tall stone wall; naturally, it too is perfectly square. Squareness seems to be the defining characteristic of this estate. Yet Carlyle's face was hardly square. If anything, his was a visage rather like the midsection of a collapsed cliff lying prone on a grassy meadow. The wife's face gives the impression of a well-formed cocktail onion. And the face of the woman guide is as round as a bean-paste bun. As I stare at her face, taking in its roundness, she launches into yet another recitative: *On such-and-such a date.* . . . I stick my head back out the window.

Carlyle: "Backwards . . . from all the other floors, nothing but leafy clumps, and green fields and red high-peaked roofs glimmering thro' them: a most clear, pleasant prospect, in these fresh westerly airs![4]

Thinking to see those leafy clumps and green fields for myself, I stick my head out

4. Thomas Carlyle letter to John A. Carlyle, 17 June 1834.

the back window once, twice, but I see no green. To the right are houses. To the left are houses. To the rear, more houses. Above everything hangs a leaden sky as slothful and apathetic as a dyspeptic. I pull my head back in. Still the guide continues chanting brightly: *On such-and-such a date in such-and-such a year. . . .*

Carlyle again: "Of London nothing visible but Westminster Abbey and the topmost dome of St Paul's; other faint ghosts of spires (one other at least) disclose themselves, as the smoke-cloud shifts; but I have not yet made out what they are."[5]

Nowadays, Carlyle's notion of looking out toward the city is an anachronism. Looking toward the city in today's Chelsea makes no more sense than looking toward your own house while sitting in your drawing room; you would simply be looking in your own direction. Carlyle, though, never considered himself to be living in London. He regarded himself as pursuing a quiet rural life, gazing off into the far distance at the grand temples of the city center. I lean out the window a third time, looking in the direction Carlyle described as being toward the city. But I see neither Westminster nor St. Paul's. Between me and the skyline are tens of thousands of houses, hundreds of thousands of people, making millions of noises: they stand, linger, move. The Chelsea of 1834 and today's Chelsea are completely different beasts. I pull my head back inside. The woman stands behind me, silent.

We ascend to the third floor. In a corner of the room I see Carlyle's bed, standing impervious. The green canopy is perfectly still, while the bed beneath lies silent and dim. I don't recognize what kind of wood it is. Some rather crude designs are carved into it; otherwise, the bed has no distinguishing features. It calls to mind the image of the person who once took his rest here. The washtub he habitually used sits nearby, as dignified as a Chinese emperor's ritual cauldron. I call it a washtub, but in reality it is nothing more than an oversized bucket. I think of him rinsing away the soot of London in this large basin, and I find myself more and more drawn to the man. I look up to see hanging on the wall the plaster mask taken when he died. That's the face, I muse. That's the face that bathed in this tub no taller than a *kotatsu* foot-warmer, that slept in this simple bed, that chided and chided the world so unreservedly for some forty years. All the while, the woman's fluid recitation continues, echoing like greetings from someone on the telephone from Yokohama.

If you're ready, sir, shall we go upstairs? the woman says. Feeling as if I were sitting alone atop a five-story pagoda, the dust and noise of London far below me, I am puzzled

5. Thomas Carlyle letter to John A. Carlyle, 17 June 1834.

when she urges me to go upstairs: can there be another floor above? *Let us go,* I assent, because it seems the higher I climb, the more powerful this strange reverie.

When we reach the fourth floor, I feel vaguely happy for no particular reason. More a curious feeling than happiness, actually. This is the attic. I look at the ceiling: it is low to the left and right but the center stands tall, like a horse's mane, and along the spine of its peak is set a glass skylight. Light streams into this attic from directly over our heads. And above, separated from us by that plate of glass, stretches the vast sky that extends across the whole world. Our view is utterly unimpeded. This is the room built at Carlyle's own initiative. He then used it as his study: this would be the room where he would seclude himself to work. It was only after he had begun closeting himself here that he realized the flaw in his plan: the study was too hot in summer, too cold in winter. Having reached this point in her recitation, the guide turns back to look at me. I see the shadow of a smile flit across her round face. I nod in silence.

Why did Carlyle go to the trouble of building this singular room so close to the heavens? As his writings show, he was a man of sudden impulses. With his short temper, he seems to have lacked the capacity to block out the impudent sounds that prevented him from concentrating on his writing. A piano, a dog's bark, a rooster's cry, a parrot's chatter: one by one these voices would chafe against his sensitive nerves, causing him agony and ultimately driving him to seek refuge up near the heavens, far above the world of ordinary humans, in this fourth-floor attic.

From a letter he wrote to Mrs. Aitken: "All summer I have been more or less annoyed with noises, even accidental ones, which get free access thro' my open windows: all the tinkering and 'repairing' has done me no good in that respect. A very despicable, very intolerable sort of sufferings,—as poor Aird and others, can testify! At length, after deep deliberation, I have fairly decided to have a top story put upon the House, one big apartment 20 feet square, with thin double walls, light from the top &c, and artfully ventilated,—into which no sound can come; and all the cocks in Nature may crow round it, without my hearing a whisper of them!"[6]

And so the study was completed more or less as planned at a cost of ¥2,000, and it seemed at first a great success—until another utterly unanticipated problem erupted within earshot of our hero. Yes, the notes of the piano had disappeared, as had the barking dog, the crowing rooster and chattering parrot: none could be heard. But alack: there were other unwelcome sounds he had never imagined from downstairs, church bells

6. Thomas Carlyle letter to Jean Carlyle Aitken, 11 August 1853.

and train whistles and other unidentifiable noises from afar that assailed his nerves, as much a curse as the noises downstairs.

Noise. The very same noise that afflicted Carlyle in England also assailed Schopenhauer in Germany. Schopenhauer writes: "Kant has written a treatise on *The Vital Powers*; but I should like to write a dirge on them, since their lavish use in the form of knocking, hammering, and tumbling things about has made the whole of my life a daily torment. Certainly there are people, nay, very many, who will smile at this, because they are not sensitive to noise; it is precisely these people, however, who are not sensitive to argument, thought, poetry or art, in short, to any kind of intellectual impression: a fact to be assigned to the coarse quality and strong texture of their brain tissues."[7] Carlyle and Schopenhauer: what a fine nineteenth-century pairing! As I muse in this fashion, the woman suggests, *Shall we head back downstairs?*

With each floor we descend, I sense the vulgar world drawing near, as if the veil of meditative reflection were being stripped away. When we reach the bottom, I lean over the balustrade and gaze out on the street; I am returned to the state of an ordinary mortal. A disinterested look on her face, the guide invites me to take a peek at the kitchen. It is located below street level. To reach it, I descend another five or six steps. Today this is the apartment of the woman who is guiding me. In the corner sits an enormous hearth. In her usual recitative tone, the woman tells me, *On October 12, 1844, the day the famous poet Tennyson made his first visit to Carlyle, the two men sat facing each other before this stove and for two hours only smoked tobacco, not exchanging a single word.* Apparently, the man who so loathed noise when he climbed to the heavens also adored silence when he descended underground.

Finally, I am shown the way to the back garden through the kitchen door. I look around this perfectly square patch of ground but see neither trees nor flora worthy of the name. According to the woman, in the old days there was a cherry tree, grape vines, and a walnut tree as well. One year, she says, Mrs. Carlyle harvested 25 *sen* worth of walnuts.[8] The woman goes on, in considerable detail: "In the southeast corner lies the Carlyle's beloved dog, Nero, five feet under. Nero died on February 1, 1860. There used to be a grave marker, but unfortunately it was later removed."

---

7. Arthur Schopenhauer, "On Noise," from *Essays of Schopenhauer,* trans. Mrs. Rudolph Dircks (London: Walter Scott, 1900), 28.

8. *Carlyle's House Catalogue* (20) quotes a letter from Mrs. Carlyle: "Behind we have a garden (so called in the language of flattery) in the worst of order, but boasting of two vines which produced two bunches of grapes in the season, which 'might be eaten,' and a walnut tree, from which I gathered almost sixpence worth of Walnuts."

This is the garden where Carlyle would ramble, straw hat pushed back on his head, pipe in mouth, still in his nightshirt. This is the garden where at the height of summer, he would erect a modest tent on the shaded stone patio and bring out a desk and chair to labor at his writing. This is the garden where on a clear, starry night he would smoke a last pipe, gaze up at the heavens and mutter, "Hah! In a little while, I shall have seen you also for the last time. God Almighty's own theatre of immensity—the infinite made palpable and visible to me—that also will be closed—flung to in my face—and I shall never behold that either any more. The thought of the eternal deprivation even of this, though this is such a nothing in comparison, was sad and painful to me."[9]

In recompense for her efforts, I place a single silver coin in the woman's palm. *Thank you,* she says—even now, that recitative voice. An hour later I was far, far away, amid the London dust, the noise of carriages, the River Thames—in another world entirely from that of Carlyle's house.

9. Thomas Carlyle journal entry, 14 October 1869.

HANDS, SQUARES, CHIMNEY SWEEPS

BRIAN
EVENSON

A REPORT ON HANDS

F., because he was not good at hypnotism, eventually decided that hypnotism was not essential to his method. Instead, he would place his palm on his patient's forehead, regard them intently, and intone the words, "You will remember!" The touch of his hand, activated by the resonance of his voice, by his gaze, would draw the hidden memory out of the skull.

The religion I grew up in has a similar technique for healing the sick, but it involves two hands. The patient—though patient is not the right word exactly—is seated facing away. The hands are placed on the head from behind, fingers splayed, as if to form a helmet. The head is anointed with oil, a sacred formula is uttered, and the patient is either healed or remains ill.

I have uttered this formula myself, willing power and healing from my hands into someone else's body through the application of hands to a head. While it was happening, I believed I was truly doing this, and that the person whose head I touched would be returned to health. Indeed, they were—so invariably that even now, as an excommunicant, to think of it still gives me pause.

Even now, fifteen years after being excommunicated, whenever someone close to me is seriously ill I wonder, *Could I do it still?* Even though I no longer believe, would it be enough if, through the pressure of my hands, the resonance of my voice, I could make *them* believe?

F. went on to develop an entire discipline based on losing his faith in hypnotism. Soon, he did not even need to touch the patient. It was enough simply to speak, and to listen. There he is, engaged in his magical act of forcing buried memory to the surface. It surges up, here a bloody head, there another white shape, threatening to disappear just as suddenly. And yet, he brings his words to bear in a way that cracks the memory open. And we do remember, we do.

But whether he heals us or we heal ourselves, well, that is another story.

A REPORT ON SQUARES

B., a poet, tends to invent an eccentric form and then faithfully repeat its gesture over and over until he exhausts it, after which he never returns to it again. He might, for instance, write several hundred poems that consist of a single line that runs along the perimeter of the page, forming a square. This square is made of a line a single character thick, enclosing an emptiness. There is no clear place to begin reading these poems and indeed, according to B., one is allowed to begin anywhere, with any word, reading the line and turning the book repeatedly at right angles, skirting the emptiness of the center of the page, until one feels an ending has been reached.

This reminds me of the painter C.'s work, which depicts, among other things, portraits of serial killers. Each time he draws a killer, he draws as well a sort of magic border around the page to hold the image in, to keep it contained. This way we are allowed to observe without fear that something will break free. In the same way, with A.'s poems, we are allowed to contemplate the void at the center of the page, to feel it enclosed, contained, if only temporarily, by words.

Writing, art, can be just that: writing, art. But both can also be enclosures, rituals, demonic circles.

Another square: the one we raise our hand to when we, in court, swear to tell the truth, the whole truth, and nothing but the truth. This too is an act of control, of binding, involving a book and a square, but what is bound this time is ourselves.

The Mormon temple garment, found under the clothing of the most devout Mormons, has four sacred marks. One, touching the right breast, is the mark of the square "suggesting to the mind exactness and honor in keeping the covenants." In the temple, you raise your arm to the square as you recite these and other words.

This mark, like the square we raise our arm to form when we swear to be truthful, is not a four-sided geometrical figure as are A.'s word boxes or C.'s borders, but rather half of such a figure: a right angle, such as the tool known as the engineer's square. Such squares are not boundaries. They are half of an enclosure. They don't enclose you, but just force you to take the long way around: one can lie under oath or one can, like I did, choose to reject the covenants and leave Mormonism. They only ensure your awareness that there will be consequences when your break your bonds. They are more a leash than an enclosure, and leashes can be wriggled free of. They don't control you, but neither do they protect you.

Which is better? To be able to come and go in your half-square, even if others can come for you or flee from you? Or, on the other hand, to be fully inside or outside a solid geometrical figure? Is it better to be the demon enclosed or the person who has summoned the demon or, instead, the person who, not really believing in magic, does not even finish drawing the figure? The person who holds his hand to the so-called square until he is tired and then lets his hand fall and hang limply beside his body?

A. the poet draws the square over and over, out of words, and each time surrounds something. But is it an empty page or, somehow, the void? Or is there any difference?

A REPORT ON CHIMNEY SWEEPS

In B.'s study of A., a hysteric, he notes that she refers to the process by which he purged her of her memories as "chimney sweeping." A humorous term, he claims.

And yet, it leads one to wonder, in what ways is the head a chimney? Does it open to the sky? Is it constructed in some way or other of "brick"? What is "brick"? Does the "chimney" heat the "house"? And, if so, what does this "house" consist of?

In the town of W., the body of an eighteen-year-old boy missing for seven years was found wedged inside the chimney of an abandoned cabin. He had, authorities believed, tried to shimmy down the chimney and had gotten stuck.

In G.'s story, "The White Wyrak," a brewery chimney is blocked. A chimney sweep sent to clear it climbs into it and then is simply gone. Another boy is sent, ascends said chimney, and never reappears. When a third boy is sent, he thinks to take not only his sweep's tools, but a hatchet.

"I saw in the half-light of the flue a snow-white being staring at me with a pair of huge, owlish eyes." This creature, "part monkey, part large frog," holds in its front claws "what seemed like a human arm." The fact that it "hung limply from a corpse" does seem to confirm that, yes, it is, in fact, a human arm.

The creature, its proboscis adhered to the corpse's temple, is too sated and sluggish to attack. It is quickly disposed of with a hatchet blow to the skull. They tug down the first body, which is the body of the second man, and then the second body, which is the drained body of the first man, now little more than skin and bone. The body of the creature itself, drawn out into the light, immediately dissolves into glittering black soot, as if it has been nothing at all.

Which adds up to what, exactly? A doctor, B., in a room with a patient, A., hypnotizing her and making her relive a trauma, and then the trauma hidden beneath that, and then the one beneath that, until the chimney seems swept clean.

And yet, as F., another doctor practicing the same method, lets slip in a later study, perhaps more than sweeping is going on. When his patient, E., complains about gaps in her memory, "especially about the most important events," F. concludes "that my work . . . had exercised a sufficiently deep and lasting effect." Though one might conclude otherwise: that the chimney has not been so much swept, as had some of its bricks knocked out so as now to be in danger of collapse.

But this, of course, is a humorous matter. Or so the sweepers would have us believe. The creature has been reduced to ash and the chimney is clean: if a few bricks have rattled free in the process, the only one to blame is A. It is, after all, her chimney.

translated by Ted Goossen

THE DAYDREAM

RAMPO
EDOGAWA

Did my daydream spawn a nightmare? Or did these events really take place?

It was a sweltering afternoon in late spring. Even the breeze felt uncomfortably hot against my cheek.

My recollection is hazy—I don't know if I was on some kind of errand or just out for a stroll—but I do remember walking on the outskirts of town along a broad and dusty thoroughfare that stretched in a straight line as far as the eye could see.

The silent shops lining the road had been bleached by the sun and weathered to a light sepia, like a washed-out summer kimono. In the shop windows, each barely a yard wide, I could see dusty gym tunics for primary school students displayed on hangers; an entire store filled with rows of shallow bookcases crosshatched like go boards whose compartments were stuffed with what looked like sand but was actually red, yellow, white and brown seeds; another narrow and dimly lit establishment with bicycle frames and tires piled to the ceiling; and a two-story building with a soot-stained votive lantern hanging behind a rickety lattice door. Through that door leaked the beguiling sounds of a three-stringed shamisen, as if the house was protesting being crammed into such tight quarters, and in such a bleak landscape.

A group of young girls, their long braids caked with dust, had formed a ring in the middle of the street and were singing: *Appuku, chikiriki, appappa . . . appappa.* The poignant melody rose into the hazy spring sky and evaporated.

The boys were playing jump rope. Their long rope looped through the air, slapping the ground in a persistent cycle as one boy, striped kimono open to the waist, hopped over it again and again. The whole scene unfolded at an unhurried pace, as if shot with one of the new movie cameras.

Every so often a heavily laden horse cart rumbled past, making the street and houses tremble.

I noticed something taking place farther down the street. A group of fourteen or fifteen adults and children were gathered in a ragged semicircle beside the road.

I could see amused expressions on all their faces, as if they were watching a comedy. Some were guffawing loudly.

Curious, I went over to see what was going on.

In sharp contrast to the grinning crowd, one pale face was dead serious. The man's lips protruded as he vehemently argued his case. His manner was far too passionate for a street vendor. Nor, given the frivolous reaction of his audience, was he likely to be a preacher. What on earth could he be doing?

Before I knew it, I had slipped into the semicircle for a closer look.

The man holding forth looked to be about forty and was wearing a dark-blue serge kimono cinched with a stiff yellow obi. He seemed at first glance to be not just well dressed but quite well educated. His hair shone so beautifully it could have been a wig, while his long pale face, with its aquiline nose and narrow eyes, was marked by crimson lips framed by a splendid mustache. A shower of spit sprayed from those lips as he appealed to his audience. His fine nose was dripping with sweat, and the feet that peeked from beneath the hem of his kimono were bare and coated with dust.

"Can any of you imagine how much I loved my wife?" he cried, overcome with emotion. He seemed to be approaching the climax of his speech. He searched the faces of those about him before answering his own question. "Enough to kill her, that's how much! How tragic that her virtue was so unreliable!" he went on, eliciting peals of laughter. His voice was barely audible amidst the hilarity. "I had no doubt she would start seeing someone else."

"I bet she found someone ages ago!" came a voice from the crowd. The laughter mounted.

"I tore my hair out," he went on, shaking his head theatrically like a Kabuki actor. "I was so worried I couldn't concentrate on my business. Each night on our futon, I would ask her to stay true to me. I clasped my hands and pleaded with her." More laughter. "Don't give yourself to another man, I begged. But she wouldn't listen. Like a seasoned geisha, she toyed with me, used her wiles to wrap me around her little finger. And I fell for it, each and every time."

"Lucky man!" came a shout from the audience, followed by still further laughter.

"Ladies and gentlemen," he went on, ignoring the hecklers. "What would you have done in my place? Would you have let her live? She looked so winsome with her hair put up in the *mimikakushi* style. She could fix it that way all by herself. Sitting in front of a mirror. The last time she did it I was ready. Her face was so beautifully made up, her lips red. She smiled as she turned to look back at me."

He lifted one shoulder and shook it in another dramatic pose. His thick eyebrows drew together, turning his face into something fearful. His red mouth twisted in a ghastly sneer.

"Now is my chance, I thought. If I act now, her lovely form will be mine forever. I had placed a needle-sharp awl at hand, and now I drove it into the nape of her slender neck with all my might. Her smile froze on her face, her eyeteeth peeking through her parted lips. She died without a whimper."

At that precise moment, a trumpet blared and a small band of musicians paraded by, the sort that advertises store openings and the like. They were followed by a ragtag group of children chanting, "Off we go to the end of Japan, a thousand leagues to far Manchuria," in time with the lively beat.

"You see," exclaimed the man. "They're spreading the word about what I did. Taro Magara is a murderer, a murderer, they're singing."

Once more, laughter erupted around me. The band was soon out of sight, but the thump of their big *taiko* drum lingered, as if accompanying the man's confession.

"I cut her body into five pieces, see. Two arms, two legs, one torso. A terrible pity, but what else could I do? Her legs were so plump, so white." The man abruptly lowered his voice. "Didn't you hear it? The sound of running water?" He thrust his head forward and intently eyed his audience one by one, as if imparting a matter of the greatest secrecy. "I left the water in my house running full blast for the next three weeks, until the twenty-first day. Why? Because I had placed her body parts in five big barrels, and they had to be kept cold." His voice dropped even lower, so we could barely hear him. "You see," he whispered, "a certain formula had come into my possession. A secret recipe, if you will. When human tissue is chilled in that fashion, eventually, it transforms into a waxen substance. 'Death wax' they call it."

I had read an article about the "death wax" phenomenon—the grainy photograph of the doctor who had written it popped into my head. But what was this man trying to tell us? Fear rose within me. My heart began to bob in my chest, like a toy balloon.

"In the end my wife's voluptuous white torso, her limbs, all of them, were turned into fetching wax sculptures!"

"Haha. So that's where you were heading! How many times have you rehearsed this since yesterday?" an onlooker bellowed rudely.

"Do you still not understand?" the man's voice climbed several notches. "How many times do I have to tell you? I know what you're thinking—that she walked out on me. Walked out on me? Well, think again. I killed her, do you hear? Surprised, aren't you? Wahahahaha."

A split-second later, as if severed by a knife, his mad laughter broke off and his expression grew serious again.

"Now the woman is mine, really and truly mine," he whispered. "My worries are over. I can kiss her when I want. Hold her when I want. My dreams have come true!

"But I must be vigilant. There is blood on my hands, and there's no telling when the police will come poking around. So I came up with a brilliant idea. A hiding place even the cops and detectives won't be able to figure out. You, sir," he said, his eyes alighting on me. "Come and see for yourself. She's on display here in my show window."

I spun around. Sure enough, right behind me—in front of my nose, in fact—was a white canvas awning with the words DRUGS GUARANTEED EFFECTIVE boldly splashed across the front in familiar Gothic lettering, and behind the plate glass window, a mannequin. So the man was the proprietor of this shop, purveying his own line of medicines!

"You see, there she is," he called to me. "Go ahead, please, take a good look at my beautiful wife."

What possessed me, I don't know, but a moment later I found myself standing under the awning.

A glass box containing a woman's head sat in the store's show window. She was smiling, so that I could see her protruding eyeteeth. The wax replica of a sickening tumor was attached to her face, but beneath that was real human skin. That skin was darker in color and—the ultimate proof no artifice was involved!—covered in downy hair.

My heart rose in my throat—I was on the verge of collapse. It took all my strength just to stagger out from under the awning. Avoiding the man's eyes, I escaped the scene.

Only after I was safely away did I notice a policeman standing at the back of the crowd. He was laughing along with everyone else as he listened to the man's spiel.

"Why are you laughing? Have you no shame? Where is your sense of duty? You heard what the man said. Go under the awning and look if you don't believe him. A human corpse is exposed to public view, here in the middle of Tokyo."

I wanted to tap the blockhead of a cop on the shoulder and tell him all that. But I didn't have the guts. I lurched off, my mind swirling.

The white thoroughfare stretched endlessly before me. In the haze, the row of electric poles undulated like seaweed swaying in the ocean.

translated by Ted Goossen

PEOPLE FROM MY NEIGHBORHOOD (THE FINAL INSTALLMENT)

HIROMI KAWAKAMI

THE SECRET

A white cloth was lying at the foot of a zelcova tree. When I walked over and picked it up, I saw a child underneath.

"What's the big idea?" The child glared up at me.

It had narrow eyes but thick eyebrows. I couldn't tell if it was a girl or a boy.

"Oops. Sorry!" I apologized. But the child kept glaring at me. "Are you playing hide-and-go-seek or something?" It shook its head vigorously from side to side.

"I live here," it said.

The cloth was big enough to carry things in if you folded it at the corners. Tall grass was growing wildly around the child's legs.

I retreated a step and turned to depart. I could feel the child's eyes on my back as I walked away. The hair on its body was thick and downy.

The following day the same cloth was lying under the zelcova tree. Damned if I'll pick it up this time, I thought, when just then the child sprang up in front of me.

"Let's go!" it said brightly and headed down the road. I didn't intend to follow, but it was taking the path that I had to walk to get back to my room, so naturally I tagged along.

The child went straight to my door. Open it, it said in such a bossy tone I couldn't say no. The child and I entered together. The room became its home.

Luckily, it didn't eat very much. And it was an unexpectedly good listener. It would listen to my tales of woe—my failures at work, my diffident lover—sympathetically, nodding as I spoke.

The child would always be excited after a shower. It would dance madly around the room naked, its little penis bobbing up and down. It appeared to be a boy after all.

Sometimes, the boy would unexpectedly disappear. After he'd been gone for a week or so, I would go back to the zelcova and find him sleeping beneath the white cloth.

"Why did you leave?" I'd ask.

"I don't know," he'd answer.

I began to doubt he was a human child. It didn't matter to me, though.

He's been with me now for thirty years.

He hasn't changed in all that time. He continues to eat sparely and to be a great listener. He still dances his funny dance after his shower, and he still disappears from time to time.

I've come to realize that he isn't human after all, seeing how he's stayed the same all these years.

Humans change over time.

I sure did. I aged and got cranky. But I've come to love him, though I didn't at first. I bought an apartment. And a dog. And three cats. I developed a fear of death.

The dog died, and the cats too. Now only the child and I remain. Before too long, he'll be the only one left.

"Why did you come here?" I asked him once.

He thought for a moment.

"It's a secret," he said at last.

GRANDMA

I can't remember her name. "Grandma" was what I called her, but looking back, she must have been in her mid-forties at the time. I would stop by her place every three days or so on my way home from elementary school. It was so much more fun playing with her than with my school friends. My friends were barbarians.

Grandma was always there by herself. She told me she was just looking after the house, so I should come on in. It was a big house. I glimpsed a little boy younger than me there on several occasions, but he always ran away and hid somewhere in the back, so I never met him. Grandma's room had a *kotatsu* table, brightly colored origami paper, a pack of Japanese *hanafuda* cards, and her tea things: a large thermos, a teapot, teacups, and a container of green tea.

We always played cards. Since *hanafuda* is usually played with three people, we quickly ran out of cards in our hands and played off the table. As a result, we amassed all kinds of bonuses that would have been almost impossible had three been playing: sets of four and even five "lights," for example, and triple red and blue "month" combinations.

Every so often, Grandma would ask me for money. "Ten yen, please," she would say. I didn't have it the first time, but the next time she asked I was prepared. She praised me that one time, but after that she seemed to take the money for granted, though I handed it to her with immense pride.

Grandma was subject to terrible moods. She would just sit there sullenly folding the same origami figure over and over again: a gaudy Fukusuke, the big-headed dwarf, for example, clad in *hakama* made from equally gaudy paper of a different design, topped off with a glittering *kamishimo* ceremonial costume. Then she would toss the whole lot into a corner.

I was introduced to the word "Hell" in her room.

"I've been told Hell smells like cod-liver oil," she announced one day. Cod-liver oil was provided at the nurse's room in my school during our lunch break, but only children whose parents had applied and paid got it. I said I wanted some too, but my mother called it "a waste of money," and rejected it out of hand. When Shimizu and Kanae came back from their visit to the nurse they said it tasted yucky, and I was lucky not to get it.

"Does it smell bad?" I asked Grandma.

"It stinks," she replied.

Then I'm glad I don't have to drink it, I thought. She had recently changed her hairstyle. The hair in front now jutted weirdly over her face like the eaves of a house, while a mini-chignon covered the nape of her neck. When I asked, "Can I touch the front?" she glared at me. Not long after that my visits stopped. "Let's play," I would call from outside her window, but she would just slide it open a crack, stick her head out and say, "No" in a cold, dismissive tone.

Grandma entered the hospital. I guessed she was dying, but she was allowed to return home after a while. I started visiting her again, but I was a third-grader by then, so I didn't go very often. "Did they make you drink cod-liver oil in the hospital?" I asked, but she just shook her head. My illness isn't that simple, she said in a patronizing tone. She was hospitalized twice more, and released both times. After that, she suddenly became a normal old woman puttering in her garden, sweeping the road in front of her house and fussing over the neighborhood children.

FRUIT

A princess moved into our neighborhood.

"She's just an old lady," snickered Michio and Akai, but we girls knew better, so we decided to launch an investigation. The Princess lived on the north side of town in a cozy little bungalow, with Christmas roses growing in the garden and wild roses arching over the front door. The walls of the bungalow were painted a light green, and the door was chocolate colored.

The Princess worked in her garden in the morning, went to the local market at noon, spent most afternoons sunning herself in the park, occasionally visiting the proprietress of the pub-cum-restaurant Love, where they would chat over a plate of warmed-over pilaf from the freezer. She would return home before dark, close her lace curtains and turn on the light. She appeared to spend a full hour preparing dinner—partway through, a delicious smell would come wafting from the house. We could see her movements through the curtains. She would eat her dinner, clean up, and then sit in her rocking chair and read.

It took us a whole month to nail down this pattern. Since we were in school all day, we took turns feigning illness so that someone would always be tailing her.

"Just as I thought!" Kanae exclaimed. "Only a princess would stick to a schedule this closely!"

For us girls, the Princess was like a figure from a storybook. Raised by mice, proposed to by a frog when she came of age, she ran away to escape him. Following many hardships, she met a prince and married. Left him in the end, and for the next fifty years lived a life of unrestricted freedom and luxury, then became an underworld figure until, tiring of that one day, she suddenly dropped out of sight, taking pains to conceal her whereabouts. Word spread that she had died; yet now, after many years, she had come to our neighborhood, far from the prince and the gangsters searching for her.

"Her life is perfect, don't you think?"

"Yeah. She even married a prince."

"And made a pile of money."

"And walked all over men, but they still followed her everywhere."

"But isn't a princess supposed to be no bigger than your thumb?"

"They say it's 'cause she got as big as a regular human being after her wedding that she and the prince broke up."

"No way," Kanae's big sister put in. You mustn't believe in fairy tales, she warned us. But none of us listened. We had other things on our minds. Like, how did one go about meeting a prince? Or putting the boot to a frog? Or becoming an underworld figure? Beset by these hidden desires, we groped for some way—any way—to draw closer to the Princess. Not one of us, however, was brave enough to approach her. Thus when the group of us came across Dolly Kawamata and the Princess walking down the street talking quietly to each other, we lost our cool.

“Are those girls from around here?” the Princess asked Dolly about us. Dolly nodded in alarm. “From what I’ve seen, children in this neighborhood are hardly what one could call sophisticated,” she went on in a condescending tone. She shrugged at Dolly and walked off without so much as glancing at us. Only then did Dolly tell us for the first time that the Princess had lived next door to her family during their stint in the United States. Night after night, Dolly revealed, men driving Rolls Royces and Jaguars had driven to visit the Princess, the sound of popping champagne corks resounding beyond her walls.

“Tell us, Dolly,” Kanae asked, burning with curiosity. “What were you and she talking about just now?”

“I asked her how to poison someone without being discovered.”

There was a persistent rumor, it seemed, that the Princess had left no less than ten bodies buried in her backyard in America. But she had assured Dolly that she had gone straight and had no plans to murder anyone in our town.

“Is there anyone here that you would like to murder?”

Dolly laughed. “Yes,” she said. “Two people anyway.”

Many years later, when a mass murderer poisoned scads of people across the country, the Princess was long dead and gone, but Dolly was in fine shape. Indeed, it was that year that the branches of the fruit trees in the Kawamatas’ backyard were so laden with fruit that they almost touched the ground.

THE WHITE DOVE

Kanae’s big sister picked up something strange on her recent school trip.

It was not a big school excursion. They didn’t even have to board a bus: they just walked northeast to where the path to the top of Mt. Golden begins and then up from there. The mountain is a mere 300 meters high. It took an hour to walk from the school to the entrance, and another hour and a half to reach the summit.

Kanae’s sister had no friends in the class. While all the other kids were doing stuff together—singing songs, getting scolded by the teacher for running around playing tag, snickering over shared secrets—she alone trudged glumly at the back of the pack, her face turned toward the ground.

“Come and walk with the rest of us,” Yamagami, the class representative encouraged her over and over again (at the teacher’s request), but she stubbornly refused. After seventeen tries, Yamagami finally gave up.

Actually, Kanae’s sister had experienced a prophetic dream the night before.

The dream had featured a little old woman and an old man ten times her size. The old man tried to crush the old woman underfoot, but she nimbly evaded him by leaping in the air over and over again until he fell on the ground in complete exhaustion. Without hesitating, she took a tiny, tiny needle and stabbed him in a vital spot, half-killing him.

"Isn't marriage wonderful," the old woman said. "You can hurt each other like this any time you like!"

The old couple had celebrated their golden wedding anniversary long before and were well on their way to "till death do us part." Yet they never relaxed their guard, each waiting for the opportunity to deliver a fatal blow to the other. Kanae's sister dreamed about them on a regular basis, about once a week.

A bubble emerged from the wounded old man's mouth. It was the size of a soap bubble at first, but it grew and grew until Kanae's sister could see herself inside. The view was hazy, but she glimpsed herself picking up a strange object from the mountain path she would climb the next day. That was why she had rebuffed Yamagami—if her classmates saw her, she would have to share whatever she found with them.

When they reached the summit, everyone pulled out their box lunches. Kanae had played a nasty trick on her just before she left the house that morning, though, secretly replacing the contents of her box—fried chicken, a small omelet and rice balls—with a mess of fermented soybeans. Kanae's sister had found out by the time she reached the corner of her street, but she didn't care all that much—her sole concern was locating the strange object prophesied in her dream as quickly as possible. She left her class to their lunch and followed an animal trail into the forest.

At a certain point the trail came to an end. All was dark. Then she saw a glow far ahead. A light seemed to be coming from a bamboo grove.

"What the hell?" Kanae's sister cursed. "All this way to find Princess Kaguya, the Moon Maiden? Who needs that?"

Looking more closely, though, she realized that the light was coming not from the bamboo but from a long squishy plant shaped something like a garden hose. She ripped the plant off at the roots. What emerged from the stem resembled a white dove, and it smelled absolutely awful. Yet it wasn't a bird, or a god, or a goblin, just a very stinky *thing.* Kanae's sister pulled out her lunch box, scraped out the mess of fermented soybeans and replaced it with that malodorous whatever.

On the way back down the mountain, Kanae's sister's classmates gave her an even wider berth. She just smelled so bad. When she returned home and removed the lunch box lid, the stinky, dove-like *thing* flapped around her room. She knew that if Kanae discovered what she was keeping, she would get rid of it right off the bat, so she kept it in the box. It never left her side after that—it went with her to school and when she went out, and stayed with her when she was back in her room.

Slowly but surely, the strange white dove-like *thing* grew. When it had become too large for the lunch box, she let it roam free. It always came back at night, though, pecking at her window until she let it in.

The strange *thing* changed shape as it matured, going from white dove to something resembling a large green grasshopper, to, quite suddenly, something shaped like a human being. It still stank, but when Kanae's sister put clothes on it, it looked like a boy about her age.

Kanae's sister called the boy "Grandpa." Each day, she would call, "Hey, Grandpa," take a tiny, tiny needle, and run around him trying to prick him in a vital spot, often attacking from the rear.

The boy was fast on his feet, though, so she hardly ever succeeded. As he grew into a young man, it became even more difficult.

Raising the youth became a freer and easier matter when Kanae went off to study in France. Until then, Kanae's sister had kept him in the crawl space under the roof, but once Kanae's room was free, he stayed there, and they engaged in lavish amounts of sex all day long. Her parents were in the house, of course, but unlike their children they were an easygoing couple, so they never noticed the young man's presence.

The young man grew into his prime, and then into middle age. Kanae's sister entered her thirties.

"Hey, Grandpa," she asked one day. "How about getting married?"

The middle-aged guy nodded. By that time, Kanae was a celebrated *itako* medium on Mt. Osore, the "mountain of dread," speaking in the voices of the dead for those who came to communicate with them. They paid her well, so she was able to build a magnificent house for herself and her middle-aged husband at the foot of the mountain. He no longer stank; to the contrary, his sweet disposition made him popular with the young women who came to hear their dead relations speak through his wife's mouth, which led to numerous affairs. Kanae's sister knew about these, of course, but she left him alone—confronting him would have been a headache, and besides, he wasn't a real person, just a strange *thing*.

When Kanae's sister was sixty years old, a huge meteor threatened the earth. Physicists had calculated its trajectory a year earlier and determined where it was going to land. The place? Mt. Golden, the exact same spot Kanae's sister had gone on her grade-school excursion.

Kanae's sister had another prophetic dream. In it, her middle-aged husband successfully turned away the falling meteor.

She asked him when she woke the next morning.

"I'm sad we have to part," he said, wiping away a tear. "But, yes, I will repel it for you."

No sooner had he uttered these words than his shape reverted to that of a white dove. He flew higher and higher into the sky, growing ever more massive as he rose, so that when he met the meteor head on, the two dissolved in a great cloud, which drifted down to earth like snow.

Hailed as a hero, Kanae's sister was greeted with wild applause wherever she went, and statues of her were erected across the country. This had been her childhood dream, but when the statues actually went up, there was no joy in her heart. Instead, she spent her days quietly thinking, her mind on the strange *thing* that was no more. When it had abandoned human form and changed back to a white dove its foul stench had returned as well. Till the day she died, Kanae's sister longed to smell that stench just one more time.

EYE MEDICINE

It was Dr. Miranda of the Miranda Clinic who taught me that some people are hatched from eggs.

I know Miranda sounds like a foreign name, but it is actually Japanese. The weird combination of kanji made it look like it belonged to someone in a biker gang, though, so Dr. Miranda decided to write it in katakana instead.

After working in a university hospital during his youth, Dr. Miranda quit for personal reasons in his early forties and traveled the world for a number of years before returning to Japan in his fifties to open the Miranda Clinic. He rented a small seventy-year-old two-story building on the outskirts of town, converted the first floor into a clinic, and the upper floor into his residence.

Opinions about his abilities varied: some thought he was a fine doctor, while others dismissed him as a complete and utter quack. Thus, while almost everyone in town knew about his clinic, those who used it were relatively few.

I went to the clinic whenever I had a cold, partly because it was seldom busy. He claimed to be able to handle all kinds of cases, so when a bug became lodged in my ear, I went there, and he extracted it immediately. I had never seen a bug like it before.

"This species is peculiar to Central Africa," he said, shaking his head. "Where did you pick it up?" Of course I had no idea. After that Dr. Miranda and I would sit and gossip when there were no patients around. He was an insect collector and was thrilled to add the bug he had taken from my ear to his collection.

It was during the rainy season when things were slow—patients suffering from allergies and the flu grew scarce then—that he told me about the egg people.

"There are quite a few around here," he said, as if it were no big deal.

"How can you tell?"

"Medical training helps us recognize the signs, but the main thing is one's doctorly intuition."

He confided to me that the Dog School principal and Michio had hatched from eggs.

"But . . . how do you know?"

"Stop and think. Both of them are a bit different from the rest of us, wouldn't you say?"

I thought it over for a minute. But I still couldn't tell.

"So then," I went on. "Human beings born from eggs aren't really human?"

"Of course not. All mammals are viviparous."

"Huh? You mean they're not even mammals?"

"Well, there are exceptions—take the duckbill platypus, for example—so I guess we could include them."

Dr. Miranda's tone had grown rather pompous. He whacked his belly like a sumo wrestler.

After that, I began looking more carefully at the people in our neighborhood. I roamed the streets studying their behavior and their faces, their tendencies and their favorite foods, before coming to a decision about who had and who hadn't hatched from eggs.

After a while it hit me that almost everyone had been hatched. Kanae and her sister, Akai, Dolly and Rumi, the lady who ran Love, even my parents—they all had come from eggs.

The one exception was Dr. Miranda.

"That's true," he moaned. "That's the reason I'm so lonely. Can you understand my loneliness?"

"No, I can't."

"No, of course you can't."

Cigarette smoke was billowing everywhere. The examination room stank of tobacco, and Dr. Miranda's nurse poked her head in from the adjoining room to complain.

"See how my staff treats me? Is it any wonder I'm so lonely?"

"I see," I answered. I found it difficult to sympathize with Dr. Miranda, however lonely he might be.

Laying eggs was apparently a very pleasurable experience.

"When they lay their eggs they secrete these special hormones, you know," he explained.

Could I lay eggs at some point, I wondered. Dr. Miranda glared at me for a second.

"Humans can't lay eggs," he declared.

"Then you made it all up?"

"Nonsense. It just means that you are a real human being. Once in a blue moon a human is born into the world.

Then might I be as lonely as Dr. Miranda? According to him, the best remedy for loneliness was an eye medicine made from a combination of antibiotics and boiled broccoli. A prescription was required for the antibiotics, but Dr. Miranda said he could give me one whenever I needed it.

translated by David Boyd

THE ELEVATOR AND THE MOON

SHIN'ICHI MAKINO

I came crashing down at the crossroads of art and philosophy, my head too heavy to hold up. I was out of breath and out of rope, lost in the desert with nothing to do but stare blankly at the sky.

Somewhere along the way, I had learned how to divide myself into three and let my alter egos run free in imaginary worlds, giving me some relief. No, much more than that—were it not for them, the mounting pressure would have made me pop like a balloon.

I named my three parts A, B and C.

First, A:

Heavenly powers rise, descend,

Passing gold vessels from hand to hand.

Think of A as the carefree artist. Always singing his favorite lines—words left behind by that great fallen poet: *Now it's this, now it's that; now in love, now in hate. Roll my barrel, on and on, like Diogenes the Saint.* Or: *Fellow men! There's no lack—today's bread white, tomorrow's black!* He spends his days running through the meadows with a butterfly net, or plunging into poetry in a corner of the Mermaid Tavern, or gazing at the stars through a handmade telescope, or surrendering himself to some fleeting love.

Then B:

If a man comes to me and hates not his father, his mother, his wife, his children, his brothers, his sisters—even himself—then he is no disciple of mine.

B is the Saint's most loyal servant. He has the blood of the Stoics, who rejected Euripides and his *River Marsyas*. Tragedy? He laughs at it. B places his faith in God and Power, nothing else. He wants only to free himself from the manacles of rhetoric, to live a plain and proper life, in harmony with reason.

And C:

Student of the legendary Scientist who stood at the top of the Leaning Tower, dropping metal spheres of various sizes to better grasp the logic of "falling bodies." C always looks miserable, not just because his experiments have yet to yield any superior theorem, but because he spends every waking hour repeating the same futile routine: ascending the stairs, dropping the balls, descending the stairs, retrieving the balls—*ad nauseam.*

One day, A, B and C got together and decided to set off on a journey to the remote nations of the world. C was less than enthusiastic, certain that there was nothing out there beyond what he had already seen. Still, he collected his possessions—his metal balls—and left for the Capital, together with artsy A and bullheaded B. It should go without saying that the three were always butting heads. Crossing paths in town, they never even exchanged proper hellos.

Having carried the idea this far, I leapt out of bed, shuddering with delight. For once, my head was clear as a summer day after a season of unrelenting rain.

O, indescribable jubilation! I snatched the Indian headdress off my wall, threw on my Indian gown and did a lively Indian dance. (But what choice did I have? I'm so impulsive—my highs and lows always come to the surface. In those rare moments, say, when I crack a geometry or algebra problem all on my own, not that I have any need to do so, I emit a strange shriek. Those shrieks often come in the middle of the night, so deafening they wake everyone in the house. When morning arrives and the others have to sleep in, I can't wait around for breakfast, so I walk down to the station to buy one of the bentos they sell on the trains. At that very moment, a savage yawp was climbing my throat, but I stifled it just in time. Yet, I ask you, after so many days chained to that bleak bed, how could I wake with such a brilliant idea and do nothing about it?)

What could give me greater pleasure than plotting a strange adventure for this unlikely band of travelers? For too long, I had been wandering in emptiness, looking after the jagged fragments of myself—always at odds, ever deadlocked. Yet what awaits them on the road ahead? What if I have A, chanting his gay tune, face off against the Devil on Bunyan's Mountain Pass? What if I have bullheaded B enter into a dialogue with the Gentleman of La Mancha? What if my frustrated Physicist were to pay a visit to Swift's Floating Island? One look inside the Academy at Lagado would scare him out of his wits! The scenarios played out in my head. Lost in bliss, I muttered: "O, accursed primitive philosophy! O, asinine arts! O, land of yesterday's countless miseries!"

Then I realized I was no longer in my room. I was on the street, carrying a whip of a sword—one of the fencing blades I keep crossed on my wall, right below my Waseda pennant. Mind you, these swords aren't just for show. I often duel with whomever I can find in the house. When I feel an unbearable sadness coming over me, a little swordplay always lifts my spirits. And when I get excited reading tales of knight-errantry, I like to bring down my trusty foil and twirl it around the room, becoming the hero's faithful shadow.

The road was bright with white moonlight. I turned around to look back at my house, halfway up the hill. My bedroom window was flung open, shutters dreamily outstretched, as if a bird had escaped moments earlier.

I brandished my sword and darted down the bright flatness of the road. My head-feathers rustled as I soared happily into the wind. I shouted back to my companions: "Ho! Poet, Philosopher and Physicist! After me! I shall see you as far as the Border Hill!" Then I thought: "Once they've left, I shall be alone—my true self once more. As of tonight, we will be nothing to each other!"

Then A, always the poet, leaned in and whispered: "Give this message to the waitress at the Mermaid Tavern. Should I find a jewel beetle on my travels, I will make sure it reaches her. I want her to pin it on her breast, as a token of my immeasurable love."

Astounding! This simple Poet, having totally lost touch with reality, was always calling that dingy dive "the Mermaid Tavern," as if it were the backdrop in some Keats poem. I suppressed a wry smile and did my best to play along: "Poet Laureate! In the window of a boutique in the Capital, you shall find a golden insect with wings of the seven treasures! If you truly wish to bind your love to the Mermaid beauty, send her this!"

But the Poet caught not a single word of my farewell. "Now it's this, now it's that!" He belted out as he strode downhill in the highest of spirits.

Then B roared, like the Athenian orator he was: "Anxiety is not a property of this world but the product of our imaginings. Tragedy befalls the fool alone. This odyssey shall be mine. Like a wild beast running from the forest, I shall embark with nothing but faith in my own power."

Fully confident that "everything flows," B marched off without regret. *Anxiety, tragedy, faith*—the words meant nothing to me. Yet B's pontification was so comical I felt I had to warn him: "Don't be too full of yourself—you might slip into an abyss of anxiety. Here, take this bow, and when you get hungry. . . ."

But B was already gone, not even looking back, so I stopped. My blade bent like a bow, I shot a wink at him, an even mixture of respect and ridicule.

C said nothing. He just trudged after the others, the balls in his pockets jangling like coins.

As the trio vanished into the distant twilight, I threw my hands into the air and shouted at the top of my lungs: "At last, a world all my own! Very bright, very bright!"

May they spend their days wandering the mountains and fields, foraging for food, and spend their nights round the fire, sharing tales of valor with the villagers. I pitied the Philosopher and his thoughts of thought, dreaming only of the Mount of Olives; I looked down on the foolhardy Poet and his rolling barrel; I bade farewell to the forlorn Physicist and his joyless staircase. I shook my headdress in ecstasy. What dark clouds might be waiting for them! The very idea thrilled me.

I unspooled like a kite and flitted down the mountain. But when I came to the bar that A extolled as the Mermaid, the waitress popped out.

"Well, well, well! If it isn't Makino-san!" she cried, barring the way. She looked me up and down, then purred: "Don't think you can fool me in that outfit. . . ." She nuzzled up against me. "Come on, what are you waiting for? I came out here for you—carry me in like always!"

"But I don't have the Poet in me. . . ."

"Stop playing games, Makino!"

"Games? Not at all—I want Shichirōmaru to take me night fishing but had nothing more suitable to wear."

"You mean you're on your way to Shichirōmaru's place now?"

"Verily! And fish or no, I shall return with inspiring tales of the sea!"

Chest out, I gave my sword a mighty swing. She punched me with everything she had.

"Liar! Who would go night fishing when the moon's out like this?"

"Right. I guess it ought to be dark out," I gasped, catching my breath.

"Isn't that obvious?"

Out of the corner of my eye, I saw the flushed face of a man peering out at me from the bar. It was Shichirōmaru. "Makino—I've been waiting for you! Stop trying to get the moon's attention and get in here!"

"Shichirōmaru! If you're here, then count me in!"

I stepped inside, feeling somehow out of sorts.

The girl ran in after me, her shoes slapping loudly on the floor. "Shichirōmaru, why are you friends with this liar? Forget him and get friendly with me."

She stepped between us and threw her arms around Shichirōmaru.

The name "Shichirōmaru" had been in my friend's family for generations; it was the name of their guild and the name of their ship, but the ship was no more. Only the name remained, though that didn't stop me from begging my good friend to take me night fishing: "Let's go this fall. . . . This has to be the year."

"It's a shame I can't oblige. You look like you're ready to go."

Shichirōmaru brushed the girl away and leaned in to fill my cup.

When it came to fishing, I was Shichirōmaru's devoted disciple. I really was dying to get out on the water. Of course, I wasn't actually thinking about night fishing when I hopped out of bed and put on this costume, but Shichirōmaru was always trying to get me to wear it to work, and the words just came out when the girl accosted me. Then again, had Shichirōmaru agreed to the jaunt, I would have gone in a heartbeat.

"I just went to your place to look for you," Shichirōmaru began. Then, all of a sudden, he started hyperventilating, gasping for breath. He grabbed my hands—his were unusually hot. "Dammit. I forgot what I was going to say when I actually found you."

His eyes were wide open, unblinking, riveted on me. Tears started to dribble down his face, then he grabbed me. I froze like an imp caught by Zhong Kui the Demon Slayer.

He began to cry like a baby.

"Shichirōmaru!" I howled, though I had no idea what was the matter. "Who would ever harm someone as good as you? Spare me the details—just give me the bastard's name!"

"No, that's not it," he finally said, choking back the tears. "Happiest of fortunes . . . the Shichirōmaru flag shall fly over the sea once more!"

There's a lookout tower over the fish storehouse on the shore, where poor Shichirōmaru—no boat to his name—has long made his living. On rare occasions, my friend would rent a boat and take it out, but he's never been on great terms with the boat's owner. For the most part, Shichirōmaru has stayed in the tower, raising and lowering flags to signal weather conditions, sounding the siren to alert the villagers when a shoal of fish has been sighted. He could only watch from the tower window as the fishermen flocked to the sea. My C wasn't conducting experiments in the Tower of Pisa; he was here, helping Shichirōmaru! Whenever Shichirōmaru looked through his telescope and cried: "OK—flip the switch!" I would do the honors and the villagers would scramble into the water, setting off a flurry of activity.

In my excitement, I'd pick up the megaphone and cheer on the brave fishermen below. Then I'd remember my friend, who wanted nothing more than a ship of his own, and return to some menial task: manning the flags or recording the weather or charting the tide. The Physicist's assistant at his passionless post. The two of us would stand at the window, grimly studying the villagers' every motion.

"Well, I'll be . . ." I had no other words. We just cried out each other's names, grabbed hands and danced a celebratory jig.

Then we hurried back to the tower, our excitement somewhat contained.

"Listen—I ran over to your house, but the door was locked and nobody was home. Then I saw that your window was open, so I cut through the yard to get a better look. All the lights were on, but I didn't see you anywhere. The room was a mess, as if there'd been a brawl."

Shichirōmaru said nothing about how he had come to acquire a ship after all these years—effectively returning the Shichirōmaru name to its former glory. Nor did he give me the chance to ask.

"Then I looked up at the wall and. . . ." He pointed to my outfit. "I saw that was gone. Thinking we probably just missed each other, I doubled back to the Mermaid to keep an eye out for you. God, how anxious I was! Then, when we heard you outside, the girl rushed out to meet you. But I couldn't move—I was trembling like mad. All I could say to you, in a calmness not my own, was: 'It's a shame I can't oblige.' But the truth is, when I saw you dressed like that, I was so happy I didn't know what to say."

Full of emotion, I looked up at Shichirōmaru's flag and asked: "How many years has it been since this banner has seen the sea?"

Only once, when we were drunk out of our minds, did we mention the flag, though it had been hanging in the tower for years. I was always stealing glances at it.

"I shall make this room my ship," Shichirōmaru had said that night, "so I might find the courage . . . with my flag flying here, just like this." He was standing by the flag, arms folded.

I got up and stood by him. "If you want it that badly," I said, "the day will come in no time! I know it."

I'll never forget it.

"When that day comes," Shichirōmaru said, "we'll share the ship—the *Shichirōmaru*—and give her all we've got!"

"I swear it!" I said with a nod.

"What a feeling! Like I'm riding Pegasus, soaring through the clouds."

With the flag whipping in the wind above us (we were so snockered the room really did seem like a ship), we stood with our arms held high like a couple of Greek statues, singing sea shanties.

"No wives until that day comes!"

"Ha! Of course! In my eyes, every woman on earth is Medusa. Zeus has given me the Sword of Perseus, Vanquisher of Women and Gorgons."

Alas, the vows we exchanged that night could never be kept. It was ages ago—

we'd just left school (Shichirōmaru was at the Fisheries Institute)—but I remember it all. Overcome with excitement, we shouted like madmen until the sun rose in the east:

"Hoist the sails!"

"Aye, Captain!"

"Raise the flag!"

We sang together:

"La-la-la, la-la-la!"

We ran around in frantic circles, then: "Time for the morning ceremony!"

We hung the flag on the wall, where it would stay for years to come.

I can't say why, but we hadn't spoken about it since, as if we'd been avoiding something painful.

One thing I ought to mention: although my A is a big drinker, sober C is the one who usually keeps Shichirōmaru company. Outside of that one surreal, drunken night nearly a decade ago, we've never even raised our voices in excitement—until tonight. That's why Shichirōmaru's tearful outburst at the bar was such a miracle. I'd never seen anything like it.

"Shichirōmaru! Has it really been ten years? Tell me, tonight, about your flag, about your dreams. . . ."

I shut my eyes and tilted my head, when—

"Slipslop!" Shichirōmaru barked as he took a swig from his cup. He got up and began pulling the flag down.

"Leave it! We ought to raise our cups beneath it!"

"No, I want to take it down with you here. Do with it what you will—but spare me the past!"

"Hold steady, the ship—the ship's moving!"

"Here we go, here we go! What monstrous waves!"

I staggered to my feet. Both of us were struggling to find our sea-legs.

As we held the flag at both ends, I shouted: "No, Shichirōmaru, you take it!"

"Nonsense! Tonight, and the day she launches, it has to be you, my friend!"

"Truly, I appreciate the sentiment, but I'm afraid I don't deserve the honor!"

"But can't you see there's no one else?"

Three sheets to the wind—or four?—we tried to hand the flag to one another. The timid Indian and the giant in the *maiwai,* chasing each other around the deck like two lions prancing among peonies in a Noh play.

(Note #1: "Slipslop." An interjection I've been spreading among the youth. As you already know, it means something like "I mock thy mawkishness.")

(Note #2: *"Maiwai."* Padded housecoats handed out to villagers to celebrate a good catch. Literally, "ten thousand blessings." *Maiwai* come in cotton, like under-kimonos; most are light yellow with vibrant designs along the hem, the Lucky Seven Deities dancing, for example, or Chinese children at play. But they aren't just for celebrations. Locals wear them year round—on a brisk evening walk or lounging at home. By the way, at Christmas, I always exchange gifts with an American woman I know. Last December, when I had no money, I remembered that the "happy" coats worn by Japanese laborers were all the rage in her country. So I sent her the brand-new *maiwai* that Shichirōmaru had given me. I told her it was the genuine article, a real happi from a coastal village in Japan, and urged her to wear it the next time she met her friends for tea. They would turn green with envy, I swore. She was grateful beyond words! But I digress.)

We tussled for some time. Then—without warning—Shichirōmaru let go. Holding his breath, he put his hand behind his ear.

"You hear that?" he whispered harshly.

The world outside was awash in brilliant moonlight. Between the lapping waves, I heard it: the rhythmic clang of wood chisels in the distance. I concentrated my whole being on that sound and let it draw me in.

All the fishermen had already snuffed out their lamps. They were fast asleep, or so it seemed. In the dark of night, the only ones still toiling away were the shipwrights in their workshop by the pines further up the coast. The workshop was no more than a roof propped up with poles; no walls to stop the curious eye. A bonfire blazing out front cast the silhouettes of the men and their hammers in sharp relief.

"They've already started?" I asked, my eyes fixed on the workshop. I could feel a storm of passion rising in me, fanning the flames.

Shichirōmaru only nodded. Then he said solemnly: "Marugen and my grandfather were great friends. Now Marugen is intent on seeing this job done while the moon lasts. Chivalrous, don't you think? They've only started today, but just look at them move! There are a good fifteen men in the workshop. As many as eight are Marugen's sons. Masters of the craft, one and all. Look, there—see the old devil barking orders by the fire? Marugen, in the flesh. Well, Makino, what do you make of it?"

In the glow of the moon, the bonfire burned bright, like a giant paper lantern; the shipwrights appeared as shadows drawn on its surface.

"If only we could hear his words. . . ."

"Not from this far away. . . ."

"But this is a most brilliant sight, isn't it?"

I was breathless.

The scene had gripped my soul. It made no difference that we were so far from the action, that the sound of the men's falling hammers only reached us when they had lifted them overhead again. I scrutinized that faraway flame intently, to witness each move the men made.

I looked up. An infinitely pale screen of moonlight—a silent canopy. A golden halo encompassed a giant, otherworldly lamp; the eye at the center of that radiant splendor, bursting with life, was like a circle of soldiers preparing for battle.

I was enraptured.

Was I staring too hard? Were my eyes playing tricks on me? The giant lantern and its human brushstrokes floated silently into the sky—transformed into a bright little moon! But I could still make out the shapes of men. Marugen's sons: Tarō, Jirō, Saburō and the rest, down the line. I saw their faces so well in the white light that I swear I could even read their lips.

"No way can we finish the job by firelight alone. Work hard while the moon is on our side!"

"Yes, Father! For Shichirōmaru, we'll work around the clock!"

As I imagined that distant exchange—Ah, how did I not realize that a dream had seized me?—I blinked. When I looked back, Tarō, Jirō and Saburō appeared as my three selves: A, B and C. Had I not just seen them to the Border Hill? Never did I suspect that they would spend the first night of their adventure in a place like this! They must have been drawn to the flame, imagining it to be the light of some village.

As always, A was singing: "Now it's this, now it's that!" Yet he swung a mighty hammer. Next to the bonfire, B was eating his lunch—at this odd hour. C was looking down, so I couldn't get a good look at his face, but he had a ruler in his hand and appeared to be engrossed in measuring a block of wood.

"What a promising beginning! I suppose I should say something, a blessing, for their efforts!"

I started to pray for the fortune of the penniless travelers. But I was unable to find the proper words, so I borrowed those of B's mentor, wishing that the road ahead be smooth and wide: "May you traverse the universe, and the surrounding vacuum, survey its forms and the infinity of time. May you comprehend and embrace the periodic renovation of all things."

Finishing my prayer, I turned to them. I wanted to share what I felt inside, so I made as if to grab the longing inside of me, threw a fistful toward them and let go. I did it again and again.

Meanwhile, new shadows entered the ring of light. They circled around the bonfire, watching the others hard at work. They seemed to be speaking words of joy.

"Well, I'll be. . . ." I muttered and blinked again. Then I saw, among the others, Shichirōmaru's father and grandfather in crested *haori.* My father was there, too, similarly dressed and scowling like a battle-hardened warrior. Youths in *maiwai* were dancing around the bonfire. How absurd, to see these men, no longer of this world, behaving in this way. Still, they looked exactly like they did when they were alive. As I watched the visitors mingling with Marugen and the others, the scene began to feel less strange. No—it was just as it should be.

"Glad to see it," I said.

"Thank you," Shichirōmaru replied, slapping me on the back, bringing me back to myself. Still, I couldn't believe that the apparitions across the way were just that. Shichirōmaru patted my back a few more times.

"Thank you, my friend," he continued. I can't tell you how much it means to me, the intensity with which you watch Marugen and the others work. I'll never forget your passion as long as I live. Oh, it's just too much—come back to the table!"

Roused from my reverie, I took a look at myself. One leg on the window sill; right fist thrust into the moonlight, like a valiant piercing his enemy's belly; back arched like a tiger's; left fist pressed up against my chin. I was as still as a living doll.

Then the bell rang.

A visitor.

"Who is it?" Shichirōmaru asked into the mouthpiece.

"Lower the elevator."

It was my wife's voice.

This room was "For Authorized Personnel Only." As always, Shichirōmaru and I had dutifully drawn up the rope ladder once at the top. Visitors had to ask to be let up. When their hands were full, they called for the elevator.

Our "elevator" was man-powered. We fed a rope through a pulley, then tied the rope to a wooden box, like a bucket in a well. We had a couple of gearwheels of different sizes; spinning the larger wheel made the load several times lighter—not unlike a bicycle—so even a drunk could operate the lift.

"You alone down there?"

"Hardly," she said. "Everyone's here—we even picked up the Mermaid on the way."

Now I grabbed the mouthpiece and peered into it. "Listen—I don't know what this is about, but if anyone down there has a beef with us, tonight's not the night. You hear me?"

"What's wrong? Did we ruin your ritual dance? We could see you miles away!"

"Shichirōmaru! What do we do?"

"Don't panic. If we've been seen, we've been seen. Get the elevator ready."

I turned the key and the wooden box slid quietly down the shaft.

"You know the rules," I said. "One at a time."

"There are six of us . . . Is that alright?"

"No problem. Just ring the bell once you're inside."

It rang.

"Ready, pull!"

Shichirōmaru gave the signal, and we moved as we had countless times before.

"Heave-ho!" we bellowed. "Pull, pull! Heave-ho! Pull, pull!"

First to step out of the box was E, a camping bag slung over his shoulder; in one hand he had some spring onions and what looked like a bottle of soy sauce. (E, R and H were young friends of my wife and my younger brother. All were residents in my village Republic. I'll tell you now—E was only the first to emerge with a bulging bag on his back; R, H, my wife and my brother would soon do the same.)

E looked right at me and said: "I took a cart into town and sold most of your books."

"What! Why? Those books mean as much to me as my own life!"

My face bright red, I started to question him—when the bell rang again. I returned to my post.

It was R this time, bearing lotus roots and burdock. "I pawned your watch for bullets. We won't have to worry about meat for some time now."

R was an expert marksman who kept us supplied with plenty of wild fowl.

"But I need that watch to do my job at the tower!" I yelped.

Next was H: "I bought us some gas," he crowed, shoving a tin of Mobiloil in front of me. "Now we can get around town on motorbike. You can make it anywhere you need to go in under an hour."

"Where—pray tell—did you find the cash for that?"

Gripping my aching chest, I glared at H. Before he could answer, the bell rang again.

It was my brother: "We talked it over and decided it was wrong that you were the only one in the house with a kimono."

"Say no more! You'll only break my heart."

I shook my fist at my brother. The thought of having my fine kimono taken from me was enough to make me cry—I am quite the dandy—but I didn't have the time. The Mermaid came up, followed by my wife, a loaf of bread tucked under her arm.

"I hate to tell you this, but that Indian costume is all you have left. Guess you'll just have to make do for a little while. . . ."

When my wife broke the news, I felt wretched.

"What should I do? What should I do?" I wailed again and again.

I burst into tears. The others stood there in utter shock, watching me fall apart. I had always talked about material possessions as if I were totally indifferent.

"It's just too much . . . to wear this outfit every day . . . I-I-I . . ."

"Everyone, listen . . ."

Shichirōmaru spoke up: "Don't be alarmed. Makino's just drunk on happiness is all. His emotions are surfacing in strange ways. He's not the only one, either . . ."

"Shichirōmaru! Have you been drinking, too?"

"That's neither here nor . . ."

My friend prevaricated, announcing the happy news—the *Shichirōmaru* would sail again. "Behold! There she is. Not yet complete, but already a magnificent ship. When she goes to sea, dearest friends, I hope you'll move your Republic aboard!"

At those words, the out-of-work Republicans held aloft the things they had in their hands and cried for joy. "Hear, hear!" they cheered.

Greatly relieved, my wife said: "Now I see! I never believed that my husband would crumble over something so petty."

She sidled up to me. "Don't worry, this look suits you. Nobody thinks it's funny. Just go about your work as usual."

I asked the others: "What have you got in those sacks?"

"Rice!" they answered in unison, almost like a classroom of eager students.

The Mermaid and my wife left to find libations. The two of them insisted they didn't weigh that much, so they could ride the elevator together. I turned the key and took hold of the wheel. I started lowering the box as smoothly as I could, when it occurred to me: "I don't think I've eaten anything but potatoes for more than a day. Guess that explains why I've been feeling so funny, and why the drinks went straight to my head."

I could hear my wife whistling down the shaft.

As I worked the wheel, the room around me brightened with conversation. Then, somewhere between the voices, I thought I heard one of them mock another: "Slips-lop!"

CONTINENTAL DRIFT

KEVIN BROCKMEIER

"A tale where two continents quietly separate and cease to share a common civilization."

—*Tales in Tanka,* Mina Ishikawa

The night the earth came apart, Maya and Lucas were lying on the hillside between their houses, toying with each other's hands. Fourteen and newly in love, they had just discovered that soft glade of skin between the thumb and the index finger where someone could work wonders simply by tracing a circle. Pleasure took you over. It came buzzing in through your pores, your joints, the sheen of hair on your cheeks. Maybe their parents would ground them for breaking their curfews, but what did it matter? They were all pulse and instinct when they were together. They couldn't help themselves.

Nearby something slipped through the grass, separating the blades. They propped themselves on their elbows to listen. A snake, they decided, or no: a rabbit. At first it moved with a sound like an expensive book creaking open, rustling and popping against its weight, and then, as it raced away, like a string of little kisses.

Lucas leaned over and said, "Know what that reminded me of?"

"What?"

"This." And he demonstrated on Maya's neck.

"*What* did it remind you of?"

"This."

"What was that again?"

"This."

An hour later and there was no maybe about it: their parents were definitely going to ground them. They traded a last kiss goodnight, and then Lucas left one way, sliding through the trees, and Maya the other, hopping over a crack in the soil. Beneath her the narrow opening sank away in the skim-milk light of the moon. To her eyes it looked almost bottomless. She fell asleep wondering how a boy she had been five with could grow up to be so desirable, so mysterious, like someone who had never worn a juice stain around his mouth, never chased her with a worm on a stick, and he fell asleep amazed that a word spoken quietly in his ear—*what?*—could register in the soles of his feet.

By the time they woke the next morning, the crack in the hillside was already too wide to cross. The two of them set out, as always, to meet each other on their way to school, and there it was, a great vertical gorge with walls of yellow dirt and white clay. Hundreds of people stood scattered along the edges. The bravest few knelt right at the lip, blades of grass bristling between their fingers. Lucas elbowed his way to the front. Though Maya had promised to meet him at their usual spot, where the dirt broke around a big gray mass of granite, she wasn't there. He scanned the other side of the opening until he found her. She was wearing the blue cotton dress he liked so much, the one that showed the backs of her knees when she stretched. He waved, trying to seize her attention, but she was too busy tracing the rift with her eyes. It reached as far as she could see, traveling north toward the hills and south toward the cornfields. When someone tossed a coin over the edge, the wind carried it back against the face of the gulf so that it fell like a rock skipping over water. She lost sight of it long before it hit the bottom.

Gradually, as the day thickened, more and more people arrived, making their way to the edge of the fissure in clusters of tens and twenties. Shortly after noon, a long file of men in work boots sliced through the crowd with the stripped trunk of an oak tree, extending it over the gap in a series of coordinated little boosts and heaves until the tip stopped gnatting around and slid smoothly onto the turf on the far side, lodging against a cast-iron bench. A spontaneous cheer went up. But just as one of the men was preparing to test the trunk with his weight, the ground spread a few feet wider and the tree plummeted into the abyss. With barely a whisper the grass let it go. The suddenness with which it vanished left a blank space hanging in the vision, an emptiness that neither Maya nor Lucas could resist filling with a picture of something else: for him it was a roof collapsing in the snow; for her, the pull-it-in-two trick her dad liked to play with his thumb.

Eventually, there was nothing for people to do but leave, taking whichever direction they could, to work or to school or simply back home.

It was mid-afternoon and a thick layer of clouds was shadowing the sun when

Lucas climbed the worn path to the top of the hill. Years of footsteps, some of them his, had stamped the dirt there to a hard gloss. The instant he left the trail, he could feel the difference beneath his shoes. By the time Maya lifted her gaze, he was already halfway home, following a soft blanket of leaves through the trees. She thought she saw him walking in the other direction, past the basin pond where the dragonflies hatched in the spring, but he was far away and getting farther, just a blur of shapes in the suggestion of a boy, and she couldn't be sure it was him.

By the next day the seawall had broken and the waters had flooded in from the ocean, carving the ground away in gigantic curved wings. Arriving at the ravine, Maya and Lucas found that they were marooned, irrecoverably, in different lands. For months they kept thinking about that first morning: why hadn't they taken a running start and tried to leap the gap? Or why, over the next few weeks, before the sides grew so far apart that people came to think of them as coasts, hadn't they boarded one of the many boats ferrying passengers back and forth across the channel? Or why for that matter hadn't they simply taken a dive and struck out swimming? But the fact was that she lived with her parents, he with his, and there were times when your future was chosen by something other than you. Lucas couldn't stop fantasizing about their reunion. Again and again in his imagination, the hillside would mend itself and they would meet there like always, landing on each other's bodies the way that bees land on flowers. Maya had fantasies, too, but hers were uglier, more jagged—dismal visions of the years of loveless isolation she foresaw for herself. Yet if her daydreams were bitterer than Lucas's, they also faded more quickly. For a few brief days, she spent the rest of her life feeling hopeless. Then school started again, and she had tests to take and papers to write, and her sadness mellowed and lifted.

For a while, after the mail began working properly, the two of them exchanged love letters, but sooner than either of them would have imagined, they became absorbed in their separate worlds. The notes they sent grew sparer, more perfunctory, all *how have you been*'s and *hope you're well*'s, *I'm tired tonight*'s and *just a quick word to say*'s, until they stopped entirely, and which of them wrote last and which failed to answer, they could not remember. Another summer went by before Maya found a new boyfriend, and three years after that she moved inland for college. Before she was twenty-five, she had finished law school, and several months later, with two of her classmates, she started a family law practice. As she grew older, she realized, her hopes were slowly being replaced by other hopes: leisure where once she had wanted possessions; anonymity where once she had wanted recognition. It had been ages since she envisioned herself as someone's wife—not since Lucas, really—but then one of the clerks at the county courthouse spent five or six months tendering his shy-man's flirtations to her, sliding her files back fingertips-first so that he could brush the palms of her hands, and somehow, by the time he worked up the courage to ask her out, she was already picturing herself in a wedding dress. In the years after they married, he was so sweet-tempered with her, so willing to listen when she had quarreled with the other partners, so ready to agree that she had done everything she could, that she reached the middle of her life, and the end of his, before she realized she had barely known him. Her second husband she knew all too well. They divorced for the same reason they had married: his openness, which gradually curdled from open affection to open disdain. She knew that the marriage had rung its note of doom when he took to beginning all his sentences with the word "actually." She resolved that there would not be a third.

For Lucas there was never a first, just the occasional hopeful entanglement that lasted a year or two without ever quite straightening into marriage. In his late twenties he had joined a structural engineering firm, and in his thirties, as his reputation spread, he had less and less time for romance. His commissions began to carry him far from home. One summer day, in a coastal city afire with sunlight from both the sea and the sky, he passed a window he momentarily believed he was seeing not onto but through and was shocked to stillness by the realization that the man inside its frame, with the red skin and the pinched gaze and the brightness rebounding through his hair, was him. Middle age: it was like a bobcat, a panther, some dead-stepping wild animal readying itself to pounce on him. All this time it had been pursuing him. But from which direction, he wondered: the past or the future? Instantly he felt closer to the end than the beginning. If only he had someone like Maya in his life again, he thought, a beautiful girl who might sit in his arms for hours, sharing in the illusion that everything was permanent and time was blowing over them like a breeze.

A few weeks later, back home, he read a newspaper profile about the retiring director of a foster care agency. Asked about the headaches of the job, she answered, "From day one it's always been the same: too many children and too few caregivers." Lucas never supposed a single man would meet the agency's qualifications, so he didn't think very hard before submitting his parenting application, but he was healthy and reasonably prosperous, and to his surprise he was accepted. He was what they called a "short-termer," his custodial duties lasting only a few days or weeks at a stretch, which meant that between assignments he was free to work long hours or to travel.

His first child was a spindly nine-year-old redhead named James, practically raccoon-eyed with freckles, who seemed to survive entirely on a diet of white bread and peanuts. One night, when James was running a mild fever, Lucas tested the boy's forehead with the palm of his hand and felt the heat of it in his own stomach, traveling down some strange secret highway of nerves. *Oh yes,* he remembered. *This.* Cora, age three, liked to help him clean the house by stuffing every object she could carry into the large cedar chest in his living room. Alan, age seven, could only fall asleep backwards, with his head resting on the bed's mattress and his feet propped against the headboard. Ben, fifteen, spent a whole month of winter afternoons on Lucas's front porch, whittling away at a wooden staff until gradually it revealed the perfect long contours of an insect: a walking-stick walking stick. Ethan, Avery, Beth, Robin, Phillip, Kendall, Melissa. Lucas might have guessed that after a while their personalities would start to dim in his eyes, to overlap, forming a single mulch-like child, some young-old girl-boy who was angry one minute and inexplicably delighted the next. But it didn't happen. He would know it was time to quit, he decided, when he stopped falling in love.

He still lived in the town where he grew up, just a few blocks from the hillside where he and Maya used to break their curfews kissing, and where these days he took the kids to throw pebbles into the ocean. Maya herself had hopscotched farther from home with every move. After her parents died, though, and she returned to ready their house for the realtor, she spent her first quiet afternoon staring out over the waves from the upstairs window of her old bedroom. The curtains were musty, and something's claws went scratching over the roof, and suddenly, in a deluge of recollection, came all the melancholy, fervor and humiliation of her teenage years: the feelings of a lifetime ago. Had the water been as blue then as it was today? In her memory it was a thousand-colored green.

The two halves of the mainland had separated so long ago that no one thought of them as a single country anymore. In big ways and small, from their weather systems to their clothing styles, they had gradually distinguished themselves—formed their own governments, nursed their own industries, even adopted their own holidays. They still played many of the same sports, but on Maya's side of the world, where the mountains were stately and the rivers treacherous, the popularity of climbing had risen and the popularity of rowing had declined, while on Lucas's, where the rivers were wide and the mountains rolling and green, it was the reverse. Over the decades, the countries had developed competing superstitions. *For good luck, spit to the west; for good luck, spit to the east. Make a wish on the first minute of the hour; make a wish on the last.* The children had built their own separate kingdoms of slang, and presumably, given time, their taunts and colloquialisms would mature into distinct languages. And then there were the marks of biological evolution. Already, it seemed, some of the moths and butterflies were showing subtle variations in their wing patterns.

Maya had witnessed every bit of it, but there was nothing so profound to her as the changes she had seen in herself. How was it possible that the girl who liked to trolley her stuffed animals around on a bath towel and say *ding, ding* was now the graying woman with a taste for strong cheeses and ristretto shots? Soon after she buried her parents, she returned to her law practice. Barely a year went by before she was appointed to the domestic relations court. She was amused by the idea that behind her robes, solemnly administering justice, was a hapless human being with all her hapless human difficulties. At the bench sometimes she would think, *The judge has a cold today*, or, *The judge isn't digesting well*, and observing the counselors and the litigants, she would wonder if, like hers, their minds were dimly occupied nearly all the time by the secret derelictions of their bodies. When rheumatism and absentmindedness made it harder for her to concentrate, she stepped down from her position, and, rather than resuming her legal work, she retired.

Sixty-nine years old. Pruning the yellowed leaves from the plants. Boiling water for tea every evening. Sitting in an armchair with a wool blanket covering her lap. Listening for the double tin pop of the mailbox, which happened between ten and eleven most mornings, though late in the afternoon on Saturdays. Paying the bills. Washing the dishes. Feeding the fish that vacillated around inside their big glass brick. Considering the way the house changed its sounds when she turned the lights off, and asking herself, again and again, whether she was merely imagining things. Noticing the ripples the wind made in the birdbath, and the way the arms of the trees cast their shadows, and how thin her wrist looked when she held it close to her eyes and the sky took big chunks out of either side of it. Watching a stray cat shy away from the sun. Reading all the books she had never had the chance to read, or never wanted to. Brushing her teeth. Moisturizing her face. Going to bed. Seventy.

Lucas was sure he would work until his heart gave out. One after another the children he'd fostered had drifted from his care. Though he knew it was foolish, he couldn't help feeling bruised when after months or years, in the park or at the grocery store, they failed to recognize him—or worse, had grown so much that when they sang out his name, he could only pretend to know who they were. A dozen times he had considered adoption, but though he submitted his paperwork to the agency, he was invariably rejected. By the time he deduced what the problem was—age, life—he was too old to foster at all.

His final romance took him by surprise. Ivy was her name, and she was an audiologist, gorgeous, with a scar across the bridge of her nose where a slate shingle had fallen when she was in junior high, which made her beauty appear charmingly unfinished, like a landscape from which the mist was still lifting. He thought about asking her to marry him, but she moved to another city to accept a teaching appointment and vanished into her faraway routines. Much later she returned, and as they sat together over dinner one night, they understood that something that had once seemed permanent between them—love, or at least the appetite for it—had fallen away. He was hardly the same man anymore. She was hardly the same woman. People say that though the body changes, the soul is constant, but what if it isn't so? What if the soul is water, clouds, mercury, ten billion colors erupting inside a lens, never one thing for longer than an instant, and we have no idea what we are carrying inside us?

The continents were like immense beasts circling the planet. For some time it had been obvious that they were going to come back together. What had been the seaside would become the mainland, and maybe its plates would buckle into mountains, or tremble with earthquakes, or shatter against their own weight—no one knew for sure. Teams of engineers, Lucas among them, worked day and night to soften the collision, designing a buffer of hinges, floats and pneumatics. He couldn't stop his mind from insisting that everything was preparing to change. This was it—the clock hands were finally going to meet—so he booked a ticket east to the opposite coast. His work on the buffer was finished, but it didn't matter. He intended to witness the moment for himself.

From her own home, across the water, Maya had joined the multitudes traveling west. It wasn't every day that two countries turned into one, and come what may, she wanted to be there when they did. Millions of faces had drifted past her over time, yet here on the slopes overlooking the ocean, in the thickness of the crowd, she doubted she would be capable of recognizing a single one. Her friends, her neighbors, her ex-husband—they would be like strangers to her, every one of them. And she, no doubt, would be like a stranger to them. Standing anonymous, with countless anonymous others, she stared out over the rising sea. The hills were advancing in great curtains of white spray. The air was busy with crying gulls. Then the flexures bent, and the cylinders compressed, and softly, indifferently, the same way they had let each other go, the continents came back together. A slow wave heaved up onto the grass, dropping webs of orange seaweed and a thousand tiny shells. Maya watched the water sift to her feet before it soaked into the soil. Then the crowd began to press past her, rushing forward across the sand. Someone knocked hard against her shoulder, and she found herself lying on the ground.

Lucas was not as agile as he used to be, and his pace was slow, but crossing the border was as easy as picking his way through a slim field of broken earth. He climbed the slope at the other end, carefully favoring his left hip. At the top he came upon a woman who had fallen. "Dear me," he said, and then, "Miss, may I help you up?"

Maya could not understand the man. She cupped her palm to her ear. "What was that again?"

The noise of the celebration surged around them, all those shouts and horselaughs and conversations, and Lucas realized she must not be able to hear him. "This," he said, and held out his hand.

The instant Maya took it, she remembered the way she used to neck with her boyfriend when she was a girl, the smell of his skin like match heads and molasses, how her heart would race whenever his fingers strayed onto her stomach. Life was long, and she had been so young sometimes.

Lucas felt her hand tightening inside his. All at once he recalled the boy he used to be, years ago, back when he and Maya were just hot-blooded kids twining their legs together on a hillside. Oh Lord for the days when they could fill the hours exploring each other's bodies with kisses, too dazzled by their senses to stop. That's what love did to you, he thought. It turned you into its instrument and it swept the strings.

translated by David Boyd

EXTRA INNINGS

HIROKO OYAMADA

My girlfriend asked me to come over and help clean out the shed.

We were serious—marriage was definitely in the cards. This was my third time going to her house, where she lived with her parents. The first time, we had cake; the next time, we made sushi. Her father hurled tame curses at the baseball game on TV while we rolled rice in sheets of nori. My girlfriend had told me that her mother had been through a divorce some years back, and the man she now called "Dad" was actually her stepfather. Still, his color commentary left me feeling like the three of them were as close as any family.

I don't know if cleaning out the family shed is supposed to be the next big step after making sushi together, but I could tell that her parents knew we were serious. I wasn't about to run out and buy her a ring, but I was sure we'd have a couple of kids within ten years or so—I could see that far ahead with her.

"No one's been in the shed in years." "We redid the whole house and meant to tear the shed down but never got around to it. Next thing you know, it's ten years later." "I had my entrance exams that year. I remember everything. Not an easy time." "The house was a mess and so were you. I was getting remarried, everything was up in the air." "We just forgot about the shed." Mother and daughter were talking over each other at a rapid clip. I did my best to keep up. They led me out back to the shed. Dad was in the living room, watching the game. It looked like he wasn't going to be pitching in.

Mom unlocked the shed door with a tiny key. Right away, a terrible smell smacked me in the face. It wasn't just ten years of stale air—more like someone had been cooking old meat, fish and rotten vegetables. But the smell didn't last long. Soon only the dry smell of dust remained. "Go ahead!" When I stepped inside, the two of them exhaled nervously.

It was cleaner inside than I had expected. There was a pile of cardboard boxes, neatly stacked. Each box had a clearly written label on its side: DISHES #1, BOOKS, etc. Behind me, my girlfriend whispered to Mom, "It's really not that bad." "No, it looks pretty clean. I'm surprised. . . . So, could you just bring them out for us? The boxes . . ."

"Me?" I looked back. They were standing just on the other side of the door. It looked like they weren't coming in. The shed was a little small, but it could have fit all three of us, no problem.

"There's dust inside." "Dust?" "Right, she's been allergic to dust since she was young." "Do you mind?" "We appreciate it."

I put on the work gloves they'd given me and got started. From the corner of my eye, I saw Mom brushing something from her daughter's shoulder.

There was one box askew, with no writing on it. It was strangely heavy. Through the slit in the top, I saw what looked like large white bowling pins resting on their sides. "Are those bowling . . . ?" I asked under my breath. "What?" Mom asked back. "Pins . . . for bowling?" She looked at her daughter and winced. Coolly, my girlfriend said, "Those? They can go in the trash," pointing at me with her chin. In that moment, she looked like someone else, like someone I didn't know at all. "You want me to bring them out?" "Yeah."

In the end, neither of them set foot inside the shed. I heard them outside, sifting through boxes, breaking them down. They were talking the whole time: "Is this recyclable?" or "Hey, check out this Doraemon alarm clock!" But they never even touched the box with the bowling pins. Sweating, I set it down next to the others. When I did, I noticed a single black ant caught in the mesh of my glove.

It was evening when I finished with the shed. "How about a bath? It's ready for you." A clean shirt was waiting for me, but there was no change of underwear. "Keep your underwear. Just make sure you toss everything else in the laundry." Then she handed me a towel and sent me straight to the bath. I almost felt like she was tossing *me* in the laundry. The water was steaming. The bathroom was pristine—not even a spot of mold. Mom sure was a neat freak. I wondered how much of that had been passed on to my girlfriend. I thought I knew, but really I had no idea.

I saw a speck of black dust floating in the water. Thinking I had probably tracked it in, I leaned over to scoop it up, but it drifted away.

The room was filled with steam. I stepped into the tub and got in up to my shoulders. More dust? No, it wasn't dust. The water was covered with tiny black dots. I strained my eyes. "Ants?" I stood up and felt grit beneath my feet. Ants at the bottom of the bath. In the drops of water dripping from my hair, in the drain, between the tiles, in the faucet—ants were everywhere.

I quickly wiped myself off, put my underwear back on and ran out. "What's wrong?" My girlfriend looked in from the living room. "Ants, in the bathtub!" Mom rushed in from the kitchen shouting: "Where?" "All over the place!" I frantically crushed the ones still crawling on me. Drops of water went flying.

My girlfriend and her mother looked at each other, their faces pale. "It's not over!" "Black as ever . . ." my girlfriend said, falling to her knees. Mom covered her mouth like she was about to throw up. "Still there, after all this time . . ." said a low voice from the living room. "Tear it down if you want, but he'll never forget." I looked toward the voice. Dad was clapping excitedly. "Huh?" Incredible! The television screamed. A bases-loaded walk in the bottom of the ninth! Well, folks, it's a brand-new ballgame now. Dad nodded a few times, then muttered: "Looks like we're in for extra innings."

translated by Jay Rubin

BEHIND THE PRISON

KAFŪ NAGAI

My Dearest Excellency,

Thank you for your letter. I have been back in Japan for nearly five months.

I was in the West as you know, but I was unable to find any fixed employment or to earn academic credentials during my time there. All I brought home with me was my collection of concert, opera and theater programs, as well as my photographs and nude paintings of female entertainers. I am a full thirty years old now, but, far from being prepared to start my own family, I continue to while away my days in a single room on my father's estate, which is located behind the prison in Ichigaya.[1] It has a rather imposing gate and a lush growth of tall trees. I'm sure you can find it easily just by asking for my father.

I will probably be here, doing nothing, for the time being. Indeed, I may have to spend the rest of my life like this. Not that I am surprised to find myself in this situation. The question of what I should do once I returned to Japan is the same old one that continued to trouble me even while I was lost in music or intoxicated by the lips of a lover, or gazing at the Seine in the evening from the shelter of spring leaves. I confess it was my inability to solve this painful problem, and not any irrepressible longing for art, that enabled a weakling like me to bear the loneliness of remaining abroad for such a long time. In a foreign country, so long as one's health is unimpaired, one need have no fear of starving. One can abandon all concern for reputation and answer newspaper advertisements to become a waiter, a shop clerk—anything at all. Without the hypocritical label of "gentleman," one no longer feels the shameful need to deceive others. One gains opportunities

1. Tokyo Kangoku was established in 1903 to hold prisoners before trial but later became a prison for convicts. The socialists Kōtoku Shūsui and Kanno Sugako were executed there in 1911. This story dates from 1909.

to observe the hidden truths of society and to touch the genuine tears of life. Oh, but once one has returned to the land of one's birth—there is no place more constricting—one's surroundings no longer permit such freedom, and one can no longer simply transcend the demands of social position. Like a skiff on a fog-shrouded ocean, I had no clear way ahead of me, no plans for the future when I landed in the port of Kobe with its low shingled houses and its monstrously twisted black pines. Perhaps I could stay there in hiding, I thought, rather than return to Tokyo where so many people knew me. At that very moment, a heartfelt cry reached my ears, the deep, strong voice of someone ascending the crowded gangplank—

"Welcome back, brother!"

And who should appear before me dressed in a university student uniform but my very own younger brother? I had naturally lost touch with my father, especially during the past two or three years, but, greatly worried, he had contacted the steamship company, learned which vessel I had boarded, and sent my brother to meet the ship.

Shamed by the extent of my father's efforts, I felt an instinctive urge to hide my face. At the same time, I was sick of parental affection. Why did my parents not simply turn their backs on a son who had proved himself so unfilial? And why did that son feel so threatened by his sense of gratitude toward his parents? Why, when he tried to force himself not to feel such gratitude, did he succeed only in filling himself with pain and dread? No, nothing in this world is as oppressive and debilitating as blood ties. Any other relationship—be it with friend, lover, wife; be it obligatory or constraining or difficult—is something one has consciously entered into at some point. Only one's ties with parents and siblings are formed at birth and are unbreakable. And even if one succeeds in severing such relationships, all one is left with is the unbearable agony of conscience. It is simply one's destiny. Your Excellency, I am certain you have seen sparrows that have built nests in the eaves of your home. No sooner do the young fly away from the nest than they escape forever from this fateful shadow. Nor do their parents make any attempt to bind their offspring's hearts with morality.

One glance at my brother's face, born of the same blood and so much resembling my own, was all it took to fill me with an indescribably cruel emotion. In an instant it seemed to sweep away the inexpressible nostalgia I felt along with the sorrow, the joy, all the vivid sense of freedom of my wandering years, leaving nothing behind. Suddenly the air enveloping me seemed to grow still, as might be imagined in a medieval monastery, cold as ice and clear as a mirror.

"The six o'clock is an express train," my brother said. "Let's buy our tickets."

I said nothing in reply. At Kobe Station all I did was stare at a few unrefined but voluptuous American girls buying bouquets from a flower vendor. After arriving at Shinbashi Station the next morning, I found myself being whisked by rickshaw to my father's estate behind the Ichigaya prison.

They held a little banquet for me at home that evening. My father turns sixty this year. He probably felt he had to give the party to keep up appearances regarding his son and heir whatever the truth of the situation. They put me in the seat of honor before the tokonoma alcove where a calligraphic scroll hung inscribed with a long string of Chinese characters that meant nothing to me. Sitting at the other end of the table were my mother and father. To my right was the brother who had been chosen to carry on my mother's family as pastor of a small church. To my left was my parents' youngest child, the brother who had met my ship, sitting there in his impressive uniform, its gold buttons gleaming. There were flecks of gray in my father's moustache, but his tanned face was more radiant than ever, and the added years only seemed to increase the youthfulness of his robust frame. My mother, by contrast, looked as though she had aged ten or twenty years during my absence. Now she was just a shriveled-up little old lady I could hardly recognize.

I would want a wife or lover and, I dare say, my mother to remain eternally young and beautiful. When I saw her looking so aged, I could hardly lift my chopsticks to join in the feasting. Sorrow, pity and a mix of even stronger emotions struck me all at once: an intense desire to revolt against the fate that dooms us to perish.

Your Excellency, my mother was a young woman until I left for the West. People who didn't know us very well used to ask if she was my sister. She was born in old Edo and raised to be a great lover of the Kabuki theater, a skilled singer of Nagauta ballads while accompanying herself on the shamisen. She also played the koto. Approaching forty, she could still sing that wonderful passage from "Azuma Hakkei" with ease, the shamisen tuned up to the high *roppon* scale: "Pine needle pins in her hair, she makes her way along the dewy cobblestones beside the Sumida River, writing brush in its case wet with ink . . ." And yet she was very restrained in her tastes. As far back as her teen years she is said to have hated the color red, and I never saw an under-kimono of hers that could be described as gaudy, even when the family's clothing was spread out to dry at the height of summer: perhaps a muted persimmon-colored grid pattern, or a pale blue Yuzen print of plovers against white-capped waves. I'll never forget all the theaters she took me to in the arms of my wet nurse: the Hisamatsu-za, the Shintomi-za, the Chitose-za, where we indulged in a rare treat of broiled eel on rice in our box seat. And those marvelous winter days in the warmth of the *kotatsu,* where she would spread out her colorful woodblock prints of such legendary actors as Hikosa and Tanosuke and tell me all about the old days in the theater! Oh, the cruelty of time that destroys all things! If only I could stay forever and ever with my mother, Your Excellency, enjoying those magnificent pastimes! For her I would gladly ferry across the Sumida on the coldest winter day to buy her those *sakura-mochi* sweets from old Edo that she loved so much. But medicine? That is another matter. Not even on the warmest day would I want to go buy her medicine.

Never have I had it in me to surrender to those ancient articles of faith which mankind has been commanded to follow. Such precepts are too cruel, too cold. Rather than bow before them, how often have I cried out in anguish, wishing that "I" and "the precepts" could be united in a perfect, warm embrace? But having despaired of such an easy resolution, I determined that I would confront them head-on, that I would do battle with Heaven's retribution. My father is a stern disciplinarian, a diligent man, a fierce enemy of all that is evil. The day after I came home, he quietly asked me about my plans for the future. He wanted to know how I intended to preserve my honor as a man, to fulfill my duty as a citizen of the empire.

Should I become a language teacher? No, I could never presume to present myself as a teacher of French. Any Frenchman would know the language far better than I could ever hope to.

Should I become a newspaper reporter? No, I can imagine myself becoming a thief someday, but I am not so inured to vice that I would treat justice and morality as merchandise the way such people do. The scandal sheets *Yorozu chōhō* and *Niroku Shinpō* present themselves as paragons of virtue, but any society reformed by them would be far darker than a society left wholly unreformed. I worry too much about this to sink to their level.

Should I become a magazine reporter? No, I am not losing sleep over social progress or human happiness to the point where I would stand up as an advocate for good causes. Nor am I the least bit bothered, as some journalists seem to be, by the cannibalistic, incestuous lives of animals.

Should I become an artist? No, this is Japan, not the West. Far from demanding art, Japanese society looks upon it as a nuisance. The state has established a system of education by intimidation and forces us to produce grotesque vocalizations that no member of the Yamato race has ever pronounced—T, V, D, F—and if you can't say them you have no right to exist in Meiji society. They do this primarily so that someday we will invent a new torpedo or gun, certainly not to have us intone the poems of Verlaine or Mallarmé—and still less to have us sing the "Marseillaise" or the "Internationale," with their messages of revolution and pacifism. Those of us with a deep-seated desire to devote ourselves to the Muses or to Venus must leave this fatherland of ours with all its stringent rules before we can begin to embrace our harps. This would be of the greatest benefit both to the nation and to art itself.

No, no, there is not a single profession in this world that will keep me alive for the days that remain to me. Should I become a rickshaw puller wandering the streets of the city? No, I have too great a sense of responsibility for that. Could I safely fulfill the demands of the profession by delivering my passengers uninjured to their destinations? And what if I became a manservant cooking rice? Mixed in with the countless grains, might there not be an invisible chip of stone that would tear my master's stomach, endangering his life? The more precise and subtle a human being's awareness, the less he can presume to take on any profession, however humble. First he must starve, he must freeze, he must numb the precision of his mind, he must be blinded by his own selfish desires. At the very least, he must ignore the teachings of the ancient sages. Oh, you who sing of how hard it is to make a living! How I envy you!

I turned to my father and said, "There is nothing for me to do in this world. Please think of me as mad or crippled, and do not press me to live up to normal worldly expectations."

For his part, my father would have found it a stain on the family honor were his son to become known as a reporter or a clerk or a servant or some other lowly worker. "Fortunately we have a spare room," he said, "and food. You can just live here quietly and keep to yourself." With that, he brought the discussion to a close.

These past few months, I have spent one blank day after another gazing out at the garden.

The hot August sunlight casts the shadows of the luxuriant trees over the garden's broad expanse of green moss. Here and there patches of light break through the trees' black shadows, trembling with each passing breeze. I find the sight inexpressibly beautiful. A cicada cries. A crow caws. And yet the world, exhausted by the scorching heat, is as hushed as at night. A sudden shower strikes, but because the larger part of the sky remains blue and clear, I can see each thick thread of rain falling in the bright light. Each of the plants responds differently to the downpour, the delicate ones bowing to earth, the stronger ones springing upward, the sound of the raindrops striking them varying from light to heavy depending on the thickness of their leaves. The shower symphony rises to a great crescendo with the rumbling bass drum of thunder that rolls through, to be followed by the gentle moderato of the green frogs' flutes and a final hush as sudden as the piece's opening. Then the entire garden—from the tiniest tree branches soaring aloft to the leaf tips of the *kumazasa* bamboo creeping among the ornamental boulders—is strung with crystalline jewels that lend a startling radiance to the mossy carpet, across which the massed trees' long, diagonal, cloud-like shadows drift until the evening cicadas call and twilight arrives. Around the time a wind chime begins ringing incessantly and the servants light our paper lanterns, from the street beyond the front gate comes the light clip-clop of wooden clogs and the laughter of young women. A student ambles along, chanting a poem, a harmonica sounds, and somewhere far away the pop of what must be fireworks. A street musician passes by, lamenting another broken heart to the twang of a shamisen. The night deepens. . . .

The insect cries grow louder with each passing day. When I lie down to sleep at night, a terrifying din travels from the closed-off garden all the way to the space beneath the veranda outside my room. What power rules these tens of thousands of creatures, what do they feel that makes them all join their voices together at once to surround me like this? I feel as if I am camped alone on a magnificent plain beneath an endless sky, waiting an eternity for the dawn to break, but when I open my eyes the dim lamp on my desk reveals that I am actually lying beneath a low board ceiling that might come crashing down at any moment, my body confined by suffocating colorless walls and blank sliding paper doors. Then a keen sense of life in Japan overwhelms me—so limited, so lacking in depth. The sudden clatter of raindrops against the ceiling sounds like someone trying to play a broken koto. I hear the night wind tearing through the trees above. But the sound lacks the depth of a lion's roaring in a dark valley, and I wonder if what I hear is the rustling of reeds on the shoreline of a great river flowing through a tropical plain. The insects cry without cease. They cry even after the break of dawn and the arrival of noon. And that is not all I hear. The rains fall day after day.

What a humid climate we have! I try closing all the shoji and lighting the hibachi in the corner of the room, but my kimono is still so moist I can't help wondering if my skin will grow scales like some fishy creature's. The fine leather binding of *The Diary of Countess Krasinska,* given to me as a keepsake by Rosalyn when I left America, has been all but destroyed by mold. The lacquer shoes in which I danced with Yvonne in a Parisian ballroom have grown a ghostly white fur. Cruel stains have formed on the summer topcoat I spread on the grass while lying there with Hélène in the Bois de Boulogne.

I hear the sad calls of vendors wandering through the neighborhood and the clatter of shutters being closed nearby as night falls. Oh, the nights in Japan! No words can describe their darkness! Darker than death, darker than the grave, cold, lonely. Shall I call it a wall of darkness—an indestructible wall that cannot be pierced by any blade of rage or despair, that cannot be scorched by any flame of rancor or frenzy? I sit beneath the only spot of light in the whole room, a single oil lamp, reading and rereading the letters I exchanged with the people I knew in those days of joy, unable to read any letter to the end before having to press my face against its pages in tears. The cries of the insects fill the garden.

Eventually, however, it dawns on me that the intense cries of the insects have begun slowly to fade with the passing of each dark and lonely night. I find myself wearing a new padded haori over my lined kimono, the smell of the freshly dyed cloth oddly sickening to inhale. The rains have ceased. In contrast to the morning and evening chill, the sunny afternoons are frighteningly hot. The leaves have turned yellow, but how strange to watch them as they flutter down through the windless air onto the garden's mossy carpet in the harsh, summer-like sunlight. I feel the deep melancholy of the French poet who sang of the South American climate, "Here the leaves scatter in the April spring." I go out to the garden one afternoon, a partially read book of poems in hand, and walk among the beds. The streaming rays illuminate each overlapping leaf of the plums, the maples, the other trees that grow in such profusion, casting their shadows like patterns on the mossy ground. Deep in this shade stands a gazebo. Beyond it is an unobstructed view of a flowering field. I sit to take in the immense blue sky at a glance. Thin white clouds spread across the blue from west to east as if painted with a brush, never moving however long I gaze at them. Countless dragonflies flit back and forth like the swallows one sees high in the summer skies of France. Multicolored cosmos, taller than the gazebo, bloom in profusion across the field beneath the harsh sun, spreading to all corners of the field, each of which is densely covered in low-growing *kumazasa* bamboo. Crimson amaranths seem to burst into flame. The Chinese bellflowers and asters retain their brilliant purple, but the white-flowered bush clover are already past their peak and bow to the ground like the disheveled tresses of a woman who has thrown herself down in tears, flowing toward my feet upon the gazebo's paving stones. In their dewy shadows, one or two surviving insects cry out in thin melodic threads.

Ah, this blue sky, this sunlight: mementos of a forgotten summer. How could one imagine it to be October, to be autumn? The barest hint of a breeze turns the pages of the poetry book on my knees until I have a clear view of the final stanza of Baudelaire's sad "Song of Autumn":

Ah! laissez-moi, mon front posé sur vos genoux,
Goûter, en regrettant l'été blanc et torride,
De l'arrière saison le rayon jaune et doux!

"Ah! let me, with my head bowed on your knees,/Taste the sweet, yellow rays of the end of autumn,/While I mourn for the white, torrid summer!"[2]

No matter what I see, even the most beautiful flower, I wonder if it is blooming only to make us think of the sadness to come when it has withered and died. The delightful intoxication of love, I can only believe, exists to give us a taste of the sadness to come after parting. And surely the autumn sunlight shines this beautifully in order to tell us, "Know ye that the sadness of winter will be here tomorrow." Now and then I become strangely agitated and, wishing to see the fading sunlight for even a few seconds longer, I leave to walk not just in the garden but through the gate and into the immediate neighborhood. Ah, what scenes the autumn sun—the autumn sun of my birthplace—has shown me!

As I said at the beginning of this letter, my home is located behind the Ichigaya prison. When I began my travels nearly six years ago, this was a tranquil patch of countryside. "You know," I would tell the girls downtown, "it's that place where the azaleas bloom." Only then would it dawn on them which area I was talking about. Now, however, it is just another new neighborhood slapped together on the edge of Tokyo. All that is unchanged are the long prison embankment that looms over the narrow street and the life of the poor who toil here beneath it.

The first thing you see across from our front gate is the long, weather-beaten wooden fence enclosing the jailers' compound and then the horrible embankment itself, casting a shadow over the narrow street and topped by a spiky thornbush hedge, beneath which no weasel could hope to burrow. The flanks of the embankment are covered by a prickly growth of frightening devil's thistle, one touch of which would cause your hand to swell in pain. On stormy September days, I would expect the wind to blow over the shabby fence around the jailers' compound, and, sure enough, the next

2. William Aggeler, *The Flowers of Evil* (Fresno, CA: Academy Library Guild, 1954) online, http://fleursdumal.org/poem/208.

morning, when the street was littered with tree branches, I would see pairs of prisoners chained together at the waist in orange jackets with numbers on their collars and wearing woven-bamboo coolie hats, pulling up and repairing the fence under the supervision of uniformed, sword-bearing guards. Sometimes, too, at the height of summer, a gang of prisoners would mow the weeds on the embankment. Passersby would stop and stare at them in silence, eyes filled with simultaneous loathing and curiosity.

The embankment runs in a long, straight line from both left and right until it curves sharply inward at the center, where it ends in a large black gate between two thick columns. The gate's heavy-looking doors are always tightly shut. No voices can be heard from the other side of the gate, and there is nothing to be seen from the outside except a narrow chimney poking up above a low tile roof, and four or five skinny cedars. The trees stand some distance away from one another, which to my eyes suggests that even these unfeeling plants are being kept apart in the prison yard to prevent them from whispering evil schemes among themselves under cover of night.

Where the raised embankment suddenly gives out some distance from the gate, the narrow street becomes a downward-winding slope, on one side of which, during my absence, some rich gentleman seems to have built a new residence with high stone foundations, while on the other side the road is lined with the same kind of rental tenement houses that have been there forever like a row of boxes, one atop another, going down the hill. The prison embankment stands behind them like a blank wall, thanks to which no ray of sunlight has ever reached the tenements. Their foundations are rotting and overgrown with moss, and worms have eaten holes through the bottom edges of the storm shutters standing outside each unit's front lattice door during the day. Two or three of the units invariably have poorly written "For Rent" signs hanging on them. And always there are signs soliciting piecework. Often when passing these tenements on a cold winter evening, I have seen on a small window's torn, soot-smeared shoji the pale shadow cast by an oil lamp of a woman with tousled locks retying her obi. And on sultry summer evenings, peering through sparse reed blinds, I have had a clear view of the secrets of these people's households. How well I recall passing by here on afternoons when the prisoners' used bath water would gush down the sewage ditches below the tenements' windows, raising clouds of foul-smelling steam. It must be the same even now. Most shocking of all were the local housewives with scabrous babies on their backs, seizing the opportunity to make use of the hot water on cold, clear days, to wash things in the ditches as they chatter away with mouthfuls of crooked teeth, or in summertime scattering the stinking water on the road.

Shabby shops line both sides of the road at the bottom of the hill—a sweet shop, a hardware store, a tobacconist, a greengrocer's, a kindling seller's—among which a rice merchant and soy sauce dealer are the only good old-fashioned establishments with thick pillars that can arouse vague feelings of rebellion. Which is not to suggest a modern socialist reaction on my part, but merely a fantasy inspired by the traditional look of the houses and starring such popular stage heroes as Jiraiya or Nezumi Kozo. Oddly, there are two old stonemasons down here, and especially noticeable of late has been the increase in the number of home-delivery tempura shops and fishmongers, proof of the day-by-day increase in the number of tenements in the area. Atop a wooden counter disturbingly overgrown with green moss sits a shallow, round wooden sushi rice mixing bowl half filled with greasy water containing fish body parts, shaved fish meat, and rows of skewered shellfish that have been dried in the sun, almost all bearing price tags of ten sen or less. As far as I can see, the eyes of the dead fish are stagnant and cloudy, the scales on their bellies have faded to a pale bluish white, and the chilled sliced fish has lost so much of its freshness that the colors in each shop front are not only unpleasant but downright depressing. The sight of dripping blood used to terrify me whenever I passed a butcher shop in the West, but here, on the contrary, the thought that this faded, cold fish meat is the only source of nourishment for the blood of most of my countrymen fills me with an inexpressible sorrow. All the more so when I turn the corner at the bottom of the hill near sundown and hear the hoarse voice of the old man at a stand there displaying nothing but fish bones and guts with a scarf tied over the top of his head and yelling, "Get your *tai* guts cheap! Get your *tai* guts cheap!" He's surrounded by housewives with babies on their backs, the women all screaming at him to bring his prices even lower.

Above the sand-whitened tile roofs, the evening sky's great expanse glows less red than an unpleasant burnt sienna because autumn is nearing its end, casting shadows more intensely black than the dark of night. The narrow road is suddenly crowded with men most likely coming home from work—rather well-dressed gentlemen, military men on horseback, passengers in rickshaws. All move as black shadows without a single light to be seen in the houses on either side of the road. Running with dizzying speed among them are children at play, waving sticks and other toys. I have seen men in Western suits stop at the fish guts stand by the roadside on their way home from the office before climbing the hill toward the back of the prison, carrying their purchases wrapped in bamboo sheathing. The sight brings to mind scenes of dinner in poor Japanese households.

The lattice door of a tenement unit clatters but shows no sign of opening, nor does the patched gray shoji behind it catch any lamplight from within. The threshold remains in darkness. One Western-suited gentleman steps out of his never-polished rubber-soled shoes, opens the shoji and steps inside to find his disabled old mother coughing beneath the window of the tiny three-mat room. The baby is squealing. Shocked to realize that night has fallen, his wife crouches down like a frog on the kitchen floor, nervously trying to fill the lamp with oil. Alerted to her husband's homecoming by the sound of the opening door, she turns her colorless face toward him in the skylight's afterglow, loose hairs from her dry-looking bun floating off in all directions. Though not cold, she sniffles when she offers him a blank "Welcome home."

Instead of answering, the husband asks, "You're only getting to the lamp now?" and he scolds her for her poor housekeeping. His old mother crawls out of her bedding on the floor and tries to intervene. Whichever side she takes, the results are the same and the argument blossoms. Just then the eight-year-old comes in wailing about the fight that sent him flying into the drainage ditch, and he has the mud-smeared kimono to prove it. Now the argument centers on him until the evening dishes line up beneath the dusky lamp—boiled beans, pickled vegetables, a stew of fish bones and scallions, and a rice tub smeared with dirty fingerprints. Gathered around their flimsy table, the family talk about uncle so-and-so, who showed up this afternoon wanting to know the cost of Mother's medicine in the spring. They talk about how the wife's father lost his job. They talk about their everyday expenses. The family's mouths were formed for only two purposes: to eat food and to complain endlessly about the hardships of life. Whether they are impoverished or not, it amounts to the same thing. The pure art of conversation for its own sake is lost on people like this. They have no need of language for anything other than seeking advice, complaining, harping on the same old stories, and quarreling.

Such are the scenes that have greeted me when I have strolled out our front gate and up the road behind the prison in hopes of enjoying the autumn light. What grips my heart still more painfully are the tragic acts of animal cruelty I see on the road. Two or three freight wagons in a row drawn by emaciated horses over long distances, some loaded with bales of rice, others with lumber or bricks or other heavy payloads, will be led through the rear gate of the prison at the top of the slope. Unfortunately for the animals, the open area in front of the gate rises at the same angle as the road itself, which causes the wheels of the turning wagons to dig into the soft, damp soil, and this makes it impossible for the exhausted horses to drag the wagons up and through the gate in a single effort. When this happens, the rough teamsters scream at the horses and beat them mercilessly with fallen branches. The men yank violently on the reins, and the horses clamp their white teeth on the bits in what seems like unbearable pain. Their manes bristle, their bloodshot eyes bulge, and finally their forelegs collapse, bringing them down on the gravel surface. Everything on the narrow slope comes to a halt whenever this occurs, but far from being shocked, most passersby stare open-mouthed in amusement. Here, then, is proof that cruelty to animals is an issue only to a few Christians, not a pressing problem for the whole of Japanese society. Is this a matter for grief or celebration? Witnessing these scenes only deepens my sense that the Japanese are a warlike people who are sure to defeat the Russians once again in the future. Oh, patriots, set your minds at ease. As long as you can make a yellow man like me believe in the white man's Yellow Peril, you should feel free to go on cursing your wives, oppressing your children, and giving three cheers for the empire with glasses held high. And so we declare: the age is still too young for us to worry that melancholy poets will begin giving voice to their ideals.

Slowly, gradually, I have come to avoid and even fear the prospect of venturing beyond the front gate. Yes, let me gaze in quiet solitude at the shifting autumn sunlight through the glass doors of my veranda.

Sadly, autumn is already beginning to fade. The intense sunlight that made the afternoons seem like summer has weakened now, and the sky is always thickly overcast. It looks like the frosted glass skylight of a large atelier, across which cloud curtains move, sending down pale refracted rays as soft as twilight. Shadows and colors seen in this light seem to have a transparent clarity that cannot be sensed in the blinding glare of the sun. The trees have lost their leaves, their crowns bare and bright, their slender black branches tracing innumerable upward-thrusting lines against the sky. Behind them, the gazebo's thatched roof and the field's withered grasses glow yellow through the black evergreens in the distance. Half-hidden by the ornamental stones beyond the veranda, tiny golden chrysanthemums bloom like stars. From there to the far end of the garden spreads an unbroken velvet carpet of moss even more lustrous than in summer. Two or three wagtails, pecking at the tiny moss flowers, move across the carpet, flicking their long, pointed tails up and down. How sharply their gray feathers and the fall colors of the dwarf sumac bonsai atop a boulder contrast with the moss's broad green luster!

No wind blows. The shifting, cloudy autumn afternoon maintains its thick silence, giving the illusion that the outlines of objects have been obliterated, leaving only their colors. On occasion, a few remaining leaves will suddenly flutter down from a tree. This unexpected stirring of the air is like the deep sigh of some mysterious creature. When that happens, every single leaf in the garden—from the evergreens' lush needles to the clumps of chrysanthemums among the stones—resounds with an inexpressible sorrow and then, a moment later, reverts to silence. Atop the smooth moss: the wagtails again, the chrysanthemum blossoms, the bonsai's fall colors. Ah, the light of a dream, the thin overcast of departing autumn.

Excellency! Since yesterday I have been reading Verlaine's prison verse, *Sagesse*:

O my God, you have wounded me with love.
The wound remains open, unhealed.
O my God, you have wounded me with love. . . .[3]

Excellency! Please come visit me once before the onset of winter. I am lonely.

3. Translated from Kafū's Japanese. The original: Ô mon Dieu, vous m'avez blessé d'amour / Et la blessure est encore vibrante, / Ô mon Dieu, vous m'avez blessé d'amour. *Sagesse* (1881) II.i. First three lines of a 46-line poem.

translated by Hitomi Yoshio

WAR BRIDE

MIEKO
KAWAKAMI

The girl was out for a walk one day when War Bride suddenly appeared out of nowhere. As usual War Bride was simply words, impossible to touch or bite into. Capturing them, the girl tried out the sounds on her lips: *War Bride*. *How nice it feels*, she thought. *Like a beam of light in this dreadful rainstorm*.

Well, I might as well turn myself into War Bride as long as the words stick around, she thought, excited by words once again. Expressions often came to her like this—they would find a void and fill it obligingly. Or should we say expression would take possession? The ceremony of naming occurred in silence. *War Bride*. The meaning remained cloaked. *But that's okay*, the girl thought. *Things that have no meaning are bound to be less damaging than things that do*. To tell the truth, the girl was afraid of hurting others, terrified really. For her, pain was never an isolated occurrence. She knew what real pain felt like after a meticulous inspection of the seams holding her together. *When you're hurt, you're hurt forever*, she discovered one day when she was poking around somewhere near her core. A single experience of pain sets off an endless process—you relive the pain every moment of your life. Though the mind may rationalize it as a thing of the past, sorrow returns again and again, grabbing hold of that distant memory. The silhouette springs back to life. That's how memory works, how it lingers. You can't remember what never happened—therefore it did. It was for this reason that the girl had renounced speech. She was afraid of setting words free. No matter what shape they took, they could always become entangled with someone's eternity. She couldn't stand the thought that her words might slip into another's existence and remain there. For all eternity.

War Bride. This was recorded in the girl's cloth-covered notebook, which was nearly blank except for a few scattered words. Five, to be exact. The girl didn't know what they meant. They weren't there to compete with one another in celebration, nor to be toyed with in spring—they were simply words that left a minty taste on the lips when read aloud. Her favorite of late was *Led Zeppelin*. Moist or dry, those two words caused the skin of her lips to slightly unravel with the friction, and the tongue—the pink that enveloped the insides—would accommodate itself as if blooming. *Led Zeppelin*. In company, she would content herself by silently maneuvering her mouth and flexing her tongue. On her own, she would enlist her vocal chords. It was the sound of "ze" that fascinated her. Also, *Firenze*. So compact and just right. *Auschwitz*. And *license*—let's not forget *license*. And *Birkin*. The way the "Bir" and "k" clang together really tickled her. The more you repeated them, the more the sounds seemed to support each other.

And so it became nearly impossible for War Bride to speak, which was why her days passed more or less as follows:

Stretched out at the massage parlor with her mother, War Bride wished the massage therapist would work a little deeper into the joints. She would have made that request without bothering to open her eyes just two years before, but now it seemed impossible, now that she realized in a flash the effect the blunt words might have on him. For who knows? He might have injured one of his fingers. Various reasons—pride, discretion, clinic regulations—would normally have kept him away, but today he desperately needed the money, not for himself but for someone dear to him. So he took himself to work, knowing that the wounded finger would hinder him from performing his usual best. *And if I were to expose the secret he had so carefully concealed to earn a day's wages, what then?* The wound might open like an eye, gushing blood. Even worse, the single moment of criticism, revelation and exposure with all the concomitant adjectives arising therefrom might set off an endless cycle of repetition. No, she could never inflict that upon him. Thus War Bride grew more and more silent, regardless of what happened to her, whom she met, what beautiful things she came across. Instead, like all the other girls who shared her temperament, her eyes would expand and expand, and if they exploded it would still be better than the cruel alternative. It was no surprise that War Bride acquired more than sixty different methods of greeting and bowing.

War Bride perfected the art of silence—at school, at pedestrian crossings, aboard all types of vehicles moving at any given angle. She always managed to slip on by, dodging confrontation with anyone's eternity, and every time she noted her success her cheeks would grow a little bit rosier. She obediently followed the cyclical passage of time—from Monday to Tuesday, then Thursday, then Sunday, then September, December, through summer solstice and the first snowfall of the season, at nine o'clock in the evening, no one noticing her eyes growing larger and larger, not her classmates, not even her own mother. Pressing her palms to her eyes at times, War Bride began maneuvering her legs and sauntering off to various places. One fateful day, on the way home from one of her outings, she walked into a bookstore and a book caught her eye—one that chronicled the life of a housewife who had abandoned all but feeling. War Bride was dumbstruck by the strange coincidence. *What could this mean, what could all this mean? Could this book be about me?* On the verge of tears she turned the pages with shaking hands, wondering whether the housewife ever reached that vast shadowy region. For the next twenty years, War Bride continued to read the chronicle. She went on leaving speech behind, overcoming it, trimming it. And just like the housewife, War Bride succeeded, after a long and hard struggle, in tearing herself away from speech and the meanings that inevitably accompanied it. Even so, her pale eyes, still brittle in some places, would pulsate violently every time her heart swelled, its volume growing oh so huge. Yet, despite it all, she felt warm inside. That tiny stone of hope—her long-held wish that she might never have to interact with anyone's eternity except her own—was at last in her possession, and she polished and refined it in a way only she understood.

War Bride continued to live like any other form of life, pressing on, tossing and turning, not just her eyes but her whole body expanding and contracting according to the rhythms of the world. Thus she became an adult in no time. She soon forgot all about her old notebook containing words for her lips, the way they would flutter. She married a salesman, an expert in carpets from around the world, gave birth to a child, and even when that child became ill and died, still did not utter a word. Speech had left her completely. On that fateful stormy day long ago she had spotted a void and wedged herself in, emerging as War Bride. Never again was she erased. Never again did she become a void. War Bride remained War Bride through the years, amid the shapes of days woven one after another. But if she never uttered a word, how do we know that she was indeed War Bride? Where within this vast world was that fact established? War Bride, however, no longer worried about such things. As she looked around, she never caught a glimpse of anyone's eternity, and though not completely satisfied, she felt content, as if she were protecting something worthwhile.

War Bride continued on. After her husband died she lived with a dog she picked up in a place covered with sand, and though she had lost much of her vision due to all the things her eyes had absorbed over time, she found teary comfort in the way the warmth of the animal's body somehow reminded her of her own past. Her dream, the last she ever had, took place inside her crumbling ribs. There, her eyes were freshly born, black and moist, amid an unbelievably immense blue sky that expanded with tremendous speed. The blue expanse was more magnificent than anything her eyes had seen, bigger than the sum of everything she had ever known. Without a cloud to obscure it, the blue washed over her eyes to coat her entire body. A robust brown earth stretched its limbs as far as one could imagine, devouring the sky from below—nothing there except for the beautiful single line where the earth and sky came together, reverberating and resounding, and there War Bride stood in the midst of the enormity, underneath and within, simultaneously. She stood on her feet, as though going for a walk with her dog. From out of nowhere, the sun flooded the world with light, piercing her eyes, and the sky and the earth surrendered themselves to the radiance as everything glimmered. War Bride stood there transfixed. After a while, she slowly looked around. She noticed something burning in the distance. As she approached, she realized she was wearing a magnificent pair of leather shoes. What was burning, what was changing shape, was a house. A tiny house, though because of the flames she couldn't see the house itself. She was enthralled by the oranges and reds, the vigor of the horrific flames that shot out and whirled and churned. The fire raged with more force than anything she had ever beheld, making her wonder whether she had ever before truly seen fire. The house burned in silence. Before her eyes, against the all too vivid blue sky and the stupendous earth, the house kept burning, but without a sound—for this world had been utterly silent from the beginning. No word, no sound, the world shone and burned as War Bride watched. Even without sound, however, she could feel the wind blowing, and though the flames made everything look bright, the wind was as cold as melted ice, so cold that all she could do was to place her wrinkled hands over her ribs. Her eyes swallowed the fire, the sky, the earth, and they grew even colder. Never again, for all eternity, would War Bride move another inch.

translated by Ted Goossen

THE FORBIDDEN DIARY

SACHIKO KISHIMOTO

PART 11
NOVEMBER–OCTOBER
DOG WHISTLE

NOVEMBER 11

Heard the municipal swimming pool has started offering jello, so I decide to go take a look. I ask Y if she wants to come, and she answers, "Yes, yes," without hesitation. Yumi and I have bonded over our great love of gelatinous things—jello, Bavarian cream, jellied broth, fiddlehead cake and so on—and we rattle on endlessly about them.

When we get there, we throw on our swimming suits and hightail it to the fifty-meter main pool. A menu is stuck on the wall:

Today's Jello:
Strawberry
Lemon
Cranberry

It's still early: the pool has just opened, and there are only a handful of swimmers. The whole fifty-meter length is filled to the brim with bright red jello. We do a full set of limbering-up exercises at the side of the pool, mount the starting blocks, focus our breathing, and then jackknife into the shimmering expanse. *Thwup*: coolness envelops my body, and everything turns red. When I surface, I open my mouth, and strawberry jello floods in. The flavor takes me back to my childhood—House Brand Ace Jello. Perfect!

I gain my feet to find my bearings, then bend my knees until my eyes are just above the surface. Stretching before them is a boundless plain of red jello. This is a

Readers: We started this series in the first issue, but you can pick it up anywhere. Parts 11–15, published here, complete *The Forbidden Diary*. The long italicized passages are inspired by Stacey Levine's collection *My Horse and Other Stories*.

childhood dream of mine, and now it has come true! I part my lips and strain the jello between my front teeth. An old habit. Strange to say, this heightens the experience even more: the flavor improves by at least thirty percent. I could suck and suck forever and never run out. It really is like a dream!

"Check out the bottom!" Yumi cries, struggling to part the red mass with her hands as she pushes toward me. The jello offers more resistance than regular water, so the going is a lot harder. "It's incredible!"

I follow her suggestion and slip below the surface. What I see takes my breath away: the jello is arranged in three tiers—red, yellow and a deep crimson. That's what the menu on the wall had meant. I squat further until my eyes are aligned with where the strawberry and lemon meet. The top half of my goggles are dyed red, the lower half yellow. I'm so happy my feet are tingling. I suck more jello through my front teeth—this time it tastes like lemon. I come up for a breather, then descend almost to the bottom of the pool, where the cranberry layer sits. Here the red is darker, like blood. It even tastes a bit like blood. I go up and down a few times in this fashion, sampling the flavors in order. Next, I pinpoint the spots where the flavors come together, swirl the jello about with my hands, and sample the result. A mixture of strawberry and lemon taste something like kiwi; while lemon and cranberry produce a more melon-like flavor.

It's a pool after all, so we figure we should do some actual swimming, but our arms grow tired after only fifteen or twenty feet.

The sweetness of all that jello lingers in our mouths, so on the way home Yumi and I stop to eat some jellied agar before we split up.

NOVEMBER 10

Again, the heat and humidity are way above normal. Mt. Fuji is Doraemon blue, with wisps of smoke rising from its crown.

When I break from my work, I sniff my upper arm and knee. A whiff of strawberry.

Slight progress on the translation.

NOVEMBER 8

Sunny skies. When the thermometer hits 100, I discover, even cicadas shut up.

I watch *Tetsuko's Room* on TV. Today's guest is "a vague uneasiness." It looks like they're running out of people after nearly eighty years on the air, so they've started inviting abstract concepts like this one.

"A vague uneasiness" turns out to be a real big shot. He hung out with writers like

Chūya Nakahara and Ryūnosuke Akutagawa in the old days, yet his manner—his aura, if you will—is moderate and reserved, on a different level altogether than your run-of-the-mill uneasiness. Tetsuko is as blunt as ever. I thought you'd be scary, she says, but you seem like a regular guy. Yet you've killed quite a few people, right? How old are you? Are you married? The flood of questions doesn't seem to faze him, though. He remains genial throughout, even venturing an impersonation of Chūya for the viewers. The epitome of worldly wisdom. Aren't you busy these days, Tetsuko asks, things being the way they are? No, he answers wistfully, the world has grown more shallow, so fewer and fewer people know what true uneasiness is.

Tomorrow's guest: "the unbearable agony."

NOVEMBER 6

I have to mail a letter, so I take the long way back from the postbox to pass by that apartment building.

The demolition is already underway. The front half of the building has been sliced off as if by an enormous knife, exposing a cross-section of the inside to public view. Even as I watch, the machine's giant arm rakes another layer off with an enormous clatter. I look up at what remains of the row of five apartments on the second floor. The middle one—the apartment that most concerns me—has already lost its wood-floored kitchen, and the six-mat tatami room that used to contain the desk and tea table is in the process of being demolished. I am startled for a moment before I realize that the room is empty of furniture or anything else. The door of the bathroom is torn off, and the porcelain squat toilet shines white in the sunlight. Then the huge claw descends on what remains of the room, stripping it from the building like a poster from a wall. As the debris tumbles down, I strain my eyes, looking for a corpse, but it all happens so fast I can't be sure.

I walk home past the wall of the elementary school. There is no sign of where the horse had appeared—I run my fingers along the seam between the concrete blocks but can't locate the slightest crack.

Translation stalled.

NOVEMBER 3

Tried to air out my bedding, but the sandals on my balcony would have scorched my feet, so I gave up. My futon haven't been aired in quite a while—it's just too hot. Maybe that's why I've been hearing those whispering voices when I go to sleep. Something is being born in there. On top of that, the voices seem to be increasing with each passing day. I better air my futon out soon or there'll be a whole kingdom living in my bedding!

NOVEMBER 1

Dog whistles are on sale in a store outside the station so I snap one up. I don't have a dog myself, but I'm dying to find out if it's true that only dogs can hear them, and how they respond. I blow the whistle to test it. Nothing comes out. All I can hear is a faint rush of air forcing its way through the hole.

OCTOBER 30

It shakes me up each time a file titled <diary.txt> appears on my desktop while I'm working on my computer. It's not my diary, so how the hell did it get in there? It's too creepy. I want to dump the whole thing in the trash, but some part of me must feel otherwise, for I always end up clicking on it.

> 5/22 (TUESDAY)
>
> I feel so much better this week! Finally, finally, the morning sickness is passing. Hooray! It was really terrible. Once the pregnancy has stabilized, I'll start going out a whole lot more, meeting people, eating good food, going to movies. I'll return to my old part-time job and resume my studies. For dinner, stir-fried vegetables, small mushrooms with grated daikon and miso soup. I order a book on Amazon.
>
> 5/24 (THURSDAY)
>
> Phone consultation with Dr. T. We talk about what I should do after the baby is born. His encouragement gives me heart: translation may not pay a whole lot, but it's a real career that I can pursue over the long term while looking after a child, so I should keep studying and not give up. I know he's right—it's important to stick things out. Beef stew and broccoli salad for dinner.
>
> 5/25 (FRIDAY)
>
> The book I ordered arrives. A bit premature, I know—a book of baby names. Actually, I've already decided on the name. Takashi if it's a boy, Takako for a girl. So "Taka" is there in either case. But what combination of kanji should I choose? There are so many possibilities. I need to consider how the kanji look, and the number of strokes required to write them. No rush, though—I'm going to take my time on this one.

OCTOBER 29

The evening news reports that a huge black hole has suddenly materialized at the scramble crosswalk in front of Shibuya Station. It swallowed a few cars and then disappeared (apparently it can move around). They filmed the spot where it happened, but all you could see was police cars and curious onlookers—no hole anywhere. When the camera panned left to the crowd gathered around the monument to the faithful dog Hachiko, for a split-second I thought I glimpsed a small liver-colored horse. I rubbed my eyes and it was gone.

I am drifting off to sleep when I hear a voice say, "Everyone get ready—we're about to head out!" I leap from my bed, grab my bedding, and lug it out to the garbage area. Spend the rest of the night wrapped in a bath towel.

OCTOBER 22

Overcast. Cicadas.

I take the dog whistle to Kinuta Park in the evening, choosing the most popular time so lots of people will be out walking their dogs. I park myself on a bench and, when a golden retriever passes by, secretly blow the whistle. The dog ignores me. I try the same thing with a part-Akita mongrel and two miniature collies, but they ignore me as well. Is the whistle broken? I try it again with a dachshund. This time the dog pays no heed but the young woman walking it spins around in alarm.

I move to the dog run. There are at least twenty dogs in all, but not one reacts when I blow the whistle. Two of their owners, however, stop and look about.

When I get home, I pull the box the whistle came in out of the trash and examine it more closely. Sure enough, it reads "human whistle," not "dog whistle." What a rip-off! I find a more detailed description in very small print on the side of the box. "This whistle emits a frequency only specific humans can hear," it reads. "A yellow whistle is audible to the very depressed, red to menstruating women, brown to those in love, black to those not of this world." My whistle is black.

OCTOBER 18

I feel like I've lost the ability to skip, but when I try I find I can still do it. So I decide to check all the other skills I seldom use. Paper-scissors-stone. Wall shadows (dog, dove, swan). Tongue twisters *(chachatsubo-chatsubo).* Arcane hand gestures. Pretzel-like poses. Radio calisthenics for beginners. Singing the national anthem. Shuffling a deck of cards. Spinning a pen between my fingers. I could never do the pen-spinning thing anyway.

OCTOBER 16

Another scorcher. No more futon that need airing, though.

In the evening, I take the train to Shinjuku for the first time in ages. I carry out my usual carpet-bombing raid on Isetan, Mitsukoshi, Barney's and Lumine 1 and 2, scoring hits on lotion, pillowcases, hair clips, socks, Thai curry sauce and a toothbrush stand. I sniff perfumes until my nose shuts down, continue on sheer momentum to raid Takashimaya, and then, completely beat (as one might expect), proceed to the Kinokuniya bookstore. I comb through shelves of new books, comics and translations and end up carrying three volumes to the cash register, where my eye falls upon a poster announcing a book signing at 6:30 on the third floor. The occasion is the launch of a new translation, and the name on the poster is mine. My heart stops. Could this have been on my schedule? Possibly, yes. I glance at my watch—it's almost seven o'clock. I run to the escalator and make my way to the third floor, where a crowd is already lining up in front of the event space. "Excuse me, excuse me," I say smiling apologetically as I push through, but when I get to the front a thin, sallow-faced woman I've never seen before is sitting at a table signing my name. Someone taps me on the shoulder, and I turn to see that it's my editor, H. "I'm sorry, but you have to line up," she says. *It's me,* I want to tell her. *How can you forget? We've been working together for ten years!* But nothing comes out. Her expression is blank. "Sorry," is all I can manage. I leave the event space and head back down to the first floor.

All I can remember after that is leaving the bookstore and heading toward Yoyogi. When I regain my senses, I find myself walking along a narrow path squeezed between a train embankment on the right and a row of dark buildings on the left. Although there are streetlights at regular intervals along one side, the ground is so dark I can't see my own feet. I consider turning around, but just then I notice a tunnel dug into the side of the embankment, not far off the ground. I peer inside and, sure enough, there is the very thing I expected to see. The dim glow of a single yellow light halfway down the unlit tunnel, and beneath that a heavy-looking weathered wooden door.

No sooner have I seated myself at the counter than a cool damp cloth is placed beside me. Mahler is playing quietly in the background. A cocktail glass materializes and a light green grasshopper is poured into it, though I haven't heard a drink being shaken. The emblem 1/1 is on the coaster. When I look up, I see the owner gently smiling down at me. His shirt is so white it glows.

I realize that someone has been sitting next to me for a while. Someone much younger in an emerald green dress. She has hardly changed since high school.

"I've been looking a long time for you," I say. O smiles, without saying anything. There are so many things I want to ask. *Where did you disappear to? Did you hear the same voice I heard every so often? What about that door in the back of the toilet in the old school building—can't you tell me anything about it? Are you really of this world?* But I can't speak. Mahler is growing louder and louder.

"Surely you know," O says, the smile never leaving her lips. "Know what?" I say, although I am suddenly struck by the feeling that I do indeed know what's going on.

"Nothing's changed. We all started in one place and then went as brides to someplace else."

I have heard these exact words before, but where and when? I look down at the emblem on the coaster in front of me.

"Let's go—to that place," O says, taking my hand. She leads me to the heavy wooden door, opens it and strides out, pulling me after her. We move quickly down the dark tunnel. It should be a very short tunnel, but we go on and on with no exit in sight. I look over my shoulder, but there's no light behind us either. The air is unpleasantly warm and humid. Before I know it, O has run on ahead. I hurry after her, trying frantically not to lose sight of that emerald green, dimly visible—where is the light coming from?—in the pitch black tunnel. The path rises and falls, steadily narrowing until, in the end, I have to lie on my stomach to move forward. Up ahead I can see O opening a trap door in the roof of the tunnel and clambering out. I follow her. I grab the trap door's frame and pull myself up and through, but there is a flight of descending steps on the other side and I lose my footing, falling down hard onto what seems to be the floor of a small, empty room. Moonlight is pouring through the curtain-less window. I look up and realize that what I had thought was a staircase is actually an upright piano. I have just exited from the piano's open lid. Looking inside, I see nothing like a tunnel, just a piano's intricate internal mechanism. Suddenly, I know where I am. It's the old P Academy's piano room. A tiny room, a glitch in the architectural plan, located at the end of the hall on the fourth floor of the main building. We called it "Anne's Hiding Place," after Anne Frank. All at once, I hear footsteps. I must follow them. When I step out into the hallway, our school's characteristic smell hits me, a funky combination of ink, old shoes, deodorant and blood. I walk past the music room, slip by the bulletin board and its yellowing announcements, and pass the ammonite fossils that decorate the front of the science room. I run on: through the open doors I see the classrooms in the moonlight, rows of empty chairs shining white, blackboards inscribed with elongated parallelograms of light. I follow the footsteps to the rear of the main building, through a connecting corridor strewn with discarded school pins, and into the building that houses the main auditorium. I pant and puff up the chilly stone steps of the gray spiral staircase. No sooner have I reached the top than there is a flash of emerald green at the far end of the corridor, but it just as quickly disappears. I follow it to the toilet directly above the stage. The moonlight pouring through the toilet's glass wall is so bright the white floor tiles appear to be bubbling. Could the words scrawled on the door of the electric panel still be there, I wonder. No way! I mean, the school buildings I'm walking through were demolished and replaced with new ones years ago. A steel door creaks, and I step into the innermost room. O is already on the other side of the swinging door. She looks back and smiles, as if telling me to hurry. But my feet are rooted to the floor. *Don't leave me*, I try to say, but the only sound is the air escaping from my throat. O's green dress melts into the darkness and the door slowly swings shut. Now I can see what someone scrawled on its front.

"Get through here to the other side!"

PART 12
OCTOBER–SEPTEMBER
COCOON

OCTOBER 10

The author of a novel I translated a while back is visiting Japan, so I head off to interview her. Our conversation will be recorded at my publisher's offices and then issued with our photos, so I doll myself up a bit first.

The building is big and quite old, located at the end of the street that winds up the slope from the subway station. I have been there before, but this time the building is entirely covered with something resembling a loosely woven bamboo basket, so that it looks like a natural sponge lying on its side.

I walk to where the front entrance should be. This is the exact center of the sponge, and the only place where the basket protrudes, facing the street with a human-sized opening that recalls the pursed mouth of a comic Hyottoko mask.

Is this where I'm supposed to go in, I wonder, whereupon a voice calls, "Hey, over here, over here!" The head of my editor, Mr. So-and-so, is sticking out of the window. "Use the side entrance," he shouts, pointing with his hand.

"What the heck is going on?" I shout back.

"It's publicity for a new art book we're putting out," he answers. "The building was like this when we showed up this morning. There seems to be a small problem with the front entrance, so please use the one on the side."

I don't see any particular problem. In fact, the more I look at the hole the more I want to enter it. I ignore the shouts from above and stride in.

The tunnel is a lot longer than I think, and the pointy ends of the split bamboo prick my face and body. To make matters worse, the roof gets lower and lower, so that by the end I'm crawling on my stomach. When I finally emerge on the other side I am in the same front lobby as always. So this is the "small problem" he was talking about, I think. Just then there is a rustle behind me and another person emerges from the tunnel. It's me. Same face, same clothes, and a look of disbelief on her—I mean my—face. I bet I have the same expression right now. Editor So-and-so comes bustling into the lobby, but when he sees the two of us he clutches his head in dismay.

"My God, I told you!" he moans.

There is the sound of hurried footsteps, and a second Editor So-and-so trots in behind him. "You should have listened to me!" he moans, head in hands.

"Oh well," the two editors sigh in unison. "What can you do." They guide us toward the meeting room where guests are entertained. I glance back and see two look-alike receptionists seated at the front desk.

More than a dozen identical white women are seated in the meeting room, all dressed in green and jabbering away as they drink their coffee. With the addition of the four of us, and the two photographers (identical too, as you might expect), the room is crammed to the rafters.

"They thought it was so cool," the two editors reply when I ask what happened, "they went back and forth a few times. Four times to be precise, so there's sixteen of them." Once again, the two sigh in unison.

But where do we go from here? It's the right novelist, no question there, but with this many which one should I interview? Who is the original? And which of the two me's should interview her? Which is the true me anyway? I am still deliberating these problems when one of the women pulls out something like a long, thick semi-transparent straw, sticks one end in my mouth, and then puts the other end in hers. What? What? I'm taken aback, but then she shoots a load of saliva down to my end. It's clear and a little sticky, tasteless and odorless; yet it carries her thoughts, feelings and moods or whatever in the most direct way possible, and I think, wow, how convenient can you get as the saliva flows and flows without end, filling me, so that finally saliva is pouring from my eyes, my nose, my ears, even my fingertips.

When I wake it is already evening. Was it a dream or did it actually happen? These days, my dreams are so strangely real I have a hard time drawing the line. I search my bag and find a taxi receipt, but have no memory of getting in or out of a taxi.

OCTOBER 9

Have been feeling totally wiped since I got up, but there's no food in the house, so I crawl to the bus and ride downtown to the supermarket.

Whenever I have one of my real-seeming dreams, the little brother growing on my hip (now actually beside my belly button) invariably acts up the next day. He is ravenously hungry which drives him nuts, so I have to feed him whatever I can lay my hands on. Perhaps I'm imagining things, but he seems to be growing bigger. I, on the other hand, have lost so much weight my ribs are showing, though I eat twice as much as I used to. I sleep more too, yet I'm always dead tired.

"Don't sweat it, sis," he laughs, stuffing more food into his mouth. "If worse comes to worst, I'll look after you." This pisses me off so much I slug him, but it hurts me more than it does him.

OCTOBER 6

It's 104 degrees. Spells of blistering heat and thunderstorms in quick succession. We had three rainbows today. I grind away at my translation.

I have been questioning my work ever since the book-signing fiasco. Exactly what am I translating? Who commissioned me? Why do I continue? I'm completely in the dark. Still I soldier on, simply because there *is* a text sitting in front of me, and because as long as I'm translating something I feel my life has some sort of meaning . . . Is that really it?

OCTOBER 4

She discovered a growth. On her body. It was speckled, and growing from a spot near her shoulder. She hated it—it was so big it pushed her clothing out, and on top of that it was damned heavy. She discovered it one morning, or was it evening, already fully developed; it was hot to the touch, and shaped like a bowl, an upside-down bowl whose corner had broken off so that oatmeal was spilling out. She cried her eyes out. The hump-like growth extended from her shoulder down her back, even reaching her arm.

Since it was on her shoulder, the skin on her back and breast was pulled tight as a drum. Nevertheless, the hump shook slightly when she moved around. Maybe it was filled with water. Even if she asked someone to check it, though—a doctor, for instance—she doubted they could tell her what was in there.

OCTOBER 1

A rare phone conversation with Okubo-san. We talk about the fixation some people have with trains: there are Riders who ride every train they can, for example, and Camera Bugs, who snap photos of trains. But what is the ultimate obsession, the one that trumps all other obsessions? The Jumpers, of course. They're the ones who dream of dying a glorious, joyous death beneath the wheels of their favorite train. It goes without saying that you can only realize this sort of dream once, so those in the grip of this mania pour their energies into simulating the event, studying the best railroad lines, the best train models, the best places to achieve the most beautiful deaths, and then meet as a group every so often to ramble on and on about their research results. They've already saved up money to compensate for the damages their death would cause.

Okubo-san has a train fixation too, but he's a Shaker, someone obsessed with learning the jerks and jolts of certain trains, although he apparently limits his scope to the Tokyo subway. "I'm a long way from mastering this thing," he says modestly.

SEPTEMBER 30

A cloudless day. Savage heat. Mt. Fuji like an upside-down plastic cone of molded custard.

The old series *Orphan Bee* is on TV. At first, I have only warm memories of the show, but then the fact that I used to see these cartoon creatures as bees starts to bother me. There is nothing bee-like about their shape. Their color is completely wrong, and their faces look human. The dark circles under their eyes are anything but cute. If I ever saw a bee buzzing around that looked like that I'd scream. And what about their size? Good heavens, they could be as big as we are! The more I think about these things the more scared I get. I run and switch off the TV.

SEPTEMBER 27

It's 2 am and I'm hard at work when I have a sudden craving for soda water. All that's in the fridge is a jug of cold barley tea, so I grab my purse and head out the door. I'm nearing the main drag and its vending machines when I see a glow of light down the block and hear the sound of music. It seems to be coming from the vicinity of the kindergarten, so I go to take a look. People are milling around the playground, which is filled with lanterns and lamps. In front of the entrance stands a sign written in fluorescent colors on a black background: "Midnight Kindergarten School Bazaar." Lured by the smoky aroma, I stumble inside. Lemon soda is being sold just inside the gate, so I buy a bottle and sip it as I walk around. Numerous stalls have been set out, and men wearing aprons over their pajamas, probably the children's fathers, are flipping octopus dumplings, hawking chilled malt syrup, and exhorting people to try their luck on the pop-gun range. Since I'm a bit peckish, I pick up a small portion of fried noodles for myself, and an order of grilled octopus dumplings for the little brother on my hip. Scattered in my noodles are alluring, light-green bits of something—my guess is luminous mushrooms.

People have formed a circle around the slide, which has been turned into a makeshift scaffold for the event, dancing Bon Odori. Adults and children in pajamas—as well as raccoons, tigers, cats and other animals, not to mention some tiny red people I've never seen before—are all dancing together, waving their hands (or paws) in the air. It's obvious how much fun they're having. They're singing along with music that is emanating from I don't know where. The lyrics go:

Good children know the beauty of the night
Hōi, Hōi!
The smell of the air, the feel of the wind
The sound of mushrooms releasing their spores
Good evening teacher, good evening classmates
We raise our joyous voices to the night.
Hōi, Hōi!

The bazaar sale items are lined up in a tent in the middle of the playground. Morel hats. Edible pillows. Firefly reading lamps. Ectoplasm cookies. Cat's eye brooches. Flutes to call nocturnal snakes. Tapes to videotape dreams.

I notice a pile of white fluffy sacks roughly the size of an adult stacked on the ground. What are those? I ask. Cocoons for the staff, I am told. From the principal on down, everyone working at the school suffers from insomnia, so they spin cocoons to sleep in and discard them every morning, when they hatch to go to work. The cocoons are marvelously light and absorbent, I am told, cool in the summer and warm in the winter. Since I am futon-less at present, I happily buy one to take home. Only ¥360, including tax.

I curl up in my new cocoon as soon as I get back. It's as good as advertised, soft on the skin yet well ventilated. They included a free firefly with my purchase, so I let it loose in the cocoon, climb in, and sail right off to dreamland.

SEPTEMBER 25

From <diary.txt>:

8/15 (MONDAY)

Had my medical exam today. Everything is on schedule, thank goodness. When they told me earlier the baby was in the breech position, everything went black—I couldn't sleep after that. But the doctor taught me some special exercises (I have to hold these really weird positions for a full ten minutes) that I performed faithfully and, lo and behold, they worked! It was thrilling to see my baby's face so clearly on the ultrasound. Maybe it's my imagination, but it's awfully, awfully cute. A doting parent already, I guess.

Dinner was creamed crab cakes, grilled deep-fried tofu, vinegared seaweed and fingerlings, and instant soup.

8/22 (MONDAY)

A hand-knit baby blanket from my mother arrives in the mail. It's white and fluffy, and feels really good to the touch. A bit premature, perhaps, but I sincerely appreciate her thoughtfulness. I fought with her a lot when I was a kid and was sure she never really cared for me, but now that I'm about to become a mother myself, I realize how much she loved me, and her love fills my whole body. Thank you so much, dear mother.

Tonight's meal was grilled salmon, boiled spinach and fingerlings, grilled smelts on a spit, and miso soup with deep-fried tofu and cabbage.

8/31 (WEDNESDAY)

My last day as a receptionist at Y dental clinic. The dentist and hygienists were sorry to see me go, and asked me to come back when I've passed through this stage of my life. I was grateful, but gave them no clear answer. They gave me a bouquet of Bouvardia and daisies on parting.

I caught a rerun of *Orphan Bee* on TV. It amazed me that an ancient cartoon series like that would still be around, but then I realized it was a remake. Somehow or other, I got so sucked in I ended up bawling over the poor bee's plight. I felt sorry for him, and even sorrier for his mother. I'm very weepy these days. Inside my belly, little Takashi seems to be sharing my pain—I can feel him moving around.

SEPTEMBER 23

Two phrases:

"So maddening Gandhi himself would kick the crap out of someone."

"So infuriating Florence Nightingale would send a patient off with a dab of mercurochrome."

SEPTEMBER 18

The hump changed her shape tremendously. Her belly became slightly hollowed out, and her hips shrunk as well. It seemed her body was doing its utmost to make sure the growth had enough nourishment—it could care less about the rest of her. Later she realized that her body might be trying to find a way to accommodate the hump, to allow them to merge together. Her shoulder and arm had swollen to monstrous proportions. Her center of gravity was thrown off as a result; that morning, for example, her balance was so bad she couldn't even get out of bed. Perhaps her body was fighting the growth on her behalf. So she thought as she lay there on her side that afternoon, listening to the sounds of traffic passing outside her window.

SEPTEMBER 16

How the hell did I end up here? When I come to my senses, I am standing on the railing of a railroad overpass. Beneath my feet, the train tracks stretch into the distance in a straight line. The sky is broad and cloudless. "Finally, the time has come," says a voice to my left. I turn and, sure enough, a tall, thin man who looks to be in his early thirties is standing beside me on the railing. He is formally dressed in a ceremonial crested kimono and pleated *hakama* trousers. "Oh, how I have waited for this day," another voice says. I turn to my right to see a chubby middle-aged man shielding his eyes from the sun as he peers down the tracks. Now that I look, there are ten or so people lined up on the railing on both sides of me. Two are women decked out in what look like cocktail dresses, their hair in a glamorous upsweep. The men are all in tuxedos or wearing coat and tails. I realize that I am clad in the white taffeta dress I wore to that college gala to thank our teachers. Where the hell did I find that thing? I see something shining in the distance, at the end of the tracks. "Right on time," says the chubby man, looking at his watch. As the shiny thing draws closer I suddenly realize what it is. My conversation with Okubo-san about the bullet trains comes back to me: the Flash is faster than the Echo, and the Hope is faster than the Flash, which means the only train that could go faster than the Hope would be the Death. Now it seems that our prediction has come true—the Death is actually in operation. "This is its first run," the chubby man says in a voice choked with emotion. "Train 001. An event worth commemorating." Now the Death can clearly be made out, its pointed nose sharp as a knife, its jet-black flank scored by a crimson line that resembles an artery. As if by unspoken agreement, all of us join hands. A whistle shrieks as the train gains speed; then a conical cloud unfolds like an umbrella around the train. "Look!" a rapturous voice says. "It just broke the sound barrier." I snap back to my senses. *Wait, I'm not a jumper. A great mistake is being made. Please, I beg you, let go of my hand.* But my words are lost. "3, 2, 1, jump!" We plunge head-first, hands joined, and in that instant when we meet with Death and our flesh is atomized by those tons of steel hurtling at a speed exceeding sound, I pray: *Please, let this be a dream.*

PART 13
SEPTEMBER–AUGUST
FOUNTAIN PEN

SEPTEMBER 10

I have tea with a grim reaperess.

She has just graduated from Grim Reapers' High School and has been accepted into Grim Reapers' University.

It was a girls' high school, she says, but the university is coed, which is making her a bit nervous. Do you have a boyfriend? I ask. No way! she says, her bony jaw clattering. Don't gross me out! She may be a goddess of death, but she's still a girl, and at the peak of her beauty. Her skin (skeleton, actually) is white and smooth, not a blemish anywhere.

She shows me a photo of herself and four of her closest classmates. They are sitting on a lawn in matching black hoods, flashing the peace sign with their five scythes arranged neatly like tennis rackets in front of them, the handles together and the blades fanning out. These are practice scythes, though—they aren't allowed to have the real thing until they've finished their training.

It's just me and the girl on the far right who are continuing on to college—the others are going into the field, she says wistfully. The field's scary, she continues, but I can't wait to have my own scythe. Her eyes have a faraway look.

It's common for girls like her to glue rhinestones to the handles of their scythes in the shape of either words or pictures. She's already settled on Hello Kitty. I mean, hey, I've been a hard-core Kittyite my whole life, she says.

When my time comes, I say, please come for me if you've finished your training.

I'm your girl! she replies.

What does it feel like, I wonder, to be mowed down by a scythe with a Hello Kitty face on it?

SEPTEMBER 7

I phone the H publishing house to talk to their man in charge of translations, H-san. "I'm sorry," the person who answers says, "but no one by that name is employed here." This isn't unexpected, but it's still sad. H-san and I have worked together for ten years, and if he's gone, then who the heck am I producing this translation for, and why?

SEPTEMBER 6

After about a week, she noticed her legs growing thicker and more muscular. The swelling was gone, but the hump was as big and ugly as ever, and every bit as painful. She quit work. Food tasted awful, and climbing the stairs seemed to take forever. Her appetite was shot. It's been like this for half a month, she thought—I guess it's time to phone my doctor.

She tried to describe her symptoms to the doctor's receptionist on the phone, and was told to come in a week.

She felt the pain worsening before she even hung up the phone—her back felt like it was on fire. The growth was expanding rapidly, stretching the skin to the breaking point. The purple capillaries she could see crisscrossing its surface were being pushed to their limit by the violent swelling. Yet the pain in her shoulder seemed to have eased slightly. It no longer hurt around the clock as it did when the lump first appeared. It wasn't completely hard either—it bounced when she walked or climbed the stairs, so that the skin around it became chafed and cracked. Maybe I should secure it with tape or something like that, she thought. I bet that's what the doctor will tell me.

SEPTEMBER 1

I go to Muji in Shimokitazawa to buy a new pen to replace my old one.

I like this brand, which I've used for years, because you can click on any one of five colors, but the pink ink and the blue ink always run out first.

The stationery section, however, doesn't have what I am looking for. They have a six-color version with red, black, purple, blue, orange and pink, but I want the five-color model with blue, pink, orange, yellow and green.

To try out their water-based pens, I reach for the pad where people test their purchases by scribbling names, spirals and other shapes in various colors and thicknesses, when my eye falls on the phrase, "I want to leave him," written in the corner of the top page.

I look about. Somehow I feel as though the person who wrote it is still nearby. I take another good look at the phrase:

"I want to leave him."

This is written in deep pink with a fine-point water-based pen in a distinctive hand, each character formed like a parallelogram and slanted to the right. A woman's hand, most likely.

Without hesitation, I tear off the sheet, stuff it in my pocket, and leave the store. Why, I don't really know. I head back to the station and take the train straight to Shinjuku. I'm determined to get the pen I want before the day is over.

I find it at Muji on the upper level of Lumine. When I go to test it on the scribble pad, though, I find this written in deep pink:

"Potato sprout soup."

I take the sheet of paper from my pocket and compare the two. No question about it. Same fine-point water-based pen. Same parallelogram-like slanted hand. A sense of foreboding rises in my chest. Someone is going from one Muji store to another trying to leave a message. Or some kind of story. I am the one who has to stitch the pieces together—that is my appointed task. I tear the page from the pad, stick it in my pocket, and run from the store.

Sure enough, I find the following in the Muji store on Shinjuku Avenue:

"Abuse our cat?"

I think I get the gist. "I want to break off with my partner, a despicable cat abuser. Better yet, I'll poison his potato sprout soup." Full of excitement, I hurry to the Muji store one block away, the one on Yasukuni Boulevard.

"Oppekepe." Huh?

This throws me off. Is Oppekepe the name of the cat? But I have no time to dwell on that. The sun is already going down, and I must retrieve all the notes left on the scribble pads of as many Muji stores as I can get to before closing time. I rush to the station and take the Yamanote Line to Shibuya.

Four hours later, I am sitting exhausted in a café in Sangenjaya. I have made the rounds of as many stores as possible in that time, and my legs are as stiff as boards. On the table before me are more than ten tattered scraps of paper, each with a scribbled message:

"Oppekepe." "Remodeled and open for business." "I want to leave him." "Awaiting your reply." "Bomb disposal squad." "Love of." "Abuse our cat?" "Early in the afternoon, in the lingerie section." "Three years from today." "Did you know, lighthouse keepers are extinct?" "Drew Barrymore." "Double again." "Dying to see you."

I arrange and rearrange the scraps. But I can't find a way to fit them into a coherent story. While I am shuffling and reshuffling them, fatigue and sleepiness begin to get the better of me. This won't work. I need more pieces of the puzzle. To assemble the whole story, I would have to visit every Muji store in Tokyo, no, in Japan, no, perhaps in the whole world. As I sit here in this café, someone could be out there, scribbling on more scraps of paper, not just in Muji stores but in stationery shops everywhere. I feel myself growing faint. I grab the edge of the table to brace myself, my glass tips over, and before I know it the words are all lost in a pink swamp.

AUGUST 31

The thermometer reaches 106 degrees. Mt. Fuji's color is Doraemon blue, and a plume of steam is rising from its summit.

I go to the station to do my shopping, but the place is in an uproar, with police cars and fire trucks everywhere. Standing on my tiptoes, I see that the station has entirely disappeared; in its place is a huge black hole. It must be a hundred feet across. Not only is the station gone, so is the station building and a few of the buildings and shops across the street, the bakery for example. Did they all fall in? When I look more closely, however, I realize that, strangely, the hole has no depth—it is pure surface, like a coating of black tar. It does not so much reflect light as suck it in. The phrase "jet black" does not do it justice; it is a black whose blackness surpasses any other in this world.

Pandemonium breaks out at the front of the crowd as the black hole begins gliding in our direction. Electric poles are swallowed whole, followed by many of the parked police cars. "Get back! Get back!" the policemen shout, blowing their whistles in alarm, and the crowd panics and runs. I run with them.

I learn from the nightly news that a number of holes popped up around the city today, swallowing a great many things. I reach down and touch the place on my ankle where a similar black spot once resided.

AUGUST 23

Cloudy. I air the cocoon I now use in place of futon.

When I flick on the TV, *Tetsuko's Room* is just starting. Today's guest is "an essayist and translator of a sprawling love story that has already sold a record five million copies."

She strikes me as familiar. Then it hits me—she's the skinny woman I saw blithely signing my name at the bookstore launch. With her smug, pale face and impassive expression, she is bragging about how hard the novel—which spans six generations of love and war, death and rebirth, and five continents—was to translate. On her chest a sparkling brooch with the crest 1/1. My name keeps appearing on the screen under her face. I have never worn flowery, fluttering clothes like that, nor have I translated a romance that covers generations of heroines. She is a fraud. A complete and utter fraud. I am about to change channels when my eyes alight on Tetsuko's hair. It is set in a bouffant hairdo as always, but today it is stacked even higher than usual. And it is beginning to writhe like a living thing. The hair at the back parts, and the head of a horse the color of liver protrudes. The horse's head thrashes back and forth, the face, neck, and forelegs twist their way out; yet Tetsuko calmly goes on with her interview, asking her questions, inserting the appropriate comments. Finally, the horse's whole body slides from her hair, as if emerging from the womb. A horse the size of a small calf, with baggy skin covered with grains of rice.

For a moment, the horse wobbles there on legs that quiver like those of a real newborn foal. Then it lets out a thin whinny somewhere between a cat's and a baby's cry and runs off camera. Tetsuko cruises along with her interview, seeemingly unaware of what has just transpired.

AUGUST 21

I believe I have been working on my computer since morning, but it's suddenly evening, and for some reason there's an online dating site on the screen. I have no memory of what took place in between.

This sort of thing has been happening recently. The reason is that my brother has learned how to match his mind to mine. While I feel tired and sleepy 24/7, his strength and energy are only increasing. Not only does he steal the nutrients from my food, he stuffs himself on rice and sweets, so that his body has doubled in size and turned a shiny pink.

—Hey, what's going on? What have you been up to while I was sleeping?

—Nothing. But the Internet sure is a lot of fun.

—What's the idea of using dating sites anyway? You're not doing anything weird, are you?

—Naw. Nothing weird. But boy, do I want a woman.

That pisses me off so much I give his pink face a whack. It hurts me the most though—he just laughs it off.

AUGUST 20

Gradually, her clothes became a problem. She could no longer button her clothes in the front, as she'd been doing. She had been squashing the growth on her back as flat as she could and then pulling the garment tight together, but that no longer worked. Regular clothes were impossible, and even the looser ones were hard. She guessed that the growth might have increased in size. Or, just possibly, her clothes had shrunk. Being so exhausted all the time meant that she had to cut her housework down to an absolute minimum, so she had started using a dryer instead of hanging her laundry on a rack to dry.

She had nothing left that fit. As a counter-measure, she slit one shoulder of all her clothes, spread it, and then patched it with blue-checkered cloth. She wore these altered garments when she went up and down the stairs. She wore them when she went out. She planned to wear them when she went back to work, too. Not just on the first day, but every day.

AUGUST 15

I spend the morning fixing myself up for the wedding of two members of our "Drinkers Without Borders" club. None of my good clothes fit any longer, thanks to my little brother's increasing size, so I choose a poncho-like dress I fashioned from an old sheet for the occasion. Luckily, the heat wave has made people very laid-back about clothing—muumuus and robes that look like Roman togas are especially popular, while some even go half-naked—so I'm not too worried about standing out. I hesitate over whether or not to tape my brother to my belly, and then decide against it. My fellow Drinkers Without Borders will be drunk from the get-go anyhow, and if his presence happens to be detected, well, my guess is they'll be tolerant about it.

The area around the station is peaceful, as if the chaos of the day before had never happened. The station itself is back in operation, but the building that housed it has been replaced by a facsimile drawn in crude black lines on a white background. An arrow pointing to it reads "Station." I go to a similarly drawn vending machine and purchase my ticket, a piece of paper reading "ticket," climb a creaky set of stairs roughly outlined by someone clearly ignorant of the laws of perspective, and catch the train heading downtown. It's an actual train, thank goodness, but looking out the window I notice the landscape is studded with blank patches. The black holes have taken a terrible toll.

The Aoyama hotel where the wedding is to be held is blank as well, and the bride and groom and their guests are all standing around looking lost. "It got us," the groom says with a drunken laugh. "Just thirty minutes ago." He is already plastered.

Thankfully, everyone got out in time. The person who was supposed to have been the wedding's receptionist takes a brush-tipped pen and writes "hotel" in the empty space where the hotel had been. Then he walks around writing "Crane Room," "Table," "Chair" and so on with accompanying rough sketches, and we all sit down to enjoy our wedding party. We drink written-in sake from written-in cups and nibble on written-in dried squid and peanuts. None of it tastes very real. We are all quite drunk, so I pull up the hem of my poncho, extract my brother, and share some of my written-in sake with him. Sure enough, no one is surprised by his presence. To the contrary, some guests come over to pour his drinks and tousle his hair. "My, oh my," they exclaim. "What a weird little brother you have!"

"I'm so happy," he tells me. "And so grateful to you, dear sister."

It creeps me out that he's calling me sister like that, so I bop him hard. It hurts.

The brush-tipped pen's ink runs out shortly after midnight, so we have to call it quits. Too soon, too soon!

PART 14
AUGUST–JULY
OFFLINE GATHERING

AUGUST 29

I pay a visit to the Word Drop-Off.

The Word Drop-Off is located at the foot of the mailbox on the corner. It's extremely small, so if you don't look really, really carefully you'll miss it.

I thought it was a mushroom the first time I noticed it. You would make that mistake too—they look just the same on the surface. A white stem and a dark blue umbrella. In size and shape, it's the spitting image of a large shiitake mushroom. I dropped a letter I was posting one day, and when I leaned down to pick it up, there it was. Strange place for a mushroom, I thought, but a closer look revealed my mistake. There was an emblem in the middle of the umbrella like you see on a mailbox and running along the side, in tiny white letters, the words:

Word Drop-Off
Words you cannot look after accepted here

Looks like they borrowed the language from the drop-off program for abandoned babies. I liked the idea, though—rather than have newborn words and phrases lie neglected and unwanted by their parents, why not give them a home with someone who really wants them? They would be happier that way for sure.

So it was that on this day I came bearing words I had created in unguarded moments, but had no hope of ever using. The absence of a slot gave me pause, but when I knelt down, brought my face close to the umbrella, and whispered the words softly, the mailbox began to glow, then quiver, then shake more and more violently. Then, just when I feared it would explode, it suddenly melted away, leaving no trace behind.

So farewell, dear "anime-conciliation" and "jell-oratory." Please forgive me for not having been able to look after you, and best of luck in your new home. I hope they treat you well.

JULY 30

It's common these days to turn on the TV to a blank screen. The problem isn't technical difficulties; rather, the station is receiving a direct report from an area hit by a marauding black hole.

Those holes are growing more and more ferocious. They appear out of the blue, swallow whatever is there, and then just as suddenly vanish. Nothing is left in their wake. Even the land is gone. All that remains is something that can only be described as a "void."

At first their domain was Tokyo alone, but now they have extended their sway, from the Tohoku region in the north to the area around Osaka in the south. It seems that the more they consume, the more they grow and proliferate: recently, they have started swallowing large buildings, entire parks, even whole city districts. Unable to grasp the dimensions of the crisis, the panicked authorities are in complete disarray.

The news report then goes on to broadcast an interview with an expert, or possibly an overhead view of Shinjuku Gardens, which now has a large coin-shaped bald spot right in the middle. Then the screen turns white again as someone reports from an affected zone. Switching channels doesn't help—they're all white. The whiteness seems to be invading me, so I switch off the TV in fear, but then I hear a voice calling *"Hōi! Hōi!"* I can't tell if it's coming from the TV or from somewhere inside my head.

JULY 28

"The Dolorous Dark Ducks," an a cappella group, come to visit.

Wearing matching white suits, they arrange themselves in a perfect, overlapping line, bodies at an angle and faces turned toward the front. Their harmony is perfect too, but their songs are so dreary and the lyrics so weird. Here's what they sang today:

The gold bug ate the rhinoceros beetle
Devoured the stag beetle, then the cicada.
The children gave the gold bug
Athlete's foot.

They're about to launch into the second stanza, but I tell them not to bother. They reply with a perfectly harmonized *doo-wah* and then slink back to their dolorous world.

JULY 27

The day of her appointment arrived, so she went to the hospital. When the receptionist saw her hump and her altered dress, she directed her straight to the examination room. A white-clad doctor and a white-clad nurse rushed in. They moved about and stopped, moved about and stopped together like extensions of a single machine. After opening and closing a number of cabinet drawers, they promptly informed her that her growth could not be removed. Attempting to remove it, they said, would put your life in danger. They stepped to the door for a moment to discuss some personal matter, then came back to explain that the growth had been with her for a long time, had possibly lived inside her since birth, although it had only become visible in the last few weeks.

She sat still on the examination table in her paper hospital gown, trying her best to maintain her posture in front of the doctor and nurse, but her hump was throbbing, and its weight was pulling the skin on her back and shoulder down with such force that even the back of her scalp was stretched to the limit. It seemed only a matter of time before the hump and her body separated. That might be dangerous to her in a somewhat different way than the danger of the hump alone. When the pendulous growth, with its tendency to swing back and forth, did finally decide to leave, she imagined the consequences: the gush of blood and warm water bursting through skin. It wouldn't happen that soon, though. After all, the hump had just formed.

JULY 25

Sunny. Temperature breaks 100 degrees again. The soles of my black plastic sandals melted and stuck to the veranda. The cicadas are so loud the ground shakes.

The little brother on my hip—well, next to my belly button now—has been fidgeting around since morning.

—Something you want to say? I ask him.

"Yeah, but you have to promise not to hit me."

—I can't promise that. Go ahead and tell me. Whether I hit you or not depends on what you say.

"There's an offline group meeting I want to attend. Will you take me? It's in Shibuya. Ouch!"

Of course I whacked him! It's appalling—he logs onto Chatbox and Twitter when I'm asleep and ends up with all these online friends—5,000 followers? Unbelievable!

Still, after a brief argument I'm the one who gives in. If he can hijack my consciousness to operate my computer, there's no telling what kind of revenge he'll take if I say no.

I slip into my usual super-cheap, extra-roomy tunic, and make my way to a bar in Shibuya, where ten or so young men and women are already seated. I join them, but then realize I don't know my—no, I mean my brother's—online handle. That's a real bummer, so I silently roll up my tunic to let everyone see him.

There is a gasp as my brother's face rises above the tabletop.

"Ah, thank you, thank you. So nice to meet you all. I am <_nyokkiry>."

"What a surprise, <_nyokkiry> san," says the rather cute bespectacled girl sitting across from us, her eyes wide. "You look just like the icon on your account!"

"Hehe, I bet you thought I ripped it off from somewhere."

After that, the questions fly. How long have you been there? How do you manage to use the keyboard? How about eating, and things like that? Who's the person behind you, your platform?

The whole thing makes me squirm, so I comfort myself with round after round of beer and shochu. As a result, my memory breaks off partway through the evening. When I come to, it is the middle of the night, and I am sprawled on the sofa in my living room with my brother bouncing up and down on my belly, his body a beet red.

"What a blast!" he exults. "Human contact is where it's happening. They want me to come next time too. And you know what? Girls like me!"

—Don't get carried away. I'm not doing this again. You can't hijack someone's consciousness like that and get away with it. I have my rights too, you know!

"I didn't hijack anything, dear sister. You drank too much of that black sugar shochu, that's all."

—Don't call me sister, either—it grosses me out.

I slug him. Later, I discover ¥10,000 missing from my purse.

JULY 24

The worst hangover in recorded history. Death.

JULY 20

From <diary.txt>:

12/15 (TUESDAY)

Finally, I've got it together enough to write this diary again. I've been in constant pain since I got back from the hospital. Fumbling around trying to deal with my new situation barely leaves me time to breathe (that's still true!). I had to have a Caesarean section in the end, but the baby was safely delivered, which is all that really matters. When the anesthetic wore off, and I held him for the first time, I was so grateful I cried. I still get teary when I look at his tiny fingernails, his hands, the tiny lashes beneath his closed eyes, the breath from his tiny nostrils—everything is just so perfect! I am full of forgiveness for everyone in this world. Even those who have hurt or rejected me.

12/18 (FRIDAY)

Went to City Hall today to register his birth. I spent a lot of time agonizing over which kanji to use, but in the end I opted for katakana syllables instead, so it's TA-KA-SHI. That's what I've been calling him in my mind since I learned he was a boy, and most of all, I feel it fits him perfectly. Will the other kids tease him because his name is written in katakana, like a foreigner's name? Perhaps. But there are weirder names these days. For example, one of the women in my prenatal group told me she was going to name her baby Tiger or Julia, and the kanji she chose were absolutely ridiculous! Compared to that, the name TA-KA-SHI is normal. What if he's teased because his name is too conservative? Just thinking about it keeps me up at night.

JULY 18

The phrase, "reverse role model."

The phrase, "Sazae-san with a fish clamped between her jaws."

JULY 10

I attend the P Academy alumni reunion. It's a really hot day, over 100 even in the shade.

I wear the makeshift poncho that I fashioned from a sheet for the wedding, but even then I'm still hot.

When I arrive at Hotel F in Chidorigafuchi, a throng of people are already walking around, cocktail glasses in hand, talking and laughing. I pin my nametag onto my poncho at the reception desk and step into the hall, where I am met with a most unpleasant odor, something sweet and fusty, like rotting fruit. But I forget the smell when I see a number of familiar faces. Some wave and approach me squealing. Nubbers, Pinner, Fippon, Nukara, Bebebe, Hebylmas, Tromley and Papoonya—none of them have changed a bit. Sure, our hair and skin and stuff like that have lost some of their glow, but I'm happy to see our essence is still the same. The organizer says a few words of greeting, one of our old teachers offers a toast, and then a torrent of conversation fills the room. It's a buffet-style meal, so circles of women carrying plates group and regroup as they share stories of the past. How E was so innocent that she thought the love hotels lining the highway were real castles. How I, who cared little about her personal appearance, wore the same ratty shoes three years running until one morning we found mushrooms growing in them. How our geography teacher, Miss Y, was mistaken as a transvestite by the custodian at the public bath and told to use the men's side. The stories are so hilarious that everyone doubles over laughing. As the voltage of the conversation heightens, the stench in the room rises to another level. Partway through, I catch sight of Moheji. Did O come? I ask. Yes, I'll bring her over, Moheji replies. Sure enough, she returns with O in tow. We stand and chat for a while. O looks great in her emerald green dress, conspicuously younger than the rest of us. So I was right. She explains that she doesn't appear in our class album because she was held back a year by her illness. She was hospitalized during our summer vacation, which was why we had the impression she had dropped out without our knowledge. I ask her about the voice we sometimes heard outside the window, and the words scribbled on the door of the toilet above the auditorium. I can't remember, she laughs. Did that really happen? That answer leaves me a little deflated, but also relieved. Alright, then. I get it. It was all in my mind after all.

Someone takes the stage and makes an announcement. *Well, it's time to sing our old school song—if you can't remember the words, feel free to cheat by peeking at the sheet of lyrics you each received.* The announcement is greeted with laughter and applause, and the piano intro begins.

Here in our cherry blossom capital
Mt. Fuji's peak towering in the distance
Hot-blooded maidens gather . . .

As our voices grow more passionate, the smell grows stronger. Sure seems like something is rotting in here. Surreptitiously, I look around me. I glimpse something moving on one of the tables. Maggots are wriggling out of a half-eaten sandwich and plopping on the plate. I am about to whisper to O singing next to me, but when I glance at her profile I see more maggots peeking from the corners of her mouth. My heart turns cold. I turn my head and witness maggots streaming from the faces and hair and clothes of all my friends—Nubbers, Pinner, Fippon, Nukara, Bebebe, Hebylmas, and Tromley. As our school song rises to the rafters, the maggots fall around us. The words echo unpleasantly around me, as if I were squatting inside some huge vase. My head spins. The stench is choking me. This is not the P Academy alumni reunion. A terrible mistake has been made. "Now for the third verse! And a one, and a two . . ." I edge backwards to the exit, trying to be as inconspicuous as possible. Then I remember. I pull the black whistle from the bottom of my bag, where I had left it. The kind of whistle audible only to certain people. Yellow for those who are depressed; red for those menstruating; brown for those in love; black for those not of this world. I blow my black whistle with all my might. The piano comes to a sudden halt, and all eyes turn to stare at me. O is staring too. Maggots fall like tears from the hollow sockets of her eyes.

PART 15
JULY–X MONTH
TETSUKO

JULY 8

I hear "Tsutaya" when the word is Russia, and say "Kobayashi-san" when I mean Tanaka-san. I'm really tired.

JULY 5

Instead of working, I lie on my sofa all afternoon, picking my nose and daydreaming about how much I'd like to accomplish something unprecedented in human history.

I don't want it to be anything exhausting, or dangerous, or overly ambitious. No solo trips to the North Pole on a cat sled, for example, or bungee jumping while shouting out the value of pi to umpteen digits. Perhaps something ecologically aware, and connected to a sustainable lifestyle? Something on a more individual, human scale?

For instance, I think, springing to my feet and trotting to the kitchen. I take a ladle in one hand and a spatula in the other, place them above my ears like antennae, and sing "Ah, Lovely Meadows" while marching in place. I bet no one has ever done this before!

Just then, the lid of my rice container opens and a little man steps out, a thick ledger in his hands. "No," he says. "What you just did was performed once before, in Taito Ward in 1965." OK, so there was a precedent for that one. I try singing the national anthem while doing Radio Calisthenics No. 2 and alternating a knife and fork with the spatula and ladle, but it turns out that has been done before too—in 1947 (in Nara), 1968 (in what was West Berlin at the time), and 2010 (in Oita). Damn! The precedents keep growing!

I keep trying, though, changing the movements, changing the objects, until it becomes clear that, no matter how utterly bizarre, even unthinkable, a particular act is, someone somewhere has already performed it. Achieving a "human first" is a wall too thick to break through. The little man places a comforting hand on my sagging shoulders. "Don't let it get you down," he says. "Just think. Is there anyone other than you who has held *that* knife and fork in *that* kitchen and sung the national anthem in *that* voice?" That wakes me up. He's right. Just being alive in this world is a "first" in human history, for me, for everyone. The irreplaceable me. I just have to be myself. A flower unlike any other. Not number one—the *only* one. The little man and I embrace each other as tears pour from my eyes.

When my thinking reaches this point, though, I have to face the reality that, in fact, I haven't budged an inch from the sofa. What the heck? When I stop to think about it, though, lying sprawled out like this picking my nose and thinking these thoughts is, in its own way, "a first for humanity." I let out a loud fart.

JULY 1

The Cabinet holds an emergency press conference to announce that, since running the calendar in reverse over the past several months has been disruptive to society and damaging to the hearts and minds of the people, and since, moreover, the national economy is reeling from the impact, a decision has been reached to abolish the calendar altogether. There is an angry outcry as reporters hurl questions and comments at the legislators: Won't this decision create even more chaos? What are you thinking? An abrogation of governmental responsibility! A woeful dereliction of duty! Can't you at least restore the old calendar? The cabinet minister wails, "I don't understand what you're saying!" and starts crying. I look more closely and, sure enough, he is a boy of about ten, with a school bag on his back. "There are cookies back in the room, dear," his private secretary calls out to comfort him, and he steps down from the podium and leaves the room. She's probably his mother.

X MONTH X DAY

I find a large, perfectly constructed spiderweb in the corner of my veranda, its reigning monarch enthroned in the middle. A careful examination reveals that he has arranged his tightly bound prey at equal intervals along two vertical strands. Perhaps the most delicious prey are lined up along this strand, and the not-so-tasty prey along that one. In a sense, then, his web is at once a place of residence, a weapon, and a memory storage device. Enmeshed in these thoughts, I squat there until the sun goes down.

X MONTH X DAY

Every day, the news reports on the increasing ferocity of the black holes.

Their damage now extends across Japan. Ranging in size from 5 to 50 meters across, they pop up suddenly and advance across the landscape, swallowing everything in their path. What they leave behind can only be described as emptiness. At this stage, every community looks like moths have been chewing on it. It is no longer strange to see entire mountains, towns, villages and hamlets disappear. According to one research center's provisional estimate, nearly an eighth of the nation has, to all intents and purposes, vanished.

The black holes have also rooted themselves in our psyches. Are there ten seconds in a day when they are not on our minds? They squat at the center of our thoughts. They inhabit our dreams. Even when we try to think about ourselves, "holes" quickly become the subject of our musings. They are the focus of our fears; yet, at the same time they mesmerize us. There are now cults that worship them as the one true God, while books, T-shirts, and coffee mugs with a hole motif are flying off the shelves.

Just the other day, *Tetsuko's Room* finally had a feature interview with one of those holes. For the first time in eighty years of hosting the program, Tetsuko took a crew and ventured outside the studio to a spot along the Kōshū Expressway, where a hole was making its slow but steady way north.

"Today's guest," she began, "is someone who, whatever one might say, has managed to capture the world's attention. It is a pleasure to have you on our show." She extended the microphone in the hole's direction, but there was no response. Its pace stayed the same. "Where were you born? How old are you? Do you have a family?" The hole said nothing, just kept moving forward. "You've swallowed up so many things, so many people. Aren't you full yet? What becomes of the things you swallow?" The hole said nothing, just kept moving forward. "Surely there must be problems and worries connected to your work. Could you share those with us? Perhaps tell us what dreams you have for the future?" The hole said nothing, just kept moving forward. "Oh yes, I've brought you a little something by way of thanks. Do you like sweets?" The hole said nothing, just kept moving forward.

Tetsuko's expression changed. Her eyes sparkled, her back stiffened. Were my eyes deceiving me—even her wrinkles seemed to disappear! I sensed I was witnessing the return of the fighting spirit that had once made her the goddess of the talk show. "Alright. I understand. You don't like superficial chat, do you. That's fine with me." Her voice was young, almost girlish. "I promise to get right to the point. And I want you to listen to what I have to say, too. I feel that I've been waiting for a guest like you all my life." Tetsuko placed her microphone on the ground, turned her back to the camera, and determinedly strode toward the hole. Her feet disappeared, then her knees, her hips, her shoulders, her neck, then finally her onion-shaped head was slowly sucked down into the blackness. The hole continued its steady advance. When it swallowed the camera, the screen went white.

X MONTH X DAY

Soon, she went back to work, leaving early in the morning, returning late at night. When she got home she left the lights off, and turned on her little radio to the news and sports. As she listened, she lay on the sofa and massaged for as long as she could the hump and the raised ring of inflamed skin around it, which was swollen and purplish in color, and cracked and scabby as well. Nevertheless, she could see no proof that the growth was bigger than before; to the contrary, over the past month it had hardened and become less pliable, and that increased hardness made it look smaller.

After a long day's work, the throbbing was markedly worse, so she got up and went to the shower to wash it, wrapping a towel clumsily around one hand and placing it over the growth. When she wrung hot soapy water from the towel over the damaged skin, however, she jumped and yelped in agony. She quickly ran clean hot water over the spot, which dulled the pain. The hump responded by becoming hotter and redder itself, so she stood there in the scalding shower for nearly an hour, rubbing it nonstop with a cloth.

X MONTH X DAY

First thing in the morning, I go out to take a peek at that perfect spiderweb in the corner of my veranda, but there is nothing there. Yet I checked it out before I went to bed! Maybe the spider moved, or maybe he died, but how does that explain the entire web disappearing overnight? It was a big spider, with beautiful black and yellow striped legs.

X MONTH X DAY

From <diary.txt>:

> 12/15 (TUESDAY) A policeman stopped by today to drop off Takashi's boots. Those yellow Sergeant Keroro boots I gave them to help their dog recognize his smell. As soon as he left, though, I threw them in the trash. The whole thing made me laugh—I mean, how can they not know that a four-year-old's shoes won't fit after six months? Can't they guess I bought him a new pair ages ago? Of the same yellow Sergeant Keroro boots? Takashi isn't gone. He's still here—in fact, he appears to me as clear as clear can be every so often. Like the other day, when it rained, I could see his boots had somehow become covered in mud. The problem is he's gotten lost in some other world and doesn't know how to find his way home. Or maybe some witch of a woman has him in her clutches. That's why I can't leave this apartment. Or age either. So that when he finally escapes from that witch he knows where to come, and who I am. For that reason I will no longer date this diary. Nor change the page of my calendar. Time has ceased to exist for me.

X MONTH X DAY

On the spur of the moment, I decide to pay another visit to the Arakawa Alpaca Gardens.

When I get off the train at Alpaca Station, one stop before the end of the Arakawa Line, I can see immediately that a great change has taken place. It had been a small, rather rundown unmanned station before, but now it lies in ruins. Weeds push through the cracks of the yard-wide platform, and the wooden station sign is covered with vines: it hangs diagonally, and I can make out only the two syllables pa and ca.

I make my way though the dust-coated turnstile and see that the area in front of the station has vanished, along with the bus stop. The long, rusty arcade of shops across the street is similarly pockmarked with empty space. To circumvent the damage, I wend my way through a daunting maze of back streets to finally arrive at Alpaca Gardens. The place is locked, the gate wrapped in chains. The handwritten sign, "Adults ¥20, Children ¥5" has come loose and now sits propped beyond the gate.

I climb over the concrete fence and venture inside. No alpacas. Just billowing brown grass as far as I can see. I go to the little concession stand. The window looks like frosted glass, it is so caked with mud and dirt, but I can see enough to confirm that there are no signs of human activity inside. The back door is unlocked, so I enter. Cookies, juice bottles, and packets of alpaca crackers are scattered across the wooden floor, everything coated with a layer of dust. The air is stale and moldy. I pick up the least crumbled packet of alpaca crackers I can find and a panda mask and go outside. I put the panda mask on, sit down, and wait quietly for any alpacas hiding nearby to show themselves. Alpacas are wary creatures, so the rule is to put them at ease by pretending that one is not a human being but another animal—thus the panda mask. I don't know what pandas sound like, so I quietly call "pan, pan." I walk around the Gardens for almost an hour making that sound, but not a single alpaca appears. Did a black hole swallow them all? Did they wander into a different dimension? Or did they form a line and trudge off to the moon? I hope the last is what happened to them.

I stay in the Gardens until the sun goes down. I sit on the fence, take off my panda headdress and nibble on an alpaca cracker as if I were an alpaca myself. It tastes of mold and dust.

X MONTH X DAY

All that rubbing made the hump itch. Not the sort of itch you can deal with by scratching, either: rather, it was the kind of itch that compels you to try and tear your skin off in strips. She began rubbing the growth with all her might, sending her wet hair swinging back and forth. She bore down, putting the full weight onto one side of her body, as sweat streamed from her pores and was washed away by the shower. In response, the growth began to glow a garish red, the color of blood but with all the darkness of blood removed. She no longer felt any pain. But the itching was driving her crazy. Eventually, though, the itching stopped, and the burning returned. With a vengeance. It assaulted her. She slumped against the wall of the shower and screamed. Now she would have to go back to the doctor, she thought. The circular spot around the hump had raised up and turned an alarming color—the blood vessels beneath the growth's thin skin were visibly pulsating.

X MONTH X DAY

The TV news reports on the volunteers trying to deal with the havoc caused by the holes. In an attempt to recreate the townscapes that have been lost, art school students are sketching shopping streets that have been entirely wiped away. They rely on maps and photographs taken before the catastrophe, but their skill, technique and materials differ, so there is little unity to the result. Moreover, each draws in his or her chosen genre—the oil painting of a greengrocer may sit beside a Japanese-style ink sketch of a clock store whose neighbor in turn may be a trompe l'oeil version of a bookstore. When the art students get carried away they add extraneous things like rainbows, jumping salmon and many-colored flowers and mushrooms, turning the work into a surrealistic dreamscape of primary colors. Still, the shopkeepers agree it's a huge improvement on the empty space that was there before. It's said that, a few days ago, a great stir was caused when a reindeer someone painted came to life and started roaming the streets. According to the story, it quietly munched on some grass and rubbed its antlers on a telegraph pole before running off to parts unknown.

At the end of the report, one of the students said that her dream was to bring the people who had been swallowed up back to life in the same way.

X MONTH X DAY

The phrase: "My Secret Garden Bean-Paste Bun."

X MONTH X DAY

I wake up in the morning to find that my brother has finally moved from the spot where he was to the exact front of my body. Alarmed, I take a good look in the mirror. He has grown huge—I can't believe how big he is!—one fist dangling heavily from just below my navel, his sleeping face shamelessly drooling. I am wasting away, my sallow skin hanging in folds, but the part of me that is him glows a lustrous pink and pulsates with vigor. My hatred for him reaches the breaking point—I grab a knife and slice him off at the root. There is no blood, no pain, and it hits me that this must be a dream. On the floor, my brother turns purple and shrivels into a tiny, lifeless ball. Or so I think, for all of a sudden he swells before my eyes. When he reaches the size of a calf, he sprouts a neck and four legs, his skin turns the color of liver, sags and, voila, there it stands, a small horse covered with grains of rice.

—C'mon, big Sis, climb on board.

He tosses his head and neighs, urging me on.

I realize that I have assumed the form of an *oiran* courtesan.

"Don't call me big Sis!" I say, but with a beatific smile.

The heels of my black enamel kinky boots hit the ground with a loud crack as I hike my gold brocade and damask super-mini kimono to the max and swing myself up on the horse's back, my electric hairpins emitting seven colors of light in all directions, like the Battleship Yamato.

"Let us be on our way, my faithful retinue," I call.

We are surrounded by an impenetrable darkness. Golden flakes dance crazily about us like snow as, protected by the 108 Girls of Earthly Desire, and surrounded by the rhythms of samba music and the classic *hichiriki* flute, I launch our merry parade, at once an *oiran*'s and a bride's processional. I see female ninjas and ladies-in-waiting, barely clad pearl divers and ballerinas among the 108 Girls, all of whom are grinding their hips suggestively while squealing *Hōi, Hōi*! The glittering tassels of the standard bearers waving in the air, the glowing lanterns everywhere, the *oiran*'s kimono, and on everything the crest 1/1 in archaic characters.

I see a faint white light far in the distance. A door. I don't know where the light is coming from, but I can read the inscription on the door's surface:

<Break on through to the other side HERE!>

This time, this time I feel sure I can make the break.

My brother the horse lets out an ear-splitting whinny as voices rise in unison with the samba beat.

Hōi, hōi!

Hōi, hōi!

Hōi, hōi!

CONTRIBUTORS

JEFFREY ANGLES (b. 1971) teaches Japanese literature at Western Michigan University. He has translated poetry by Mutsuo Takahashi, Hiromi Itō and Takako Arai, among others. He is the author of *Writing the Love of Boys: Origins of Bishōnen Culture in Modernist Japanese Literature* (University of Minnesota Press).

SAM BETT (b. 1986) writes and translates fiction. In 2016 he was awarded Grand Prize by the Japanese government in the 2nd JLPP International Translation Competition for his translation of "A Peddler of Tears" by Yōko Ogawa, which appears in this issue. He is also a founder and host of Us&Them, the quarterly Brooklyn-based reading series devoted to showcasing the work of writers who also translate.

MICHAEL K. BOURDAGHS (b. 1961) teaches Japanese literature and culture at the University of Chicago. His book *Sayonara Amerika, Sayonara Nippon: A Geopolitical Prehistory of J-Pop* was published by Columbia University Press in 2012 and has been translated into Japanese.

DAVID BOYD (b. 1981) holds a master's degree from the University of Tokyo and is currently in the East Asian Studies doctorate program at Princeton University. He has translated stories and essays by Hideo Nakai, Riichi Yokomitsu and Naoyuki Ii, among others.

KEVIN BROCKMEIER (b. 1972) is the author of eight books of fiction, including the short story collection *The View from the Seventh Layer* and the novel *The Brief History of the Dead*. In 2014 he published *A Few Seconds of Radiant Filmstrip: A Memoir of Seventh Grade* (Pantheon). "Continental Drift" was inspired by one of Mina Ishikawa's tanka poems, which appeared in vol. 2 (2012) of *Monkey Business*.

ANDREW COWAN (b. 1960) is a British novelist and Director of Creative Writing at the University of East Anglia. Among his books are *Pig*, *Common Ground*, *What I Know* and *Worthless Men* (Sceptre). "Seals" appears for the first time in print in this issue.

RAMPO EDOGAWA (1894–1965) was a mystery writer instrumental in promoting mystery fiction in Japan. His pen name (Edogawa Rampo) was inspired by Edgar Allan Poe.

Many of his novels and short stories were made into films. His translated works include *Japanese Tales of Mystery and Imagination,* translated by James B. Harris (Tuttle), and *The Early Cases of Akechi Kogoro,* translated by William Varteresian (Kurodahan Press).

MICHAEL EMMERICH (b. 1975) teaches Japanese literature at the University of California, Los Angeles. An award-winning translator, he has translated books by Gen'ichirō Takahashi, Hiromi Kawakami and Hideo Furukawa, among others. He is the editor of *Read Real Japanese Fiction* (Kodansha) and *Short Stories in Japanese: New Penguin Parallel Text*.

TOH ENJOE (b. 1972) is known for his highly metafictional, self-referential and allusive writing, which he characterizes as straightforward fiction. His novel *Self-Reference ENGINE* was translated into English by Terry Gallagher (Haikasoru). "The Thousand and One Tongues," one of the twitter stories that appeared in vol. 5 (2015) of *Monkey Business*, was included in *The Best Small Fictions 2016* (Queen's Ferry Press).

BRIAN EVENSON (b. 1966) is the author of more than a dozen books of fiction. Among his recent books are *A Collapse of Horses*, a collection of short stories (Coffee House Press); the novel *Immobility,* and the novella *The Warren* (Tor Books). "A Report on Chimney Sweeping," "A Report on Hands," and "A Report on Squares" appear for the first time in print in this issue.

HIDEO FURUKAWA (b. 1966) is one of the most innovative writers in Japan today. His novel *Belka, Why Don't You Bark?* was translated by Michael Emmerich (Haikasoru) and his partly fictional reportage *Horses, Horses, in the End Light Remains Pure* was translated by Doug Slaymaker with Akiko Takenaka (Columbia University Press).

TED GOOSSEN (b. 1948) teaches Japanese literature and film at York University in Toronto. He is the general editor of *The Oxford Book of Japanese Short Stories* and has published translations of stories and essays by Hiromi Kawakami, Haruki Murakami, Yōko Ogawa, Sachiko Kishimoto and Naoya Shiga, among others.

HELEN GURI (b. 1983) is the author of *Match*, which was shortlisted for the Trillium Book Award for Poetry, as well as the poetry chapbooks *Here Come the Waterworks* and *Microphone Lessons for Poets*. Her poems and essays have been published in Canada, the U.S., and Australia. Based in Montreal, she edits poetry for Book Thug and Brick Books.

HIROMI ITŌ (b. 1955) is one of the most important female voices in contemporary Japanese poetry. English translations include *Killing Kanoko: Selected Poems by Hiromi Ito* and *Wild Grass on the Riverbank*, both translated by Jeffrey Angles and published by Action Books. "Evil Flourishes But Itō Encounters Jizō" is the fifth chapter of *The Thorn-Puller: New Tales of the Jizō Statue at Sugamo*, her semi-autobiographical novel published in 2007.

HIROMI KAWAKAMI (b. 1958) is one of Japan's leading novelists. Counterpoint Press has published two of her books: *Manazuru*, translated by Michael Emmerich, and *The Briefcase*, translated by Allison Markin Powell. Powell has also translated *The Nakano Thrift Shop* (Portobello Books). "Banana," which appeared in vol. 4 (2014) of *Monkey Business*, was included in *The Best Small Fictions 2015* (Queen's Ferry Press).

MIEKO KAWAKAMI (b. 1976) is a novelist, poet, singer and actress. Her awards include the Akutagawa Prize, the Nakahara Chūya Poetry Prize and the Waseda University Tsubouchi Shōyō Emerging Voice Prize. Her work has regularly appeared in *Monkey Business*, and "War Bride" was included in her 2012 award-winning collection of prose poems.

SACHIKO KISHIMOTO (b. 1960) is known for her translations of Nicholson Baker, Judy Budnitz, Lydia Davis, Thom Jones and Miranda July. She is also a popular essayist; her latest collection, *Some Kind of Reason*, appeared in 2012.

SATOSHI KITAMURA (b. 1956) is an award-winning picture-book artist and illustrator. His own books include *When Sheep Cannot Sleep: The Counting Book*, *Millie's Marvellous Hat* and *Lily Takes a Walk*. He has worked with numerous artists and poets.

CHRISTOPHER LOWY (b. 1986) is a PhD candidate in Japanese Literature at the University of Washington, Seattle. His translations regularly appear in the journal *Genron*. He was awarded a Japan Foundation Doctoral Fellowship, 2016–17.

SHIN'ICHI MAKINO (1896–1936) wrote many novels and a number of fantastical short stories. He studied English literature at Waseda University. Following his suicide, he became a cult figure. As far as we know, this is the first time his work has been translated into English.

AOKO MATSUDA (b. 1979) has published four collections of short stories and two books of essays, and has also translated Karen Russell's *St. Lucy's Home for Girls Raised by Wolves* and *Vampires in the Lemon Grove*. English translations of Matsuda's work have appeared in *Granta* and *Monkey Business*.

TAKI MONMA (b. 1933) is a novelist and short story writer. Her stories "Splinters," "White Socks" and "Botchan and Tsuru-san" were translated by Ted Goossen and appeared in vols. 3–5 (2013–15) of *Monkey Business*.

HARUKI MURAKAMI (b. 1949) is one of the world's best-known and best-loved novelists. All his major novels—including *Hardboiled Wonderland and The End of the World*, *The Wind-Up Bird Chronicle* and *1Q84*—have been translated into dozens of languages. "On Writing Short Stories" is the second half of his conversation with Motoyuki Shibata, published in vol. 9 (Summer/Fall 2016) of the Japanese literary journal *Monkey*.

KAFŪ NAGAI (1879–1959) is considered one of the most important Japanese novelists from the early twentieth century, known for his evocations of fading Edo culture. English translations of his work include *Rivalry: A Geisha's Tale*, translated by Stephen Snyder (Columbia University Press), and the excellent selection of his writings, translated by Edward Seidensticker, in *Kafū the Scribbler* (Stanford University Press).

SŌSEKI NATSUME (1867–1916), a founding father of modern literature in Japan, is still read and revered today. English translations of his work include *Sanshirō* (Penguin Classics) and *The Miner* (Aardvark Bureau), both translated by Jay Rubin. Michael Bourdaghs's new translation of *Ten Nights of Dreams* was published in vol. 6 (2016) of *Monkey Business.*

YŌKO OGAWA (b. 1962) is, with Hiromi Kawakami, one of the most highly regarded novelists in Japan. Translations of her work have appeared in the *New Yorker* and *A Public Space,* among others. Four of her books have been translated into English, all by Stephen Snyder, including the best-selling *The Housekeeper and the Professor* and *Revenge: Eleven Dark Tales* (Picador).

HIROKO OYAMADA (b. 1983) is one of Japan's most promising young writers. Her story "Spider Lily" was translated by Juliet Winters Carpenter and published in the Japan issue of *Granta* (Spring 2014), and "Lost in the Zoo" was translated by David Boyd and published in vol. 6 (2016) of *Monkey Business*.

JAY RUBIN (b. 1941) is professor emeritus of Japanese literature at Harvard University. One of the principal translators of Haruki Murakami, he translated *The Wind-Up Bird Chronicle, after the quake* and *1Q84* (co-translated with Philip Gabriel). Among his many other translations are *Rashōmon and Seventeen Other Stories* by Ryūnosuke Akutagawa and *Sanshirō* by Sōseki Natsume (both Penguin Classics).

TOMOKA SHIBASAKI (b. 1973) is a novelist, short-story writer and essayist. Her books include *Awake or Asleep*, *Viridian* and *In the City Where I Wasn't*. She won the Akutagawa Prize in 2014 with *Spring Garden*, which has been translated by Polly Barton (Pushkin Press).

MOTOYUKI SHIBATA (b. 1954) teaches American literature and literary translation at the University of Tokyo. He has translated Paul Auster, Rebecca Brown, Stuart Dybek, Steve Erickson, Brian Evenson, Laird Hunt, Kelly Link, Steven Millhauser, Richard Powers and Charles Simic, among others.

SEIICHI SUZUKI (b. 1962) has designed every issue of the Japanese *Monkey Business*. The logo is also his creation. He is the most sought-after book designer in Japan and has designed more than eight thousand books. His tardiness is legendary, but he always comes through in the clutch.

MAKOTO TAKAYANAGI (b. 1950) is a poet and has published numerous books of poetry. His complete works appeared in two volumes in 2016. *Aliceland* was his first publication, in 1980.

TAKORA Kimiyoshi Futori (b. 1972) is a visual artist. The trademark cover art of Monkey Business is his creation. He has designed numerous posters, clothes and even cash cards. To see more of his art, visit www.graphictakora.com.

HITOMI YOSHIO (b. 1979) earned her doctorate at Columbia University and currently teaches at Waseda University. She has translated stories and essays by Mieko Kawakami for *Denver Quarterly*, *Granta*, *Monkey Business*, *Pleiades* and *Words without Borders*.

BARRY YOURGRAU (b. 1949) is a writer of very short stories. His collection *Wearing Dad's Head* was reissued in 2016, and *A Man Jumps Out of an Airplane* in 2017 (Arcade). His memoir *Mess: One Man's Struggle to Clean Up His House and His Act* was published in 2015 (Norton).